PENGU

The Rooms in My Mother's House

Olga Lorenzo was born in Havana, Cuba, in 1959. She grew up in Miami and studied at Washington University in St Louis, Missouri. She worked as a journalist at the Melbourne *Age* where she met her husband, cartoonist John Spooner. They have three children. This is her first novel.

OLGA LORENZO

The Rooms in My Mother's House

PENGUIN BOOKS

Penguin Books Australia Ltd
487 Maroondah Highway, PO Box 257
Ringwood, Victoria 3134, Australia
Penguin Books Ltd
Harmondsworth, Middlesex, England
Viking Penguin, A Division of Penguin Books USA Inc
375 Hudson Street, New York, New York, 10014, USA
Penguin Books Canada Limited
10 Alcorn Avenue, Toronto, Ontario, Canada M4V 3B2
Penguin Books (NZ) Ltd
182-190 Wairau Road, Auckland 10, New Zealand

First published by Penguin Books Australia 1996

3 5 7 9 10 8 6 4

Typeset in Goudy by Post Typesetters
Printed in Australia by Australian Print Group

National Library of Australia
Cataloguing-in-Publication data:

Lorenzo, Olga.
The rooms in my mother's house.

ISBN 0 14 026115 X.

I. Title.

A823.3

This project has been assisted by the Commonwealth Government through the
Australia Council, its arts funding and advisory body.

To my family. Especially, to my mother.

Acknowledgements

I am indebted to Jill Hickson and Gaby Naher, Bryony Cosgrove, Hilary McPhee, Luis Garcia, Thelma Englert and Prof David Hadas. Also to the Literature Board of the Australia Council. Special thanks to Dr Lilit Thwaites, and to my editor, Meredith Rose.

For their love and support, I want to thank Caroline Odell, Anita, Ellen and Matthew, Manny, my mother Olga, and, especially, John.

Mother, I love you so.
Said the child, I love you more than I know.
She laid her head on her mother's arm,
And the love between them kept them warm.

Stevie Smith

                        O to be self-balanced for
   contingencies,
To confront night, storms, hunger, ridicule, accidents,
   rebuffs, as the trees and animals do.

Walt Whitman

Contents

The Generations

María, born 1873, died 1958

Dolores, born 1904, died 1981

Consuelo, born 1928

Ana María, born 1959

María and Elena María, born 1985, 1986

PART ONE

The Hairless Tongue

There were always more people living with them than they ever encountered, just as there were rooms in the house that they dared not enter. They did not allow themselves to know to what extent their past was there.

But still we crowded their lives. We forced them into a smaller space. We curtailed the possible.

We were there, neither appeased nor unappeased, neither watchful nor neglectful. We were the blood seeped into the ground, the bones drifting in white clouds. We were the faded but not forgotten smiles, the caresses of their infancy. We were the soft hands in the evening breeze that soothed their brows. The memories of other lives that came upon them when they stood in their front yard looking down the road. That rose up when they were most unsuspecting, when they were asleep.

But we were also the sharp hand. The edge, and also the pit. The darkness. The endings so that there could always be a beginning. We were the smell of jasmine and gardenias when there were none there. But also – es verdad – the chicken heads left in the sun.

We were Ana's Consuelo. And her Dolores. And her Marías. And her grandmothers whom she never saw.

We were with her. As yours are with you.

Australian Nights

Some nights Ana dreams that she is back in Cuba.

She dreams of Havana, of driving through a sweet balmy evening along a road that follows the line of the sea, past old and peeling terraces whose balconies sag and whose wrought iron is the hair combs and mantillas of tired dancers, aged *bailarinas* many years past their time of dancing.

She is searching for people who knew her the first years of her life, people who loved her before oceans came between them.

It seems to her that the family she's looking for lives in a mortuary, a sky-blue house that is also a mortuary, but a plausible place, with the blue paint thin and scaly and dirt etched on the concrete balustrades that run up to the door. She stands on this threshold, looking up, her foot poised to step on, but gets no further. It is as if she were about to breach a hidden barrier beyond which is a room she doesn't really want to explore, and only wakes herself just in time.

Tonight she finds she can't sleep again, for thinking about her mother.

Consuelo, who is sick.

She has been pushing the thought away all day, but she wakes knowing that her mother is ill, that the hints she dropped the last time they spoke – that her weight was still falling, that she could no longer read Ana's letters – have to be taken seriously.

Her mother is sick, she wakes knowing that she is sick, and she knows she won't be able to sleep well again for a long time.

It's been a long hot night, but not at all like the nights of her infancy and childhood in the near-tropics.

Here the heat is dry, it is the baked crust of the centre of this continent, borne by the wind onto a seaside city.

It is a high, dry fever.

It is discordant: a summer fever.

Ana opens her eyes – impossible to fall back asleep – and turns to the window and stares out. And then the window slides her thoughts from her mother to Dolores, her mother's mother.

Open windows at night do that – they make her nervous. Too often what pours through is the past.

The curtains puff and whip, breathe and sigh, the light from the streetlight skips across the fabric, and after a while she can't stand the tension any longer. She gets up to close the window.

This fear of the night is something Ana got from her Abuela Dolores, but not in the way you might think.

Dolores lived with the family when Ana was growing up.

Oyeme bien – listen carefully, she would say. And so begin a story of Cuban nights deep as a sea, swirling with vipers, vampires and spirits.

The old woman never admitted that she was afraid of the dark. It was not in her to give any explanations, to ever give anything away. Regally, she simply refused to be alone after sunset, to be out at all at night.

Yet when Ana closes the window, it's not for these reasons. It's not that she believes those stories of her grandmother's. Not exactly.

It's what she said later that still worries Ana.

If she's alone, the night coming in through the window reminds her that eventually Dolores's stories changed. When Ana was twelve, Dolores began to tell her, over and over again, that after she died she would not rest.

The two were fighting to see which one would get to live in Ana's mother's house, where there seemed to be less space every day. When Dolores saw that Ana might be winning, she became desperate.

I will always be with you, Ana María. My death will not part us. I will haunt you all your days, she said.

Oyeme bien.

Towards day, just as she might finally be dreaming, she becomes aware of the birds calling in the trees. She imagines she smells smoke and steps outside in bare feet. She walks up to the road and looks around. Everything is milky white and ghostly, like a stand of white-barked gums. Wattlebirds, magpies and honeyeaters fill the dawning day.

There is no smoke that Ana can see and she goes back to bed. It is the fire season.

Then, in that in-between time, neither night nor day, memories well up, more scrambled than dreams, and Ana drifts in and out of them. I'm drifting, she thinks, and a tune comes into her head, a children's song that her mother Consuelo used to sing. A lullabye . . . *Había una vez un barquito chiquitico . . . que no podía, que no podía, que no podía navegar . . .*

There was once a little boat . . . too little to navigate . . .

Then she is no longer in Australia. She is in Cuba, she is three. She is six. She is in Miami, she is four, and the dress she is wearing is too short; her bloomers, plumped by rows of lace at the back, peep from underneath her dress. They are at *la bodega*; she is tired. She wants a *pastelito de guayaba*.

He is there.

She is four. She is five. She is playing *sortijita* in a doorway with two other little girls. They pass the pebble from one set of prayerful hands to the next. One will end up with the stony ring with its promise of marriage. The pebble slips into Ana's hands. It feels heavy, damp and hot. She looks up. *He* walks past.

Había una vez un barquito chiquitico . . .

She is three and a half. She is straining to see over a table, to see the hands washing dominoes. A smell. *His* cologne. She looks up and he is there, across the table. A smallish man, hair gleaming stiffly.

Memories from a time before she knew what faces went with which names.

She is five. They are visiting Pipo, a friend of her father's, a good man, a man who has sometimes helped them when there has been nothing to eat in the laundry room that is their first home in North America.

They are in Pipo's front yard. Lots of people. A big yellow poinciana tree over the whole place. Ana is running around the tree. Chasing. Chased. Nothing can catch her. Nothing can stop her.

Something does. She stops.

He is there.

On a chair, near the low fence. Coral rocks, friendly to spiders. Talking, quietly. *Bahía de Cochinos. Playa Girón. Bahía de Cochinos. Playa Girón.*

He is a hero.

She sips water from the glass in her hand. Puts it near him.

He doesn't drink it.

She is six, and she has walked with her father to *la bodega.* The many smells of this crowded shop, the smells of *lechoncito asado* and *coco rallado* and ripe mangos and roasted *yuca*, billow over the front steps. Pedro stops to buy *un cafecito*, leans forward, talks into the bosom of the woman who serves him, hitches up his pants. Ana pulls on his sleeve, waits for him to look down so she can beg for *un Peter*, and then realises *he* is there.

She stops. Stares at his face. Gazes frankly.

She forgets about the chocolate bar.

Pedro slaps the man's back, detains him with a hand on his arm, insists on buying him *un café.* Pedro talks, and Ana watches the man, and only listens when he starts to talk.

He says that he is going back. That they leave next month.

The other men at the counter fall silent. The music stops. The wind stops. The cigar smoke dissipates.

What stays with Ana, what is still with her all these long years later – as she tries to sleep and drifts between dreams and memories like an unpiloted boat – is his hands. The image of his hands, so fine, white, smooth, almost a woman's hands. Almost her mother's hands.

And the look that was in his eyes as he stared into the distance.

Consuelo Watched the Road Behind

Consuelo Santiago was one of those people who had a love once, and lost it, and spend the rest of their lives haunty-eyed, mercurial and distant, forever gazing backwards from the front of the car, out the back window at the receding horizon.

She was a woman who needed great intimacy, but she was, for historical reasons and, perhaps, personality, beguiled by the faraway, the receding, the spaces between, the breach.

She saw him from time to time, those cruel first years in Miami, and so did Ana. But Ana was too young to know what she was looking at, and anyway she was never told who he was.

Consuelo, of course, did know who he was, knew only too well where he should have been – that is, by her side – and she carried the guilt of that, as well as the full knowl-edge of how impossible that had always been.

She had loved him, loved him well, and she had never given up the habit of loving, and she sat next to Pedro in the battered old Chevy and craned her head around, ostensibly to look at Ana, but really what she was seeing was the past, unrolling behind her.

But Consuelo had never been able to hang on to anything, except Dolores, whom she had not liked from the very first moment her baby eyes clapped on her. Dolores. Just Dolores. No one and nothing else had stayed. Not her mother's house. Not her grandmother's plaited hair. Not a friend's purple-gummed smile. Not a red-roofed house brooding behind a lacy iron fence. Not her lover. Not his hands, not his shoulder, not even his music.

Pedro Santiago never noticed that the hero in their midst, the only man who could make the other *cubanos* stop their tirades mid-word just by shifting his weight and preparing to open his mouth, had eyes for his wife. He never noticed the look on her face when he entered a room, never heard the name she moaned in her sleep. Pedro had his index finger up in the air in front of his face, eclipsing the sun, as Cubans say.

And still he hung around her, her former lover, if not from the force of his will then certainly because of the force of their love, which kept their paths crossing routinely. And this despite the fact that Consuelo had by then reached that time when a woman can, with some assurance, put her babies' diapers to better use as monthlies' rags. She sighed a lot, and at least some of those sighs were relief at something finally winding down, something held too tight too long finally being let go. The hairdresser became a friend of the past unless there was a wedding or a first communion, and on Saturdays and Sundays the rollers gave her head the look of assiduously planted fields and her housedress was stained and wet at the armpits. Everything about her spread a little, including her hips which no longer wanted to samba. And her breasts, so recently purposeful, became during that time socks stretched from too many launderings.

But in truth Consuelo never was a dancer, although with him she had once – many years before – stepped into Havana nightclubs and tried, and why not? But she was no dancer. It was as if the vital part that attaches most of humanity to the herd, some ageless urge to move in unison, had skipped her. She was always totally, fully alone. She could never, even if she wanted to, move in step.

But there must have been a deep attraction, something that kept him on the periphery of their lives. Because Consuelo was married, to the loud and irascible Pedro, and her hands were full with Ana and Carlos, and for her to constantly be running into her love could only appear as a cruel mockery, life's jest, a nonsense.

Until one time became the last time, the finally lost time – a visit to a friend's house for a barbecue on a coquina slab, a final unexchanged glance over a frothing Budweiser. And then he was gone, and Consuelo was back again in the gutted laundry room that was the smallest house she had ever lived in, that first house in what had been promised as the new and better life. Wandering in a space six by eight, spending her nights again plying a dry sea on a drifting raft.

She did not see him because he left precipitately, and Cuban jails rarely surrendered their catches, having learnt a lesson in 1953 after releasing the leader of the Moncada revolt. She did not see him, but she dreamed him. If, by some unfathomable tug or some inexplicable twist, she and Pedro touched in the night, interlaced, and held on briefly, then she would fall asleep uneasy and he would come, and speak: mysterious utterances, elliptical reproaches.

She must have wondered sometimes whether he haunted her or she haunted herself. She did wonder – I heard her say it once, even if it was in another context – if she could never reach for happiness, if it only had to meow at her door and show its white tail on the porch for her to pick it up and bash it into the wall.

Because sure enough by midday, if it was a Saturday – earlier if a weekday – she and Pedro would have killed whatever happiness they had spawned the night before in a floorquaking, shitkicking, namesplattering brawl.

She did not know whether or not he was in prison, although she embraced the possibility like a sweet desolation. But she also tortured herself with the obverse – he was free, he walked, he danced into someone else's eyes, he lifted a limp curl from someone else's face to tuck it behind someone else's ear.

And never again did Consuelo move without that empty nothing feeling in the centre of her that she had had as a child when she wondered who her father was and where her *mami* was and never again did she look long into any-one's – anyone's – eyes.

So Dolores raised her kids. Consuelo got a two-bit job at the South Miami factory where Pedro worked and left Carlos and Ana in the not very benign care of Abuela

Dolores. Consuelo was too shrouded in Dolores's webs to see that she should not be near her children.

Dolores did not live with them at first, but she spent the interminable and always summer daylight hours in the old weatherboard farmhouse on 25th Street in north-west Miami.

At the factory Consuelo shuffled papers for a man running from bankruptcy, who kept snakes in a burlap sack in the filing cabinet and let an iguana roam the office, destroying her nerves. By late afternoon, around 5.30, she and Pedro would be back at 25th Street, arriving bad-tempered from manoeuvering the little battered Chevy through lunatic traffic along melting streets. Dolores was there to meet them at the door, to inform them of all she had done for them that day and what trouble six-year-old Ana had been (it was Ana who was trouble; Carlos's misbe-haviour came from nervous energy and was therefore benign, was tolerable, but in Ana Dolores saw something malevolent). She told Consuelo what dishes were cooking on the stove before striding from the house, an ill-used old woman. Well before nightfall she would be back in the two-roomed duplex around the corner with her husband Montero – who was not, who it seems could not possibly have been, Consuelo's father.

People said Dolores and Pedro had been lucky to find a place for her so close by. The old farmhouse, a fossil in a now suburban street, and the duplex were both rented from the same *yanqui* landlord. All the houses on the block were unfenced, which meant that the dog, Happy, a German shepherd, lived tethered to a chain at the foot of the ficus tree. Ana could stand by her back door and look across the unfenced yards straight to Abuela Dolores's door.

Dolores taught Ana to sew. Rolling her jaw sideways to wet the length of thread in her mouth, she held the needle up towards the light from the verandah, screwed up her left eye and passed the damp thread through the needle, knotting it at the end so it wouldn't slip out in Ana's clumsy fingers.

A *ver, mija, óyeme bien*, she commanded, and Ana studied her old woman's hands – dry, red, criss-crossed with silvery lines.

Dolores saw her hands as symbols. She was careless, even brutal, with herself, and her hands were always injured, shredded during her hours in the kitchen and bearing slug-like blisters from the stove, as well as scars from ancient wars. A thin white tracing near the ball of her palm, exactly in the shape of a fish-hook, was a gift from a Cuban scorpion. The flap of skin over the festering wound had taken a year to heal.

Mine are the slave's hands in this family, she declared when she was angry, holding them up to be viewed like a fisherman holds up lobsters. Or: I am the bad finger of this family – *el dedo malo* – she sang out, in a tone that had an edge of satisfaction. Carlos and Ana smiled.

Ana was a beautiful, brooding child. She had almond-shaped eyes, heavily lashed, dark at their centres and luminously white all around, and the contrast reflected her nature. Above all, she was intelligent. But she had acquired the habit of silence, of staring mutely, of watching. Consuelo had made a great mistake when she thought Ana might be simple, when she scarcely spoke by the age of four.

Consuelo took her to old Doctor McDonald, who despite his Anglo name was Cuban and had delivered Ana back in Havana.

Doctor, she hardly ever speaks, Consuelo had complained. Doctor McDonald examined Ana's ears and noted that the child's hearing was perfect. He saw the intelligent look in Ana's eyes and Consuelo's harassed face. He rightly surmised that Ana's muteness was not the issue. She was merely quiet. Worrying about it had become a diversion for Consuelo, different from a stroll through the park but more effective. In truth there was always too much happening for Ana to waste words. She was preparing for the day when she could speak with sufficient gravity. And she was dreamy.

Dolores tried to wake her. She wanted to prepare her for the life of domestic bliss of a Cuban housewife.

When you have *un nene*, she said, knotting Ana's final stitch and snipping the thread, you must leave the scissors open under his pillow, like this, forming a crucifix. That does two things – it cuts the bad luck in the child's life. And keeps vampires away.

Ana tried, but found she could not imagine herself, grown up, bending over a sleeping baby's pillow with open scissors in her hand. Nor did she think there had been vampires at her own crib, which she knew had been in her mother's spacious and airy and clean bedroom in her fine marble-tiled house in Havana. But she looked at Dolores's face as she talked about coconuts that chatted and nodded and sent messages from the past, and women who were half-fish and still had scales under their armpits and in the

17

moist part between their legs because they were our ances-
tors who had gone to our island before us, and *patriotas*
hanging from gallows who would never rest in their graves
but crowded the homes of their murderers' descendants to
this day. She imagined a dark and overgrown place where
there were no bright greens or blues, only drab olives and
greys, and nights were always tenebrous. She saw a rough
crib – a crate – in a dark hut, and a baby – her mother
Consuelo – whose little fists did nothing to frighten the
vampires that flapped in her skies.

As Dolores's voice droned on, Ana embroidered the
image. The velvety swishing beasts with their little pug
faces all looked like Dolores.

Dolores wanted to spend more than her days in their fat
sprawling house on 25th Street. It was a dwelling as closely
resembling Dolores's person in its incongruities and hidden
recesses as was possible. And perhaps that played a part in
why Dolores was so drawn to live there, campaigned for it
so hard and was so willing to rid herself of Montero. But she
had to wait two years, two long Miami years of zipping back
and forth between the duplex and her heart's desire. She
finally came to a stop at 25th Street that year that Ana was
six, the spring before she started school and the afternoon
that Montero died.

It was a strange house. Only a few months earlier Pedro's
best friend from the old days, Cheo, had arrived at their
doorstep. This was on a Saturday and he had with him his
daughter Rosa, who was also six, his wife and the clothes

they were standing in, and a travel bag given to them by the American Red Cross with a tablet of soap inside and a first-aid kit but nothing to sustain a Cuban refugee with not enough money for *un hamboogar* or *una* Coca-Cola.

Pedro had greeted Cheo with a manly hug and many claps on the back. *Dios mío*, Consuelo, look who's here, he exclaimed, bending over in happiness, slapping his knee with such joviality that anyone who didn't know him well would have been misled about his true nature.

Por Dios, Consuelo, get my *compadre* here *una cerveza!* Don't be a *guajira, mujer!*

Pedro invited Cheo and his family to stay until they could find a place of their own. He led Cheo through the eccentric hallways connecting the rooms of that former farmhouse, and then on through the back door and to the yard to sit in an aluminium chair and drink his *cerveza*. Ana, tagging behind, first became aware, through her father's eyes, how wrong the house was. With every step, he made excuses for their home.

The Santiagos liked modern things. The very new – wood unpolished by centuries of human touch and jewellery untarnished by sweat – was what they took, given a choice. Perhaps it came from living in the tropics, where things were more likely to be ravaged by heat and discoloured by mould and warped by torrential rain and nothing – nothing – could keep out the damp. But even so, that didn't account for the fact that no one Ana knew had the slightest interest in any sort of antique or heirloom, in anything older than a year, nor would they wear anything second-hand. All in all, very little except pain was ever passed down.

The house embarrassed them. It was old, it was a relic, and ugly. A lumpish thing, unadmired and unloved. It had a false tower on one corner, a round, blind turret that led nowhere, a preposterous thing. And it had a fireplace – what an incredible phenomenon! Why would anyone risk lighting a fire in the middle of their house? And another thing, it had a roof that caught the edge of a wind, that beat it into a wail – the steep roof of those houses that waited for snow many miles to the north – and under this roof was an attic, dark and unfriendly, reached by pulling stairs down from the back verandah that refolded themselves like the arms of a praying mantis.

And even worse – *¡Qué horror, muchacha!* – there was a basement under the house. *Un sótano* – even the name sounded dank and fetid and evil, like the word 'sewer' in English. It had a basement, a hollow, a hole where the house's foundations should have been. On stormy nights, Consuelo dreamt that the house collapsed on itself and fell into its pit.

The house had only two bedrooms, only two rooms that seemed fit for the purpose of sleeping, but it had many strange rooms: a useless room next to Consuelo's bedroom that was wedge-shaped, that could not fit a bed or even a table and yet was too large to use as a closet. And another room past the cavernous bathroom that was a dead-end place, where no one wanted a closet, much less living space. The other rooms of the house meandered off corridors and had only the weirdest logic, the kitchen behind the second bedroom and the dining room in front of the lounge room.

It may have been a dairy at one time, because it had a grey barn, with paint peeling in curls like perched butterflies, and a loft, and a shower room large enough to wash a cow.

All of these things were unusual and unjustifiable. The Santiagos and their friends didn't call it a barn; they called it *el garaje*. A barn, for *habaneros*, was nothing to be proud of. The country look held no nostalgic appeal for them, Cubans whose families had only one generation ago surged to Havana pursued by the misery of the countryside.

Carlos and Ana and, for the short time she was with them, Cheo's daughter Rosa, never went into the attic or the basement. It was not just that these places were forbidden – almost everything there was to do in that house transgressed some family bylaw. They never ventured up or down because those parts of the house oppressed them, frightened them, were dark and scary and filled their mouths with cobwebs. Corridors led off corridors in a maze that kept Cheo's family confused all the days they stayed with them.

The house unsettled everyone with its mysterious potential. There was more space than could be accounted for, spaces that were locked in like the secret tombs of the Pharaohs, dead spaces that no one could reach scattered throughout. Fake walls trapped sound so that the secrets whispered by Dolores in the house's dark closets echoed back to Ana many years after they were spoken.

Consuelo, Pedro and Dolores considered that it would have been better to live in a house without so much history, without the baggage of a past. They would have loved a

21

small, modern house set in a treeless lot, a house under control, not old and fat and sprawling. They dreamt of houses that were open and light and breezy like the ones they left in Havana, that they had lost, that they said had been torn from them by *El Déspota*. They would have liked to own such a house again, even knowing how easily it could be stolen in a social whirlwind. But we are *refugiados*, Pedro said, we have been betrayed by Kennedy – *ese hijo de puta* – and we have to take Uncle Sam's crumbs.

The noises Cheo and his wife Gloria heard in their first night in *los Estados Unidos*, the squeals in the ficus tree which spread over the back of the house, over the verandah and the roof of the second bedroom, the scraping sounds in the attic and the thumps under the windows, Pedro explained in the morning, scoffing at Gloria's fears: This certainly is not *La Habana, mi negra!* Here it is more like the countryside, *compadre: pues* there are squirrels in the trees! *Sí*, and an animal like the ghost of a cat, they call it *un* opposum, *sí, increíble!* There is no civilisation here, *mi hermano*.

Carlos and Ana took an immediate dislike to Rosa, a plump little girl Ana's age with fuzzy orange hair. That first afternoon of their acquaintance Ana spent bailed up against the rough walls of *el garaje*, hands splayed out on either side, her face screwed up in a mute wail of apprehension. It agitated Happy, who strained on the end of his chain and whined. Indeed, there seemed to be something canine about Rosa. She sniffed Ana and smiled into her face, wagged her tail, headbutted her in what Ana did not realise was a friendly suggestion.

She only wants to play, smiled her parents, already embarrassed by their flagrant imposition on the family. Ana looked at their daughter and thought she had never met anyone like them.

Eventually Carlos rescued her. He studied Rosa and realised her potential. He led Rosa to Consuelo's room and took the box of talcum powder from her dresser.

Look, it's snow! he said, shaking it vigorously over Consuelo's white chenille bedspread. You try it. It's good.

Rosa hesitated, but they sustained her in her moment of doubt, initiated her into the games children played in the United States, coaxed her to shake, just a little: *Así*, Rosita, don't be afraid. And then left her in the powder-coated bedroom when they heard footsteps.

¡Ay, *Dios santo!* ¡Ave *María purísima!* screeched Dolores, clapping her hands together in front of her face and lifting her eyes to the ceiling. What a creature!

Her calls to the avenging angels had to be heeded, and it was one of the few times Cheo ever struck Rosita.

Rosa and her parents did not stay long but somehow they became a focus for Ana. She first saw the house clearly during their visit. And it did not stop there. Rosa touched her in ways that always surprised her. It was in a dream many years later that Ana realised Rosa's life had become the story she told herself, for contrast.

But their visit, if eye-opening, was only the briefest interlude in the house on 25th Street, and, after they left, life refolded itself around them like a worn garment that falls into place along its tired creases. In the mornings, Consuelo and Pedro and later Carlos hurried out of the house and Ana was left with Dolores. The days once again unrolled in an endless monotony of hot quiet sunshine outside, and Ana's grandmother's voice, her grandmother's radio, her grandmother's food and her grandmother's hands inside.

Dolores had fierce dark eyes and a small heart-shaped mouth. She had never been beautiful, although she once had a certain severe, stark handsomeness, judging by fading and creased photographs. But she herself claimed to have been one of La Habana's greatest beauties. She boasted that she had always attracted men, that they had gathered around her like flies around a ripe mango.

No one in the house contradicted her, even though by then, in her twilight, and with Montero in custody in the duplex, she bore no resemblance to her boasts. If anything, she went the other way – she punished the eye.

She forced over her bulging lines Consuelo's discarded clothes, so that skirts stretched around her belly and her rear, sliding back sharply towards her stick legs, and sleeveless blouses cut into her armpits.

Sometimes, as she shoved around in the kitchen, as she raised her hands towards a high shelf or to plead with God for something or other, they got glimpses of the conical brassières she made for herself from sewing scraps. A stiff, textured polyester purple or a motif in green winked from her blouse.

She had tight bits of permed hair that had once been pitch-black but were now different shades of brunette, depending on which hair dye Consuelo had bought that month to be shared between herself, Dolores and Pedro.

24

Pedro, in his prime but grey, said he needed the hair dye for work, needed to colour his head to keep his factory job. He said old men were flicked away. And maybe that was true, but Consuelo also knew that he did it just as much for the ladies at the *bodega*, where he spent his evenings padding about in his polished moccasins, or airing his political views (she called that sort of talk *descargando* – flushing the toilet) with one foot on a stool in front of the counter stacked with Cuban pastries and a hand on a paper thimble of coffee that he never quite drained. (But still she slushed the foul-smelling yellow-black basting brush around his head, and wiped the splatters from his face.)

Carlos, who was seven and in First Grade at Fairweather Elementary, was woken early by Consuelo or Pedro to prepare for school. Dolores arrived just as Carlos was bringing up his breakfast. The vomiting was not seen as a result of anything that happened in the house. It was considered a part of his heritage as a refugee. Some time after the revolution – that storm which had descended on them that year Carlos was one – between the times of crisis and bombings and counter-revolution, of despair and exile and soul-searching and hunger and a truer discovery of the meaning of despair, Carlos had got into the habit of vomiting. Dolores, Consuelo and Pedro saw a connection between Fidel and Carlos's sensitive stomach.

Rosa's mother Gloria, when she had stayed with the family, had observed that perhaps Carlos didn't need a cup of hot sweet milk and coffee with his breakfast. Perhaps it added to his nervous hyperactivity and unsettled his stomach?

¡Muchacha! Dolores had exclaimed. Don't talk nonsense! She had pulled the tin of coffee from the cupboard and showed it to Gloria, leaning into her. Look at this! *¿Qué dice?* Nestlé! she answered herself. I drink it myself. Don't talk nonsense.

Consuelo, who had had the same argument with Dolores many times before and always lost it, pretended not to hear. She was thinking of the office, of how the iguana had yesterday flicked its tongue at her when she encountered it unexpectedly, asleep in a beam of sunshine that entered from a high window and penetrated under her desk. She could not question Dolores in front of Gloria. Dolores would be affronted, would scream in toxic self-defence, and everyone would be embarrassed. Tomorrow, Consuelo knew, Carlos would be given strong coffee and would vomit again. She thought about other things.

In *el exilio*, she had to work. Pedro did not make enough at the plaster factory to support the family, so every day she hurried out of the house, leaving Dolores to deal with Carlos in the bathroom.

At the factory Pedro filled moulds with plaster. He eased home the religious statues that had hairline cracks or were imperfect in some scarcely discernible way. Angels, crucifixes and plaster Marías swarmed on their walls. Some had little crevices for flowers; these Dolores stuffed with red plastic roses from the Five and Ten.

On the disingenuous morning towards the end of May when Dolores left the duplex for the last time, Carlos had vomited early and was watching *Captain Kangaroo* on the television. Dolores flung a few crisp words at Consuelo's and Pedro's departing backs and urged Ana out of bed with quick flicks of the old belt she wore buckle up at her side: it hung to her ankles and writhed when she hurried. She then clicked on the radio in the kitchen and stood at the sink washing black beans for a *potaje*, swishing them around with her clawlike hand, setting them to soak in a deep speckled cauldron on top of the stove.

This was in the days when she still ate with the family what she had cooked, before she started eating her meals mushed in a saucepan, and before she took, in her last years, to defecating in different places in the house, occasionally even in kitchen pots, so that they had to hurry after her to keep clear what she had used for what that day. But already she cooked carelessly, sloshing the beans in the bottom of the pot, picking out deficient ones with impatient gestures. In between she talked to her friends on the phone and listened to her *novelas*, the soap operas on the radio that were as important to her as life – that at times she took more seriously than the life around her.

An enterprising Cuban woman drove a station wagon past the house every morning at 7.30 to take Carlos to school. Cubans would not let their children walk alone to school like the uncaring Americans did. Instead, twelve to fourteen children would be ferried each trip, and if Carlos had not already lost his breakfast, he did it in the car. By then *Captain Kangaroo* had been switched off and Ana wandered the empty rooms of the house on 25th Street.

The day warmed and stretched ahead of her, the house creaked and settled, and Dolores's radio tried to fill the morning with the blare of Cuban music and the emotional, self-important male voices guiding housewives through their work.

Towards mid-morning Dolores made a *sofrito* of onions and green peppers and six cloves of garlic, ground the beans into it with an effort that left the fat on her arms swinging like the hammocks she strung up in the back yard, and put it all to boil in a couple of litres of water in the big green *olla de presión*. She favoured the pressure cooker, relished the frenzied shaking of its little button top and struggled with its lid, grunting as she forced it open amid the hiss of escaping steam.

Ana was underfoot. She heard the harangues to the pots, watched as Dolores stopped to scoop a handful of scalding rice with her fingers. She swallowed without so much as breathing on it first. Then she tilted her throat towards the ceiling to gulp down a string of raw meat, and extended another towards Ana. *Hija*, take this! Blood, to give you strength!

But Ana was bolting towards the daytime stillness of the part of the house that was in front of the kitchen. Picking up a basket of tiny plastic dolls, she hid in the long closet of the room she shared with Carlos. There, nestled amongst clothes that had fallen to the floor and boxes of blankets stored for the winter, she played with the dolls, manoeuvering them first gently and then harshly and murmuring reproofs for several hours.

Around two o'clock, long after Ana and Dolores had finished their lunch of steak fried with onions, white rice, Cuban bread and black bean *potaje*, Montero ambled over, slicing across Old Man Mathers's back yard and hauling himself up the three steps of the house.

28

He sat down at the kitchen table – a table squeezed onto the verandah of the house, just beyond the kitchen – and stared around, blinking pale red-rimmed eyes, as if not quite sure he was in the right place. Then he was asleep, his head thrown back, his face turned towards the attic stairs that folded themselves into the roof. His scantily toothed mouth was a foul hole. A half-dead cigarette balanced on its edge, jigging in time to his breathing.

Dolores called Montero a doubled-over, empty sack of a man. He wore his few strands of greasy hair pinned to his scalp with brilliantine. He was not so much old as useless, having entered early retirement, Dolores said, soon after adolescence. He was the sort of man people ignored, she said – the sort who even in his youth was never clapped on the shoulders in the vigorous greeting of Cuban *machos*.

He moved among them like a spirit, leaving no trail to prove he had been there, no fingerprints on the cutlery and no imprint on the mind, no wake at all except a smudge of ash where his *cigarrito* had twitched, and the lingering personal smell of helpless, bovine poverty that was like a door into the Cuban countryside.

Ese cabrón, Pedro called him. As in the English 'bastard', *cabrón* had connotations of 'poor bastard'. At other times it could be pronounced so that it carried nothing but contempt.

Pedro told Consuelo he didn't know who was luckier, *ese cabrón* Montero who had never done a day's work in his life yet had found in his old age a woman who put food into his mouth as if he were a child, or his mother-in-law Dolores who in her late years, when no trace of her former looks

29

could be gleaned, had a man who never answered her, never, in fact, said a word, but kept her company at night. (The existence of a third lucky party, themselves, was not canvassed. But Montero was useful, because although they fed him *de gratis*, he did them the invaluable service of providing a respite from Dolores, at least at night.)

Dolores came up behind Montero with a steaming dish of black bean *potaje* and prodded him with her elbow. He started; his cigarette fell to the floor where it was left to make the marks Ana confused with cockroaches at twilight.

At quarter to three they left him with his spoon slowly travelling from plate to mouth. They walked the ten blocks to Fairweather Elementary where they met Carlos.

It was on the return trip that Carlos suddenly yelled 'fart' in Spanish. *Peee-ooo* hung for seconds in the hot still air.

Maybe he did it for the fun of it, to irritate and test Dolores, or perhaps just because it expressed something he felt about the afternoon. Carlos stopped and turned around and looked at Dolores, a mischievous grin on his nervous face. Dolores's features were even grimmer than usual, but she didn't deign to react on the street. When Carlos thought he had gotten away with it, she whispered to Ana, Wait until we get home.

By the time they had cut across the alley Dolores was ahead of him. She stepped inside two seconds before he did and had enough time to take off her belt, double it, and grab his arm as he passed through the door. Carlos hunched as the belt came down on his shoulders, and cried out, and curled into a ball on the floor. But Dolores did not hit him more than half a dozen times before she paused. There was something wrong in the room.

Ana, who had been watching quietly, followed her gaze to the table. There Montero sat slumped in his chair with his face in the deep bowl of black bean *potaje*, from forehead to nose, so they couldn't see his face at all, only whisps of hair clinging to his shiny scalp.

Dolores crossed herself, murmuring *ave María purísima*. She wouldn't go near him. After a minute the belt slipped from her hand and she sank to her knees on the floor where Carlos had recently been and stayed there, crossing herself and quietly repeating *ave María, ave María purísima, madre de Dios*.

Carlos and Ana walked stiffly to the telephone and Carlos, his face the colour and set of the plaster Jesus crucified, for the first time broke the rules by dialing the number of the factory. He asked for Consuelo Santiago. When they heard her anxious voice, they yelled into the mouthpiece, Mami, Mami, Montero drowned in his *potaje!*

Where the Living Slept

Ana spent the rest of the day hiding and watching from under the skirt of her mother's sewing machine, and Dolores never again went home.

Doctor McDonald came to look at Montero and declared that his blood pressure, never too good, must have slipped dangerously.

But surely that happened before he died? said Pedro, who was by then back from the factory.

The doctor peered at him from above his glasses, wondering if he was simpler than he had previously seemed, but decided he was nervous. *Sí, sí, sí,* prior to the death, he said solemnly.

Pedro stared at the corpse, shaking his head, and exclaimed, *¡Qué fenómeno más grande!* – what an incredible phenomenon! He stayed with Montero as Consuelo walked the doctor to the door. *Qué fenómeno más grande,* Pedro said again, as if faced with a head-breaking puzzle, as if Montero's death were a fantastic thing, unintelligible, incomprehensible – impossible, really.

It was his phrase whenever anything happened beyond his ability to cope. Then he blamed the event on the freakish indocility of nature — what an incredible phenomenon! – as if such things just didn't happen in the normal course of life. *¡Qué fenómeno más grande!* he said if the electricity went out, or the car broke down on South Dixie Highway and he had to open the hood and look inside.

Dolores and Consuelo began scrubbing the house, concentrating on the kitchen and verandah. Night had fallen, a night redolent of fried onions and stagnant water. The hacking of the crickets outside was sad, squeezed out by the heavy air. From time to time, Consuelo would sigh, *Ay, Dios,* and pause. She arched her back with her hands around the mop, then bent over to press it into the linoleum again. Ana, hiding under the homemade skirt of the sewing-machine table, half listened to their murmurs and mutters and rags of talk. She became more alert when she heard Dolores say she would sleep in Ana's bed that night.

She thought about how Dolores smelled – of the garlic pinned inside her blouses, and of the onions always in her hands and of her tomcat-vinegary sweat, and other things that Ana, at six, wasn't able to identify.

And she snored.

Bueno, Mami, Consuelo said. That little room is already very crowded . . . You could sleep here. Cheo's family passed their time here very happily, and the Gutiérrezes never complained.

Consuelo crossed the verandah, grabbed the edge of the curtain that hung on rusty metal rings from a pole, and drew it. The whole area – the formica-topped table where the family ate and the part of the verandah on the other side of the pole, with its sewing machine under which Ana was hiding, and the ironing table, and the high shelves above the windows where games and toys were stacked – was the centre of life in the daytime.

But the place reminded Dolores too clearly of other curtained-off rooms where she had lived, half-rooms in boarding houses through which people walked to get to their own rooms, their prying eyes and feet and hands *manoseando* your life. Where, she said, you couldn't fart quietly enough – and no one else bothered to try. She would sleep in a proper bedroom, with a door. If that meant sharing with two children, she would do it. What were two *chiquillos*? But she would not be pushed ever again into a curtained place. She would not squat, let strangers see her bottom, or let herself be manoeuvered. *¡No Señor! De eso nada.*

And although she would never have admitted it, it must have seemed to her too close to the scene of the day's fatality, too far from the rooms where the living in the house slept.

Here I am, destitute, a poor widow, and the daughter who sprang from me – *que me salió de las entrañas* – says there is no room in her house for me!

No, Mami. Don't be stubborn. Of course there is room –

I will not sleep there. Because I don't feel like it. Because – and here Dolores said something that is hard to translate, that Ana only ever heard *her* say. She didn't feel like sleeping on the back verandah, she said, because the urge did not spring from her loins – *¡Por que no me sale de la papaya!*

Whenever she spoke of her *papaya*, she would put her

34

hands on her lower stomach, just above her legs, and press up and down so that her stomach jiggled. *Paaa-paaa-yaa*, she bellowed. It was a gesture that appalled Consuelo.

Ana peeked. She was interested in the image of her mother bursting from the place Abuela had been jiggling.

I will sleep with the children, Dolores declared. Or my name isn't Dolores Gutiérrez de Tacoronte.

Pero, chica, said Consuelo, still trying to reason with her. That room only has one window! Can't you see that Carlitos and Ana María are already crowded in there. That they are growing up, they need more space, if anything!

Dolores didn't see. Her face was livid; her eyes shot sparks. Damn all of you! she intoned. Why didn't you tell me I wasn't wanted before I gave up everything – *todo, todo, todísimo* – to be with you in this cursed and Godless exile?

That was one of the things they fought about. When the family came to Miami in 1962, Dolores had stayed behind with Montero in Havana. That year was the only time since Consuelo's childhood that she had managed to put any distance between herself and Dolores, and they disagreed over whether Dolores had subsequently come of her own accord or had been summoned.

Dolores claimed that Consuelo begged her to come, that her tearful letters to Havana stated she couldn't cope with her children alone. Consuelo furiously denied ever writing such a thing.

Whatever the two had wished to convey in the letters that had criss-crossed the Florida straits must have been lost in the formal niceties of written Spanish. Or else Dolores read into them what she chose. For she had come, and now Montero was dead, and a place had to be found for her to sleep.

Now here I am, raising your *chiquillos!* While you waltz away with your husband to make plaster angels. I am treated worse than a servant. I am the sick finger of this family, *el dedo malo!*

Dolores parked her face hard up against Consuelo's so that her spit could reach its target. You treat me like *el culo del negro* – the black man's ass. Demon that I pulled from a garbage can! Child of bad sperm!

The words tripped a landslide of jagged feelings in Consuelo – released from half-submerged memories of things Consuelo would have liked to forget if only she had been able to forgive. A bed in a slum tenement, an open window, Consuelo staring out. Not able to get up because she was tied, calflike, ankle and knee.

A train coming to her pueblo, and Consuelo with nothing more solid to cling to than a single strand of hair. Wrenched from the only person who ever loved her truly, her four-year-old's tears dampening the dust.

Consuelo pushed Dolores away, unbalancing her and sending her skating across the wet floor. Dolores came to a stop against the Frigidaire.

You've killed me, you've killed me, she hissed, her chest heaving with asthmatic breaths. Wait for me, Montero! I'm going with you!

Get up, get up, urged Consuelo, tugging at her arm. *Por Dios*, Ana María, get out of there and help me!

When Dolores stood, half dragged and still yelling to Montero to wait, it was obvious that she was not dead. But at that moment Consuelo knew, bitterly, that Dolores would always in the future refer to that day as: The time they flung me across the kitchen like a *puta's* underpants.

You make my life impossible! You have always made my life impossible! Consuelo wailed. You followed me here because you bullied me for thirty years, and no one else, not even Montero – whose balls you always clutched in your fist – was as satisfying for you!

But when the floor slipped out from under Dolores's feet, Consuelo lost her moral ground. That night Ana shared her bed with Abuela Dolores.

Why is it that images are acid-etched onto our memories, smells can conjure up great chunks of the past, but once a voice is gone it's gone for good? Ana can remember the qualities of Dolores's voice: grating, shrill, above all, commanding. Perhaps she should be grateful that she can't actually hear her. But she remembers her words.

No one could ever best her in an argument; she was simply too clever. Her ability to ridicule left people either helpless with laughter or determined to hate her forever.

You are a condom on the penis of progress, she snarled at Pedro.

Radio bemba, she spat at a woman at the *bodega* who was gossiping, implying that the woman's thick lips – her *bemba* – were akin to a radio transmitter.

I am independent and sovereign, she proclaimed to the household.

Such was her strength that no one ever thought of her as

having fears. But she did. She was beset by fears. In all the hot years of Ana's childhood, after all the long and tiresome trips to Crandon Park, Cape Florida, Haulover and Miami Beach, Dolores never once went near the sea. She sat in an aluminium chair that they took for her, as far from the water's edge as possible, and kept her eyes on Ana as she bobbed and played in the warm and gentle waters of the Atlantic.

Ay, hija, ¿y por qué? she exclaimed when Ana ran out, water sluicing off and salt in her eyes, to pull Consuelo's hand. Dolores reminded Consuelo of what the salt water would do to her periods and, trying to dissuade Consuelo, drove her into Ana's arms. And it wasn't just jealousy, although of course that was there too. But the sea for Dolores was a liquid night, a slippery, treacherous dimension.

She courted that endless darkness in her own fashion. No one understood why she compelled doctors to perform exploratory surgery on her six times. Each time they found nothing, but gave her the satisfaction of a new scar. At thirty-two she had cast off her reproductive organs, at thirty-six she had enjoyed the removal of her appendix; she divested herself of her tonsils when she was forty-three. She craved the knife, she craved the anaesthetic, she needed to feel pain.

Above all, she needed to remove something from inside, something deep inside that she had carried for a long time and which was so painful for her to focus on, so unthinkable, that at times she thought it was a section of her colon, or something here, in *el vientre*, or here, right under the heart. (It moves around, Doctor, it is intolerable, you don't

38

know what I suffer . . . Your pain is incurable, Señora, it is caused by the cicatrices of your earlier operations – it comes with your history, Señora . . .)

Dolores proclaimed herself undaunted by life and unafraid of death. But when she gazed at the airy space in the back verandah, she saw only the windows that would let in the night's vapours. Perhaps she was afraid of Montero. Perhaps she felt guilty when she thought of him. Who knows? She never mentioned him again, never, not once. That day he passed from their lives completely, a character in a forgotten dream.

After a few nights, Ana refused to share her bed. During the day she told Dolores that she wouldn't sleep with her, that she didn't like her. And at bedtime, with Consuelo standing next to her, she threw tantrums, screaming that she hated Dolores, that she would sleep with her mother instead.

To avoid these scenes, she was allowed to watch television with Consuelo until she fell asleep. They would lie on the living-room couch, Ana in front, both stretched straight, two planks of a vast floor – Consuelo's liquid hand never resting, stroking away at whatever scrunched Ana's forehead.

Eventually the television images turned to fuzz and Ana's head swirled with disconnected thoughts and she slept. Then Pedro carried her to bed, where she woke to a new day in a bad mood, squeezed against the cold wall behind Dolores's towering bulk.

Ana challenged the old woman. Get out of my bed, she demanded.

And where should I sleep, *desgraciada chiquilla*? Tell me

that, *fiera*, malignant spirit, heart-of-concrete. Where should an aged and dying woman like myself lay down when night comes?

Ana stared and did not voice her thought. She would have gladly had her sleep in the street. Cruelty coursed through her veins and she was ashamed and uglified but she stood her ground. There was not much that had ever been hers in that ramshackle house. She thought she would win because justice should prevail.

But she lost. Consuelo and Pedro went to Jackson Byron's one evening after work and came home with a package half the size of a real bed. It was a fold-up bed, which they called a *ping-pang-pung*. Every night it was wheeled out and wedged at the foot of the other two beds, in front of the chest of drawers.

In a last-ditch effort to enjoy a solid bed, a bed one could fling oneself on day or night, in happiness or sorrow, Ana begged for bunks, which she had seen at Jeffrey and Linda's, the American kids from the other side of the alley.

Those deathtraps, Pedro said. We are not *americanos*. Never – *jamás. Jamás, jamás, jamás*. Again and again he grasped for the finality he longed to express. He had nothing but disdain for *los americanos*. *¡Esa gente!* Do you think they love their children? Do you think they sacrifice themselves for their children as I do, digesting my lungs every day in that cement factory? He wagged his head sideways, so wound up that he could not stop repeating his point, carried on wave after wave of indignation. His lips pouted into a *bemba*. His right hand cut the air like a windshield wiper, in rhythm with his head.

Mourning Montero

After Montero's death, Dolores swore she would wear black the rest of her life. At first she seemed to enjoy the drama of the moment, the lights on her, the phone calls, the condolences in the letterbox. Pedro always said she had missed her true vocation, that with her great memory and dramatic talent, she should have been an actress.

But she soon tired of the expressions of sympathy from friends and acquaintances. She listened to them with pursed lips, suffered their courteous inquiries, and then, despite her prodigious talent, wearied of the effort of feigning distress.

Her fourth husband had hung heavy on her hands for some years, providing little by way of entertainment or relief in his decrepitude. And he had stood in the way of what she had been ready for, which was to be reunited with Consuelo and live under her roof and manage her affairs. She had always hated the moment she stepped out of Consuelo's house every evening, leaving Consuelo to live her own life, make her own decisions. At such moments she had felt a profound insecurity.

While Montero was alive she had had no other choice. Pedro would not consent to them both living in the house on 25th Street while the government was disposed to help with the rent of the duplex. So Dolores felt that Montero's dying was the finest thing he had ever done, an intuitive realisation of her deepest desire. In the end – and only in the end – he had stepped aside for her *como un caballero*.

She had other reasons for abandoning black. She could not stand the reminder of her own immortality. In this – and many other ways – she was like her son-in-law. Ana often heard Consuelo and Pedro, late at night or behind closed doors on a sultry Saturday, arguing over the question of life insurance. And if something happens? Consuelo would demand. If a bag of cement falls off a truck and crushes your empty head? Then what, tell me? *Como siempre*. You don't change. Your finger up, obscuring the sun.

No comas mierda. Nothing, but nothing, is going to happen to me. What shit. Leave me alone.

The insinuation that you might be mortal is an insult, eh? So. You'll live forever. Jesus Christ! Poor me. Poor me. Poor children. Imbecile!

But whereas Pedro could only stalk out of the house, hounded by Consuelo's fury, Dolores had all sorts of tricks to cover her deep fears. With her indomitable will she replastered the chink in reality that allowed death to happen at all, that had allowed Montero to slip through. Right after his funeral service she abandoned her raven's costume, forbade the children to ever mention Montero's name again, and tried forcefully to forget he had ever lived.

She did not know that she was already missing him. She was not the sort of person to admit such a thing to herself. But she was agitated.

Perhaps it was the surprise of being free once again, and yet finding no takers around, no male sniffing her wake, no one remotely interested in her. It was like a challenge, a thrust by life that had to be parried. Anyway, for whatever reason, something half-dormant in her awakened and roared.

She had never before lived without *un macho*.

After her third day of mourning, she pulled on her bright, tight dresses again. But as the weeks and months slid past, these, too, were dropped in a corner. Dolores discarded all pretence of widowhood and began to wear more and more exotic and tasteless things. Her favourite was a diaphanous flowing gown in vibrant colours with which she hoped to attract the male.

Musty, musky odours wafted through the house. At first no one knew from where they were coming. Consuelo put Pedro's shoes on the steps outside the back door each evening when he came home from work. On Saturday morning she handed Ana an old toothbrush and showed her how to brush around the lilac ceramic taps and the edges of the purple tiles in the bathroom. Everyone showered more frequently, Pedro directly after the sultry drive home and again after watering the lawn, before going out on his evening prowls.

But the smells persisted, eventually permeating the house. It was Carlos and Ana, who lived closest to her, who first discovered that the slightly stale and vaguely unsettling smells were being swished and dispersed by their Abuela's new wardrobe.

Pedro's male friends – his *socios* – sitting in the kitchen of the house on 25th Street on a humid evening, shifted their buttocks nervously on the plastic covered chairs, put their hands up in polite refusal of hospitality and fled as soon as they could. Even such a staunchly Cuban *macho* as Pedro's friend Pipo, who had fought at Girón and been imprisoned by Batista and knew his first prostitute at the age of eleven, and who was sure his being resided in his *cojones*, even he, when he felt the urgent pressure of Dolores's fingers on his shoulder, found the joke he had been telling dying on his lips.

Pedro's bad temper worsened. He became confused, and very soon was beside himself each time Dolores's bosoms swung before his nose as she bent to serve him coffee. The whole house was intimidated by her fierce femininity.

In those months following her bereavement, she began to more and more resemble a stout little pressure cooker. Sexual organs featured in her stories: the length and shape of a man's thing, the colour of a woman's bits, the size of the neighbour's dog and what the cat had in mind for the night were all open for discussion with her.

Ana learned things. She learned even though she was torn, half repulsed, reluctant to give up innocence, half thirsty for understanding.

One oppressively hot June afternoon as they sorted laundry on the back verandah, having been chased inside by a sudden storm, Ana said something about the *cigüeña* – the stork Consuelo had told her delivered babies – and Dolores laughed.

Vamos, chica, don't be a cretin. Surely you know how a man and a woman make babies?

Ana did not know.

¡Dios santo! How can you not know?

No one has told me.

So what? Don't you have two fingers of forehead? I would have figured it out for myself.

There was a moment when the only sound was the tapping of rain on the roof, while Dolores waited for her reproach to sting, and then she plunged.

She pulled Pedro's sock from the laundry basket. Look, you know, a man's *pito* is like this, she said, stretching the slack blue sock to an amazing length.

You know how he puts it inside the woman?

Ana shook her head, her eyes never leaving Abuela Dolores's face.

Vamos, ¿cómo no? You're six years old! *¡Una señorita!* Don't you know the man puts his *pito* inside the woman, here – she said, gesturing down below her waist – to make babies?

But how?

Well, *vamos*, I'll show you.

She led Ana to Consuelo's bed.

There, on the frayed and yellowing chenille bedspread, as the rain tormented the house outside, Dolores demonstrated ten positions for intercourse.

Like this, with the man on top, or here, from the side, she said, turning and twisting on the bed with an invisible companion. The smell deepened, but Ana was mesmerised by her jiggling, cratered belly and her hairy shanks.

The woman puts her leg up like this, and he puts it here. Or like this, or from behind, here, thus . . . You see now?

———

45

Dolores often said that she did not fear anything on earth and that was mostly true. The nether worlds of the sea, the realms of dead souls – night – terrified her, but in the world of things that could be seen she was brazen, almost lawless.

She had an entire wardrobe of names and aliases, run up because it had suited her to become a different person at different points in her life – for personal reasons, to forget a disappointing past and start afresh, like someone else might buy a red dress after a love affair gone wrong.

But legal documents became enmeshed in her histories, so that one document, here, showed she was Dolores Teresa Gutierrez, a widow, born in 1904, while this one proved she was married to Ramón Sillas de Céspedes and certified her birth in the Cuban country town of Güines in 1910. That this or that husband was unknown to the family was explained by Dolores with *el cabrón se largó* – the bastard took to the highway – expressed with the sound of two hands smacking together and one hurrying off. And the *cabrón's* actions were always due to the human male's infidelity and had nothing to do with her, Dolores García.

Pedro and Consuelo gave no more weight to one set of names than to another. Consuelo had suffered from Dolores's games in her childhood, and now refused to delve into them. Her response to Ana's questions about Dolores was a long-suffering sigh and the cryptic words of, God knows what the truth is. Your grandmother has forgotten, and so have I.

Consuelo was unhappy. Ana knew it then, of course, but they were all unhappy and Ana doesn't remember a time when things were different. So in another way she did not realise that anything was wrong at all. And her own problems were encompassing enough.

She looks at photographs from that time and is shocked by Consuelo's face. Dolores was now with her, in the house, day and night, and they were all squeezed in more ways than one. But no one as much as Consuelo.

She was putting on weight. She was eating too fast, scoffing food down, going through *empanadas* and *bocaditos* as if you could put faith in nothing but the moment's grace. As if too much had been snatched from her and more was slipping by every second, before she could savour it.

Consuelo trusted no one – not Pedro and certainly not Dolores and absolutely not life. Nothing whatsoever except – perhaps, possibly – the hearts of her two children.

She was mean in ways that would surprise you. The house had too many rags – no faded T-shirt or child's outgrown dress was ever passed on. Books she had somehow acquired and didn't want – Vonnegut and Saul Bellow and other tough social commentaries which left her bewildered – she stored in boxes in the garage loft. She gave no one presents except Carlos and Ana. When she had to bring something for the Christmas exchange at the factory she considered taking a cracked plaster angel but Pedro wouldn't hear of it. *No seas mierdera*, he bellowed. So she shopped all Saturday, agonising over an extra forty-nine cents. In the end she bought a $1.99 box of soap, not because it looked like value for money, but quite the opposite. There had been better possibilities; she chose this one because it best expressed her conviction that whoever received it did not deserve a gift from her.

It was not that she thought she was the poorest of the poor, although the taste of that was still in her mouth, and hot moonless nights – and how many aren't in Miami? – could still spin her back to the laundry room, their first home in North America. Rather, it was that she had been born with less than her birthright, and life, pulsing through Dolores's hand, had been pushing her back ever since. She bitterly resented Dolores being firmly ensconced in her house again. She bitterly regretted marrying Pedro. She was trapped, and poor, and scared of being poorer, and she was alone and scared of being abandoned.

Some people give because they know there is always someone worse off and the thought inclines them towards charity. Consuelo's hand was stilled by the thought that there was always someone better off.

Let *them* give.

Dolores also felt desperate, even though she had gained Consuelo's house. She was aging, and the fact that no man wanted her or would even slow his step for her, no matter how refined her tricks, made her realise that a darker night was drawing near.

You could sense her fear in the games she played after Montero's death. She said she was alone in the world, *desamparada* – a word Ana thought meant she had been left without a lamp, a concrete image of abandonment. She said that she was *huérfana de madre y padre* – a total orphan.

She said these things not in a self-pitying, weak tone – that was never her style – but in a dramatic, grim way, as if girding her loins. Still, those feelings of being alone and abandoned affected her, and suddenly she was playing games with the government of the United States of America. She suddenly had twin sources of welfare. It was almost as if she had split herself in two – as if, officially, there were now more Doloreses than ever. She had a mysterious income and it all had to do with her living with them in the house on 25th Street – but not really, and perhaps she was still living with Montero as well.

Things seemed to go well for her for a while. She bought Ana a 24-carat gold bracelet inscribed with 'A. María'. She had ordered the jeweller to obscure the first name because she had never liked it, and to emphasise the 'María', the name of her own mother – a saint! May she rest in peace! And she bought gold because that was what saved you, one of the few things that had value, she said, in a political holocaust like the one they had just come through.

She bought Carlos a gold ring, too big and ridiculously heavy for his finger, with his name embossed on a platform. And she bought a stereo for the house, the first they had had, although there had been a television in Havana in 1957, years before most people in *los Estados Unidos* – but then pre-revolutionary Cuba had been a civilised place, something the world liked to forget, Dolores said.

All this was possible after Montero's death, until the day a Spanish-speaking welfare worker, a Señorita Remedios, came to the door and asked her was she Dolores González Tacoronte.

Soy yo, said Dolores, chatting cordially with the woman, as one must with government people, but careful not to let her past the front door, and watching as she craned her neck to look around, to see what the family owned and who lived in the household, and other things which were none of her business.

Then the woman asked who was Teresa Dolores Gutierrez, and as Dolores couldn't say that that was also herself, she said it was a sister; yes, the same name, with her they put it in the middle. Well, my mother, María, may she rest in peace – she was a saint, Señorita! – said her daughters were formed from her pain; that is why she named each one Dolores. There were ten of us all together, imagine it! She bore ten children and saw two die, and now two more are in Heaven with her. And I? I'm an orphan, Señora. *Así mismo. Así mismito.* Orphaned of mother and father, these last seven years.

Eh? What was that? *Sí, sí*, Señora. My sister lives at that address, with me; my husband died only a few weeks ago. Yes, yes, thank you, it is terrible. Excuse me now.

Dolores, as if overcome with grief, tried to close the door but the woman would not step back. We have no record of immigration for your sister, she persisted.

Well, someone has not been doing their job! Yes, she too had to flee Cuba, I told you, she escaped the clutches of *El Déspota*. No, no, I don't know where she is today; perhaps she's shopping.

Tears welled in her eyes as she thought how good it would be to have a sister live with her and share her work. Señora, she is a saint. Just like our mother, María, may she rest in peace. *Sí, sí, claro*, I'm certainly sure she isn't home today.

La señorita wanted to come in. Dolores said it was not possible, she was just leaving herself, this was her daughter's house, she had an appointment and had to hurry. Well, she spent her days here, looking after her daughter's children. But please have the courtesy to excuse me now, I have said that I am in a hurry.

La señorita stumbled, was at a loss, but said she would return next Friday and could *la señora* arrange to have time to see her. Abuela Dolores said *Sí, sí, seguro, con muchísimo gusto.* And hastily made other plans.

True, she later told Consuelo, she had nothing to worry about, being innocent of any wrong-doing.

I am good. Totally good, she proclaimed. I am one of God's innocents.

Still, it pays to be careful, Dolores said, recounting the measures she had taken. *Eso sí.* One can never be too careful. Any fool knows how government officials can beat the truth into *merengue*. How easily a face wrinkled with smiles can turn nasty, and then they have done a *numero ocho* on you, a number eight, and you discover you have been screwed in more places than you ever considered or enjoyed.

It scattered her complacencies. Never before had anybody taken the trouble to gather so many diverse documents about her. And it wasn't just the papers. It was the things that Dolores had closeted, cold hard facts that she had put aside many years before, that part of her never thought about while the rest of her knew nothing else. So she found Señorita Remedios to be like canefields lit in a high wind: hard to handle and boding catastrophe. She thought she remembered her face, perhaps from Cuba, where so many of her neighbours had been members of the

51

Committee in Defence of the Revolution, which Dolores had called the Venetian Blinds Committee.

That week she played thirty-seven on the lottery, which stood for an unwelcome visitor, and forty-five, which she said was the number for government papers but was also the number for babies and children as well as for thieves – but that part of it she wouldn't discuss. She gave the numbers to Pedro, fronting him directly he arrived from work, always the wrong time, but Dolores was rendered even more imperious by her need. She pulled the scrap of paper out of her bosom, which was as full as some people's wallets, and thrust it at him.

¿Qué's eso? Pedro demanded, as if he never played the numbers, as if they stank warmly.

Ah sí, said Dolores bitterly. As if I met you yesterday! Jacket, I knew you when you had no sleeves!

I haven't played the numbers in six weeks, spluttered Pedro.

Six weeks, eh? Your six weeks is anyone else's night. *Mira, hombre,* don't mess around with me. Put this on the numbers tomorrow – *mañana, óyeme bien,* and save your lies for whores.

Her anxieties never lasted more than three days. During that time she appealed to the saints for help. Specifically, she appealed to San Dimas, the patron saint of lost things, more commonly invoked when Ana María's sneakers or Carlos's homework was lost. San Dimas, San Dimas, pass by here, she called out. Each time she would have some sort of bond ready, and when it seemed likely that the saint hovered near, Dolores would tie him down, refusing to release him until he coughed up the lost object.

Now she tied San Dimas to every available fixture in the house, every doorknob, table leg, the handles of the clothes hamper, cupboard hooks. She used Ana's skipping rope, Pedro's singlet, Consuelo's stockings, Carlos's magnets, Ana's hair ribbons. She pushed and pulled on the bonds, punishing the saint while beseeching him to help her. Ana watched through almond eyes, not knowing what her grandmother had misplaced nor what she wanted to find.

What did you lose, Abuela?

Vaya, chiquilla, I've lost time. Go play with *bolitas de gofio.*

In her frenzy Dolores herself did not know what she was praying for. At times she was looking for a document, a piece of paper which would prove that her blood tie with the family was direct, a document which had never existed except in her own forceful, half-crazed will. At times she was searching for babies she had lost, for alabaster cheeks and angel fists long ago buried unceremoniously, now taking the form of the plaster angels on the walls of the old house on 25th Street. From where they watched her, choosing propitious moments to tumble and shatter at her feet.

But Dolores's remorses were subterranean; her heart had too many twisting chambers. An idea anchored in her mind and all she could do was pursue it unto death, never admitting an antithesis. So, intent on finding a document that never existed, and petrified of what the government woman might have in her office, whose evidence only the non-existent document could have contradicted, Dolores tied San Dimas to a pot handle. She set it on the flame with rolling potatoes. The saint failed her again and whatever

53

Dolores had lost remained lost, and what was worse, her numbers didn't materialise either. None of Dolores's powers helped her through this mysterious crisis. And then Dolores had to accept her fate and resort to other games.

So began the days in the closet. When the woman was expected, Carlos was kept from school, because Dolores said the government woman was crafty, that she was really a thin woman who only appeared fat because she was swollen with cunning. Dolores worried that the woman would approach in the afternoon, just as they were walking Carlos home, and waylay them, and extract something from the mouths of babes as deftly as a dentist removes a rotten molar.

Her friend Aída agreed to help. Aída lived on the same block, on the other side of the alley. She lived with Armandito Ramírez's family, and Armandito was in Carlos's class at Fairweather Elementary. The two women had met one afternoon as Dolores, returning with Carlos from Fairweather, felt her breath catch in her throat and her face turn mottled purple. Instead of reaching for her vaporiser, she stopped, gripped the arm of the lady coming up to her, looked into her face and croaked, Asthma. *Auxilio. Por favor*, if you are a Christian, help me – I am dying. Thus easing into a long friendship with a woman with an equal flair for melodrama.

Aída Pulpeta perched precariously in the Ramírez household. She was not related to them by blood, so she could not define herself as a relation exploited as unpaid help, the description so loved by Dolores. Neither was Aída hired help. She was a spinster who had worked as Señor Ramírez's

54

secretary before the revolution, when he had been a successful young capitalist, and he had made rash promises to her when he saw his world crumbling. In Miami, where Señor Ramírez filled cement bags in a factory and had no need of a secretary, Aída dressed his children, brewed coffee, folded laundry, and tried hard to appear victimised.

She stayed because she was not told to leave. But it was not a happy household. In the small weatherboard bungalow also lived Señora Ramírez, who had little else to do than look after her house and her husband and her two children, Armandito and Gloria. But Señora Ramírez had tolerated the situation for too long and could not bring herself to act. And Señor Ramírez seemed to like having the two women in one place.

Dolores and Aída sought each other out. They had things in common. They also had differences. Aída, younger by at least a decade, was thin and aspired to elegance. She wore her hair aerated in a silver mass on top of her head, accentuating her height. She ate only two saltine biscuits for lunch every afternoon and picked up the crumbs from her tight skirt with a moistened finger. She washed every item of her clothing by hand, even the pair of shorts she wore for two hours in the morning while relaxing. And she bragged about these habits. I have to go home and wash my hair, she sighed in Dolores's kitchen. I have an appointment this afternoon for a shampoo and haircut at the salon.

The other *cubanas* of the neighbourhood considered her *estirada* – stretched to pretentiousness – but not Dolores. She enjoyed the company of anyone with difficult domestic entanglements.

On those days when Dolores expected the government woman's visit, Aída arrived at 25th Street early, as soon as Consuelo and Pedro went out the door. From that moment and for the entire day, she was left to entertain herself in the house, awaiting the unappointed hour of the woman's visit.

In the meantime, Dolores led Carlos and Ana into the very long, very narrow closet of their bedroom, whose single door allowed limited access to its farthest recesses, so that unused clothes and winter blankets were tied in bundles and stacked topsy-turvy there. They sat on those bundles all morning, in that dark theatre of the absurd, with Abuela Dolores the magic carpet of the imagination but still firmly gripping the doorknob, controlling the flow of air and preventing their escape. She let them out for a quick lunch with Aída, and since Señorita Remedios preferred afternoon visits, they returned to the closet.

It would seem almost impossible to keep two energetic children – and they were raucous as hounds – shut up in a closet for the better part of a day. But here Dolores put all her virtuosity into play. She made up long rhyming poems on whatever subject they requested. They were hilarious poems, custom-made, on the spot, just for them.

About a frog, Abuela! About a shoe!

Shh, shh! *Cuidado, muchacho*, the witch will hear you. She is probably out there right now! (And they would wonder who they were hiding from, a witch, a woman from the government – she was probably hovering nearby, how almost frightening, but quickly their Abuela Dolores would switch them over to another channel.)

All right, let's see, a frog . . . And she would draw breath, pause only to draw breath, and immediately would come, in perfect rhyme, stanza after stanza of inventive silliness that left them squirming with joy.

And she told stories. She was a born story-teller. Her favourite setting was Cuba, the Cuba of her childhood, her favourite characters the cast of her youth.

In the closet, the Cuban countryside became real. It was a place where it was always night, like in a dream. Later Ana realised that Dolores's imagination – born in a time before electricity relieved the pressure of pure night – was the sister of Francisco Goya's; she had long ago conjured for her the witches astride sticks that suggested more than broomsticks between their thorny shanks, the demons and the farting bellows and all the handmaidens of a nether world, *Los Caprichos*.

In the darkness of their bedroom closet, through Dolores's rasping voice, everything became immediate, intimate, plausible – the family's history, its future, death, and even the phantoms in Dolores's mind.

Ana was too young to tell where memories ended and fantasy began in the stories told in the closet.

⎯⎯⤙

Bueno, let's see. Did I tell you about *la americana*, Henrietta? No, she was not a witch. That was the other one. Henrietta was a very rich American lady whom I knew when I was a *señorita*, and so was she. She didn't have anything to do with me, she was so rich; she lived in a palace. I was more beautiful but Henrietta did not care

57

about such things. She had only two things on her mind: the humanitarian rights of women and learning to fly.

This was in our pueblo, Olvidados, in the year nineteen-hundred and twenty-one, when General Gerardo Machado was in power. He was in league with Henrietta's father, a Mr Douglas, who owned the sugar mill, and the town, and our souls. They were all in league.

Henrietta and her girlfriends, a little circle of three or four rich girls, could have anything they wanted but every day we saw them sitting on the steps of the town hall, making a spectacle of themselves with signs saying garbage about female rights, and let women run the country, and *arriba*, Barbara Romero.

This was in the time when women still wore long dresses, but Henri, as they called her, wore hers up to here, you could almost see everything, the way she sat on those steps. Those soft shiny clothes she wore, in so many unusual colours, and her curly yellow hair – no one had ever seen anything like her.

We used to see her up in the air also, taking lessons from the German. The two went so high together and looked so small, we called her La Mosquita.

The men, tired as they were, old and young, couldn't sleep at night with thoughts of Henri buzzing around their heads. The worst to be struck with this malaria was my brother Ramón, the oldest of my four brothers, who because he was the first he took out all the best my mother could offer. *¡Ay, qué guapo era!* But foolish, as you will see.

He had a dream he told me once. It was no small thing,

but I didn't know it then. It was dawn, he was setting out to work in the fields. I handed him a cup of coffee and he told me he had dreamt he had a baby on his chest. He said he was lying down and playing with his child. That he could feel the baby, there, on his chest – filling it to breaking point. A full sweetness like milk in his chest. And that he woke with the conviction that he wanted great things for this unconceived child.

Muchachos . . . that baby became the seed of his destruction.

Because that baby, talking to him from the other side, put it into his head to confront Mr Douglas. And Ramón went to *el* Señor Douglas, knocked on his door, asked to see him. And he talked to him, face to face. *Muy macho.* He made demands. He said men were men. That they had certain rights. To read, to write, that sort of thing. *El* Señor Douglas listened. Ramón told him that the children of the *campesinos* – his future child – should have a school. He carried on a lot about the school, said it was needed to lift people out of ignorance. *¡Imaginate!* By the end of the week Ramón was in jail.

Well, I was living in Olvidados, so I was used to Henri, but Ramón lived in *el campo*, working with our father. That day when he was thrown into that cage like a rabid dog, he looked out the window and saw Henrietta sitting across the dusty street with her girlfriends and their placards. And he was so impressed with her skin and her figure and what he could see of her underwear, and felt so strongly that he was imprisoned and being kept from all that was for free and desirable out in the world, that he could not bear it. In an effort to get out of the prison and come closer to Henri, he stood on his cot and put his *pito* through the bars of the window.

It was like this – thick as my forearm. And as long.

They say that Henrietta's aunt was walking past just at that moment and immediately took in the situation, and was heard to say to her companion, Oh my, I wish he wouldn't do that! Henrietta is *so* impressionable!

But even as she spoke, it was clear that Henri had seen and was fascinated by the first she knew of Ramón.

The authorities were informed, and four men entered Ramón's cell and tried to subdue him, but such was his strength and his excitement that he overpowered them and ran out into the street and across to the Johnstone warehouse and vaulted into the rafters, because he was so strong that if he could reach something with his finger-tips, he could pull himself onto it. And he disappeared into the countryside.

They sent six policemen from La Habana to look for him. But no one saw him, and then fifteen days later Henri also disappeared.

She, who had never before been in love, known a man – even dreamt of one – now found the experience of Ramón more ecstatic than flying.

Well, he had a prodigiously long manhood. It was the talk of the family. When he made love to a woman he had to tie a towel at its base, to keep from disembowelling her.

Carlitos, you are like him. It is in your blood. I am telling you so that you will not hurt your bride on your wedding day. Because by then I may not be at your side to counsel you . . .

But you know, happiness for those two was ephemeral. They were cursed and had no hope of lasting happiness. A man who was a vampire, an intimate of *Satanás*, who lived in a lonely *bohío* up on the part of the mountain that never saw the sun, betrayed them to her father. May the curse of infertility fall on the testicles of the descendants of that Lazarillo de Tormes.

They dragged Ramón to town and killed him . . .

Hijos, there are some things I cannot talk about. May he rest in peace.

¿Y Henrietta? Well, imagine it! She went to live in La Habana. I didn't see her again for years, and by then I had your mother, my Consuelo.

Then Henri was like a raisin, all her juices had dried, she never married. She kept a great library of books and campaigned a little for the humanitarian rights of women, but half-heartedly, you know. She never got excited about anything until she met your mother, who was like an empty vase, ready to be filled with life. And because of Ramón's memory, Henri opened her heart and her house to Conchita and gave her books and paid her school fees. And the wedding dress that *tu mamá* wore when she married *tu papá* with the train that stretched from the altar to the door of the cathedral was given to her by *la americana*.

She's dead now, *la pobre*, may she rest in peace.

All right, be still, I'll tell you about the witch now.

What They Had

Some people keep mementoes. They have relics from their childhood, they keep their children's toys long after their children have grown up and away and are wandering the world as vagabonds. They hoard the past. In their hands, a white lace tablecloth whisks you back to places you never saw – a clump of white-washed cottages by the sea; fat old ladies dressed in black sitting in doorways, sewing lace with arthritic fingers and looking up only to gaze over olive trees to the little village harbour where they last saw their son, their daughter.

Serving a special dinner they remark, This was my grandmother's. Despite the casual tone you know what it means to them, and you grip the chipped platter with the fading roses, the little china cup. They are testimonials to the past wealth of the family, to its substance, or merely to the fact that it *was* – there was a past, and here is the link, we've held on to this, this small piece of evidence.

The Santiagos had nothing like this. Inside the house on 25th Street everything was plastic, it was cheap, it was cut off from a human past. And it was not just because they were Cubans and loved the new, the flashy and the glitzy. Because even Cubans are Spanish, are European, or African, with ties to ancient cultures and a will to preserve them.

Pedro never once hauled out anything that his father took from Ourense, from Galicia when he sailed across the seas for a better life as a Cuban carpenter, because his father never gave him anything except *gaznatadas* on the head. He had nothing from his mother, who left a seaside town in Asturias to accompany her brothers when they made the crossing and then didn't live to see her son take his first communion.

Pedro had nothing from his childhood, not even a photograph, not even a picture of his parents, and nothing left from his fleeting time of proud young manhood and affluence. But at least he had facts. He knew he had once made it, made it big, and it was Fidel – *ese hijo de puta*, he always said – who had stolen it all. He knew who his parents had been, why they left Spain. He remembered his mother telling him about her native village, from where she could look out over the fields and see Los Picos de Europa – snow-covered, she had said, even in summer.

And Dolores had stories, knew stories about a woman named Henrietta, an *americana* who had nevertheless lived, like themselves, in Cuba. Dolores knew a lot of things about this woman, things it was hard to imagine how she could possibly have known. And she told the children those stories as if airing suits from a bygone day stored in trunks in an attic. But what was there were bits of gossip, more often than not a remnant, never a whole wedding dress, just a few rags . . . She aired them, even embroidered them, there, in the closet, while they hid from the woman.

And thus she handed them down, stories that came to no conclusions, that Carlos later forgot and Ana remembers now only in fragments, and when she takes out these rags they are different – Dolores would not have used those words, and her rhythms and patterns have altered, frayed with time. But then again, how could you remember who put what into that closet all those years ago?

Still, Ana has something from the past. It is only her mother, Consuelo, who never got anything. It was Consuelo who was the most impoverished. Consuelo had no residue. In this sense she was light. She was more than light – she was empty. She was transparent. The generations that should have made her solid, should have stood behind her like innumerable shadows that in the end add up to a substance, were not there. All that was there were unanswered questions, even unformed questions, and doubts, and rumours, and memories of an agony of a childhood and adolescence. She was insubstantial.

⤙

We must intervene here. That is not totally right, although she can only tell you what she knows. And it's true, Consuelo had questions when she should have had facts. She should have known her parents. We crippled her, for reasons of our own which there is no divining, when we let her go without that knowledge.

But she had us.

Because of what we had taken from her, we clung to her. Because we had once abandoned her, we could never let her go.

We watched her closest.

We stay near not because we have been hurt by the living, or hold grudges over slights, no matter how cavernous. Nothing could be further from the truth. We are forgiving. Few realise just how forgiving we are.

No, we are hobbled by the breach. By the things we didn't do. The gaps that cannot be filled. The tasks unfinished. What we withheld. How we withdrew when we should have charged.

You think we need appeasing. We do not. We want your peace. We crave your wholeness. We need your happiness, to free us.

So Consuelo held us to her. Her migraines were ours. We dashed around her bed at night, frenzied by her dreams. The questions in her eyes haunted us.

⟶

Ana stood next to her father's chair in the lounge room of the house on 25th Street. It was night – the light had sur-rendered the streets and taken refuge in the houses, and because the café curtains on the small high windows were not drawn, the blackness lapped up against them and they became mirrors.

In those little mirrors you could see the lives in the house more clearly than if you were looking straight at them, because their perspective was closer to the truth. They were small people. The father slumped in his chair, his shoes kicked off near him and the smell from them sharp, heavy and mouldy. Ana ignored it and hovered behind him.

He wore only a singlet and pants and the singlet looked belligerent, looked a bit aggressive, and Ana was unsure why she wanted to ask her question, even whether she really wanted to ask it. But the night had just begun and the music of *Bonanza* or *High Chaparral* or *Branded!* was coming from the television set in the corner next to the fireplace and Ana said, Papi! Papi, would you like me to comb your hair?

Her father's stern face dissolved, like that, in a snap. He laughed his deep friendly laugh and bent down towards her, extending his cheek, and she kissed it and he tapped her nose affectionately like he did the cat's nose – *un toque narizal*, he called it – a nasal touch. She ran through the house to fetch a comb and a brush and a bowl of water and the round mirror with the pink rabbits on the handle that Aída gave her for Christmas.

Ana dragged the little table of plastic wood with its thin tapering legs to the chair where he was sitting and placed on it the bowl of water and the brush and comb and mirror.

Ana concentrated, her tongue darting in and out of her mouth. She wet his hair, sprinkled it like the priest sprinkled holy water, and all the while he sat still, a surly look on his face even in repose, his eyes on the cowboys shooting their guns at each other.

She stroked his large round head. She wet the comb in the bowl and passed it through his hair. She patted the wet hair down and studied it and then undid her work and began again.

For an hour or more she combed and brushed his black shining hair, practised different parts, combed it back and forth and across the globe of his head. She smelled his smells, the brilliantine in his hair, and the hair dye, and the men's cologne he used after his afternoon shower. And the smell that was so strong under his arms, the pungent smell that always lingered in his singlets, even the clean ones.

She combed back and forth and across. Every so often she handed him the mirror so that he could admire himself. He took his eyes off the screen reluctantly, smiled at himself and said, Wow! in a way that Ana found both silly and gratifying. And then he handed back the mirror and his features recomposed themselves into a scowl and Ana resumed her work.

The big orange tomcat came up to him and he rubbed his fingers together, hissed, Miso, Miso, Miso. Miso leapt into his lap and the image of the two – the cat and the man – was caught high in the little square windows as they sat contentedly on a sultry Miami night, purring as their heads were stroked.

She loved walking with him. He was so tall, taller than all the other men. Six-foot two, he always said proudly. He had a huge stride. She went to the park on Saturday mornings to watch him play baseball, stood with fingers in the wire mesh until Carlos came up to her and pinched her. Stop staring at the men.

He was only a year older, why did he get to be boss? It was insulting, she was not staring at strange men, she had been watching Papi. She hit him with a balled up fist and he hit back and they fought until one of the wives of the other players laughingly told them to spare each other. Embarrassment quelled their rage.

She watched her father. Pedro's hands were calloused

and cracked from handling wet cement. They healed slowly, leaving his palms like soles. They sprang out in the lithe swing of a true athlete. Monkey hands.

Ana's mother never attended the baseball.

Ana trotted next to him as the family walked along Bayfront Park to the memorial to the Cuban martyrs. She was proud to be the only one who could keep up with him. Carlos and Abuela Dolores and Mami were hopelessly behind, they were only now emerging from the front of the City of Miami Library. She loved the way his shirt sat across his broad shoulders, and the power of his body that came from so much baseball and the work he did at the factory.

It was Sunday morning and she was still in bed but not in her usual one. She was wedged in the big bed between them. She must have come some time in the night, found her way in the darkness through the maze of hallways and picking up the covers at the foot of their bed slithered in between the two of them. She had done this many times and never did she remember in the morning the journey during the night.

What she knew was that they did not mind. They liked it. They welcomed her always and the first thing she heard in the morning – what actually woke her – was his laugh, deep and sonorous.

You came in the night like a little mouse, he said, enfolding her in his bear's embrace. Consuelo smiled and stroked Ana's hand.

He had already gone out to get the *Sunday Herald* and now he read Ana the comics. Carlos was also in the bed and so was Consuelo. (But not Dolores. Never Dolores!

There was no place for Abuela Dolores in Consuelo's bedroom on Sunday mornings.)

He took off his shirt and told Ana to go find a hairpin.
She ran to the dresser in the other bedroom and returned
clutching a handful of thick brown pins. Now he and Ana
took the opportunity to squeeze the pimples on his back,
the white juicy ones that gratified them both with their
deep volcanic spurts, and the tiny black pinpoints which
were dry and hard and had to be squeezed against the
curved tip of the hairpin until they slithered out, tiny white
worms with dark faces.

The stories in the closet continued while the threat of the
woman shadowed Dolores. The stories thickened and then
unravelled and retied themselves around some mystery that
Ana didn't understand. Ana guessed that Dolores feared
Henrietta Douglas. She felt, dimly, childlike, that Henrietta had some hold on Abuela Dolores, or Dolores on
her – why else did she always talk about her so much? It all
had something to do with the government woman who
wanted to ask Dolores questions, who wanted to know too
many things. Dolores had secrets, and stories, and visions of
the future as well as memories of a past that had not fully
been put to sleep. Carlos and Ana entered the closet with
the old woman who called herself their grandmother to
dream her dreams. More and more, Henrietta Douglas was
a presence there as well.

Henrietta had a cat as a child.

She had had other pets – a monkey that sat on her shoulders and put his long thin forefinger in her ear and then chortled with delight when the maids screeched, *¡Qué atrevido!* And jagged-edged iguanas who strolled in the yard amid the cool grevilleas and thought jaded thoughts, blinking wearily because they were ancient creatures who had seen too much.

But it was the cat, the white girl cat, the summer-house cat at Cojímar that Henrietta had liked most. Not loved, but liked, her feeling dampened and distanced by a cool admiration that sometimes tilted towards envy.

So she could never be sure whether or not she should have known – had known – that the cat was in the boat-shed that day towards the end of summer when Henri had come in off the water peeved that her boots with the buttons like thin shells had been ruined in grey mud.

She tossed the boots into a corner and slammed the door.

The white girl cat cried out angrily at dusk that first week, after the long thirsts of the hot days. One of the maids, at Henrietta's orders, called her every evening – Misita, Misita, Misita. The answering meows were desperate and pitiful, but went unheard.

It took a long time for the blue eyes to penetrate Henrietta's thick indifference, staring knowingly at something in her. Then Henri dreamt of a pair of blue eyes shining like twin gems in the darkness, staunchly unblinking despite what lay ahead.

Henrietta finally insisted on returning to Cojímar. She

ran all the way to the boatshed, but all that was left were scraps of fur and a clean white skull alongside the ruined boots that had been gnawed and not even a smell let alone a strip of flesh let alone life. By then it was November.

It should have stayed with Henrietta. Her cat should have told her something about herself. But somehow the fine silks and linens she wrapped herself in also kept her from feeling with any depth, and her emerald jewellery drained the warmth from her eyes. And after Ramón died, he took the small amount of holding and caressing, the paucity of gentleness that was all she had ever had. All she was left with was her hardness.

Each day after his death she rose and ordered a straight-backed chair be taken outside. Henrietta sat on her father's wide verandah, facing the sea. She found that the sea air cooled her mind, and it got up and went wandering of its own accord across the sky. It skipped across whisps of cloud and soared freely but then, more often than not, it would trip on a protruding jaggedness. Then she would feel a little stab at her side and she would think about cancer. Only two days after his death, before he had even been buried, she became convinced she had cancer.

She believed there was a malevolent thing growing inside of her, that only she knew about. She confided in her *criada*. She told the maid that she knew exactly when it sprouted in her – the moment she looked at Ramón's corpse, split open like an overripe fig. It was this that planted the malignancy in her, in her womb and in her breast and in her mind as well. It was because of her father. He was responsible. If not his hand, then his wish.

She would never look at him clear-eyed again. She could never get past the sight of her beloved – shredded, multi-coloured.

She did not speak to anyone but the maid. She hardly ate, would not wash, could not sleep, did not rise from the chair she sat in, on the verandah of her father's *casona*, on a rise facing the sea.

Herman Douglas was a stocky, sallow man, living in his mind well beyond his time. He was interested in velocipedes and gramophones and light magnifiers and distorters, which he collected, and in all the advances that could benefit industry, not only those pertaining to sugar cane. He had filled his houses with air coolers and mosquito traps. He encouraged his family and servants to smoke cigars to (rightly, as it turned out) ward against yellow fever. His personality won over his Protestant heritage; its style was inimical to his. He was born in the east of North America, exactly what state and city was hazy, but it was known he was exiled for numerous romantic transgressions (the last of which he was compelled to marry). And he raised his only daughter in the Spanish style, lavishing her with some things – caresses and endearments and gifts – but withholding others. Things she needed more: compassion, understanding of her spirit.

He had enlarged the modest fortune he was given. He could concentrate. But his manners, his mind, his pleasures were male, and he knew there were things he did not understand. His mother, it was said, had been a sad

woman. His maiden sister, for whom he had been responsible, had fallen into the habit of walking into the sea on
December nights. When her nocturnal baths were discovered and her room locked after supper, she had turned
to wandering the beach in the mild winter sun. She
looked for sealife, for gelatinous things whose aqua and
magenta and saffron hues caught her eye. She gathered
them into the hem of her skirt and took them daintily to
her room where she squeezed the iridescent jellies and
gritty sponges, played with them, and finally ingested
them through various orifices, puzzling everyone with her
decreasing vitality, until the day she was found dead and
the doctor was able to probe the sources of her poisoning.

With such a history, Herman had felt the responsibil-
ity for the women in his life like a hot hand on his shoulder, and he had stumbled. He knew Henrietta blamed
him for her lover's death. He repeated his decisions in his
head, manoeuvred himself along the course he had taken
in the white rapids of events. He could not fault himself.
He didn't even understand why he felt culpable.

He offered her lover an exalted burial. He prized
Humboldt's history of Cuba; kept it as a source of wisdom
in all things. He paid for Ramón to be buried in the manner of Hernan Cortés in Cortés's second internment.
Ramón was shrouded in a winding sheet of cambric
embroidered with gold, fringed with black lace four
inches deep.

His poor mutilated corpse, thus disguised, was placed
in a wooden coffin enclosed in one of lead. This was put
in another of crystal, with crossbars and plates of silver.

Herman Douglas made sure his daughter discovered the lengths to which he had gone. Henrietta remained unmoved. He did not see her cry. Neither did she speak.

She watched the sun set on a looming horizon. She envisioned her cancer as a seed of hate she hoped would soon blossom, so that she too would sleep in a glass case in a silver coffin. And that would be all.

Henrietta sat without moving day after day, and the household, in fear of her temper, tiptoed around her. Her maid pushed an amulet into her bodice and anointed her with *hierbabuena* that she had procured from a *santero*. She covered her mistress with lambswool blankets and shrouded her in nets as the sun disappeared, uncovering her again in the morning.

Herman Douglas put up with the charade until the day he walked past her on the verandah and, glancing down, saw a pool of blood at his daughter's feet. And then, looking up, he noticed the red stain blossoming on the green of her skirt.

Confused by his disgust, remorse, and a terror that he could not acknowledge, he wrenched her up by the arm and slapped her full on the face. She awakened long enough to spit at her father, a dry foul gob spattering his face. He considered her reaction a victory but still he had to lift her bodily and carry her to a bath, where her *criada* undressed her and washed her in chamomile water that turned a rusty rose red immediately. She was anaemic.

Some of Us Gulp Tears

Apúrate, muchacha, apúrate, Dolores demanded night and day, racing six-year-old Ana towards a future she was never ready for. When she played with the little American girls in the neighbourhood, Dolores warned her of the dangers of lesbianism: Don't fall in love with that Linda. *Mujeres* who love *mujeres* don't grow *tetas,* she said, cupping her own bosoms in her hands and shaking them up and down in admonishment.

Apúrate, muchacha, she hissed, getting Ana up in the morning and urging her into the bathroom with quick strokes of the folded belt. She followed her inside, insisting on supervising her washing. Oblivious to her own emanations, Dolores warned Ana that she must learn to wash better – Or your husband will sicken and die from the smell of codfish.

I'm not even married!

Huh! *¡Claro que no!* And you never will be! Who would want a *chiquilla* like you, whose smell would kill a canary?

Ana began to watch for times when it was safe to go to the toilet, when Dolores was busy with a cauldron on the stove, or when she was on the telephone talking to Aída.

Ana stood up awkwardly, clutching the taps and the sides of the bath. She had heard the refrain that if she slipped she would kill herself many times. Her movements were curtailed by the warning, *¡Cuidado!* and the grim forecast, You'll kill yourself! She scarcely dared move.

As she reached for the towel, as her fingers grasped the tip and pulled on it and it fell to the floor, the door of the bathroom swung open and there was Dolores, filling the doorway, moving forward quickly.

Abuela Dolores had come to help her – there was a towel over her shoulder and so maybe there was nothing to worry about. But there was also a fat arm outstretched.

Wearing a fixed smile and mouthing the sort of slippery words people say to babies, she reached to stroke Ana. She murmured pet names and teased her about her immature baldness: How lovely, *puchita*, so hairless, not even one little hair!

Ana tries to remember. Is that all that happened? It feels as if there must have been more – more than a hand taking liberties. But perhaps that was enough.

Dolores threw her hip into the bathroom door just as Ana tried to close it. She followed her in. She dosed her for the rabbity little pebbles Ana managed to squeeze out after much effort, standing next to her as she strained, urging her on. Hurry up, *muchacha*. You have been there an hour. If you're not careful, your intestines will fall out. I've seen it happen. They'll drop into the water there, ploop! Ploop! *¡Oyeme bien!*

They battled over the foldaway bed, which was wet in the mornings as often as not. Dolores woke Ana through hissing teeth: *Desgraciada chiquilla*, you will never be *una señorita* – words that stung like her belt.

The light from the bare bulb on the ceiling drew them around the table, narrowed their scope. As the darkness enfolded the house on 25th Street they moved about inside a little less assuredly. Ana carried the plates to the table, Consuelo brought the tall frosted glasses and Dolores the *cazuela de ropa vieja* – old clothes – what a name for a dish of canned shredded beef! Even the name made it clear that it should not be eaten, and the smell was portentous. Even the colour was unnatural – so orangy. That was the paprika, Dolores's hand must have gotten away from her again, *a la abuela Dolores se le fue la mano*. The grease lay there in clear little orange globules and already Ana dreaded the meal.

Pedro tore off a chunk of Cuban bread and plastered it with margarine and opened wide his mouth. He took another, pushed it into the steaming *ropa vieja* in front of him. He was holding forth. He was recounting a long story about a man he called *Ache-Pe*. (Years later Ana realised *Ache-Pe* were letters, 'HP', with the same meaning as SOB.) It was another instalment in the saga he continued every evening at dinnertime. *Ache-Pe* was Pedro's superior at the factory.

Ana reached for the shrinking loaf of bread, but Dolores hissed, *No te hartes con pan*. Ana picked her fork up and stirred the shredded beef. She feared for herself.

And I told him he was *un Ache-Pe!* Pedro bellowed. He smacked the table with his open palm. He was furious even as he told his story, which Consuelo received as if she were not there at all, her eyes cast down, eating silently, her movements all gentle, all quiet, always refined. She never slurped or yelled or banged.

I called him *un maricón!* A queer! *¡Así mismo! ¡Qué coño!* He doesn't know who he's fucking around with! *¡Sí, Señor!*

Pedro paused in his retelling of the day's events only to command, Hand me the salad. Bring me the salt. Pour me a glass. *Alcánzame. Dame. Tráeme.* And, *Oyeme lo que te voy a decir* – listen to me, for I am about to tell you something.

Consuelo ignored him, left him talking to himself, yelling with himself, his own best audience. She knew it was highly unlikely Pedro had jeopardised his job by doing any of the things he was claiming to have done. He was reinventing. Relishing the reliving of every acrimonious moment at the factory, because in the retelling Pedro had incredible *cojones*.

Consuelo murmured to Ana to eat but Ana leant towards her and whispered, I don't like it, Mami – the last word a whimper. Consuelo glared an instant – don't make trouble – but it was too late. Ana had Dolores's attention.

Eat, *muchacha*. Don't tell me I slaved over that stove all day for nothing. Eat it, *desgraciada!* Already she was removing the belt from her waist and doubling it in her hand.

Ana's heart stuttered and she looked for escape, but the

only possibility was the dish with its steaming offensive smell. She gagged – it was not possible – and Dolores's belt left a hot red trail.

Ana picked up a forkful and tried to put it in her mouth but she was crying too hard now. The belt arced out again, and again.

Pedro stopped talking. He squeezed his bread into the puddle on his plate. The only sounds between the screams were the clink of silverware and the munching of food.

Ana's arms flew to her face. She leant further from Dolores, leant so far towards Consuelo that she was in her lap, she was practically in her chair. But she could not leave the table, she was not allowed, she would never get away.

Dolores's arm went up again. And now Consuelo leant away from Ana, giving the belt a bit more scope. She hitched her chair up slightly and slid a few inches away. And now Consuelo picked up her spoon and resumed her meal.

Some time in her life, I imagine, Ana may have to confront the image of her mother and demand of that tense, faraway woman why she let all of it happen.

But Ana knows. Very clearly and easily she can recall this scene:

Consuelo is lying on her bed, on her stomach. Her skirt is pushed down around her knees. Ana is startled by the gleaming white roundness of her body. Two beautiful soft quivering orbs. Ana has never seen her mother undressed before.

No one knows she is watching. Dolores has something in her hand. She approaches Consuelo, something silvery and sharp in her outstretched hand. She prepares to deliver a suppository.

Dolores lead Ana to the Fairweather Elementary School office and pushed her ahead through the door. They waited for one of the office workers' attention.

Tell her that you are Ana María Santiago and you are ready to start school, Dolores ordered.

The office lady eyed Ana sceptically. How old are you? When Ana whispered six, she asked, How old are you, *really*?

Six.

The woman turned to Dolores, talking quickly in words neither Ana nor Dolores knew. Dolores shrugged several times. Me no speekee Eenglish! she said, affronted.

It seemed to Ana to go on forever. The office ladies talked and Dolores said, Eh? Eh? Then turning to Ana, *¿Qué dicen*, Ana María? Until a teacher who spoke Spanish was called. She informed Dolores that it was illegal not to start children at school when they were six. She is six! Dolores interrupted.

How can she be? She is so big! She is at least eight! Her parents could be prosecuted for keeping her from school.

Mujer. She is tall. And strong. You are too used to teaching anaemic *americanitos*. But she is six, or my name isn't Dolores Fátima!

The women studied Ana sceptically. They told Dolores to return the next day with a birth certificate.

Dolores hurried Ana through the streets, spurred by

indignation. What do they think, she fumed. That I raise rachitic children, like the Americans, who see a *bisteck* once a week, if they're lucky? And she used one of her phrases for those moments when her integrity had been questioned: History will absolve me! Mark my words, they will render to me an apology, or my name isn't Dolores Tacoronte.

School would eventually be a refuge from Dolores, but that was still a summer away, and a summer is a deep and dangerous lake when you are a small boat that can't navigate. And even when school did come, it was a forbidding place, in the way new things are always more frightening than the devils you've lived with.

The strangeness announced itself in waves, beginning with the smells. Hotdogs and hamburgers and boiled green vegetables and melted cheese sandwiches and peanut-butter cookies have a unique aroma. Ana and Carlos noticed it – it was a pungent pall around the Fairweather Elementary School cafeteria. It hit them when they were still a block away, it nauseated Ana on the monkey bars and it wrenched her stomach as she climbed the cafeteria steps at lunchtime with her class. Ana only ate the dessert. Carlos threw up if he ate anything.

He would spark a chain reaction in the other children. When the teachers grew tired of wading in vomit, they called Consuelo to the school. They informed her that Carlos was reacting to what was in his brown paper bag: You must give him something else for lunch. Or else let him buy his lunch like the other children. The minced ham sandwiches you give him make him vomit.

Consuelo did what she was asked out of respect for teachers. Carlos ate Cuban bread smeared with butter. But Consuelo knew the Cuban ham hadn't been the problem. It was the smell, that foreign American food smell.

At three o'clock Carlos and Ana would run to Dolores, who waited by the school gate. Dolores walked them home. And knowing they would have had little for lunch, she placed before them the usual deep bowl of strained black bean *potaje*, which, despite the fact that it had killed Montero, she had not stopped cooking every morning.

Oh, no, *not pooo-taaaa-je!* Carlos and Ana made their voices low and mournful, like the *moo* of a cow. It wasn't that they made dire associations. It was just that, hungry though they were, they still couldn't stomach a piping bowl of black bean stew on a hot and humid Miami afternoon. They had about five minutes of toying with the mercurial puddle of olive oil that floated on the stew's purple-black surface before getting down to the serious business of avoiding Dolores's belt as she tried to compel them to eat.

It ended, often, with Dolores gripping Ana by the wrist, wrenching her from her chair, and dancing a mirthless dance with her in the kitchen. Ana ran around Dolores, chased by the belt.

Afterwards, the *potaje* half gulped between sobs, half spilled on the table, Ana hurled herself on her mother's bed. She calmed herself by picking out the lines of fluff on Consuelo's chenille bedspread, placing her little harvest on the battered nightstand in which Consuelo kept the important drawings her children did at school.

After a while she sat up on the bed, wiped her face on her T-shirt, and walked to the dresser. She examined the contents of the centre drawer where Consuelo kept the enamelled wooden jewellery box that had come from Cuba in her suitcase. It had little of worth in it: nothing of value had been allowed out of the country. But Ana loved to touch the contents, those symbols of her mother, arranging her pastel bead necklaces, mock-pearl earrings, a pendant shaped like a strawberry, and three turtle brooches, smaller than a dime, with fake jade shells on their backs.

From other drawers she pulled out shiny nylon scarves and silky black underwear, folding them and returning them neatly. Consuelo wouldn't mind. Ana knew she would be pleased that Ana had tidied her drawers, would praise her sense of order, would not begrudge her explorations.

As she played she chatted to herself. *Bueno*, you can see she is not really my grandmother. Well, perhaps she is related to Papi. She is very much like him. But she cannot be my mother's mother.

She is a witch. She lied to Mami. My mother was adopted. They don't look the least alike.

Nada, nada, nada igual.

The barn that was not a barn, that was a garage, had a side room where the Westinghouse washer was kept. Next to it, a tortoise Carlos had found in the alley scratched in a wooden crate where it was fed on strips of prime beef.

The laundry room was Ana's place, that last summer of freedom before school. Here was the doll's high chair and the rocking cradle and the miniature stove with pots and pans the size of sand dollars. Dolores rinsed her emptied cans and gave them to Ana. They rusted on the high shelves above the washing machine.

Ana would cross the alley and stand outside Linda's back door and holler for her. Sometimes she was invited inside. Linda's mother baked chocolate-chip cookies in the afternoons. Mrs Gaylord stood in a cloud of white, fat arms gloved in it, sliding a tray into the oven. It seemed to Ana a wonderful thing to have a fat American mom who was home all day baking cookies.

Linda never came into Ana's house. Its eccentricities, compounded with those of Dolores, had earned it the reputation of being haunted. None of the Santiagos understood why the children's playmates wouldn't come in. They put it down to Gringos' prejudice against Cubans.

They'll eat my food, grumbled Dolores, walking a platter of minced ham sandwiches and ham *croquetas* outside. Their *puta* mothers tell them to come here to glut themselves on real food. But they have scruples – *ieso sí!* They won't come in, the little bastards! Dolores said that what Linda's mother was doing was criminal. Kool-Aid! Cookies! She's malnourished, she huffed. Rachitic.

When the Cuban playmates wouldn't come in either, Dolores and Consuelo declared their neighbours snobs. The Santiagos lived too close to the ghosts in the house to see them.

Ana watched as Linda ate her mother's warm cookies.

When the last fragrant morsel was gone, Ana chased Linda. She caught her by her blond-brown curls, hung on until Linda fell, and then she sat on her chest and hit her. Linda hit back but she was out of her league. Ya crazy Cuban! Let goa me!

Ana only stopped when Linda started crying, snot dampening the crumbs on her face. She got up and let Linda run home.

A few days later, as Ana hunted grasshoppers in the alley, Mrs Gaylord appeared from nowhere, a black turtleneck stretched across her stomach, her hair in a ponytail. She must have been watching for Ana.

Come here, miss. Listen up! You've been beating up on my Linda, haven't you?

When Ana shook her head Mrs Gaylord grabbed her arms and shook her so that her head nodded.

Don't you ever go beating up on my Linda again. You hear me? I better not hear you ever beat up on Linda, you hear?

Ana played alone. She played with Gavicito. He was her son. He had been born in Cuba and a not quite three-year-old Ana had carried him into exile under her arm. His little pink smile never wavered. She loved him hard and hit him hard, pulling his brown pants down and spanking him. When that didn't seem enough she tied him to the doll's cot and whipped him with the rope she wore around her waist for the game. Sometimes she took the round blue box of salt from the kitchen and rubbed salt into his bottom. It was something she got from one of the stories. Dolores said this was what really hurt. It gave her a funny feeling. It

85

made her squeeze her legs together when she ground the salt into Gavicito's rubbery bottom. Gavicito smiled his little pink smile. Don't you look at me with that horseface, she muttered. Shiteater. She untied him when she finished the game. She didn't want the others to know.

She wandered across the back yard.

Carlos was crouching in the worn sandy patch alongside the driveway, his knees into his ears. He had a stick in his hand and was delicately probing a grey ant mound.

There was something bothersome about him. His lower lip – it was getting fat because he tickled it with his pillow at night. And the way his new front teeth jutted out. They bothered Ana.

Her big toe nudged the edge of the ant mound. She considered what she could do to provoke him.

He looked up and sneered, knowing what was on her mind, sensing her need. He mumbled, *Pata podrida* – rotten leg – a nonsensical taunt against girls with María as a middle name. Ana María, *pata podrida, guarda los huesos para la comida* – Ana María, rotten leg, keeps bones for her evening meal.

Shut up, Queer.

He studied her from his crouching place. Your nose is full of boogies. Why don't you pick it?

It stumped her. She was ashamed. She squinted into the sun, searching.

Man, you're so stupid!

Ana hadn't noticed Pedro on the other side of the blue Chevy cleaning the insides with a small broom. Certain things could set Pedro off, could throw him right off the curb – but nothing pushed him harder than the words 'man' and 'stupid'. He heard 'man' every day from the blacks at the factory. It was the only part of their speech he understood. As for 'stupid', Carlos and Ana prudently never asked him why he hated it.

Ana heard his bellow. What have I told you about those words? You shiteater! Come here! I said come *here!*

She saw him shaking, his hands trembling about his body like a scarecrow in a wind. They fumbled at his belt and it slithered through the loops in his pants with a hiss.

She ran for the laundry room, thinking she might make it and close the door behind her. But she glanced back and it slowed her.

The legs. His legs. So big, so hairy. Like she'd never seen them before. Pumping out from Bermuda shorts. Coming for her.

The ground shook and she grew roots. It seemed too late to run any more, and each second it was later.

Ana remembers that day, has hung on to it like a vision, although I don't know what was so special really, the legs came plenty of other times. And she remembers the later part, the crouching in the corner part, wedged in next to the doll's cradle, the air still swimming and spinning with some woman's pleas of Stop, Pedro, you'll kill the child! – was it Dolores? Consuelo? Let's say it was Consuelo – and Ana's own screams, Please Papi! Oh, no, no, Papi, stop, please stop, no! And then just yelps and sobs because Pedro never stopped; when Pedro got going he beat his children as if they were made of rubber.

Then there was a sound that is harder to recall. And the

thought rose, even then, that it was a very strange noise, a rattling gasp that shook her.

As the gasps tapered she took stock, noticing how the bruises had begun to take on the first tinges of what tomorrow would be lurid colours, the bumps were rising on her head, the scratches from the corner of the garage and then the laundry sink were raised red streaks bordered by white. It amazed her how he could transform her.

They are visiting the house of a friend of her father's, a man called Pipo. They are *haciendo visita* in his spacious front yard, under the cool umbrella of a yellow poinciana. There are many men sitting in a wide circle of chairs. He is here – the man that she likes.

The yard is enclosed by a low fence of coral rock. He is sitting on a kitchen chair, the centre of the circle. The men mostly wear *guayaberas*. There are several dogs lying in the dirt, wandering up, nosing about. There are children playing, there are strident women carrying platters of food. She is chasing another little girl around the tree. She stops to listen to him.

He wears light-coloured trousers and a black shirt. His legs are open as he sits. He talks, quietly, of what happened at Girón.

She goes to the kitchen and asks Pipo's wife for a glass of water, and when no one is looking takes a sip from it, making sure that a tiny trickle of her saliva slips back into the glass. It is not something that anyone taught her to do, not even Abuela. It is ancient, ageless, an instinct. But then she doesn't dare to offer it to him, there are too many adults around and she is in awe of him. She leaves it on the small wooden table next to him.

She watches. He never touches it.

The fat man sees her staring and holds her cheek between his thumb and forefinger and shakes her head for her. It hurts and makes him laugh. She knows she is supposed to smile. She doesn't. She stares, and then hides her face behind Pedro's back.

She listens.

He answers the other men's questions. He talks about Playa Girón, and Bahía de Cochinos – the words always on the adults' lips. He fought on the beach, was trapped when the retreat was called. She hears the whir of helicopters. She imagines a cliff, although she knows there were none. He says his best friend lost his glasses before touching land and very soon lost his life. He says he was taken prisoner. She feels a bayonet poking her back.

He hints that he will be returning soon. There will be more missions. He will not rest until he regains the past.

He speaks modestly – so different from Pedro's ravings. Whereas Pedro always appears to be arguing, spoiling for a fight, challenging his listeners with his blazing eyes and his intimidating posture to question any point – *cualquier cosa* whatsoever – this man sits quietly recounting tales of such heroism – it seems to her – that even her *papi* is silenced.

In prison, says the man, I wrote in the dirt.

In prison, I kept sane by taming a lizard, he tells Carlos. The lizard became so trusting it would walk into my hand and rest quietly there.

She imagines a prison, a man in chains on a dirt floor, his body racked, his hand extended towards a small grey lizard. She imagines him hiding the stick he uses to write on the ground.

Cheo had found his feet, so to speak, in the early spring of 1965, standing in a *bodega* and working as a grocer, and very soon Rosita and her parents had left the Santiagos alone again in their fat sprawling house. By late summer Cheo announced that he was ready to buy a house for his family. Pedro was astounded, almost offended. The Santiagos were still in the rented house on 25th Street where they had, only a few months earlier, enjoyed taking pity on Cheo. What bank did you rob, *compadre?* Pedro asked his old friend. It seemed almost impossible for a refugee to have the wherewithal to buy a house so quickly. There was much speculation that Cheo had somehow managed to smuggle wealth out of Cuba – an unheard of thing in 1965. And then Cheo, audacious Cheo, ignored all wisdom and spurned the advice he had received on arrival from Pedro and from every other Cuban in Miami – Don't work in *factorías* or live in Hialeah. He bought a tiny, freshly constructed cement cube of a house in Hialeah, a low and spongy suburb west of Miami. It was very bad for Pedro, *un golpe de estado*, like a slap in the face. Carlos and Ana, who didn't know anyone who owned a house, sensed the adults' confusion and became convinced Cheo was rich. (Rich! Rich! Rich beyond our wildest dreams!)

Driving home from inspecting Cheo's new house, Consuelo was quiet while Pedro criticised his friend, talked of the times Cheo had failed to stand up to *El Comité*, had been thick with *los comunistas*, sold out, shown he had no balls, *casi mariquita*. And he spoke of the days when Cheo first arrived in La Habana – just like when he arrived in Miami – when Cheo had not had two coins to buy a sheet of paper to wipe his ass with, and how he had had to come to him, Pedro Santiago, with his hand outstretched on that and many, many, many other occasions.

But Consuelo suddenly exploded, turned on him, told him to stop pretending, told him he couldn't spend his life keeping the truth from himself, *tapando el sol con un dedo* – putting his finger in front of his face to block the sunlight. And she offered him her few crisp truths, told him that he had squandered the money on the numbers lottery that would otherwise have afforded the family the modern luxury of Cheo's cube. And not just the money – the time! The time it had taken her to save it, the days months years of her life, wasted next to him, squandered! He was the sort of anchor that sinks a boat! He was as useless as sand! He was as bright as a spent globe! Bitterly she exclaimed that she would always have to work side by side with him at *la factoría*, that she would always be a slave to his errant ways, unlike Cheo's wife Gloria who spent her days *echándose fresco* – pouring fresh air on herself – in her new home.

Pedro told her to stop eating *mierda*. Consuelo's eyes flashed and her face took on a steely cold look and she and Pedro exchanged words like *imbécil* and *no me jodas*. Ana watched in terror, as if caught in a lightning storm out in the open. When Pedro stopped at a red light, Consuelo opened her door and got out of the car and pulled Carlos, who had been sitting between her and Pedro, out after her.

Ana always rode in the back seat, next to Abuela was her place, and the traffic whooshed past on that side. She was trapped and began to cry.

As Pedro drove away, Ana stared through her tears at Pedro's head, so big and round and gleaming with brilliantine. She imagined Abuela's knife in her own hands.

Abuela's *machete* sings through the air, it swings in an arc and thwacks into Papi's head, it sinks into his head, bites into the gleaming blackness of his hair, it splits Papi's cranium cleanly the way Abuela opens coconuts.

——•——

There is a place of sun and sea and easy breeze, and there we meet them, away from the house for once. Just the three of them, standing stark against the azure sky, the sky that is as fresh and blue-cool as the sea, and the sea and the horizon merge into each other on this translucent day. This day when anything is possible, when even we can leave the attic, when we can dance.

Today the sky, she says, is bluer than the eye of a cat.

They are standing on a grassy knoll, staring out to the sea, an endless breath of sea air filling them.

These are ours. Our niños. *They are bright and light and good children, the boy with his short sheared hair, his* cucarachas *where the scissors clipped too close to the scalp. But his thin face is not screwed tight with unhappiness now, his body is not tight with tension now. He is running with the wind, and we are running by his side. He is chasing air, pulling great slabs of blueness into himself, squealing with delight as we toss him about, as we chase him into his mother's orbit.*

And look at la niña. *She is slower than the boy, a bit clumsy. But her face, also, is turned towards the light, is spilling over with laughter, is brimming with a delicious sweet airy nothing from deep inside her, and it brings smiles to even the grimmest, most haunted of us.*

All this because she has taken them to the park, to Crandon Park to fly a kite, just the three of them because the father is playing baseball with his socios.

She stands on the faint mounding facing the blue blue sea, stands in a triumph of light. She is wearing a cotton dress cinched at the waist, a dress of tiny flowers which the little girl loves because it is the only thing she wears which makes her look young and girlish. (Certainly not the purple polyester pantsuit, or the white polyester dress that are her uniforms, worn with a severe and worried look, daily to the factory.)

She holds a ring of plastic red in her hand, a large spool from which stretches a thin nylon string, stretching forever, so high even we have trouble following.

Listen to the kite line singing with its high-pitched whine. Look at her, our love. See how she holds the wind in her hands?

When you can't stand the happy sight of her another minute, throw yourself on the grass, roll on the grass down the hill, spin and spin and let yourself go. Never mind that the grass is itchy, that you don't roll straight. Let yourself spin out, because when you hit the bottom you can stand and she will still be there, still in her cloud of light, flying the wind and sky.

When Ana climbs back to her again, Consuelo says to her, smiling into her face, When I fly a kite, Anita, I feel close to God.

We smile, but some of us gulp tears.

The House on 25th Street Sleeps

A Saturday afternoon, and Ana lying on the old shapeless couch on the front verandah with a book in her hands. It was the kind of book she most loved, one with no pictures. Thick and musty with creamy yellow pages and letters that marched like black ants, marched on and on, leading her away.

She also loved it because this sort of book made her unusual, because she had surprised her First Grade teacher, Mrs Fuchs. (What a name! sighed Consuelo. Consuelo never spoke to Ana's teacher, fearful of mispronouncing her name.) But she had not surprised Consuelo. Consuelo said she always knew Ana was like that.

Late afternoon. It had only just stopped raining outside. The storm had come like a fully opened faucet, had poured tubfulls and stopped just as suddenly and now the sun shone. Abuela said the devil had been singing.

And certainly something seemed to have been recently singing. But not the devil and not anyone on the radio. WQBA – *La Cubanísima* – had been snapped off and there was that feeling of humming clarity as the last note reluctantly left the room.

The house had been cleaned in the weekly Saturday morning frenzy; everyone had taken broom mop brush or rag and the house on 25th Street had been polished.

Before settling down on the couch Ana had walked through the house, had circled it like a dog, inspected it from one end to the other. Sniffing the wake of what had happened, the lemon Pledge that she had rubbed into the coffee table after carefully lifting the three-pronged molten glass ornament that came from La Farmacia Tres Milagros on Calle Ocho y Biscayne – a thing of orange and red like a flame that sat in the centre of the house to be admired.

She noted the shine on the speckled surface of the dining-room table, the cheap aluminium and formica table that was never used, being a notch better than the one in the kitchen. She surveyed Consuelo's bedroom, pulled on a corner of the white chenille cover to straighten the line that met the floor. She adjusted the Barbie that sat on the shelf in her own room, pushed her back so her legs came together. Sit like *una mujercita* or I'll give you a smack – *una nalgada*.

She breezed through the spotless house, admiring everything, content because it was at peace, like a child who had been bathed and rubbed dry and oiled and perfumed and dressed and tucked in, tucked in all around its corners, and now the house napped peacefully in the fresh afternoon and Ana could pass through it like a mild breeze.

Finally she came to the the front verandah and before flopping on the couch she paused to admire this room as well. Here the bright light of the washed afternoon rico-cheted off the half-dozen aquariums at the south end of the

95

room. Carlos and Ana had changed the water in the aquariums and the morning's emerald murkiness was now a crystalline splendour.

The aquariums were Pedro's hobby from Cuba and he had thrust it on the children. It was their job to rub them with salt and rinse many times and refill the glass cubes with clean water. Now the gouramis and the prized angelfish that glided like black hands, and the swordfish and black mollies with their pregnant companions, and the guppies with their peacock tails all swam in crystal waters and all this pleased Ana.

The windows had been closed when the rain began and the sound of the neighbours' radios was muffled. The house stood independent in the quiet. Pedro and Dolores had gone to the *supermercado* and Carlos was playing with friends. The afternoon was unusual without the blare of WQBA and only the occasional drum of rainwater when a breeze rustled the branches of the ficus tree and it scattered its catch on the roof. The house was dozing a siesta and its soul was still and this was as close to peace as it ever got.

As Ana read she absentmindedly kicked the door jamb. It was one of her nervous habits; she had an excess of energy in her legs. Her rhythmic pounding on the wall was one more pleasure that afternoon.

Consuelo was soaking in the bath and eventually the vibrations reached her through the napping house and she called, Anita, stop that. Anita, come here, *por favor*.

Consuelo was the only one who ever said please.

She was in the bathtub with the curtain pulled around her, the plastic curtain with the violet swans that matched the violet tiles in the bathroom. Anita, do me a favour and get me the tweezers from my dresser.

Consuelo never told Ana what she did with the tweezers in the bathtub. When Ana brought the tweezers, Consuelo put a hand around the side of the curtain. Ana tried to glance beyond but all she saw was her mother's neck and shoulders and a washcloth draped over her chest.

The bathroom was sweating from the heat of the bath. Consuelo's discarded clothes were in a pile in the corner but even here it was clean and sweet-smelling. Mami, what do you do with the tweezers?

Tell me what you were reading, Consuelo countered from behind the curtain. Ana went to fetch her book, brought it back and pushed it through the damp plastic. Consuelo looked at it and Ana took it back.

Do you want me to read to you?

Bueno, cariño, you read so well. Have you got time?

The praise was as invigorating to Ana as Kool-Aid on a hot day. Consuelo loved books as much as Ana did – more. She had loved them first and then gave the love to Ana, her gift to her. But it was always a funny thing, how she could say something like this to Ana and still there was a space between them. Not a gap, a missing thing, but a positive space, a bit of pasture. Ana didn't feel forced, obliged to perform, trapped in her mother's expectations. Consuelo always made her feel that she expected her to do well in life, the way she expected the oceans that divided countries to be deep, and her children to breathe in and out. Some intangible in her manner told Ana it would come effortlessly and the success would be all hers – not

97

Consuelo's. It was Ana who always handed it back to her, her gift to her mother.

She sat on the toilet and read aloud and as she read, her voice droning through the steamfog of the bathroom, reverberating in the quiet of the dozing house, she developed the feeling that Consuelo was using the tweezers on her thighs. As she read she pictured her mother plucking the hairs from her thighs, the black stragglers that Ana sometimes saw just below her bathing suit.

Ana plucked words and Consuelo plucked black hairs. She placed them carefully in rows, tiny black soldiers, on the edge of the scrubbed bathtub.

Ana knew the little black rows of hairs were there, even though she couldn't see them. *Hay que verlo para creerlo*, Consuelo often said, but that wasn't always true. Sometimes you knew things that you couldn't see.

That fall Consuelo saw his name – brave and black and bold as maracas – in a newspaper story. He had spent the summer underground, in Santiago and Cienfuegos and Camagüey.

When she saw that he was in Miami the thought came like distant thunder that she could call him, walk up to him, walk into his life. And she opened the telephone book and found his name.

But she did nothing. The pleasure, perhaps the right, certainly the inclination, she clutched to herself, held in reserve. Because in truth the reality of their meetings at night was better. She was dreaming him, every night, night after night. And it was better, more real, and she thought it was the most she could hope for and that it was enough.

But she was drifting. She was receding, she was nowhere near even when she was in sight and Carlos and Ana missed her.

A hot low swampy place is the wrong place to live if you are living a melancholy dream and if you aren't sociable, or musical, or at least graceful. What is there to do in such a place but relax, feel sensuous, let the heat pound at you and soften you and melt you in rhythmic waves? What was there for Consuelo to do?

And what is there to do on a hot night but gather with friends for a cold beer and hot music and laughter?

A cold windswept place would have been better. Perhaps that is why she had chosen this particular house, that sat like an exile from the north, misplaced in the tropics. In a cold place, Consuelo could have learnt to spend most of the year fighting snowstorms with cups of tea and reading novels by the fire until her dreams became narrative.

But vinyl chairs stick to your skin and a whirring electric fan makes it difficult to turn the pages of a book slowly. Windows and doors thrown open to catch a breeze also invite people. It becomes hard to live a quiet, solitary, closed life. And if the material in your genes was not entirely from the tropics in the first place, the heat is grim indeed.

Pedro had Carlos interested in tropical fish. Carlos was a collector – of marbles and rocks and magnets and comics and books on the stars and books on how clocks worked, and of insects which he kept pinned to felt boards. Carlos was a scientist but he was not an athlete, and the sight of him in front of an ant mound, poking and stirring with a stick, infuriated Pedro. Pedro told him that he would be better off playing with a little stick and *mierda*. That he was growing up among the women, he was becoming one of them, he was *un mariquita* and he would grow up to be *un maricón* if he didn't go outside and play baseball.

Carlos ignored all this. He was terrified of Pedro but he hated baseball, and football. Although he said he would prefer to get nothing at all rather then clothes for his birthday, what he wanted least was a bat and a catcher's mitt – what Pedro had said he would have.

Carlos's only narrow peninsula of common ground with his *papi* was the aquariums, which Pedro had kept in La Habana in those days when he had been wealthy and the future hung before him like a rosy mango. Then the aquariums had lined the courtyard of the house, that first house Consuelo bought with the money she had been saving since she began working at the age of seventeen. The aquariums had been huge, the size of sofas, and they had stood in the shade of the house behind the ornate black iron gate.

Carlos kept his allowance to buy chemicals to turn tap water into seawater. Pedro and Carlos prowled Haulover Pier and the Biscayne causeways with homemade nets and took home two-inch trophies for the saltwater aquarium. This aquarium in particular was important to Carlos and a slender tie to his *papi*. Yet towards the end of that summer, on a hot and still afternoon, Dolores ground her foot into the tank lid that lay on the floor. Her stout heel shattered the hood with its ultraviolet light that Carlos had bought with money he had saved over five months.

Carlos and Dolores had been fighting about something as Carlos cleaned the aquarium – no one remembers what. Their relationship was different from the others', they had private pacts and private conversations and he was *el macho*. But still, as her heel ground his heart, Carlos gave his Abuela Dolores a shove. Ana came into the room just as Dolores flew across it. Her bottom crashed into the glass of the aquarium, where it embedded itself. Forty gallons of saltwater gushed past. Clown fish and butterfly fish and sea-horses flopped hopelessly on the floor.

But it was Carlos who pulled Dolores out from the jagged mouth of glass that had bitten her. Ana was there to witness the front verandah under an inch of seawater, the tide lapping around Dolores's calves as Carlos went into her arms, whimpering that he hadn't meant to do it. Dolores kissed his short shorn hair and murmured, *No te preocupes, mijo.*

Ana was there to help the two of them clean up the glass and dry the floor, but it was too late for the sea creatures, who all died that day.

When Consuelo and Pedro came home from work Dolores met them at the door and told them she had had an accident, she had slipped while walking across the room and had skidded into the aquarium but she would buy Carlitos a new one, *el pobre*, poor boy.

And when she visited the doctor at the Refugee Centre the next day for the pain in her back, and in the many years that the pain in her back manifested itself, it was always caused by the time Consuelo and Pedro had taken her out to celebrate the New Year in 1956 and had callously kept her, an old, arthritic woman, out in the cold Havana winter air until dawn – *dawn*, señor! – while they sambaed and cha-cha-chaed and *se echaron fresco*, poured fresh air on themselves.

In the elastic summer that is a Miami autumn, Ana fell sick.

Her temperature soared until she floated high above the little fold-up bed. Here she stayed suspended throughout the long bright day, while the neighbourhood howled and children squealed and the house muttered and groaned.

Some time in the late crooning darkness of the tropical night she began her descent.

She sank. She sank deeper than the bed, right through the mattress, sank so deep that she seemed filled with something much heavier than blood and bones, something so heavy that it kept her asleep for days . . .

Ana pulls down the attic's folding steps by standing on the kitchen table where Montero died. She climbs the stairs as if led by a string.

When her head is level with the hole in the ceiling Ana discovers that the attic is not one small room but many rooms, of magnificent porportions, larger than anything in the middle kingdom of the house.

Ana climbs in and begins to explore. The farther she

goes, the more rooms open up to her, revealing their nature. And this is a vastness, an opulence – a wonderhouse stuffed with rich red velvet furniture, drapes and ornaments and beds with deep scarlet and gold coverlets.

Ana is excited by the possibilities that are uncovering themselves for her, by the unexpected discovery of treasure, here, within grip. It will be her finest gift to her mother ever – the family need never again be cramped, or poor, or angry!

Ana explores the rooms tremulously, willing to believe, brimming with anticipation.

Until she opens one more door and finds a woman – a thin, groomed, bejewelled and powerful, poised and controlled and cold and unspeakably bad presence.

Evil sits in the unexplored attic rooms, squats there, waits in the rooms no one knew were there. And Ana recognises Evil the second she sees it, not by any quality it has but by the feeling inside herself.

Ana flees, disappointment surging to fill the space where there had previously been hope.

She runs from the rooms, slamming doors behind her. She leaves Evil trapped there, in those voluptuous rooms. She realises that she will not be able to offer her *mami* the delight of their magnificence after all.

The heat woke Ana. She was amazed at how wet her bed was, but it was just sweat. It was the middle of the day and she had been fighting under the immense, suffocating weight of half a dozen blankets.

She drifted again. After an endless, tiresome night of many days and many visits to the extra rooms upstairs and the plush red furniture, and the evil squatting there, she awoke again late one morning and called out to Dolores.

Aaa-buela! Aaa-buela!

Dolores came. She sponged Ana's face, changed her damp clothes. She tugged gently, supporting her head from behind. She helped her into fresh soft pyjamas. She spoke to Ana quietly, then sat by her side and stroked her hand. She began a story about a witch and a tree that had no end.

That afternoon, Dolores brought her toast trimmed of crust and cut into ladies' fingers, grated apple sprinkled with cinnamon, and orange segments stripped of all fibre and topped with sugar, so that the orange bubbles exploded sweetly in Ana's mouth.

For two weeks she was too sick to get out of bed, and the world was bathed in the faded yellow light which would thereafter always let her know when she was running a temperature.

Then late one morning Dolores declared that Ana was better, and led her to the big purple bathtub in the violet-tiled bathroom. She soaped her, the flannel caressed her shoulders, and Dolores sighed over their thinness.

You are disappearing, she lamented. But you'll see, *mijita*. I'll soon make you strong and beautiful again. Like a sun.

She dressed her in loose shorts and a T-shirt with a picture of Bambi on the front. Ana had never noticed how white and soft it was. Dolores strained to bend over, puffed asthmatically as she buckled Ana's sandals. And then took her outside for some fresh air and sun.

They sat together outside the back door, on the top step, the old woman and the little girl.

When Ana emerged from that early autumn visit to the many rooms in her mother's house, she gazed at a world with a giant old ficus whose root tendrils fell like hair to the ground, and from whose branches little brown birds flitted and soared and darted and called to one another. At her feet long lines of ants marched, other insects scurried around, the sun shone, the sky was the purest, loftiest blue, and clouds rolled slowly across it, massing and then dispersing. She was acutely aware of the sound and motion and vivid colour of her back yard. It was the first time that she experienced the world as an achingly beautiful place. She wrapped her thin arms around herself, embracing the warmth of midday.

Eventually she became too hot, she began to sweat, and to her amazement she discovered that her skin seemed to be rubbing off, that the little grey cigars she could sometimes find in the crease of her arm on a hot day were now everywhere, could be rolled into large fat cigars before they slipped from her palms. She looked at Dolores.

Eso no es nada, don't worry about it, that happens to lots of people after a long illness. It's just the skin burnt off by the fevers.

But Ana wasn't reassured, and soon the day grew cloudy and too warm. She wondered at how quickly bright blinding light could slip under cloudy greyness. She was tired, and went back inside for a nap.

Then there came a time when Ana loved Dolores, after

Abuela had nursed her so lovingly. Despite the tension that had been increasing between them in those years of Ana's childhood, they tried, for a short time, to weave a quiet spell during the day, rarely raising their voices at each other. But there was something in Ana, some nebulous perception that she didn't actually form into a thought – that this peace wasn't real, that it was feigned. It was as if, embarrassed to fight, they were forcing themselves to behave.

The Woman's Nerves

Yo no tengo pelo en la lengua, Dolores often said. When she referred to her tongue as hairless, she wanted it understood that she was not afraid to say anything. But actually Dolores had many secrets, there were plenty of things she would not talk about. She never spoke of Consuelo's father, never said what he had done for a living, or why she had married him. When Carlos or Ana – shut in the closet those long afternoons – asked a direct question about the past, about the cast of characters in her stories and how they related to any known history, she would snap closed with the words, That I will take with me to my tomb.

And even if she did tell them something, and assert that it was the truth, it was still, after all, one of her stories.

—◦—

Henrietta stayed in her father's country house, an elegant *bohío* with a thatched roof and white walls set in the midst of a stand of royal palms.

The house nestled in the hills between Regla and Guanabacoa. It was where the monied people of La Habana had been going for two centuries, to breathe a purer air whenever there was yellow fever in the capital. In the cool nights, the boats crossing the bay left tracks of phosphorescent light behind them. These hills above La Habana were an enchanting, rustic place; a place to lose bad memories and acquire good ones.

But that year all Henrietta acquired was the intense desire to follow her lover to the grave. The illness that she hoped would soon kill her was making her weak and dizzy, bloating her arms and legs. She ate almost nothing but still her stomach grew, extended, protruded like the stomachs of the starving *guajiritos* begging on the steps of the capital. At night she was tormented by vicious cramps and poundings from inside. She welcomed the malignancy, revelled in it, eagerly awaited the moment when it would suffuse her.

The servants dropped hints that it was life, not death, that was extending her stomach. But Henrietta still bled once a month and she was not so ignorant as to think you could be with child if your legs were regularly awash in red.

So she was unprepared for the dawn, after a night spent harvesting cramps, when she hurried to the bathroom and felt a tremendous urge to pass something very solid. What eventually she pushed out was a monstrous thing, covered in white gossamer slime and purple and green but still recognisably human.

It cried, it was alive and it squacked and Henrietta stared at it in horror until she finally managed to recover something of her wits. It was Henrietta herself who cut the pulsating cord with her nail scissors and wrapped the creature in satin-lined towels. Eventually she found the strength to pick up the bloody bundle and stumble with it to the garbage dump at the farthest end of the property.

Where her daughter spent her first morning, sustained by the warmth of decomposition and breathing a moist air.

Until one of the maids heard her.

———

Dolores strode across Bayfront Park into the tall spired building of the Refugee Centre. She entered through the basement cafeteria, and when Ana tugged at her arm Dolores hissed, Leave me alone, *hija*. *Bueno*, we'll see how things go. Perhaps afterwards we'll buy you *un pastelito de guayaba*.

Dolores led the way up dark stairs that twisted away from the cafeteria's aromatic gloom. She heaved herself up with one hand on the bannisters as if she were scaling a mountain with a rope, her other hand twisting the fleshy part of Ana's arm whenever she touched the wooden rail. *¡Muchacha! ¡No seas idiota!* Don't you know there are millions of microbes there? All the old men who come here! Who finger their noses and then stroke that wood! See if you can walk like a young lady!

She was panting by the time she arrived at the first floor. Her lips were compressed into a tight sphincter, her eyes malignant. *Al que mucho se agacha, se le ve el fondillo* – he who bends over too much shows his ass, she muttered.

La Señorita Remedios, she rasped at the first desk in her path. She was directed, then redirected, up and down, across and all around the ancient building.

They crossed waiting rooms packed with fat, strident women, sickly children, sad men in loose *guayaberas*. The smoke from their cigars rested solidly on the back of Ana's throat until she had to swallow.

Dolores's stout old lady's shoes tap-tapped heavily and her face was becoming redder. Her patience gone, she rounded on a woman in a uniform. Let's see if you can tell me where *la* Señorita Remedios is in this mansion of Satan. Do they only employ cretins here?

La Señorita Remedios wore a navy-blue suit and a wide stretch hairband. She was middle-aged and heavy. She spoke English badly and Spanish with a foreign accent. Ana had not seen her when she had come to the door of the house on 25th Street, and did not associate her with the government woman Dolores hid from in the closet.

Dolores greeted her cordially, panting and coughing from the exertion of finding her. She lowered herself into the chair in front of the woman's desk without waiting for an invitation. *La* Señorita Remedios, flustered, said, *Buenos dias. ¿Como estas*, Señora?

I'm dying. It sounded like an accusation.

Vamos, Señora. No one is extending their lives.

Bueno, my case is more serious, if one can believe your doctors. They say I am rotten with tumours, but they tell me these things calmly, complacently. What should I think?

Dolores coughed and the air she was breathing whistled inside her.

How can I help you today? asked the woman.

Bueno, there is little anyone can do to help me. I have

110

very little time left to me. Look at this, Dolores said, lifting a specimen jar from her handbag. See that? There's not much hope when you see that, is there?

The woman refused to look. She kept her eyes on Dolores's face. Forgive me, but I am very busy. I am not a doctor, but I have many people to see today. Is there anything I can do for you?

Dolores dropped the jar back into her handbag. I have come here to help *you*, she said. We met some months ago, when you came to my daughter's house. Perhaps you do not remember me, Dolores Tacoronte? You are such a busy woman, and so *amable* . . . Dolores smiled benignly, encouragingly, all simplicity.

Sí, Señora, sí, I think I do . . .

Señorita Remedios had a poor memory for faces but recognised the name on one of her most difficult cases – at least one of the names. She had been trying to track Dolores for months, had gone to her daughter's house in north-west Miami half a dozen times. She was happy to hear Dolores say she believed there was some confusion about her file that had been worrying *la señorita*, and if *la señorita* would be so kind as to show her the relevant documents she believed she could clear up any mystery because she was not long for this world and did not want to be any trouble to anybody.

Señorita Remedios brought out Dolores's file and spread it on her small desk. She pointed her sharp pencil and said she needed to know exactly what Dolores's maiden name was, and also the names of her husbands – there seemed to have been several – and any other aliases she may have had. But as she said this Dolores's cough became more violent and her chest heaved. She was forced to grip the edge of the desk as her back arched and she fought for air.

Her face was darkening and she managed to wheeze, I'm suffocating, I'll die right here, while plonking her handbag on the desk. Her hand searched in it desperately, rummaged like a rat in the dark, and then pulled things out – pill bottles and vials and flasks and the specimen bottle. Somehow the vaporiser wasn't there.

A glass of water, she rasped. Señorita Remedios, who had been hovering anxiously, hurried away.

My back, Dolores commanded. Ana stepped forward and obediently patted the curving expanse of fat to help activate her lungs. Dolores's trembling hands stuttered as they riffled through her bag, grasped the desk again as she heaved desperately, and reached for the bottles on top of the file. She opened several and perhaps she could barely see what she was doing because of the severity of the attack, for she also opened the specimen jar with its brown and slimy lumps and her tachycardial hands knocked it over.

The stench was fresh and sharp. It pushed Ana away just as Señorita Remedios returned with the glass of water. She stopped at her door and stared, aghast. Dolores finally managed to get her puffer to her lips, and pulled on it to save herself. The plummy redness began to drain from her face almost immediately.

Dolores found a space to breathe and turned around a bit, shifted her bulk, looking towards the door where Señorita Remedios and Ana stood, unable to come closer. When Dolores could speak again, she exclaimed that that was the worst attack she had ever had, she was sure she would die. She heaved herself up from the chair and picked up the file and the specimen jar and its spilt contents and carried it to the plastic-lined garbage can. She stuffed it in and knotted the top with knowing hands.

I hope you will never taste the bitterness of being ancient and infirm, she said grimly. *Vamos*, Ana María, before they have to roll me out of here on four little wheels. *Buenos días*, Señorita.

The stories in the closet ended after Dolores devastated the government woman's file and the government woman's nerves. After that there was no more need to crouch in the dark for hours on end, and no more was heard of Henrietta. It was a pity, because Ana had begun to look forward to the sessions in the closet, to relish the tugging at the knots of the mystery about *la americana*. But Carlos was bored with it, wanting to hear about witches and vampires, wanting even more to play in the sunshine. And the stories had been building up to something, had come perhaps to too many conclusions already. Dolores had reasons to fear her own hairless tongue.

A Storm

Dolores claimed to keep track of her age by the hurricanes she had survived. *Sesenta y cuatro*, she boasted, fixing her listeners with the unwavering eye of a mad hen, daring a contradiction. And it was true that in her hometown of Olvidados the storms came almost every year between August and October, relieving the *campesinos* of everything except their *pellejos* – their thick skins.

Moving north scarcely changed her country habits. Although she left *el campo* almost as soon as she began to menstruate and always lived in cities and towns afterwards, she remained essentially a *guajira*. It showed in her reverence for the almanac on the wall, in the way she went outside several times a day to peer at the sky, in her eating – a smackery of lips and crunchings, slurpings, sucking, sloshings. The Cuban countryside was in the twisting corridors of her heart.

Even in Miami, in *el exilio*, Dolores knew when the storms were coming. She waited for them each autumn. She read the auguries in the skies, drawing meaning from the morning's nervously jostling clouds, from the crescent-moon formation of birds fleeing the copper evenings, from the way the night winds could not shake the leaves from the ficus tree.

She was anxious about the radio. She anticipated the moment when the house would be isolated, retasted the terror of other endlessly thick nights. She wanted a new transistor radio.

She felt no remorse about the old one. It had been a gift from the family for her birthday, but Dolores had hurled it at Ana one apocalyptic afternoon. It had hit Ana squarely on the head. Static now interfered with the broadcasts from WQBA.

Dolores conceived the idea of ringing up *La Cubanísima* and throwing herself at the mercy of its listeners. The plea she dictated was heard several times in the next few days: *Anciana en necesidad* – ancient lady in dire need. Requires a radio to stay in touch with the outside world.

Some were mailed in boxes, most were delivered personally. Dolores received them all gratefully. When her benefactors seemed surprised at the robust and youthful *anciana* who came to the door, she quickly reassured them by reciting a catalogue of her illnesses.

The radios continued to arrive, like rain showers, for months. They crowded tables and chests of drawers, jostled on the kitchen workbench and melted in the sun. Carlos spent days exploring their insides.

The house braced itself for the coming storm, and the souls inside felt the tension. Consuelo grew listless and needed quantities of *tilo* brewed for her night and day. Dolores sent Ana out to look for the flat round seeds, the weed that grew among the trash in vacant lots.

Happy, chained to the ficus tree, howled day and night.

This year *el huracán* will destroy everything; it will come ripping out of *Satanás* himself, Dolores warned at breakfast on the first day of September. The pronouncement frightened Pedro enough for him to thump the table.

¡Basta! Enough of your shit! I'm sick of your *guajira's* tales! Stop eating *mierda!* Nothing, but nothing, is going to happen. You think you know more than the damn scientists. You sound like a *santera!*

That was in the morning, in the gloom before dawn, because he always insisted on leaving an hour earlier than was necessary, wherever he was going. At seven, as Carlos and Ana were trying to work out which holes in their shirts their heads went through, he opened the door to say, You're going to be late, and then he was gunning the engine and roaring away with Consuelo.

Sometimes, in the ripeness of that fall, the sun rose and kept on rising, and after the others had poured out of the house Dolores went to her pots to prepare *pollo asado* and cream of rice. Sometimes the house slept through the noonday sun, or crept past the hours, trying to stay in the strips of shade cast by its neighbours, and nothing disturbed the afternoon siesta. In the afternoons, after school, Ana would go outside to a patch of sandy dirt beneath the kitchen window and turn the hose onto it to make soup. Fingers like fat worms travelling through and around and stretching and oozing. Revelling in it and squelching for hours. Her voice drones on in my ears. Neither gladness nor pain, just a child's chatter to herself – it must have been contentment.

But to say that that was what it was like would be wrong and you already know that. That time was – well, not even like a coiled spring, or a cocked gun, or a machete too scrupulously sharpened. That would imply a long wait.

There were no long waits. Their peace was bought expensively. And was rationed parsimoniously. They moved in that house in spasms, through noisy hot hours, past glum gulped meals and into somnambulant nights. Ana cried in her sleep, fought through her dreams. In the mornings they would advise her that the night had been filled with her shrieks. *Demonio.*

And if the first to break the daytime peace was Pedro or Carlos, Dolores or Consuelo, what did it matter? Each shattering boxed Ana's ears, pinched her flesh, left her uglier and quieter. Because, you see, in the end it was always her. Her doing. Her undoing. Her badness.

That's what it feels like to be a child in an unhappy house. Don't you remember?

So Pedro came home on the first day of September wound tight with the day-long ringing of Dolores's words in his ears. Happy's barking sent him pounding outside. The dog cringed from the moment he sensed Pedro, lowered his head and front paws, presented his rear end and whimpered, but still Pedro grabbed his collar and beat him with the doubled length of hose he kept just for that. Happy yelped high little screams. Pedro grunted with the effort and beat him some more.

Carlos and Ana stayed inside, played their rabbit game of

making themselves invisible, of blending into the light brown stucco walls, and were glad it was the dog. Carlos, even more than Ana, was learning to keep a light finger on Pedro's pulse. More and more he tried to withdraw his own personality, hoping to evoke nothing in his father.

But he always forgot. Then Pedro would stalk outside just as Carlos crouched over a pile of dry leaves, a magnifying glass in his hand, or stirred an ant's nest with a stick. It stirred Pedro. No son of mine is going to be a queer, he roared, smashing Carlos's play.

Pero Papi, said Carlos, standing up but reluctant to emerge from his daydream, to confront the danger.

¿Pero qué? demanded Pedro, looming closer, challenging him.

Carlos looked down, daring only a *tsk* in protest, but even that was too much and Pedro was on him.

Don't fry eggs at me, he howled. No son of mine is going to be *un maricón. ¡Qué coño!* That's what they're raising you to be! *¡Un maricón!*

And then it didn't matter what Carlos did, where he looked, how he pleaded, Pedro was dragging him away by the collar, kicking him in the seat of his pants, his leathery palm everywhere. When Carlos lay crumpled before him, his face dissolved, Pedro ordered him to stop crying – Don't get me started again. And then, as his hand began to ache, as the cold in it turned to stinging warmth, he felt guilty and that confused him. He searched out Carlos, who by then had pushed himself into a corner of the closet where Dolores told stories. Pulling him out by the ear, he ordered him from the house.

I'll make a man of you yet! Go and play baseball like a real boy! Don't ever let me see you poking in the dirt like a queer again!

Pedro singled out Carlos because he saw in Carlos something he had once had, which had been taken from him, and beholding that was intolerable. Just as Dolores saw in Ana a version of herself – perhaps an earlier self, not yet grown a carapace of scars – and punished anything still quivering softly.

Pedro carried around the house on 25th Street his white-hot rage which he kept in constantly smouldering coals, to be fanned into life any second. He was angry, he was furious – with a fury he had inherited on the packed dirt floor of the *bohío* into which he was born. And where he was soon after disciplined by his Asturian mama for crying, for touching his penis that was never diapered, for touching his *caca* and the mud around him – the only media for creativity in his blank and lonely life.

Rosario Espinosa had been sent to Cuba to look after her brothers and help them escape the misery that was all they were going to inherit in Spain. With her back twisted by childhood polio she was lucky to have found a man at all, even such a bad-tempered and unreliable *gallego* carpenter as Fecundo Santiago. Her back was constantly inflamed by her work, and she was already suffering from the cancer that would kill her before Pedro was ten. But despite her pain and tiredness, Doña Rosario lived only to work and when she had dealt with the interminable chores, she covered her head with her shawl and deposited Pedro for safekeeping in a wooden crate that her husband had discarded in the courtyard of their shack.

She left him there to be baked by the sun and to struggle to control his bowels while she went out with half the family's dinner, to distribute it among those of her neighbours who had no dinner at all that night, and to clean the houses of those who were sicker than her – a *guajira* having a difficult pregnancy, whose legs had swollen to the size of an elephant's, or an old mulatto woman who had given her life in service and now was dying alone.

Doña Rosario did this to negate her own poverty and pain, to deny its existence; she beat it into submission the only way she knew. In the hovels of her neighbours she was well off and strong.

When she'd finished caring for the more afflicted, this pious woman dragged herself to church to confess her sins to the old *gallego* monster who served as a priest, whose bad temper and bitter displeasure with life rivalled that of Don Fecundo.

The boy passed the long hours in his wooden prison, and eventually could not help but defecate in a corner. Out of mindbending boredom, he put his little paw in it and messed it around, knowing he would be beaten for it but unable to help himself.

And still Pedro carried the additional rage of losing his mother when he was ten, because he found out then that life could be even harder. He spent the rest of his life idolising her, describing her as a saint – pronounced a saint by all her neighbours who survived her. But he mentioned her rarely, because he could not touch his childhood, could never bear to take it out and examine it. And he had not seen a photo of her since leaving Cuba: the six photographs of Doña Rosario in existence had been kept from her only son, distributed among her relatives and the women she had helped. And these were the very people who put the saint's son in an orphanage when Don Fecundo remarried, turned their backs on Pedro and left him there to further his education with fresh beatings at the hands of the *jesuitas*, while cherishing the image of his mother and praising God when they mentioned her name.

Ana does not remember the old *gallego* who was her only grandfather, although she was told that Abuelo Fecundo galloped her on his knee and brought her *pirulís*. But Pedro could not forgive something he could neither examine, and when he left Cuba he never wrote to Fecundo, and he had good reasons.

Consuelo was mostly sad. She was mostly depressed. Softer and weaker by nature than Pedro and Dolores, her pain, equally untouched and unexplored, rinsed through her periodically, leaving her crushed and listless for days, her fawn's eyes clouded and confused. An inertia like the weight of destiny pinned her limbs to the joyless bed she shared with Pedro.

But Consuelo, too, had her streak of rage; she too was a survivor. Never defeated, she could mine her lode of rage and emerge fighting, her mouth spitting oaths and her hands doling out pain to rival Dolores and Pedro.

As Consuelo and Dolores prepared the evening meal that first night of September – fried plantains and *yuca* and black beans with rice and fried steak – Pedro went out again and came back with a hurricane lantern, a flashlight, and plywood to cover the windows, all things that would disappear from the stores once the panic was on.

121

Dolores watched from the verandah. As he walked past she breathed out a slow, quiet hiss.

The rain began two days later, skittering showers that WQBA said were associated with a tropical depression originating south of the Cape Verde Islands.

Within a few days they heard that the warm Atlantic waters had nursed the infant storm into a fury. The warning services named her Betty. They said Betty's trajectory would bring her to the New England coast within the next few days, and Consuelo sang with relief. She and Pedro had no confidence in the weatherboard farmhouse, so much older than the neighbouring houses built on its pastures.

But Dolores mocked them. Wake up, cretins, she rasped. No one can save us from this one. Of that I'm sure, as sure as my name is Dolores Fátima.

That night the always passionate voice of the Cuban newscaster had an hysterical edge as he warned listeners that the storm, incredibly, had done a loop-the-loop in the middle of the Atlantic and was bearing down on Miami with winds approaching 180 miles an hour.

By the following morning Betty had crashed into the Bahamas. Like a terrible magician she whipped the cloth from beneath those islands' humble tablesetting, and when everything descended again the landscape had been trashed.

Instead of finding the images on Channel 7 sobering, Carlos and Ana celebrated. As the waves pounding Miami Beach became more erratic and the waters of Biscayne Bay were churned, so were they.

Outside, palm fronds swished and groaned, their trunks compelled towards the ground. An untimely gloom descended. All of this excited them. The wind shrieked louder and so did they. Nature was having a fit, but they were inured to fits. Carlos and Ana revelled in release.

They saw Pedro outside with their neighbour, Old Man Mathers, struggling together to place a plywood sheet over the dining-room window. Pedro's round face was red with the strain of hanging on to the wet wood. Nails sprouted from his mouth instead of a cigarette. He glared at them.

They hurtled away, careering from room to room, knocking past Dolores who was turning drawers inside out looking for rope, for pills, for the things that would keep the impending castastrophe at bay. She struck out at them – at Ana, her favourite – but they were moving too quickly.

Consuelo pleaded. Behave yourselves. Don't you realise people die in hurricanes? Then, as if actually finally seeing them, exasperation took over. Shut up! Be still!

They danced away, skipped off to jump on Dolores's bed. Hur-ry, Cane! Hur-ry, Cane!

Consuelo and Pedro scurried between the hardware store, 25th Street and the grocery, hoarding tinned food and lumps of fuel. They argued with Dolores over whether to leave any windows open for the moment when the air pressure inside became greater than the plummeting pressure outside, when the house might explode. Consuelo caught Ana and put her to scrubbing the lilac bathtub. She filled it, the sink, and anything else – pots and buckets and bowls and even the garbage pail – with water for when the taps ran dry.

That evening they ate in the delightful unnatural darkness of the shuttered house. Ana struggled to swallow runny plantain soup and to eat the *tamales* Dolores had taken out of the freezer. Consuelo brought out a carton of *mamey* ice-cream and loaded their bowls. It was no use putting anything back.

The rain lashed the house, the wind screamed, and Ana and Carlos waited for the electricity to fail so Pedro could light candles and lamps.

They were innocent. There had been other years when the lights had gone out. Each time the storms had only touched lightly on Miami, offering a rowdy caress to an indulged and favoured child, having battered Haiti or the Bahamas. But as the night grew longer, the realisation dawned that Dolores was right: this one would be different.

Despite the coverings on the window, the noise grew frightening. There was a shriek in the night that had never been heard before. Consuelo said it was the wind encircling the house.

Ana did not believe her. She imagined a being out there, the evil in her dreams. She imagined the malevolence of her dreams roaming the night, set loose by the tempest, bent on destruction.

The clocks stopped at 10.38, the refrigerator shuddered and ceased its hum, the radio's incessant drone finally faltered. In the sudden hush the noise from outside swamped them like a wave. They hurried to push against it, to push it out, switching on transistors in every room. Ana clung to Consuelo.

Everything sprang up strangely, washed in sickly yellow tones and constricted by the circle of light from the lamp. Tall thin shadows sambaed on the walls.

They clotted in the living room. WQBA warned listeners not to leave shelter, and repeated the news heard earlier in the day – Cuba had been spared a direct hit.

At Pedro's order, Carlos and Ana lifted the phone from its cradle. It was dead; they were alone. Returning to the living room, Ana looked up and thought she saw a wild-haired, angry face in the high window Pedro had left uncovered.

Did you see that? But Carlos looked blank and said, ¿Qué?

Ana pointed to the black square of glass which seemed too vulnerable for what was happening outside. I saw someone.

That night she felt the presence in the attic wander loose outside, prowl about their daytime domain, try to make its way into their downstairs lives. It knocked on doors, pounded walls, pushed its serpent hair into the steaming window. Ana looked at Pedro, looked at her mother, and seeing their fear, ran away with Carlos, away from the windows, away from the adults who offered so little comfort.

They went to Consuelo's bedroom, the room in the centre of the house, the family's Sunday morning room. Where Ana once saw her mother with only a blouse on, lying on the bed, her white *nalgas* mooning the ceiling, big and round as the balls they bounced outside, waiting for Dolores.

Carlos and Ana cowered under the chenille cover. They chewed their nails and whispered and fell into the kicking game. They joined the soles of their feet together and bicycled, slowly at first, picking up speed until their legs were pumping like pistons, until their feet slipped apart and they were kicking one another.

They were startled mid-kick. Something large and solid hit the house. The walls shuddered, things crashed. They ran back to the living room.

A plaster Jesus, crucified, had been knocked from its nail on the wall and smashed on the wooden floor.

Dolores and Consuelo gathered around the shards, desultorily picking up pieces. *Ay, Dios santo. Ave María purísima.*

Estamos fritos – we are fried, Pedro offered.

Carlos and Ana dared not leave the room again. They sat on either side of Consuelo, pushing their faces into the rough fabric of her dress like kittens, seeking the comfort of her stroking hands. Carlos asked what time it was: it was only a few minutes past eleven. Time seemed to pass differently that night, seemed to barely go forward at all.

Pedro was at the formal dining-room table, chain-smoking – an ominous sign. His mind had narrow parameters but they contained a thing untamed. It was best for him to be eating or sleeping, and if not then he should be in motion, pacing the factory, pitching a ball, or tapping one of his *socios* on the chest as he made a lucid point about the Cuban political situation. Pedro unoccupied, Pedro quiet, Pedro staring, was a portent.

They made a space around him, a walkway without safety rails that they erected hastily while still compelled to remain with him, because the thing outside seemed more threatening.

It was a rhythm, and in that sense normal, the way in all families people will draw close together, and then away, and closer and then further, until the tangent lines take you off to other neighbourhoods and faces that were never in your dreams.

Still you keep swaying, closer and then further, never a well-timed arrow, but a motion like the pull of tides, because after all it is their blood in you, and now their darkness too, and now their love, and now their rage. Until you realise, ultimately, that there is to be no pulling away at all.

But a child is new to the game, and knows only its feelings, and watches darkness gather up its house and try to prise it from its moorings with no equanimity whatsoever.

And indeed the house on 25th Street creaked and groaned, wept and shook. Water began to trickle down the walls, from window edges and from the corners of the ceiling. Trickles turned to streams. A crack appeared in the plaster below the dining-room window. It grew, stretched, as if a snake waited to slither out.

Pedro stood with clenched hands, his eyes wild, and something inside him seemed to sort itself out. The house is going to go, he pronounced. We have to leave. It won't stand the second part.

Consuelo's face was an agony.

But Dolores had no doubts. Fool! she hissed at Pedro. Cretins!

They were the first words she had spoken in hours and they rang out the more loudly because of that.

She sat in a squat red armchair in a corner of the room, her hands gripping the armrests, a portrait of royalty.

Listen to what I'm going to say. I've lived through many hurricanes – *muchísimos*. She bent forward slightly, raised her forefinger and proclaimed, This one will also pass. You will find nothing out there.

Pedro stared but didn't hear. *Ven acá*, Ana María. *Tú*, Carlos.

Ana thought of the terrible thing out there, thought to refuse, but when Pedro called, her feet went – they were his. Consuelo's face was ashen, her hands frigid as she poked their arms into raincoats. Pedro strung them together, tied himself to the front of the line and Consuelo to the back.

He stood on the threshold of the front door and crossed himself. Dolores stayed in her chair, her mouth pursed in scepticsm.

Pedro fought to open the door, pushing against the wind with his shoulder, and they pushed with their hands beside him. When the door opened it flew out of their hands and slammed against the wall, and once outside they battled for minutes to close it again.

They straightened and looked around – they were somewhere they had never been, with only inconsequential and tangential relations to reality.

The cumquat tree in the front garden was bent and broken, was only a shadow squatting several feet away. Beyond, nothing was recognisable. Vague shapes flashed by, glinting for seconds and then disappearing.

Pedro was saying something. Ana could see his face, only inches from hers, knew he was screaming by his distorted features but could barely hear him above the noise.

He pointed along the street, towards the nearest corner, and they put their heads down, were forced down by the wind and rain. They were pitched and blown, pulled and then raised up, but struggled forward by slow inches.

Things flapped past, boards and shapes flew by. Branches and dirt and rain pelted them. Ana could hardly keep her eyes open, could hardly breathe.

She thought despairingly of Abuela, sitting in the house, warm and dry.

She hated him.

And then she was stumbling, clumsy as always; things were twisting between her and her mother. The four-foot length of rope twisted between her legs as if it had volition, brought her down like a calf. The gutter was a river, gushing, engorged, carrying a household of rags and crockery, a spoon a radio an alarm clock, coconuts and tree branches and sheets of metal and wooden things. This roiling river was swamping her and Ana was caught, the rope twisted around her, pulling at her chest. She was spluttering, and the water was gushing into her face, blinding her, drowning her.

And then Consuelo stopped tugging on the rope and put her arms around Ana and heaved her up. She tried to carry her, but her weight and the wind were too much. She put her down and held her upright for a second. Ana stopped crying, caught her breath, looked at her mother's face, found her eyes.

Consuelo began to walk again, but this time she was pulling her back, turning around, pushing her back towards the house. Ana went without looking behind for Carlos.

Seconds later she knew he and Pedro had also turned, that they were following, because the rope still held them together and when Carlos stumbled on the front door steps

Ana fell.

Then they were inside the house again, in the front verandah, and Pedro was behind, pushing the door shut.

Dolores stood in the doorway to the living room. She stood silently, nature's consort, her arms folded across her chest, her black eyes sparkling. Some time in the night, Ana fell asleep with her head in Dolores's lap.

The morning was scarcely brighter than the night but its relative hush was reassuring. Betty had sheared across the Florida peninsula and was in the Gulf of Mexico.

They were allowed out in the afternoon. They put on damp raincoats and ventured into the drizzle.

Most of the houses stood but many were roofless, or had entire walls missing. Twisted bits of metal and wood clung by nails, by threads, twitching in the wind, enlivened by the memory of what they had once been.

Trees had been uprooted, pitched into houses, or lay sprawled across sidewalks. Those standing had been stripped of leaves, branches, even of bark. Lakes had formed in the streets and these were full of dead birds, squashed fruit, unrecognisable things. Cables writhed on the ground.

They saw a car guillotined by a piece of plywood which had flown through the night like a razor, slashed through the hood and embedded itself in the dashboard. Roaming further, they came to a cordoned corner where people were considering a Volkswagen that hung intact ten feet above the ground, its front wheels caught in the partially caved-in roof of a timber house.

Sirens bleated in the distance and the rain and cold penetrated their coats. Nagging them home was a notion that they might have gone too far, stayed away too long. But Papi didn't say we had to stay on our block, they reassured each other.

Still they hurried back, pausing only to gather coconuts, the ones whose internal swish and gurgle promised juice. They saw mangos, rosy red and large as footballs, lying by the dozen in front of a blue house. They took the best ones.

They found a small wooden crate and filled it with their windfalls. Lemons, *sapotes*, a ripe *papaya*, a handful of small green guavas.

Their arms ached and fruit spilled and had to be picked up again as they struggled home. Tired, glowing, they sang, Hi-ho, hi-ho, it's home from work we go!

They came through the front door yelling, Look what we found! Mami! Papi! Abuela! Look what we found!

Pedro's footsteps pounded through the house, shook the house. It was their only warning – a familiar warning that plugged their throats. A second later he was upon them, grabbing Carlos and hurling him against the wall.

Ana also flew, her head hitting the opposite wall, her ear momentarily freezing, then burning.

No Papi, No! Please don't!

¡Qué no, qué no! Let's see, now! Shiteaters! You little shiteaters, you can't even wipe your own asses, yet you have the temerity to wander away for hours, worrying me and your mother out of our heads! Shiteaters!

His words refuelled his wrath and he lashed with his belt

at one while the other cowered. They bounced from wall to wall, huddling where they landed.

He seemed to be winding down when his eye fell on the fruit. His rage was not yet spent; he resavoured the time he had been worried about them, what he had told himself he would do, and found he had not done enough.

He hurled fruit at them. *Sapotes* and guavas bounced off the children's backs and arms. He ground the mangos and avocados with his foot. Enraged by the mess he had made, he threw the remaining fruit at the wall. It struck with sickening thuds.

When only coconuts were left, Consuelo and Dolores ran forward, imploring him to stop.

Por Dios, Pedro, you'll kill them!

He finished with his hand. Red handprints everywhere.

Yellow mango slime dripped from the walls. Avocado pulp clung to the curtains. Their bodies oozed.

⊷

The house creaks and strains.

The echoes of the voices of the day don't die, but dwindle in diminishing circles that float towards the roof like rings of smoke.

They are caught in the roof. They are trapped. They accumulate, season after season, life after life, generation upon generation, the condensation of all the heat that passes underneath.

That is why Ana dreams about the attic. At night, when the mind expands, when the mind follows the dwindling rings, when it wanders away to fill the nooks and open spaces of your houses, this is what it follows.

This is how it finds us. This is why we wait here, shifting rest-
lessly on our haunches. This is what feeds us. This is what ties
us to this plane. This is the why and the how of all the haunting
there is.

The emanations of human discord. The trail left by rage,
solidified.

———

After the hurricane it occurred to Ana that perhaps
Dolores offered a tough wisdom that could be trusted. She
was inclined to think that she needed alliances, would not
survive without them; that perhaps Consuelo's love was not
enough. She considered the possibility of an alliance with
her grandmother.

But a few days after the hurricane Dolores woke from a
nap with a sharp intake of breath and called to Ana,
urgency trilling in her voice.

Come here, *mija*. I just had a dream about you. This will
interest you greatly.

I saw you walking through a neighbourhood of brightly
painted houses in a strange land on a sacred day – Good
Friday.

You were happy despite the sadness of the day, and you
walked proudly, your head held high.

You opened your mouth to sing, but an egg filled it,
rolling up from your throat and blocking your tongue.

How that scares me, daughter.

Ana looked at the brown wrinkled face, the sourness and
irresistible force of it, and tried to pull away, but Dolores
held her hand and drew her closer.

Suddenly a huge wind sprang up, she said. Day became night. The heavens opened. Houses flew up and were thrown down again like so many blocks in a child's hand. I saw the railroad ripped from its anchorings and I watched the locomotive sail over your head. You clung to a tree but it was pulled up by its roots. I watched as you soared away.

She paused for a second, considering the meaning of her dream. Shook her head.

Pobrecita, I am so sorry to have to tell you this vision. It is a very bad omen. *Muy, muy malo*, she said sadly.

Ana twisted out of her grandmother's grasp and ran outside.

She played fiercely, punishing Gavicito for the slightest misdemeanor, without compassion.

The Back Yard

In November, the month of her birthday (in almost all documents), Dolores announced that she was going to see an American doctor, a Doctor Hughes she had heard about from an acquaintance.

You've exhausted the Cuban doctors in Miami, said Pedro. Crooked as they are, they can't find anything else to remove from you.

They are feeble-minded, like you, scoffed Dolores. I feel what I feel.

Ana went with her to the American clinic. She had thought she was a connoisseur, but this waiting room was a revelation. Here was sunshine, here was quiet. The air was cold and the room smelt of the springtime that came in a spraycan. The chairs were deep and comfortable. There were children's books to read. She hoped Abuela Dolores would go far with Doctor Hughes.

But the waiting was as long as at *el refugio*. Ana began to feel oppressed by the American matrons who peered at her above their glasses and then looked away again. She felt stifled by the silence of the two children sitting by their mom, like her, staring into space. Only a baby acted naturally in this frozen environment. Yet no one chuckled at the baby's antics, clucked, or remarked on the bow in her hair. No one broke the ice.

Abuela, why don't *los americanos* talk?

Están amargados. Sour. They have been soured.

At the time it did not seem a strange thing for her to say. At the time Ana did not think of her as bitter and incomplete and soul-dead.

She could see Dolores's point. This was in the days of national hysteria about NASA, and in the games the children played they sang to each other, Zap! I got you with my laser beam. You're dead!

No, I'm not! I pressed the button for my invisible force shield!

Ana decided Americans had ready-made buttons for invisible force shields. This was the layer they wore just beyond their clothes, and never went out without it.

It occurred to Ana that *americanos* didn't know about *confianza*, the state of easy intimacy that Cubans so often discuss: Right away, I knew that she and I had *confianza* . . . My house is your house. You and I have *confianza* . . . I don't know how he dared. I had never given him any *confianza*.

Confianza was a quality one could possess, like self-confidence. But unlike self-confidence, one only had it when one shared it. Even as a concept it was elastic.

Confianza was what Ana most wanted with Consuelo. She adored Consuelo, but Consuelo was an endless enigma, never there enough, never strong enough, slipping through Ana's hands.

If my mother's personality was a many-roomed house, Ana said years later, some rooms cramped and mean but others splendid, then surely I spent most of my time in her drafty corridors, waiting to be admitted inside.

Unlike Dolores, Consuelo told few stories. Her past, her history, was a void. Ana had hundreds of questions but Consuelo refused to answer the simplest of them. The hardest – the ones Ana knew Consuelo did not want to hear – went unasked, unvoiced, even to herself.

She did not know why she wanted so badly to mother her, except that Consuelo so obviously needed mothering.

Consuelo lies on her bed in the fragrant noisiness of late afternoon. She lies straight, her arms slack at her sides, the faded bedclothes creamy in the gold light of the departing sun. Her eyes stare out from smudged wells on her face, glowing so darkly that when her daughter enters the room she almost instantly steps out again. But in that instant she sees – she sees too much. Consuelo's eyes burn Ana like a memory, singe her with their strange unnatural docility, their deathlike resignation. It panics the child.

Ana runs to her *casita*, wedges herself into a corner. She picks up her foot and examines it, the dry dirtiness of it, even takes it up to her nose to smell it. She tears the skin off a ripe blister, tastes it, chews on it meditatively. Keeps pulling, working from the edges. A white patch, soft, dead-looking, maps the place where she has been gnawing.

As the year drew to a close, the house started falling apart. Too many roof tiles had taken flight like startled birds the night of the hurricane. Water dripped from the ceilings even when there had been no rain for days, for weeks, for months. On calm evenings the *peck peck peck* of dripping water reminded Pedro of a woman's tears and drove him mad.

The acrimony within the house increased that season; the jostling souls found less room to escape one another and came into more and more painful contact. The house carried the scars, in weals that opened up in the floorboards, cracks in the plaster, chunks lifted from the bathroom tiles and postules of paint everywhere.

Maldito el día que te conocí, Consuelo snarled, spinning Pedro into a whirling rage. She cursed the day she met him, and he retorted by sending her to eat *mierda*, and later to *el carajo*, and so on in escalation. Neither had any idea exactly which day their misery had started. For they had met so early in their lives, when both were growing up in the same *barrio* in the poorest district of Havana, that they could not say whether they first spoke to each other at the age of five, or seven or ten or fifteen. They had always been on each other's canvas but it was Consuelo's mistake, as far as Ana could see, to have married Pedro, and not the other way around.

Then there was the night he came home late from shuffling dominoes and shuffling with the whores he met at the bar on Palm Avenue. Beyond the reek of rum was the taint of cheap perfume. He stopped at the kitchen sink and relieved himself. Consuelo walked in midstream, prepared to be furious but not prepared enough.

Hijo de puta, she said, low, almost a whisper but meant to be heard.

You're the bitch! You're the bitch! What the fuck! Who the fuck do you think you are? They scuffled in the corner until he caught her wrists and his lips wetted her eye thickly. He hissed, *Ahora sí*, let's see if I am *hombre* or not. Or some such nonsense that was in his mind and sprang from the devil knows where – it wasn't from me. One hand took turns fumbling with his trousers and then slapping her face whenever she tried to bite him. It didn't take long. He left her to crumble like a whipped child on knees turned to jelly by fury, not fear.

He never came home the next night, or the next. He was shy of her rage. When he finally came back it was in clothes aged from having been lived in too long, and holding a ream of clot-red roses in green tissue paper as well as *el pan cubano* and the gallon of milk. He was still not too sure of his footing. He set the flowers on the table next to the groceries and stamped through the house, calling out brusquely to Ana to set the kitchen table because he was hungry, but really waiting to gauge Consuelo's temperature, still not sure whether two days' disappearance had lowered it enough.

He only got his answer when the knife that everyone associated with Dolores thwacked into the table, once, twice and again. Nothing was said, the decapitated stems were eloquent and Pedro could only hustle out of the house flinging *¡Estas loca!* behind him, because only to call her a lunatic, he knew, could sting sufficiently.

Neither said a word to the other for the rest of that year – two months and six days – right up to December when they talked about what Carlos and Ana needed for Christmas and where to hide it.

After the months of drought the words, when they came, hailed like misguided missiles until they stopped hitting the house and its walls and began finding their marks on human beings. So that the moment came when Ana and Carlos were woken late at night by the sound of their fury, and got up to witness their father's hand meeting their mother's face in the kitchen of the weatherboard house on 25th Street.

That was the night Consuelo rushed to her room and swept her arm across the top of her dresser. The china bird in its cage flew off the end with the little bottles of perfume and the framed photographs and crashed down in an explosion of glass.

Consuelo ran from there to the living room to the kitchen, sweeping anything breakable down – glass crashing, crashing, crashing until nothing precious or fragile or beautiful was left, even as Pedro tried to hold her arms and Dolores screamed, *¡Dios Santo! ¡Estás loca!* Curse the day I knew you! And Carlos and Ana stared and whimpered, because their mother was mad.

The night of broken glass ended with Pedro's clothes going out the back door and Pedro slamming the front door and disappearing into the dark.

But that was not really the end – it was a beginning.

Because that was the night Ana realised she had to take care of her *mami* – no one else did and she was as fragile as the glass things that were now strewn in shards throughout the house. Ana remembers sitting with her on the couch on the front verandah, in the darkness, as Miami slept. Consuelo takes Ana's face in her hands – or did Ana take her mother's face in her hands? – and she talks to Ana of all that is wrong in her life, Papi, Abuela, *el exilio*. She leans against Ana's shoulder, weeps into her blouse, and Ana pats her, her heart clogging her throat.

Her *mami* says that she waits for the day when someone will come to the door to tell her that Pedro has been killed in a car accident on LeJeune Avenue, or shot down by *un mafioso* as he crossed Calle Ocho, or stabbed from behind by a jealous husband. She whispers, sobbing, that she cannot imagine she will stay married to him forever, that she had not foreseen her life could be so bitter, and that she waits for his death daily.

Her *mami* stares into space and whispers that she has moments where she remembers the future, and is sure she once dreamt that it was on a sunny afternoon, after the children had been drinking a pitcher of Kool Aid and she had been cleaning the violet tiles in the bathroom, that the knock on the door came informing her that she was to be a widow now, and she saw that she would grieve and worry and then emerge into happiness. But always the moment passes, the *déjà vu* proves treacherous. She hears instead the jingle of his watch chain mixing with the change in his pocket and his heavy tread on the floorboards.

She tells Ana that there are married people who do not

love one another, where the husband thinks his wife's nipples protrude like light switches and her breasts remind him of fried eggs, which he dislikes. And there are women who feel their husbands' hands are greasy and hot and their ears stick out from their round heads like warm pot handles.

Ana makes an enormous effort to understand, tries so hard to understand that she convinces herself she has understood, because she needs to and Consuelo needs her to.

This is the night she realises that if anything were to happen to Mami, she would be left with Papi and Abuela. This is the night she realises she could go mad. And turns her back completely on Pedro and Dolores and resolves to save her mother, because more than her mother's sanity is at stake.

Ana María slept in the foetal position, curled like a leaf with a worm in it, at right angles to Carlos, each head drawn to the other's. Ana's fist was clenched, turned, impossibly, under her chin, just as Consuelo did.

Under their light cotton pyjamas the children have tucked what will be most important to save when disaster arrives in the night. A fire. A plane dropping out of the sky. An unforecast storm. A bomb – a missile – following the route of other Cuban refugees, skimming like them over the water, following the scent of *gusanos*, crashing into the land. *La invasión*.

Cuando salí de Cuba, dejé mi vida, dejé mi amor,

Cuando salí de Cuba, dejé enterrado mi corazón.

Carlos clutched his pillow, the one made for him in *los Estados Unidos*, a replica of his infant's pillow left in the blue enamelled cot in La Habana, the safety rail drawn up. It was the pillowcase's edge that comforted him. He rubbed it against the fleshiest part of his lower lip, tiny creases going grey as they spun under his fingers, the sensation controlled, perfect. His last act of the day was always to tuck it inside the elastic waist of his pyjamas, half over his crotch, half over his chest.

Ana slept with a red plastic wallet in her panties. In the morning it was never there, but somewhere else, under her pillow, under the chenille cover, under the bed. She found it, carried it to her face, just as she sometimes cupped her hands to carry the odour of other body emanations to her nose. It smelled of the crease between her legs, the acrid smell she didn't dislike.

In her wallet were silver coins. Some of them she had slipped into her hand at school. Miss Fuchs had announced it was lunchtime and everyone had to put their money on the top right-hand corner of their desks. And then desks were being cleared and children were rushing for permission to go to the bathroom, or handing in their work or putting away their crayons. There was a flurry and under this cover, keeping her eyes on the teacher's face, Ana walked, her eyes only there, her hand moving alone. The fat boy, Angus. Or the thin brown one with the round head drooping from its slender stalk. Oscar. The fat girl with freckles and pigtails. Debra!

Soon someone would be crying, anticipating missing

143

their lunch. But I put the money right here, Miss Fuchs! And Ana would keep her head down, or if need be, raise her quiet, innocent eyes to her teacher.

Some of the money came when she deprived herself of lunch – the twenty-five cents too round to spend, willing themselves to be added to her hoard. My father forgot to give me lunch money today. The free carton of milk she drank instead was cold, slightly sweet.

The money would be spent on a present for Consuelo. For her birthday. For Valentine's Day. Mother's Day. Easter. Christmas.

She counted the days with the fat red pencil on her desktop, rubbed it out with her thumb. She planned. A gift. A reward. A bribe.

Consuelo needed the extra coins, needed for anyone with the slightest bit of goodwill towards her to put a fifty-cent piece near the sacristy at morning mass. She could use whatever benevolence could be gotten from a spluttering *novena* candle.

How far her mother was drifting became clear to Ana late one Sunday night. She had spent the evening hours outside, rollicking in the grass, chasing and being chased, her heart pounding so merrily that all thoughts of the house and its many infelicities had been driven from her mind. When she could no longer ignore a need to pee, she burst into the bathroom. She was in before she realised that someone had forgotten to lock the door. By then it was too late – there was Consuelo, caught with the tweezers in her hand, her legs raised. Her thighs were a great bubbling expanse, a field stubby with small red potholes where her tweezers had been, where she had dug out tiny hairs before they had even broken through the skin. She had been unable to wait for their eruption, and had dragged them out, unwilling, from their little nests of skin, leaving small bloodied pools.

Consuelo, in the grip of some ineffable despair, was no longer just plucking hairs. She was attacking herself, plucking flesh now. Her legs, her thighs and abdomen, were an expanse of scarred skin, mottled purple and bloody.

All this Ana saw in an instant, in the briefest second, in the time it took to say Ay! and close the door again, and go outside to do the *pipí* in the bushes behind the old barn and pretend she never saw what she did not want to see.

In the closing days of 1965 Ana had a dream of such vivid intensity and poignancy that she never forgot it.

She dreamt that as she played in the streets she came upon a child, a small child, perhaps a baby, very sad and bedraggled and lonely, but nevertheless beautiful and sweet with long dark eyelashes and pale skin and honey-brown hair – perhaps a boy but perhaps a girl and yet also the baby left in the rubbish heap by the strange woman who lived on the island but later haunted her grandmother's stories.

Ana played with this little boy-girl child in the back yard of the house on 25th Street until night came and she had to go into the house. And then, because she could not take the child inside with her, and because it was precious and beautiful and needed to be safeguarded, she dug a shallow hole for it, and put it in this hole, and covered it over with dirt, tenderly, suffused with the feeling of care, of caring. She kept the feeling when she went inside the house. Saved it. At her grandmother's table she stole scraps of food, carried them outside, shielding her love from dangerous eyes, and kept the child, her love, alive, in its hole in the back yard . . .

Ana doesn't know if she dreamt this twice or six times or almost daily. But isn't it amazing, she says now, that one can hold on to a dream like a memory of one's life when so many more solid occurrences slip away and are lost forever?

When she woke that first time she thought the child was a newcomer, no one she had known before, an other.

She dreamt again and saw the child was her mother, or perhaps Ana was its mother and someone else was the baby – the feelings were slippery and twisted, were all good and bad mixed together.

Many years later, when she no longer dreamt the dream, she came to believe the child was herself.

The city had been built on a swamp, a place where the plants were tangled and unpredictable, like mangrove knees, and life was hidden under thick water and the air was always too hot. Where the tyranny of sun over water produced a monotonous cycle of rain and evaporation, interrupted only by fire in the sawgrass.

They came from the north to kill the shy Indians and to live in their swamp in little houses of coral rock that comforted vermin, and they shoved railroads across it and eventually mixed cement with the water to dry it all and straighten it all and get rid of the murky parts.

And they gave their children an ugly city, with so little to catch the eye, so much space, and light, and heat. So stark. Only the children and old people and the desperate walked the city's streets in the daytime.

In the daytime glare, the empty houses twinkled and napped.

Sleeping, too, in back yards were dogs – many dogs, almost a dog in every yard, and sometimes two or three. They were German shepherds, mostly, but also other breeds crossed with German shepherds, catching up on their sleep after a night spent howling, kept chained to the spigot of a hose or to a hook in the wall, or to a tether in the bare concrete meant to remind the Cubans of the paved courtyards of their former homes.

Now the air was redolent of cooking from four o'clock onwards. The women made well-spiced dishes, *rabo encendido* – tail on fire – and *patas andaluzas* – Andalusian legs – so that their aromas could waft out of the houses, to encourage their tomcatting husbands home from the factories, home for a brief visit, before they re-emerged after dinner, shaved and showered, to prowl the streets of Little Havana and visit their *mujeres*.

In this place fathers came home from work in shoes covered in white powder from the siftings at the cement factory or the plaster factory or the lamp factory or the factory where they made statues of tortured saints or of La Caridad del Cobre to set on front lawns. The fathers arrived wrapped in noise, gruff barkings of extreme irritation and pent-up

147

frustration, and the children scattered at the thump of their boots on the floorboards of the houses.

The noise within the houses drove the dogs wild with longing. They howled without pausing, a soundtrack of hell.

Now the early evenings were full of sound, were stupid with sound, and amid the cacophony there could be heard a song.

Well, it was not really a song, it was nothing but a jingle really, on WQBA, that station that called itself the most Cuban of all. Ana is remembering that little jingle, *El patio de mi casa es particular, mi mami está tranquila y yo puedo jugar*, a bit of nonsense advertising chain-link fencing that was played over and over again, so that it stayed in Ana's mind, so that it is still in her mind nearly thirty years (and thousands of miles) later.

The back yard of my house is very private now; my mommy is calm while I go out and play.

It stuck because she wondered why there were so many things out there that the adults feared, that made the *mami* in the song want to keep her child inside a fence. Because there was supposed to be something menacing out there, more than fathers coming home jowly and irascible from the factory, more than the savage dogs barking at their chains.

Ana can only wonder now, as she did when she was six, what there was that was so frightening.

What could have been worse than the heat trapped under Ana's roof?

Ana suspects that something happened that year, something which she can't quite recall, but which is essential to her story. Her stories.

A small photo of Ana taken that first year of school seems to turn up everywhere she goes – in a wallet that has no other photos or on a mantelpiece where she can't remember putting it.

Everywhere she finds this small picture of a black-haired girl in a red plaid dress with a white Quaker collar, an unsmiling little girl with large serious and thoughtful brown eyes.

Sometimes Ana thinks that little girl is still her. Sometimes she thinks she is the very essence of her.

The house where they lived in this city on a drained swamp is a fixture of Ana's dreams. She revisits those rooms, searching for something she left behind, some vital clue which always escapes her.

PART TWO

On the Pier

Looking at Cuba

To celebrate the last day of 1965 the family squeezed into Pedro's little blue Chevy and drove across the score of stepping stones that are the Florida Keys, across the Ten Mile Bridge which made everyone nervous lest Pedro swerve and they go swimming, until they arrived at the point closest to Cuba that is still American soil. As they stood at the end of the pier that pointed at their lost land, only ninety miles away, Consuelo's eyes brimmed over. Looking at her face, Ana thought she must have found something in the hazy distance.

Mami, can you see Cuba?

Don't be silly, *hija*. If you could see Cuba, all the Cubans in *los Estados Unidos* would be standing here looking.

Two decades later, Consuelo and Ana again stood together on a salt-sprayed pier looking out to sea. This time, they were on the far and underside of the world, awaiting the birth of Ana's first child, Consuelo's first grandchild.

When Ana had gone to live in Melbourne she had not thought about how Australia was as far from her childhood as she could get. She had not felt she needed to move through space as well as time for healing to happen – she was simply drawn to the other side of the world. Vines curled here along the trunks of trees in the opposite direction to the northern hemisphere. Water gurgled down the toilet in a clockwise swirl. In her adolescence, in moments of acute despair, Ana had sometimes climbed a tree, or found a beam or a rail or a bar from where she could hang upside down, like a roosting bat. One evening in her senior year of high school she had tried, ludicrously, to hook her legs over the door of her closet. She had felt, somehow, that hanging upside down would clear the fog in her mind. She did not remember this, either, when she had grabbed the opportunity as a student to go to Australia.

Dolores had foretold that one day Ana would walk in strange neighbourhoods under distant skies. And she had promised Ana that she would always be with her. But Ana only remembered that long after she had arrived in Australia. When she had made the decision to leave America, it had seemed she was going somewhere, not running away from something. It took her a few years to understand that you do not fall in love with a new country unless you want to leave your past. And it was to take even more years before she came to see that no running away was possible. That, as Dolores had predicted, she was always with Ana.

Mindful of her grandmother's threat, she had already resolved to name her unborn child María if it was a girl. Dolores had loved her mother, María, with a love, it seemed to Ana, more wholesome and respectful than she had ever had for anyone else. She had always pronounced her mother a saint, and even in her last years of life she was still composing poems in tribute to María. Dolores would not harm a child named María. And if the baby was a boy, Ana reasoned, Dolores would not hurt him either. She had always liked boys.

Consuelo had felt the absence of her daughter as a great physical pain, like an amputation. She had been even more depressed than usual. For her, Ana's migration had been like a death. Yet when her daughter had asked her to come to Australia, to be with her for her child's birth, Consuelo had hesitated. It was so far – and her inertia was so deep.

She arrived a week before the baby was due, but apart from a sharp pain as Ana unpacked the gifts from family and friends that made her mother's suitcases worth hundreds of dollars in customs taxes, the baby showed no signs of emerging.

They spent hours walking under these new skies, trying to get things moving down below. On days when the hot winds blew from the north, they kept cool by walking ankle-deep in the shallow waters of Port Phillip Bay.

While Melbourne's Victorian terrace houses reminded Consuelo of La Habana Vieja, to Ana they were still vaguely new and strange. If the beach was not Varadero, it was not Miami Beach either, and the seawall was not El Malecón, nor any wall either could remember.

As Ana waited for the new life inside her to stir, to awaken and begin to fight its way out, that other child of hers, Consuelo, began to talk for the first time about her childhood. For almost three more weeks the baby clung to

Ana, perhaps feeling that its mother had not yet prepared her place in the world. Perhaps Ana's child (who would turn out to be so like Consuelo that even her Australian grandmother was struck by the similarity) also wanted to hear the stories.

As they walked and Consuelo talked, Ana's heart, which had always been Consuelo's, seemed to break. But even though her story overwhelmed Ana, she also found herself growing resentful. She was beginning to fear for her unborn child. She was wondering whether the baby's birth would ever happen as long as Consuelo kept talking. She needed to concentrate all her energy on her baby, to help her emerge, to bring life forth into the light.

But her mother needed to tell a story she had carried inside for half a century. She told it mostly dry-eyed, steadily, as they walked arm in arm along the Melbourne coastline.

Ana found herself resenting Consuelo's past, which had made her so needy, which had washed her up on these shores, pouring her need into her daughter's ears.

The first place I knew in this life, the place where I spent my childhood, was in *el campo* near Olvidados, my people's town.

Olvidados was bounded by cane fields to the south. To the north and east, swamp and scrubland led to the sea. The town – a huddling of *bohíos*, a police station, a store and a train stop – had only two streets. La Calle de Milagros – the Street of Miracles – led to the train station.

It was bisected by La Calle Olvido – the Street of Forgetting. An ancient tree stood in the square where the two streets crossed. A few kilometres away was the plantation, owned by an American, where the people worked.

Olvidados in those years just before the great world depression was not a place where the living rejoiced in life. The first I knew of the world, the place my people are from, is as desolate as the edge of the world, as dark, compressed as a dot.

I remember the heat. I remember the marshes. I remember being small in a place of relentless extremes, as if everything there was pulsing towards the sun, tilting, sliding towards heat and sun. And nothing flourished there, nothing except the reeds of the swamp, the treacherous cane, the cockroaches and the scorpions.

There is nothing so dark as night in *el campo*. There is nothing to equal how quickly it descends, how stealthily it absorbs all light, how it steals your sight, how you sink into it, how you swim in black ink.

Unless you make friends with it, unless your soul is peaceful, *el campo* can drive you crazy at night.

I think that is what happened to your Abuela Dolores. She never made any peace with her nights.

My early life was full of insects. Insects shifted in clouds above the grasses and flapped in my face as I walked. The dry thatch of our *bohío* hid a murmuring, restless, scratching city.

At night, brown cockroaches took flight, batting on yellow wings against the thatch. Outside, the green fluorescent lights on the backs of thousands of *cocuyos* – fireflies – mirrored the spread of stars in the skies.

Flocks of birds on their way to the sea paused to rest in Olvidados, to perch on the only trees from one horizon to another, and to feast on our insects.

Perhaps that is why the earliest dreams I can remember were of flying, of taking to the endless skies. Of soaring.

Those first years of my life in Olvidados were my simplest, and in many ways my happiest. If I have described the place as harsh, it is because it did something to my soul, those empty horizons. But I was not unhappy there.

In the end it was not the bleakness, the poverty, the silence beyond the buzz of insects, or the monotony of our lives that mattered. All that mattered was that I was loved.

Almost every day María and I cooked my grandfather's lunch and set out across the fields to find him. We walked through swamp, through clouds of mosquitoes spawned in the heat. We walked hand in hand, the tiny bent *viejita* and the little girl.

I was her shadow. Always behind her, imitating her movements, learning by following. Neither one of us took a step without the other. I kept my hand in the dry ropy hand of my grandmother, who I believed was my mother, and I was perfectly content.

I never knew my father. I was told that he had been a soldier. (Later Dolores told me something entirely different, but that was what I believed then.) People told me he had been a tempestuous man, strong in spirit, but not very tall.

Years later, when I was nearly grown, my Tía Encarnacíon told me he had died in a Cuban prison, having been unable to endure his tortures. I was told he had been the illegitimate and unrecognised son of an American sugar baron and a Cuban country girl. I paid attention because I had never mistaken Lisandro, my grandfather, for anything else but my grandfather. But I was sure my *mami*, María, was my mother.

Our thatched house had only two very humble rooms – one for sleeping and one for eating. Mami cooked outside. El Abuelo Lisandro worked in the cane and on the neighbouring farms and looked after other people's animals.

We were poor, Lisandro and María were old, and Lisandro got very little for his work. We lived from the money that their grown children who were in La Habana sent to us from time to time, and the food the grown children who lived in Olvidados brought to us – a bit of maize, a few tubers, some plantains.

Everyone except María and I was scared of Lisandro. He had beaten his children regularly and hard, once leaving Domingo bloodied and unconscious under a *cocotero*, so that at first it was thought he was dead. But by the time I knew him Lisandro had mellowed: Mami said his thick Galician blood had been replaced over the years by the beer she brewed from cheap cooking wine, sugar and cinnamon. Even so, my aunts and uncles were amazed at the audacity with which I climbed onto his lap and pulled on his long white hair to say *Arranca*, and pulled on his long curving white moustache or his red ears to say Whoa.

I slept in their bed, a mattress of pine needles, curled into Mami's bony crescent. I played with her hair day and night, her long white *trenza*. I sat on her lap to eat, and we ate from the same plate. It wasn't that there weren't any other plates – although perhaps there weren't. Even when I was grown, I never saw Mami sit down to eat if there was a youngster around without pulling the child onto her lap and sharing her food.

We lived in *el campo* near Olvidados but I rarely saw that pueblo. I was more intimate with the pines around our *bohío*, the mud churned by generations of my people in which I happily played, and my many aunts and uncles and cousins who came to visit and who always were kind to me.

And I knew the animals. Lisandro put me on a horse, they said, before I could walk. Chorizo, the old mule, pulled his lips back to smile when I passed. I played with a rooster who was so fond of his green neck that he twisted himself in a knot to look at himself. I held a mirror up and he kissed himself.

Later, he grew less self-centred, and would chase me and hug my ankles. *Se enamoró de mí*, he fell in love with me, this raunchy little rooster whose head could not support the sagging length of his wattle. He perched on the tree where Abuelo hung hands of bananas to ripen and his eyes swivelled to catch mine as I played in the mud. He stood on my shoulder when I helped María plait palm fronds. He even insisted on following me into the house. Mami declared the little beast had a human soul which had to be respected, so she named him Paco and she accorded him respect by scattering maize for him.

But Lisandro had never respected any suitor that came to his house, and he fired stony missiles so that Paco only called on us in the light of day and scurried off when Lisandro's heels vibrated the dirt floor.

I played with Paco and stirred the mud and traced María's footsteps. That was my life.

He came in the winter, that first time.

He was not known as El Caballero then – that apposite title was only bestowed on him years later when he went to the city and the more sophisticated folk there recognised him for what he was.

In my childhood El Caballero de París had another name that everyone later forgot.

In the centre of Olvidados the branches of an Algerian oak made an airy room, and here the old men gathered to wait to die and scrawny dogs sniffed each other and chickens pecked in vain because nothing grew in the giant circle of that umbrella.

The oak had sprung, according to legend, from a seed carried in the coarse hair of a slave. The woman had been brought to Cuba by Algerian traders and bought by my grandfather Lisandro's father, a *gallego*, the first of my forebears on the island. Like so many of the males on my maternal side, he was a fierce man, an almost crazed man, a soldier who was determined to find his fortune in the Pearl of the Antilles. They said he battled with his slave's wild spirit but could not conquer it. They said he beat her into the ground at the spot where the tree later grew, fertilised by her flesh. Her dark bony hands appeared around the tree as roots.

El Caballero camped here, at the intersection of our two streets, and set out his wares, bringing out from his wagon, like a conjurer, plants that no one had ever seen before and books that no one could read or afford, and all the latest gadgets and implements and wonders of modern science – egg-yolk separators and mango peelers, chicken-leg holders, navigating devices for finding a path through swamp, bird decoders and imitators, and practical things as well, *machetes* and cooking pots and lanterns.

He was thin, with smiling brown eyes and long hair, and he was kind and gentle, with a courtly flair and an eye for the women. He bowed when he offered a *campesina* a white carnation, addressing all as *señora*.

And I don't know how many times he came. He came in summer and winter, in times of harvest and during drought, the year I was two, and three, and four. Always Mami and Abuelo Lisandro took me into Olvidados when he was there.

Consuelo's grandfather worked slowly, in rhythm with the droning world, swing bend toss, slashing alone at the solid walls of humming cane, the stalks flying up, slapping his face and him slapping them back down, killing them for good.

And when the sun was at its highest and the ache in his back became a fury, and he felt he could wring the neck of any living creature that came near him, anything at all – if only anything dared – there was María, with the food she had carried in a folded sombrero. He gulped it without speaking to her, while she waited at his side, and her meekness, the bovine quality that he demanded, enfuriated him to an even greater pitch. So that when he drained the liquid in the old vinegar bottle he turned towards her with the mad look in his grey-green eyes that had frightened her that first time thirty-seven years ago, but did not now that her hair was white.

Consuelo sat a distance away, at the bottom of a small hill, keeping what she knew out of the front of her mind, the part that chatted to her *mami* and chanted nonsense songs and talked to the friends that no one else could see. She sat still and squinted at the cane in the distance and at the sun and at anything that helped keep away what she knew – what she had known as a baby lying in a basket and as a girlbaby toddling after a hornet and as a child chasing the wind.

Consuelo knew without looking, watched without seeing, and did not run to her grandparents even when a cloud of mosquitoes dense as a December day moved towards her and feasted on soft brown skin until she was forced to surrender the seam at the bottom of her hillock and begin a wild but still wide circle around them.

They were her grandparents, that much is certain. María and Lisandro were half of her, even if not the half Consuelo had been told. In reality, not even María knew the full truth. Dolores had lied even to her, and her lies had been cunning.

Lisandro and María's blood gave Consuelo her dusky hue. The same as that of her father who lay, intolerably youthful and achingly undecomposed in a glass coffin. While her mother sat, composed and dead, in a fine marbled terrace in that part of the city known as La Habana Vieja. Where she tried to blot out any memories at all, and for the most part, succeeded.

Only when Dolores was talking to someone else did Consuelo allow herself to look at her. She did not look like her aunts from Olvidados, or any of the *campesinas* she knew.

She was dressed in a tight red dress. Her breasts were sharp, not rounded and pointing to the ground like those of the other women in Consuelo's life. She had on red shoes with high heels. Consuelo had never seen shoes like that. She had never had any shoes herself.

Dolores had a slash of red paint across her small, well-shaped mouth. Her eyebrows had been plucked and phantom ones redrawn high on her forehead. She was colourful, sharp and severe; she reminded Consuelo of a very thorny rose.

Consuelo no longer remembers what Dolores first said to her. Only that she insisted she was her mother.

For several days she stayed in María's house, trying to make friends with Consuelo. She showed her a silk ribbon she had brought for her hair. Consuelo knew Dolores wanted to take her away. She did not want to go. She felt sure María would not make her go.

Nails on the walls held their clothes. Lisandro's pants were stiff from dirt, sweat, slobber and horseshit, but to Consuelo they were inoffensive because they were the smells of her babyhood. She could only ever remember wearing the clothes she had on. María had a black dress, a sweater, and a grey undergarment that once was a dress.

Consuelo snatched at Dolores's ribbons without letting hand touch horny hand. She ran with her booty to the *hórreo*. Her safety lay in the past's clutch over Dolores's imagination – Dolores would not follow her. The granary frightened Dolores. Lisandro's father had built his grain store in the *gallego* tradition, a long stone corridor blocked at each end, a man's height off the ground. Just in front of this *hórreo* he had dealt with a constable who was coming to collect a tax, perhaps a debt, or a peasant's profit from a business dealing with a cunning *habanero*. And since all the family's wealth was in scraggly poultry and sinew, the constable had come, really, to force the old *gallego* back across the Atlantic to his verdant *aldeas*.

The old man could not be rounded, only cornered. Lisandro helped his father put the policeman to ripen with the sausages in the *hórreo*, and only the family knew the different smells of drying pig and human blood. The *hórreo* still stood – how could it not? – a sepulchre, a reminder for Lisandro of the nature of his inheritance.

Dolores, so close to that legacy, would not go near the place. Consuelo was safe there, under decaying thatch and shadows deeper than ordinary walls could throw.

Consuelo's rooster had no such refuge. Dolores had taken a dislike to Paco. It was partly jealousy – she would never be able to allow anything or anyone a room in Consuelo's heart. Perhaps because her own place there was so tenuous, perhaps because she felt herself to be unworthy of a great love and so despaired of inspiring it in the child.

María knew her eldest daughter, saw how she fixed Paco with a long and bitter look as if staring at distant and infertile horizons. María put her bony hand on Dolores's thickening forearm. I will not forgive you easily if you cook *arroz con pollo* tonight, she warned in her mild mumble.

Dolores would not openly incur her mother's displeasure. She lived her life trying to pretend to María that she was *good*. So she did not wring Paco's scaly neck, but her hand shot out at the bird at every opportunity. The bird, not familiar with the secrets of the past, did not know to shelter under the crumbling *hórreo*. At every encounter with Dolores, Paco lost a few feathers.

Consuelo wailed when she saw how he was moulting. On the third day of Dolores's visit, María sat on a chair under the pouting eaves of the *bohío* and began to knit a covering for Paco, a rough yellow shawl to be tied around his middle by its two ends.

At night, despite the emotional turmoil of those days when Dolores came to claim her, Consuelo slept dreamlessly.

As always in *el campo*, throughout those first years of her life she entered into a black sleep, a sleep like a soothing amnesia. She slept innocent of all demons and awakened before the sun, cheerfully, to await Paco's raucous song.

So it was that, asleep on the bed of tightly bound pine

needles which she shared with her grandparents, the soft snores of a stranger on her other side, Consuelo did not sense the little beast that crawled out from the moist edge of the *bohío* and sidled towards her.

It climbed slowly onto the light blanket that half covered the sleeping child, and then stopped, stalled on her bare thigh, and rested there for several hours.

Eventually the light of the moon made its way in through the single window and gazed on it, and spurred it on. It scurried down Consuelo's side and onto Dolores's hand.

Just at that moment, almost at midnight, Paco crowed in the yard. Dolores roused slightly, enough to feel something on her, but not knowing its nature she moved her hand in her sleep, rubbed it lightly against the mattress. The scorpion, maddened, raised its tail and then brought it down, burying its stinger in the fleshy ball of her hand.

Dolores's screams awakened the countryside. She swept the thing from her hand and pounded it into the dirt. Lisandro doused the sting with *aguardiente* and María wrapped the hand in cloth. Before it was wrapped, Consuelo saw it, a furious wound, pulsing, growing, a sun setting on Dolores's paw.

Dolores was ready to go. Enfuriated by the scorpion's sting, her throbbing wound, sick with the poison that was emanating from it, that was bloating her, she put aside all pretence of humouring Consuelo. This one is mine, she declared, and packed her change of underpants, her blouse.

Consuelo allowed herself to be dressed, to be led to Olvidados, mute, tractable, all the while trying to find some way of avoiding the fate that seemed implacably hers.

They stood waiting at the station, cowering under a flapping awning which provided the only shade. The horizon was oblivious, the clouds cool and uncaring. Little puffs of dust rose here and there – it was winter and the ground unusually dry. Dolores stood apart, glowering into the distance. The concavity of the landscape afforded the impression that they were the only beings in the world.

When Consuelo heard the train whistle she dissolved. She threw herself at María, her hands digging into her tortoise neck.

Don't let her take me! Don't let her take me. Don't make me go!

Turning her head towards Lisandro, seeing hope. Abuelo! Please, please Abuelo. Please, Abuelito. Stroking his arm, a desperate caress. Seeing his head sink, her hope dribble down the front of his shirt, Lisandro suddenly an old man. Stroking feverishly. Abuelo!

And then, Consuelo's final grasping: Let me stay, Mami! I'll be good! What did I do wrong? I won't pull your hair any more. Look, gentle hands. Gentle hands.

Her little hands patted, gentle *torticas*, wispy mudcakes on her grandmother's loosely fleshed arm. María's face stayed empty, her mouth loose, her arms slack. Consuelo dropped her hands. The insubstantial mudcakes slid to the ground. Dolores picked the child up, sat her on her hip.

The train was bellowing its approach, a wounded bull

expressing its rage. María emerged from her trance. Don't cry, *hijita*. Dolores will take care of you. She will bring you back to see me soon.

Consuelo stared at her creased face, her empty gums, through swampy eyes. For a moment, for the first time, it occurred to her that there was something she disliked in that face, some weakness she had never noticed. It was a thought she could scarcely afford. She searched for some sign, some clue that would mitigate the betrayal she felt.

I am scared of the train, she panted.

Don't be scared of the train. It is nothing but a big animal who will sing you to sleep. Listen carefully, he will be singing a song to you from me. He will chant, Conchita will return to her *mami*. Conchita will return to her *mami*.

Consuelo tried to see her through the flood in her eyes.

But how will I sleep?

It was coming in, struggling to brake in front of them. María gazed at the child. Finally, her fingers flew to the long white plait that hung down to her waist, separating the strands. She plucked out a single white hair, a yard long. Handed it to Consuelo. A ribbon.

Adiós, little daughter! *¡Adiós!* she cried, as the train screeched and snorted, pawing the ground. As Consuelo's heart broke and she clutched that single hair like a lifeline and shrieked and held her other hand out to her *mami*, who stood, tears running down her cheeks, the gums inside her toothless mouth churning around. But still she stood, resigned, unmoving, as Consuelo was torn from her childhood.

⁃

Imagine it.

The child leans away from this stranger who has declared herself her mother, this unknown woman who has swooped down and stolen her. She twirls a single long white hair through her fingers, gently, ever so gently, but still it breaks and breaks again, forever diminishing.

She looks at the woman's shoe, the way it is full, bulging, and the streaks on it where it has been scuffed. She looks at her own bare feet, her chipped nails, her brown legs, and then she lifts her head to stare out the window of the train as it stops at the furthest outskirts of the city.

She sees cobbled streets and squares lined with palms and women who look like flowers. She sees grilled door-ways, and behind these she glimpses fountained courtyards and steep stone staircases and women whose parasols allow her to imagine the possibility of luxury for the first time in her life. She sees the throbbing heart of her country.

And as people push through the door and others shove onto the train there is the noise of traffic, of many horses and horse-drawn conveyances and of automobiles, too, and the call of vendors and of the street women and the chat-ter of ordinary people going about their way. The girl realises that there are people everywhere and buildings everywhere and there is no open sky, no horizon here, no vast spaces. It is terrible, and it is good.

She puts her hands to the V between her legs and presses there, partly from excitement, partly for comfort, and she is sitting like that as a man dressed in a soiled white *guayabera* with a floppy woven sombrero moves up the aisle towards the door of the carriage where a *guajira* is standing holding a plucked chicken. And as he pushes through the crowd his hand touches her breast, skims over her bottom and darts underneath. Before anyone has the time to move or shout his hard brown hand has poked around – *manoseando* the girl – and there is satisfaction smirking on his face and then the hand is flying with him off the train.

The *guajirita* who has been *manoseada* turns to find a corner to hide her face. People scream, ¡*Desgraciado!* at the man's receding back and mutter tutt-tutt to themselves. Dolores's face is mottled and she looks down at the little girl sitting next to her and sees her hands where they are pressing. She slaps Consuelo, a single slap, quick and cold, with her unbandaged left hand, but so hard that the child drops the strand of hair in her hands. As she draws breath before crying, as she gazes at Dolores in astonishment, Dolores hisses, her breath rancid in Consuelo's face.

Only a *puta* touches herself there.

A House of Many Small Rooms

I had not known there were so many people in the world. I did not like the buildings, I did not like the noise. I did not like the house Dolores took me to.

Many people lived here and Dolores told them all I was her daughter. But I never smiled or talked to anyone, and I wouldn't eat.

Dolores beat me with her belt to make me eat, and I had never been hit before. My fits grew fearsome. I think in the end Dolores was embarrassed by me, and afraid I would get sick and die if I did not eat.

She sent me back to Olvidados with one of my uncles, Domingo, whom I knew from Mami's house. He picked me up and carried me away like a sack of oranges on his shoulder. When we were on the train, he laughed and chucked me under the chin. Well, so you showed Dolores what were *cajitas de dulce de guayaba* – little boxes of guava sweets. I knew this meant I had had a victory over Dolores – a rare thing. You be careful with Dolores, Domingo told me, that one has bad fleas.

After that, life was never the same in *el campo*. I never knew when Dolores would swoop down again to take me for a visit to La Habana. María was never again mine in the way I needed: she was lost to me like a scrap of paper borne towards you by a gust of wind, then, just when it seems within your grasp, swept away again by another wind. They said I was reknown for my fits of temper, when I would scream and hammer my head against the floor. They said that no one had seen anything like it.

The house Dolores always took me to was called a *casa de huéspedes* – a boarding house – but this was really too fancy a name for it. It was a house for the very poorest people of La Habana. Many families and also others – strange people, dangerous people and desperate people without families or friends, people who would make you cross the street if you passed them on a dark night – lived here, all one on top of one another. On top of me.

I suppose if I had been older I might have been disappointed in the house, considering the clothes she wore to get me in the country, and the way she acted. But I was too young to expect anything, except that I would be sad and lonely and very frightened, that I would hate anywhere where Mami wasn't.

It was a two-storey house which perhaps had been white once, had been a fine home for a Spanish merchant, with ornate balconies where his daughters had sat and brooded on the lip of their genteel prison. But when I knew it, it was neither fine nor genteel. Its rooms had been divided and divided again and again – and again – so that some were barely bigger than a packing crate. It was *un solar* – a tenement – where there was never peace, day or night.

In the daytime the women fought with their men, and

the babies cried and the children yelled and laughed and sang and cried. At midnight you would hear the clatter of the prostitute's high-heels on the stairs, and their high-pitched squeals, and the hoarse impatient grunts of their customers. And you heard doors slamming, and beds creaking, and the noises they made – the slow drumming, the groans and scrapes and also the thumps and cries and the screams and the running feet, and all the noise, so that the house shook with it all night and I couldn't sleep until nearly morning.

The business of going to the toilet was a problem, too, in that house. The others used a hole at the end of the courtyard, behind an old wall that was crumbling – *el excusado*. Dolores forbade me to use it.

It is not for you. It is full of disease. You go in the hole inside, she said, twisting my ear.

I was ashamed. The place she wanted me to use was in the middle of the house, under the only tap. It was the drain for the tap. Here we got water, to drink, to wash things – there, in the hole. And the people prepared their food in this room, cooked and gathered and talked, and there were always children underfoot and chickens pecking, being kicked out and returning again, and the people of the house sleeping there – the men slumped on a chair with their mouths hanging open but their eyes never quite shut – the people talking, talking, talking, there at all hours and pouring food into their mouths, a woman hitching up her blouse to feed her *nene*.

The little children did *pipí* and *caca* in the hole, and wiped themselves, if they knew how, with corn husks. Can you imagine? The poverty, the stench, the ignorance! The shame.

But how could I? I waited and waited and ran outside and came back and squeezed my legs together and waited some more and it seemed the urge had gone but then it was back and I had to run to *el excusado*.

What did I tell you? It is not for you! Rats live there. A girl's holes are just right for rats to crawl up. Do you want rats feeding on your entrails? *Oyeme bien, ¡desgraciada!* I am your mother! *Tu madre*, do you hear me?

The house was owned by one of her cousins. Many of the people had come from Olvidados and were related to me. One of her sisters lived here, Josefina, and her four sons, my cousins.

For all it was terribly cheap and filthy, we were made to feel that we were lucky to be allowed to live here. In the 1930s, Cubans were dying of hunger on the fine promenades of the capital.

Dolores earned five cents a day cleaning houses for the rich – even then, there were plenty who were rich – in El Vedado.

When she went to work in the mornings, I was left in Josefina's care. And Josi – *pobrecita* – life had been cruel to her and she had been broken, early, by Lisandro, who prepared her for the beatings that her musician husband later continued, until one day *se le fue la mano* – her husband's hand got away from him and he went too far, and her brothers had to smash his guitar over his face. And so *el cabrón se largó*, as Dolores used to say. The bastard left her to raise her sons alone, and my cousins were as mean and shiftless and musical and stupid as their father.

Dolores had boyfriends, who sometimes gave her presents, and sometimes when they came over she sent me outside, told me to go and buy *un guarapo* or *un pirulí*. And I would run down the street to the corner where a man always stood, a small roundish man, selling cigars and cigarettes and sweets. And always he gave me the *pirulí de gratis*, and there was a kindness in him that I thought was what a father should have and I began to think he was my father. And then I was sure he was. I asked her one day and she said he was. So I looked at him more closely than ever and played near him and waited for him to call me, but he only gave me the *pirulí* and smiled at me, and then other little children came and called him Papi so I stopped going, he was someone else's *papi* and you could never believe anything she said.

The men who came to see her would stare at me, would whistle long and slowly when they first saw me. They embarrassed me and I didn't know where to look, but I felt proud, also, and happy because they noticed me. They said, ¡Coño! This one will be even more *guapa* than her mother! And I knew, when one looked at me like that, when he said that, that he was not my father.

People stared at me. I knew they stared at me. I knew I was different, strange; some said beautiful. Now my eyes are tired and my lashes seem to have shrunk, as my eyes have shrunk into my head. But then – then! Then I ate up the world with my eyes! They were honey-brown, they were unusual, framed by long straight black lashes, darker than my hair. They told me my lashes flapped down like Spanish fans. And my hair – not this *pelusa* I have now, this fluff.

My hair then was golden-brown, thick and curly, it made a *trenza* as thick as your wrist.

But for all of that, I did not consider myself beautiful. I only wanted to look like everyone else. I wanted to have dark eyes and black hair. Finally, after all, I would have preferred to not look a bit *mestiza*, like *una americana*.

And then the time came when I got too much attention, when I began to hate the attention I got from men and to wish that I was ugly, when I walked with my face down, looking always down – at the filth in the street and the gobs where the men hawked and spat. That was better than the looks on their faces.

It was about this time that I first saw El Caballero de París again. He had grown a bit less lean – he was as well-loved in the *solares* of La Habana as he had been in *el campo* and housewives vied for the privilege of feeding him. Even jealous husbands could not be angry with this good man and he was welcome in many more households than he could visit. When I saw him pushing his cart full of flowers through the street and singing and calling out to everyone by name I stopped in surprise, because he was like a memory of my past marching through the streets of the city. And El Caballero parked the long handles of his cart and rummaged in its side, and brought out some sticks and bright paper, *un papalote* – a kite. He smiled as I skipped away to find a park to fly my kite. I forgot to thank him.

Another time El Caballero de París gave me a pair of skates – the kind that you adjusted with a key. Then I spent my days flying on the streets of La Habana, through el

Parque de la Calle G, along the stately Avenida de los Presidentes, the oleanders a pink blur to my right, dodging *las ayas* who walked lace-clad babies in carriages. But my knees became one great scab that would never heal because I always skated down the terraces of the park, my eyes fixed on the blue beyond El Malecón.

Dolores worried about me. You are the only thing I have in life, she said. To prove this, to prove how she valued me, as my value increased in the eyes of the men on the streets, she began to tie me up at night. In our room, which was almost completely taken up by the bed, she would tie my leg to hers with a rope. She would wrap this rope around my leg, under and over, and then pull and grunt, satisfied, *Ahora sí!* No one will take you! *¡Qué se vayan a singar!* They can go play with themselves!

She tied me with the same rope she hit me with when I wouldn't eat. *¡Vamos!* So you don't like it! *¡Vamos, condenada!*

I had a nervous stomach. She ruined my stomach.

I hated to sleep with her.

My life with my grandparents had turned me into a sensualist. My days had been filled with the soft and melancholic moan of the wind in the pines, the slow shuffle of my grandparents and their benevolent contemplation of me. I used to like to stroke their flesh, exploring Lisandro's thin ropy arms, feeling the calouses on his worn hands. He used to laugh and say to Mami, Look how Conchita kneads my skin. *¡Coño!* Give her a pound of flesh and she returns it tingling.

At night Mami's body had curved perfectly around mine.

The nights had been sweet, with only the familiar noises, the scratching crickets, the haunting cries of the owls and the swish of the palms and the whisper of the pines. My eyes would feel intolerably heavy and I would drift to sleep stroking Mami's soft wrinkled skin. Mami had felt sorry for me because I was weaned onto a *tetera* of goat's milk when I was only a few weeks old, when Dolores had left me with her. In recompense, she allowed me to stroke her soft old *teticas*, which she called her *masitas*, hanging softly as they did like little strips of roast pork. Mami used to call my fingers her evening spiders, crawling as they did up and down her all night.

But above all, it was her hair I missed, pined for and mourned – the soft white hair that hung like a plaited rope to her waist, that was imbued with her scent, that was soft and silky and redolent of her and which I had adored and kneaded and stroked and sniffed and tasted since infancy. Whose loss I felt as keenly as if my hand had been amputated or the part of the inner ear that gives you balance had been drilled out.

Dolores's body was not like Mami's – was so different that it was unbelievable they had once been one. Unbelievable!

On a hot sullen day when the trees and the clothes on the improvised lines stood like everyone else, slack-armed, despondent, I made a friend in the boarding house, a woman called Pura. Some people called her Pura la Puta, or Pura Puta. She made a small amount of money as a prostitute. A *mulata*, Pura was very fat; she was a mountain.

Although Cuban men like their girls plump and juicy, Pura went way beyond this. Mostly she had curiosity value; her clientele was extremely specialised.

We got to know each other one evening, when I was putting off the hour of going to bed. I sat on the bottom step outside the back door, which opened into the court-yard leading to *el excusado*. There had been *sopa de maíz* again that night and although I had pretended I wasn't hungry, I sat listening to my stomach, which made the same hollow gurgling noise as the drain.

Pura came outside, her steps pounding slowly through the house. Sighing, she lowered herself onto the steps and spread her legs, trying to cool the core of her body in the still evening. Her fat ran down from one step to the next. Even though she sat with her feet apart, her legs were so massive that they came together just above the knees. It was hard to see how anything could push its way between them.

Conchita, how lucky you are to be young, she said. She sighed and fanned herself and looked at the night. I stared at her until she looked back at me and smiled, a sad smile, an effort.

Be a good little girl and get me a glass of water. *Pura se sofoca.*

I heard the pant in her throat, saw how she struggled to breathe, and I knew it was true; she was suffocating.

I found a glass inside. I had to stand with my legs wide to keep out of the drain, but only my fingertips reached the tap. As I stretched and strained my foot slipped and I fell in.

180

A pain shot through my foot. The glass flew from my hand and lay in shards. There was blood on my arm. My foot throbbed. I was frightened – I was always scared. I had broken the glass and I was dirty and I was terrified Dolores would find me.

I heard Pura coming instead.

¿Qué te pasó, chiquitica, hijita, probrecita? What happened to you, *mi alma*, my soul?

She plucked me out. Panting, her chest heaving, she bent over me, her soft hands a blur around me. She pulled off my dress, dressed me in her own black slip. Wrapped me in it several times and then washed my dress.

This will dry very quickly, she said. *Vamos.* We will wait in my room.

Pura sat me on her bed and fed me crackers spread with guava.

Why are you so fat? I asked my friend.

¡Ay, hijita! I love guava paste, and *chorizo*, and all the island food. When I am sad it cheers me up to eat. I often feel sad because I am so fat and the men don't like me, so I don't have money to buy myself nice things to eat.

But you will never have more money because you will always get fatter!

She laughed. *Sí*, that's true, *mijita*. God in the sky didn't pass you by when he handed out brains. Do you know any songs? Sing to me, I love music.

Purita was sad that I did not know any songs. It was she who taught me 'Las Mañanitas del Rey David' and 'El Barquito' and the other songs I sang to you so many years later.

I knew when she had had a good night because she gave me a *piruli* the next day.

When Dolores beat me, Pura would come hurrying into the room and stand between us. The two would hurl insults at each other.

¡Desgraciada!

¡Puta!

¡Mala madre!

¡Demonio!

Pura was so big that she barely fit in our room. Dolores could not fight her but she hated her fiercely. Sometimes I would be caught unawares when Dolores's hand shot out and slapped my face as I walked beside her or stood dreaming.

That's for your friend Pura.

Eres mía, she would say. You are mine. No one and nothing is going to take you from me.

I wondered about what Pura had said, that I was lucky to be young. She was wrong. With every ounce of my being, I longed to run back to Mami and *el campo*. But how could I find the train, get on the right one, let it take me back into Mami's arms? It was impossible.

Dolores would not give me anything I asked for, not the blanket on the chair, not a sip of water. Do you think I am your black servant? Am I the ass of that *negra* that you love so much?

I became sickly. More and more I was sick with fevers and colds and vomiting and diarrhoea and I couldn't eat and I grew thinner and thinner. Dolores left off beating me and began to go to great lengths to encourage me to eat.

She bought oranges, or *sapotes*, or a few mangos or

papaya, which she would cut into slivers and sprinkle with sugar and feed me with a spoon like a baby. She gave me the soft inside of bread loaves, keeping the crust for herself. And more and more she told me that I was the most valuable thing she had.

Eres mi todo. Mi vida. You are my everything. My life.

But it was Pura I sought out, as soon as I was better, as soon as I could run from that room of waking nightmares. It was Pura I spent time with, doling out small cups of revenge to Dolores which she had no choice but to drink.

A Cautious Daydream

The *casona* was built by Fernando de Miraflores, a coffee merchant, in the last part of the eighteenth century. The original wooden colonnades remained on the second floor, but the once stately lower columns of brick and mortar had been prised away one by one as the house slept through a time of war and pestilence, so that when it awoke it found its second storey half-collapsed, the wide balcony sagging like a petulant lip.

Once the house was broken, was homely and unthreatening, it attracted people. They ebbed and flowed on a tide of beer, playing a hand of cards, gathering, conversing, dispersing by some indiscernible natural law.

With the people came other vermin, mice and fleas and rats and especially cockroaches. The house was especially kind to cockroaches. They sauntered brazenly and eavesdropped like the whores who never hurried or worried. But on certain nights they clipped on wings or discovered them under their dirty black capes and then they made Consuelo's nights a misery.

The gallery's bare and broken supports formed a jagged Z at the collapsed corner. On this wide tilting stage Consuelo skated on those days she was well, throwing herself from one corner to the other. The burr of her skates, the sudden arrivals at a precipice, and the rolling precariousness of it all echoed other things in her heart.

Consuelo lay awake under the window. She listened to Dolores's breathing, the long rasping inhalations, the rambling exhalations. On this night Dolores had wound the rope around her right calf to Consuelo's left ankle. The belt was cinched loosely around their legs further up, at thigh level.

When the breathing turned to snores, Consuelo moved. With spidery fingers she reached down her leg, found the belt buckle, pulled the loose flap, eased past four notches. Dolores's breathing quietened; Consuelo froze, waited for the snores to strengthen again. Then she sat up a bit, and with great delicacy slipped her ankle out of its winding cuffs.

She lay back for a long time, waiting. She was waiting to grow up, she was waiting for the moon, she was waiting for Pura's heavy tread in the hallway. Waiting for Dolores to die. She was waiting for her life to begin. She knew by then that Dolores did not tie her up at night for her protection. She understood it was one more weapon in Dolores's arsenal.

Some time during the night, Consuelo stretched out her arm again. She pulled the greasy hem of curtain. She parted it. She pushed the grey shutter on the outside of the window. She anticipated its creak, deftly oiled that dangerous moment.

A wash of soft light entered the room, distant music, closer voices, discordant sounds, footfalls. Night lights chased across the walls. An image of Pura rose up.

Pura sticking her fingers into a can of sweetened condensed milk and licking her great grey paw. Holding a dinner plate up to her dinner-plate face, washing it. Laughing as Consuelo tells her a sad story. Licking the tears streaming towards the corners of her mouth when Consuelo takes her a joke. Grabbing the place between her legs when she's excited. A great mound of a child, large enough to hang onto, to believe in, to love.

As an anchor, she was unrivalled. As a wall, not even Dolores could look over her. As a house, she was warm and solid. Her arms were boughs from which Consuelo rock-a-byed. The other boarders thought her simple. She was the butt of their jokes. Consuelo knew better. Pura was her cave with more than one entrance, more than one escape route. She was Consuelo's home.

Consoled by the images, Consuelo slept.

Consuelo was in a cautious daydream on *el excusado* when Pura pushed open the door. The sight of Consuelo hurled the fat woman into an indecency of laughter.

What had tickled her began with the child's face, so serene, almost happy. She was crouching on the edge of the plank, held up by two wooden crates, over the hole. Her knees were bent up next to her ears. She had found a way of using the toilet that solved the problems of contamination. Her feet were neatly spaced. Between them were her panties, held by each fat toe and its neighbour, two sturdy wooden pegs on a clothesline.

Pura hooted, *Alma de Dios*, what a child! and Consuelo smiled shyly. Pura laughed sonorously, drinking in the lovely, quirky spirit of the child like a long rum in a cool glass.

Her cackles reached Dolores, whose head darted to a window; she saw Pura retreating, and the look on the *mulata's* face, of benevolent humour, enfuriated her suspicions.

Seconds later she surprised Consuelo, her folded belt in her hand, and the child's terror gratified her, fed something in her that was old and twisted. The buckle left streaks on Consuelo's thighs.

She stepped over corrugated iron scraps, mounds of rotting vegetables, cardboard, and bits of clothing too sodden and deteriorated to be recognised. She picked her way through gutters running merrily and others sluggish with slime.

A team of oxen passed by, pulling a cart piled ludicrously high with cane stalks. Consuelo stopped to watch. The driver nodded under his straggly sombrero, but it was from fatigue – he was not Lisandro, nor any of her uncles or cousins.

An emaciated dog with a drooping tail stopped to sniff Consuelo. She stood still to reassure him. A minute later she was mumbling a little song about cut lemons and sweet water and sinking boats to a mangy cat, until a sudden booming sound above the normal noise of the house startled it and it darted into a gap in a wall. Consuelo returned to her tentative hopping. She scampered over an abandoned oil drum, once used as a piece of furniture, stepped clumsily onto a pile of rotting sugar sacks that squelched under her feet. Idled this way around the house's corner and into the courtyard. Singing her tuneless song as she haunched down to poke at the mucousy stuff in the open drain, placing a leaf like an open boat to see if it could float along. And then looking up, listening for danger, for Dolores's footsteps, her attention was caught by a few bricks and rocks recently removed from the heap in the corner – she knew this place, her world, that well – and there, right there, the perfect curve of an alabaster cheek, but it should have been light brown.

Consuelo stepped nearer, removing a brick here, a rock there. A little hand appeared as if in appeal, as if beseeching, while the other bravely crossed its tiny chest, tucked up in a Napoleonic gesture.

Consuelo ran with the news, but who to tell – not Dolores. Tell Dolores nothing. Tell Pura, or if she isn't there (Consuelo knew she wasn't, saw her going out with a shopping *jaba* and a happy purple turban) tell Josefina tell Madrina tell Casucha . . .

In the house the women were unwrapping ham just bought from the *bodega* and Josefina led the way. *Cálmate muchacha*, calm yourself girl.

God knows why the women felt they had to obscure the writing on the greasy sheets – the price of two pounds of ham scrawled by a butcher – but it was all part of the frenzied effort to get rid of evidence. And the fat loud women and the scrawny beaten loud women of the house were quiet now as they emerged with sheets of stained paper to hastily cover the baby, to release it from the rocks and deliver it to the dirt.

———

Some people have their own angels and they don't share them with anybody and their lives are sweet. Consuelo's angels were always busy elsewhere, so older souls who had been angels once but were now walking the hot pavement had to look out for her. But Pura the whore and the gentleman from Paris were not enough to pull her out of bed once the light around the door put ideas about oblivion into her head.

We watched, helplessly, when Consuelo shut her ears to the happy squeals of other little girls playing sortijita *on the sidewalk in the fragrant twilight and instead let herself go, go so far, so deep and far that by morning her lips bled and her skin was hotter than the rising sun.*

Slowly she was willing herself backwards in time, back to María's arms and if need be back to a time before pain and even back to a complete and palpitating darkness – willing herself back towards us. And when she did that, even the angels couldn't touch her, let alone Dolores.

But it was not her time. Morning came again, with the chirp of sinsontes and the bugle call of the city buses and the cries of the peanut vendor and the mop vendor and the tobacconist and the grumble of the maids off to work and the chatter of the children preparing for school. Then Pura made sure Consuelo left smiling, before returning to her own bed.

But human angels have a hard row to hoe, and Pura was in poor shape. Sometimes she was roused from a deep afternoon sleep by what she thought was the sound of the child's weeping. She emerged reluctantly from dreams of Elysian fields in Camagüey, sat up listening, and finally, goaded by conviction, she pounded through the house, calling out, What is it? What happened por Dios? ¡Cariño! Seeing in her mind's eye Dolores gone too far, Dolores's belt buckle bloody, and something in the child broken beyond repair.

But Consuelo had only been swinging her legs over the lip of the tilting verandah, a few pages of a magazine she'd found in a dry gutter flapping next to her, feeding her hunger for the written word. She looked up in surprise. Scrambled up. Put her too thin, too white arms around dark flesh. Leant her face in. It's all right, she sang, it's all right, she soothed, in the tone others use for babies. Pura stood, swaying, her mouth sleep-dry and eyes unfocussed, taking comfort. Whose death had she been dreaming then? Pura, mujer, go light a candle, leave a coconut before Santa Barbara, poke a knife through the three soft head holes and twist and let the sweet milk run down your face. Go settle your debts, Señora, pay out what retribution you can, get what's owing to you. One cannot dream one's death too many times and take no notice. We should know.

~

Pura's face was smooth and coffee-coloured, coffee like a *cortadito*, slashed with milk. She wore her hair pulled back from her face, sometimes in a turban, like a *negra*, like Aunt Jemima on the Quaker Oats boxes. Other times she wore it oiled back sleekly with a thick hairband. The smooth skin of her face and arms turned into waves of fat around her waist, and became bubbles of fat around her massive *nalgas* and the *jamones* of her thighs.

I knew these details because I became her dresser and attendant. Pura had a terrible time reaching around to clip her brassière and bending down to put on shoes. Her face would become mottled with purple clots, and her *tetas* would heave up and down from the exertion. I would come in the mornings and help her dress, becoming intimate with the tents that were her wardrobe. I would stroke her arm and guide her into her clothes, saying the things Mami had once said to me: *Pon una patica, la otra, qué bonita. Vamos, la camisita. Así, mi amor.*

Pura was careful of her appearance because she had a love in her life. He was a little man called El Clavito – the little nail – a chihuahua of a man, as lean and small as his lover was mountainous. He was faithful to his Pura, visiting her several times a week, and because they were lovers she did not ask for much money from him, and got less than she asked for. What she wanted from him was a ring for her finger, she told me, but this he would not do.

Es un cabrón, como todo los hombres – a bastard, like all men – she complained as she wept when he stayed away for too many days. But always he would return, seeming thinner than ever, his little head like the tip of a nail, to lose himself in Pura's warm and generous love.

Other times I asked her why she loved him so.

Mija. You will understand when you are older. I cannot talk even to you of these things.

Vamos, Pura, somos amiguitas, ¿no es verdad? Dime, por favor. Why do you love him so much?

She would tell me everything, reluctantly.

I've known many others, but none as sweet as El Clavito

when we do all that. Those that make fun of him, they don't know what they're talking about. He is *un hombrecito*.

Indeed, the people of the house who always hung about on the path and *el portal* never tired of teasing El Clavito.

Don't get lost tonight, they said.

Clavito! *¡Compadre!* We will need a hammer to pull you out of *tu negra* one of these days.

El Clavito was always drunk when he came to Pura, always brought rum with him, and the two would spend the night drinking and smooching until they drifted into unconsciousness. On those nights, Pura didn't need me to help her undress but I would pad softly to her room and push the door in quietly, to make sure she was all right and determine whether she was alone or not, before I went to wait for Dolores and her ropes.

As her anxieties increased, Dolores began to follow me in the daytime, walking a block or so behind me when I thought she was cleaning the houses of the *yanquis* of El Vedado, or at home resting from her labours.

This is how she found out about the men and boys and dogs who trailed me, or waited ahead to surprise me with visions of their artillery.

I walked the streets of La Habana with my head down, ignoring these sights, calm in the knowledge that whatever they could show me was always less than what I had seen elsewhere, if not in human form then certainly between the donkey Chorizo's flanks.

But Dolores was not so unperturbed when she noticed the effect I had on males. The first to feel her wrath was Pepito Sánchez, whom people called El Niño, although he was a fat, fully grown but dim-witted man. He had come running up a lane to confront me, seeing me from Calle K as I walked along Calle J. Still, he was not so dim as to not put his thing away when he saw Dolores coming up behind me.

What are you doing, *come-mierda?* she demanded.

Nothing, Señora, I was looking for my dog.

But even as he spoke, Dolores's handbag was arcing out, a flash of silver and black which cracked him solidly in the face.

As his hands went up to his face, her knee sank into his loins.

Here's a bone for your little dog.

The attention I got never ceased, but came in waves, receding when she shadowed me, so that if I went several blocks without incident, I would begin to glance behind searching for her.

At home, my life had a sort of routine, the routine of hot boring days and long childish reflections on the shapes of snails' shells I found on the floor. Until the cold December evening that I walked into Pura's room for the last time.

I don't know why I went. Forever after I have wished I hadn't. Some misgiving which I was too young to understand compelled me to make an extra round of her room that night.

I had known Pura was with El Clavito, both of them drunk because I had checked earlier and the smell of the room had hit me like a wave at Varadero beach. But when I returned, what I beheld was Pura's face turned towards me, only feet from where I stood in the doorway.

I saw a dead puff-fish on the edge of the sea. Grey lips

that should have been purple, and eyes that stared too steadily. I saw El Clavito, sound asleep and snoring loudly, inexplicably comfortable beneath her dead weight.

I saw it all in less than a second, in the time it took to open the door and close it again. I went to my room, walking through thick air, pushing through dream air, taking off my clothes and getting under the stained blanket Dolores and I shared.

¿Qué te pasa? she said, sniffing, suspicious, gauging my life by my scent, the colour of my face and the size of my eyes.

Nada, nada, Mamá.

That night I dreamt of dolls. I saw a doll on a shelf in El Encanto, a doll that begged me to take her down, to play with her and give her life. But I said, Not today. *Espera* until I grow up.

I tried to close the cupboard but her fat dimpled doll's knees bounced the door back. Her pumpkin face pleaded with me to get her out, to bring her down from the shelf and play with her.

I grew ornery. I have never had a doll, I yelled, pushing the glass door.

But then the door shatters, and the Pura-doll falls through the air in a shower of glass. When she hits the ground her porcelain face scatters in all directions, and all around there is blood, buckets of blood. And I don't know if the blood is from the cuts I received from the exploding glass, or from the doll, which was perhaps human, and I ponder this as morning comes, as the songs of *sinsontes* pierce my dreams. I dream that I am trying to make sense of the dream, afraid to sink back into sleep but equally reluctant to wake up, because I know there is something very bad that happened in the night and I don't want to know what it is, but it has to do with my friend Pura, my only friend, and with me . . .

And indeed Pura had not been able to wait for me to grow up.

As the house began to stir, the people were drawn to her room by methodical thuds and hoarse muffled calls. It was El Clavito, banging his feet against the wall with what small freedom of movement he had left, his face almost covered by his lover's breast.

I did not go. I did not have the strength to confront what I already knew.

They said they found El Clavito nailed beneath his lover. Pura's corpse, rigid and heavier than ever, had clamped about him. Awakening from his drunken sleep, he had found he could barely draw air, that he could not move out at all from under his lover. They said he was lucky to have survived the night, that he was forever cured of his fetish for large negresses.

Consuelo was often sick after Pura's death. She spent her days reading, and was in no position to choose the literature that came her way.

Much of it was inane, often nasty, and the constant peering into those other lives upset her. She woke up heavy with strange feelings, other people's thoughts piled on top of her own frustrations. She lowered herself into this vortex willingly, but was always surprised by the grip on her ankles when she shut the book.

It seemed she only had to be walking past an open door, and spy an unmade bed, a shank of sunlight over the rumpled sheets, for something to thrill inside of her. A surrender! How lovely it must be, she half thought, to be that defeated person, convalescing in the noonlight.

And that evening she would fall asleep heavily, befogged by the books in which she had spent the day. She would dream those lives, and wake late, cold and listless. She could not eat, those mornings. She would pretend to herself that she was not waiting for the fever. But when it came she welcomed it, held the door wide open, took it in, showed it to the bed and lay there with it.

The whores' voices receded, and those of the teachers at school, and of her uncles, and even her grandparents. Even the boarding house dozed in the daytime. Consuelo was inside a more private room, an inner sanctum, and scarcely noticed Dolores's hands on her brow, her clouded eyes, her worried looks. Dolores stepped quietly out, to go clean a house in Miramar in exchange for the black bean *potaje* and the pork bones that might have been able to strengthen Consuelo if only she would consent to them. But of course she didn't.

That year that I was ten the Chief of the Armed Forces of the Republic, Colonel Fulgencio Batista, was invited to attend Armistice Day ceremonies in Washington. The newspapers reported that Batista saw snow there for the first time, and feasted with Roosevelt. When he returned to La Habana there was a public holiday. Shops and banks closed to honour Batista and I did not go to school. I set out with Dolores to the waterfront, along with a hundred thousand others for whom Batista had grown in stature after he had reviewed the West Point cadets at Arlington.

I had not wanted to go. I awoke with a headache that morning, and aches as if I had just been beaten, and I cried that I did not feel well but Dolores wrenched me from the bed, her rope in her hand, declaring I was better off with the multitudes in the street then hanging around a house full of *putas*.

The boulevards were jammed. Families streamed out of every building and hurried towards the seawall. As Colonel Batista, on the gunboat *Cuba*, entered the harbour and the guns of the Cabaña Fortress fired a salute, the crowd went mad. They surged towards him in a reckless stampede. I was torn from Dolores's grasp and pushed forward so that I could not even turn my head to look for her. In the heat of noon the press of bodies around me was the only thing that kept me upright. My feet scarcely touched the ground as I was rammed onwards, as that solid ranting mass hurried towards Batista, who had disembarked at Caballería Wharf. I feared that at any moment I would faint and be trampled to death.

The bad taste in my mouth turned into a mephitis. I felt weak and dizzy. I tried to breathe, and in desperation I hung on to a corner of marble. Looking up, I realised I was at the foot of one of the ornate lamp posts on the edge of El Parque Central.

I tried to climb on it but did not have the strength. I stumbled and clawed at its foot before I felt hands clasp my waist and raise me up through the air. I searched the thronged faces. I recognised, under a wide sombrero, the smile of El Caballero de París. But even he was being pushed towards the Presidential Palace, and he waved his hand in the air at me in a jaunty salute without realising my predicament.

From my perch on the lamp post I could see the crowds surging ahead, a wave rushing to the sand. I clung to the post, a bit of human debris left behind. I saw that the wretchedly poor of the city had not been invited to the fiesta.

Two old women slept on a wooden bench, there, at the edge of El Parque Central. Their bodies were skeletal but their feet were swollen and straight as an elephant's. They dangled over the edge of the bench at improbable angles.

I thought of my grandmother. The need to be with her had never been greater.

To my left a thin woman in a dress of rags sat on the step of El Centro Gallego, a fine, baroque old building several storeys high. The woman's thin arms dangled around a sleeping toddler. At her feet, on the hard cold speckled tiles, lay another child, dreaming in a posture of utter abandon. His shirt was hitched up around his waist and his genitals were exposed, a cluster of grapes on the creamy platter of his skin. Another brother, slightly older, was sitting stoop-shouldered on a bench a few feet from me.

A well-dressed family hurried by, trying to catch up with the crowds. The woman was pulling a little girl by the hand. The child had a short scalloped dress, shiny black shoes, and an oversized floppy bow on the top of her head. In her free hand she carried, like so many others that day, a small posy to throw at Batista's feet on her mother's command.

The boy on the bench watched until the little girl was level with him. Then he leapt up and snatched the posy from her hands. Before anyone could stop him, he had stuffed the violets into his mouth.

The girl started to cry and her mother dragged her away, calling out to the woman on the steps. Have you no shame? But the woman on the steps seemed to barely have the strength to raise her eyes to look at her.

The scene made me tremble. I tasted the bitter violets. I heard in the distance the excited chants of the crowd adoring their leader. The faraway roar was indistinguishable from the wind in the trees and the pounding of blood in my ears. The street shimmered, the strength in my arms ebbed, and I knew I would fall.

They told me later that El Caballero de París, returning from the Presidential Palace where he had been selling *maníes* to the throngs, found me near El Parque Central. He lifted me in his arms and staggered with me to Dolores.

They told me that I was sick for two months. That a brown fuzz grew on my throat and tongue that people recognised as typhoid.

Dolores did not call a doctor. Her relatives feared the authorities would quarantine the house and then no one would work. Anyway, there was no money for a doctor. Josefina and Dolores nursed me. I was too sick to know anything.

The weight I felt on my chest night and day was death pressing on me. I remember the heaviness as it insinuated itself. I could hear Pura and Dolores fighting, and once Pura sat on my mother and squashed her. Sometimes she leaned over too far, leaning on my chest, on my face, so that I couldn't draw air and couldn't move away. I begged Pura to move but she didn't understand. She kept telling me that I was the lucky one.

Once they put me on a train and its wheels sang, I'm taking you to Mami, I'm taking you to Mami. But the canefields were ablaze and the fire spread onto the train tracks and I was hot, I was too hot, I was being consumed, and no one would save me. At long last, a great bird swooped down and plucked me from the roof. The bird carried me over the burning fields, over the hills to the mountains beyond. The bird was my mother. But when she put me into her nest she turned out to be the kind with a bald head and black wings, her beak bloody from grazing on my heart.

Dolores made many *promesas* to Jesus and to La Caridad del Cobre, *patrona de Cuba*, and to the other saints for my salvation. She promised that she and I would wear white for two years – nothing but white clothes – if I were saved. She procured chickens, a goat, and had them slaughtered for my sake. No matter what, my fevers did not abate. When I began to breathe shallowly and stopped coughing, Dolores did not know what to do. She was afraid she would lose the only thing she had in the world. In desperation, she went to a rich American woman whom she had once known, a woman called Henrietta Douglas, and begged her to help me.

Upstairs in a Fine House

At the hospital Dolores stood to attention at Consuelo's side, her handbag folded into the thick crease of her arm. The child's fever was rising; she complained incessantly of thirst. Her overly bright eyes stared at a distance – at a swampy bubbling vastness that was not there. A dead mouse odour, the cadaverous taint of typhoid, already hung in the air around her, exhaled with each shallow breath. Dolores leaned over her, put her face up to her ear. Cough, she commanded. *Por Dios, hija.* Cough.

Dolores stood unmoving next to the bed but her mind devoured itself. She muttered darkly. She insulted the young nurses and *médicos* who entered the room. Who are you? she demanded. A student, she snarled. Don't touch her. *¡Lárgate!* Get me the senior doctor here! Cretins! Can't you see the situation is grave?

A doctor stalked into the room just as Consuelo, propped up by Dolores, coughed up a stream of dark red pulp and clotted mucus. Garlands of highly coloured phlegm hung from her chin, festooning the bedclothes.

Doctor Cordero moved closer, studied the child's pulse, inspected the skin under her eyelids, groped her abdomen.

Consuelo barked like a whipped puppy. Doctor Cordero straightened slowly, gazing generously on his patient and the worried woman standing next to her. He imparted the news that the situation was serious – extremely serious.

Señora, there is little hope. I have to tell you that she is dying.

Dolores looked at him and if the chips coming from her eyes had been less ethereal he would have been in danger. Where did you get your degree? she demanded. And before he could answer she put her hands on the bed and leaned closer to the doctor's face.

Don't be ridiculous, *hombre!* Pull yourself together! You have before you a case of typhoid, complicated by pneumonia. Don't be a coward!

The doctor, an important, corrupt man who had not been scolded since he was eight, went coldly white.

Bueno, Señora. It seems you have made your diagnosis. Tell me, where did you get *your* degree?

En el campo, at the bedside of my dying brother. I have seen this before. In the *bohíos* of the interior, typhoid roams, as the saying goes, like Pedrito strolling through his house.

And then, astutely changing tack, Dolores softened her voice. Doctor, this is my only child. All I have in the world. She has typhoid. It masquerades as other things – colitis, nephritis, meningitis, endocarditis. Even influenza and malaria. But it is typhoid. And it is curable. She need not die.

The doctor looked at the *guajira* before him. He was astonished. He looked at his patient with a quiver of interest, but with confusion. He did not know how to treat typhoid fever.

Dolores correctly interpreted his feelings as they rippled over the contours of his well-fed face. She needs glycerine, she said softly, to bathe the sores in her mouth. And you will need sulphate quinine, carbolic acid, calomel and sodium tablets. Constant liquids, she added. And cold compresses.

The doctor listened. Her words prodded distant memories. He wanted to speak to his father, also a doctor. He wanted to open an old textbook that sat on a corner of his desk. He was embarrassed, and unused to the emotion. He turned and left the room.

Dolores dipped her handkerchief in a basin of water that stood next to the bed and bathed Consuelo's face. The child called out to María, and Dolores whispered, *Aquí estoy*. Her touch was soothing, was recuperative.

Mami was brought to me from *el campo* by my aunts Encarnación and Esperanza. She looked smaller and more ground down than ever, like a small bone washed up on the sand that is bleached and dry and brittle but still clings to the memory of what it once was. But I could not really be ashamed of her, ever, and I could always deliver myself into her arms – the only homecoming I ever knew.

She brought with her Paco, who had pined for me so much that Mami had taken pity on him and tamed him in her arms. They had consoled each other for my loss and now Mami brought him back to me, cradled in her arms, to help me recover.

But Paco had aged quicker than I had, and no longer

looked at me with ardour in his small revolving eyes, and I had little left of the innocence that had allowed me to give my heart to a chicken. And besides, the nurses said he could not stay, and hissed, *Malditos guajiros* in audible whispers as their eyebrows flew to the ceiling, and said aloud in the hallway, *¡Qué ignorancia, muchacha! ¡Imagínate!* as their hands fluttered near their cheeks in outrage. Even Dolores felt ashamed that her family had brought a fowl to the white starched walls of this expensive hospital.

When *las tías* and Mami left and Paco stood trembling in the corner under the window, Dolores gripped him tightly by his poor long wattle, gripped him in a way that my ears knew well. She left with him under her arm, and I prayed to La Virgen del Cobre.

But as I fell asleep I had the sensation of a flash of cold silver at my throat. Dolores visited that afternoon, bringing with her a fragrant *sopa de pollo*. I turned away and wished that I had died. Then I was very sick for two more weeks and once again they thought nothing would save me.

During my second, slower, recovery I became fond of the fan over my bed, whose revolving silver blur drew me into a sort of peaceful trance. The only thing that worried me was my hair, which was falling out in swatches.

I became aware of Miss Douglas in stages as I emerged from my death-sleeps. She was *una americana*, light-skinned and papery, but she dressed in long-sleeved blouses and long dark skirts, as if to show contempt for the Cuban heat. She disapproved of everything and especially, vehemently, disapproved of Cubans, and so she was respected everywhere she went. *Sí*, Señora, and *Sí*, Señorita answered her every utterance.

She came to see me, sat down in a chair several feet from me. Good morning, Consuelo. How are you feeling today? Then, before I could think of anything to say to this *yanqui* woman who spoke Spanish so well, she said, That's good. My name is Miss Douglas. I am going to take an interest in you from now on.

She pulled a package from a leather case.

Open it.

Inside were books, the first I ever owned. The words were in English and there were no pictures. One was *Jane Eyre*, and the other was an English translation of *Les Misérables*.

You may just look at these for the next few days. As soon as you can sit up I will begin to teach you to read. Goodbye.

She never smiled and never touched me. She asked questions but did not wait for an answer. Whatever I had to say was inconsequential. It was as if we were players in a drama and only she had the script. She said her lines and that was all.

Dolores also came to visit and brought me white clothes. You have been saved by a miracle, she said. It was *la mano de Dios* – the hand of God – at work. You and I will wear white from now on.

Then, as if she had to convince herself, she muttered, It is a fine colour – the colour of brides and nuns and nurses and other pure things.

I found out the lessons were to continue. Dolores had an odd attitude to *la americana*. I had never felt she respected anyone, except Abuelo Lisandro, yet it was as if she were scared of this woman. But Dolores also wanted to take advantage of her. *Estamos cogiendo mango bajito*, she said –

we are gathering low-hanging mangos. And, She has reason to care for you. After all, *sangre americana* runs in your veins. But let it not be forgotten that you belong to me. I am your mother, who bore you.

People began to call me *la americanita*. I was learning English. Or perhaps it was because Henrietta stalked around me. But more, I think, it was because I was different. There was a cool shyness in me, even I knew that I was quiet, and I had an analytical quality – and a restraint – that made me an island in the sea of noisy, merry *cubanitas*.

Scabs formed around the sores on my body and I picked at these, slyly, under the covers, encouraging them to fester. I found in myself a desire to remain in the hospital, to cocoon myself in the white sheets, to remain in this place where I mattered little to anyone and did not have to speak, save a few meaningless noises to Miss Henri.

Dolores had always lived in the downstairs rooms of boarding houses. She had a terror of heights. She did not know it – she would not have admitted to it. Her fears of the sea, of night, of heights, were what eventually kept her from accompanying Consuelo the day a Pan Am plane took her from Cuba.

The library that belonged to Henrietta Douglas was on her *casona's* second floor. Consuelo pulled herself up to it slowly, leaning on the handrail, which was gummy. She did not realise that Dolores's fear had contaminated her.

Visiting the house shamed her. María, sweet María, so loving, so passive, was still a *guajira*, but this sort of shame had nothing to do with a childhood's worth of nights spent batting cockroaches off thatch. It was rather that María had tried to form Conseulo as a peasant is moulded to the land. One clips, one prunes, one tucks in any growth. Snip clip tuck prune, even when it callouses the hand doing the pruning. The branch will grow, but need less, need only damp swamp and crisp sky and wet rain. Won't need midnight light, won't believe anything is for the taking, won't stray.

How else does one marry daughters to men as brutish as any in their family? A man who shifts his weight to release wind as you hand him a plate of rice, without even the modesty of looking down at the floor? But what else can you do? Better that than they find out in the city that their dreams were bigger than the space between their legs. How else does one grow a *guajira*? ¡Mujer! Don't talk to me about it!

Consuelo could ask María any question, any question whatsoever. Mami, where does the train go when it leaves Olvidados? Why, why is it called Olvidados? Who was forgotten here, what is there to forget? Can we have *fideos* in the soup? Can I have a dress one day, Mami?

And the answer had always been the same, had lost all significance because of its predictability, yet its meaning shaded Consuelo's life. A loving reproach, a mild *gaznatada*. ¡Mujer! She was witless to ask, implied the tone. She was small, took up too much space. Snip, yank, tuck. Cicatrixes are preferable to starvation.

That's what stuttered Consuelo's hand on the door's lion knocker. That, and her neck. How can one keep one's neck clean enough in a *solar*? Her neck was dappled, and she knew it. A sleeve mended so often it recedes into an armpit, a white dress too roomy for a child that has just fought off vultures over cane fields – that could pass. But even a blush won't hide an unwashed neck.

And there were still more reasons to hesitate. Consuelo wondered what this rich white woman had to do with her, why she bothered. What was she, Consuelo, doing in such a cold and quiet house?

Henrietta had a way of teaching Consuelo, of being companionable, that seemed like punishment. She disciplined her mouth into a straight line: she offered nothing, neither praise nor reprimand, warmth of friendship nor the heat of animosity.

Consuelo could not have known how Henrietta was afflicted by certain memories that rose up from her shrouded bed.

Behind Henrietta's taciturnity was rage. She was furious that her lover had died. She was furious that life had not fulfilled the fantasies of an indulged childhood. And she was furious at herself for her weakness, for her failure to cope, for her own silent sinking into despondency.

She would have preferred not to be in Consuelo's life at all. She came from puritanical stock; she endured. But she could scarcely bear the sight of her lover's eyes staring at her from the child's face.

For a year Consuelo travelled weekly to La Habana Vieja to study with Miss Douglas. She learnt an excellent, old-world English. She learnt nothing else. Eventually she stopped seeing the woman, although she still visited her library to borrow and return books in English. By the time she saw Henrietta Douglas again, in the street several years later, Consuelo had grown into a beautiful young woman.

She was walking along San Rafael, thinking of which books she would take from Miss Douglas's house, wondering whether she had read everything by Dickens, thinking of an image of love on the streets of London, seeing those streets and not the hot white cobblestones where her feet were stepping.

She was in herself like this when a distance ahead there was a commotion, a rush of air, a scream, a rocketing of tension in the street. Consuelo stopped, stepped back – her muscles drew her back to where she had been a second before.

And then there was a sharp hot barking explosion and many more screams, and for a while – perhaps only a few seconds, perhaps several minutes – there was almost no sound or movement on the street except for a muffled scuffling up ahead.

But the moment passed and people began coming out from everywhere, emerged from the barbershop and the *cantina* and from recesses in walls and from behind iron gates. People were leaning over balconies and standing with arms crossed all along the street. On all their faces were expressions of angry perplexity.

The scream of a siren and plump smooth-faced police in braided uniforms filled the street. The crowd surged forward, calling out, Cowards! What happened? *¡Maricones! ¿Qué pasó? ¿Qué pasó?* Batista's henchmen had murdered on the street again, and Consuelo let herself be pushed along by the tide of emotion.

A mulatto youth lay on the cobblestones in a white shirt seeping red. His dead eyes were open and his white teeth grimaced. Near his hand lay a thin curved knife. It had done him no good in the end.

Consuelo's heart pounded in her ears, rivalling the screams of the people clotting around the dead boy. Policemen barked orders which everyone ignored.

And then Consuelo saw her benefactress, her Miss Douglas, clip-clopping towards them, her long bony head with its cool sharp thoughts held proudly erect.

There is something so strange about her, thought Consuelo. I think she despises everyone.

Henrietta Douglas walked past, as coldly removed as a cat, offering nothing to the living around her, nor to the dead. She did not so much as look down at the young man who gazed so desperately at the sun.

As Consuelo wrenched herself from the scene and plodded on towards the Douglas residence, she was repelled by a memory of that house's gloomy rustling decay. Still she walked on, sustained by the promise of books, in their thrall. And perhaps she dwelt on Miss Douglas's face, studied it in her mind, considered the serious expressionlessness on it, the look of someone withdrawn from life, totally alone.

But she never saw the ways in which Henrietta Douglas's face resembled her own.

The Springtime of Her Soul

He saw her daily for several months before he came to speak to her.

At first she was someone of whom he was barely aware, a perplexing glitch in his consciousness, stored to be processed through a dream one oppressive night – but he did not remember the dream on awakening. So she remained a girl he watched pass by, not sure what it was about her that caught his attention, aware only that she was different but not yet drawn to her.

Strange would have been too strong a word for someone so beautiful. But Cuba – and especially La Habana – abounded with Spanish beauties. Whole armies of men made it their business to sit on wrought-iron benches in the formal lushness of the city's great parks and watch them stream past. Businessman, stevedores and gangsters, yesterday's *guajiros* and *yanqui* sailors – all were, in La Habana, entitled to idle in dusty corners and talk of important things, interrupting themslves to gaze impudently, and often to remark, upon the virtues of the passing Cuban womanhood.

But this one was different. Although men paused and

211

lost their train of thought as Consuelo breezed past, seldom was a man so coarse and insensitive as to salute her with the traditional murmurs of *¡Guapita!* and *¡Qué linda!* – an exhalation at the end of an indrawn breath.

Consuelo imagined that all of La Habana was aware of the threat her mother posed to the city's men. She thought the fact that men grew quiet when she passed had to do with Dolores's fierce reputation. But this was not so. Those incidents of her childhood had been long forgotten, except perhaps by the moronic Pepito Sánchez. The beatings Pepito had received from Dolores's handbag were still one of his few true memories.

Sometimes Consuelo allowed herself to imagine that she was not beautiful, that she no longer stirred the passions of men as she had done as a child, but this was partly because she was too young, at seventeen, to understand her power. Moreover, she was too injured by her childhood and Dolores's grip to ever fully comprehend her true nature.

For Consuelo stopped men in their tracks because of her astounding beauty, and hushed them because of intangibles that had evolved over time, an unconscious process whereby certain traits were retained and others discarded. What was distilled – her bearing – was a defence, to keep at bay the embarrassment of watching Dolores brawl in the streets with a man.

It is impossible to say what she would have been like had she had a different history. Perhaps her straight back was simply part of her birthright, acentuating her lovely figure. Perhaps her eyes, no matter what, even if she hadn't spent the first years of her life gazing at a swampy vastness, would have always had that soft, serious, unfocussed gaze, as if she were always in a half-dream. But even at seventeen, what Consuelo signalled as she walked was that she was a good woman, a serious woman, someone fine, someone not to be trifled with. And there was about her also an air of sadness – one might almost say self-indulgent melancholy, because, after all, other girls emerged from La Habana's tenements with their insouciance and *joie de vivre* intact, if not their virginity.

Daniel Cancio, the third son of a wealthy family, was studying music at La Universidad de La Habana. But he spent his evenings and most of his days at the Crystal Salon café, at the corner of Prado and Virtudes, the meeting place of many aspirant artists. It was in this neighbourhood that he first noticed but did not take note of Consuelo, as she made her way home from her classes at La Habana Business Academy, on San Lazaro at the end of El Prado, a half-block from El Malecón.

He noticed her again, that winter of 1946 one breezy afternoon not long afterwards as she walked along El Malecón, her favourite route because she could look out to sea, look out endlessly, her mind empty to all but the sensations of sun and wind and saltspray. Her hair fought to escape the confines of a gauzy green scarf which matched her green-and-white striped blouse, her dangling green paste earings. He thought of a cat with green eyes and white fur, a swish classy feline being. She did not, of course, look at him as he watched her stroll past. He thought that she seemed somehow familiar.

A few days later he saw her a third time. She and an

older woman were coming out of the Fin de Siglo department store as he went in. The woman was annoyed, she had a sour expression on her face and was hissing something in the girl's ear. The girl had a stony look on her face now. The older woman, although the right age to be her mother, looked nothing like her. She was short and jowly with a deep forehead and small eyes. He was sure they had been arguing, and wondered what about.

He began to notice her daily, as he wandered east from El Vedado into her territory. He found himself waiting along San Rafael where he knew she would cross the street, where he knew that she would have to interrupt her waking dream to check the traffic and he might have a chance to meet her eyes as she prepared to step down from the curb.

From unconscious twinges she grew into obsession, becoming the excuse for him to not attend classes. Anticipating his family's response to her, he was disrespectful to his mother, a stout, strident woman intent on clinging to her place in La Habana's social strata. He argued with his father and stormed out of their fine home in El Vedado, heading unwittingly towards the decrepit building on an ugly street where, he had discovered by following her, Consuelo lived.

Desperate for an introduction and a chance to speak to her, he began asking about her. There was little to be learnt. She kept to herself. She kept to her books. She was often at the Asturias Club library – this he already knew. Her name was Consuelo and her mother was a dragon. An acquaintance, an aspiring musician named Esteban who had once lived in her building, agreed to introduce them.

It was not a success. Esteban hailed her as she walked past, using the over-familiar 'Conchita'. She looked at him as if she did not recognise him. In fact she didn't. She would never have any sort of memory for faces, mainly because she had long since got in the habit of not considering her surroundings, of living in her imagination.

Esteban looked at Daniel, who was fuming with exasperation, and raced after Consuelo. Consuelo, Consuelo, *soy yo*, Esteban, he said, planting himself in her path. It's me, Esteban. I have a friend who wants to meet you, over there. *Se llama* Daniel.

Consuelo paused and half turned, looking for the briefest second at the young man Esteban pointed to. Without smiling, her beauty masked by the severity of her expression, she murmured, Glad to meet you, and walked on.

¡Qué chiquita más rara! marvelled Esteban.

But in that moment Consuelo had become aware of Daniel for the first time. She now began to notice him everywhere, until there seemed to be a companionship, a strange unspoken intimacy brought about by the fact that each spent so much solitary time wondering about the other.

Their first conversation was about a book. It had occurred to him much earlier that the way to this girl's heart was through literature, but he spent months trying to decide on the right book. In the end it was Hugo's *Les Misérables*.

He approached her as she walked past the Cuban Telephone Company building, heading for El Parque de la Fraternidad. She liked to eat her lunch under its massive

Fraternity Tree, which always reminded her of the tree back home, in the centre of Olvidados.

Consuelo, excuse me, it's me, Daniel.

Yes, I know. Consuelo smiled, but kept walking.

I have something for you. A present. He extended the book towards her. She took it without hesitation, turned it over, read the title and looked briefly into his eyes. Thank you, she said, honouring him with a radiantly perfect smile, and started to walk on.

Disconcerted, the poor suitor thought to ask if she had read it before. Of course, many times, came the gay answer.

After that there was no questioning their friendship. He was Consuelo's first love and she was Daniel's most intense passion. Now she came to him throughout the city, sheared through traffic to reach him, walked by his side with a half-smile on her still dreaming face.

After that she would associate their rendezvous places, the city's stern majestic monuments set on beautiful broad boulevards – the Maine, the statue of Maceo, the memorial to Martí – with wet panties.

At first she was perplexed by the state of her underwear. She thought she was becoming incontinent. She thought she was so moved that she had lost control over herself, but closer examination revealed creamy puddles at the centre of the wetness. She realised that she had heard too much about sex, too little about love. She began to learn. She gave herself up to her studies.

Daniel was a quiet young man, a short man, with a grave smile. He had brown eyes in a face that was more round than oval. He would have been considered devastating had he been taller. He was the same height as Consuelo, five-foot six, an unusual height even for a man of that generation.

He had straight rich black hair. He parted it down the centre as was the style of the day, but a shock of it always fell determinedly onto his forehead, shading his slow, sardonic but gentle smile. He played the guitar, but not as the *guajiros* and *chulos* played it. He was a classical Spanish guitarist; his hands could do things others couldn't.

Music now filled her days, her nights, her dreams. The music of Lecuona. The love ballads of Tito Rey. The music he played to her, his soft eyes studying her happy face. The music they heard in parks, in cafés, the happy frothy rhythms of her gay country.

She graduated from La Habana Business Academy and got a job with the *Havana Post*, the best English-language newspaper in Cuba. She wore shorter, tighter dresses, brighter colours. She wore smart clothes, coquettish hats, stylish suits in expensive fabrics that she bought with the money she was earning and sewed for herself on an old Singer. She wore dark glasses, cool shades, and she played with Daniel in the cool froth of Varadero's beaches.

She loved the sea during this time of her life. She realised that she was slim, long-limbed and velvety; she was happy in bathing suits. She felt more at ease running to catch a beach ball than dancing at a nightclub. But she did both, did everything she could, accepted all invitations.

She drove with Daniel to El Pico Turquino to fly a kite in the flapping wind. She stood at the top of the world, embraced an ancient gnarled tree that reminded her of Olvidados, of María. The wind whistled through the palms and stirred something inside of her that was like dry leaves, stirred up a delicious exciting feeling of a lifetime's promise. (It was a feeling she would have often in that season, and then hardly at all for the rest of her life, except once in a while, unexpectedly, when a cool breeze might blow somewhere, and she would remember . . .) Daniel stared into her eyes for a long time, reached up and drew aside the wisp of hair on her face. She embraced him, pressed her long body tightly against his, and gave herself up to sensation. ¡Ay, Dios! Those hands!

A photograph from this time in her life, taken at the beach, has a three-storeyed clubhouse behind her, collumned and balustraded and awninged in the style of the day. She is wearing a two-piece bathing suit, the top held by a V that nips at the middle of the tight piece of cloth around her breasts. And she is leaning her hands on a low wall, bending forward at the waist, beaming straight into the camera. She seems unaware of the seductiveness of her pose. She is tanned and relaxed. She is looking into the future with a happy, confident carefree look, a sweet and charming and unassuming, wholly optimistic look.

Such was their passion that there began to develop around them a field of electrical charge; Dolores felt it and went out and bought herself rubber shoes. They were flat nurses' shoes which, because of Dolores's inability to correctly state any numerical parameters associated with her person, were two sizes too small. After the first day she cut them open at the top like a sardine can, but nothing could relieve her of the nagging, poisonous thought that she was losing her grip on Consuelo.

Everyone noticed that she was changing. Where before she had gone through life quietly, sombrely, a serious young lady whom people thought beautiful but strange, they were now drawn to her, eager to become involved in her life. Neighbours who had never spoken to her now called out chummily, called her Conchita. *Oye, Conchita, eres candela.* I saw you with your *novio* at the theatre.

Conchita, how are you, *mi amor?* And how is your mother?

She whirled in new circles, drawing others to her centre. She even acquired, for the first time since Pura, a best friend. Carmen, a girl she had known at school, now became someone with whom to share confidences.

Consuelo put her books aside and dove into life as though it were Varadero beach on a calm and balmy day. She came out bedazzled and bedazzling, fresh and splashy and playful.

With Daniel she celebrated everything. Their nights were soft and satin-smooth, their skin stroked by the perfumed breezes of swishing royal palms. Their nights were luminiscent and tumescent with promise and with the heavy sweet smell of gardenias.

Consuelo felt herself to be in the springtime of her soul, identified this time with a vision of throngs of birds singing in the palms and date trees, then rushing up suddenly to fly in ebullient clouds of gold-dusted colours. It was 1946, a world war had ended and although Cuba had not been directly involved La Habana was a cosmopolitan city, jostled by the ripples of whatever happened in Europe, and in the United States. And despite the atrocities coming to light, there was a soaring hope – for peace, for prosperity, for life itself.

She had imagined a man's touch would be heavy and hot. Daniel's hands were cool, dry, his touch was infinitely delicate. His hands fascinated her. They were slim, white, with not too much hair, yet manly. Not tapered, effeminate hands but angular, well-shaped hands. They were hands that left her body feeling like a finely tuned guitar.

She had thought that a lover would be noisy, intrusive, a gushing river of maleness that would overpower her. Instead she was swept away by his intelligence, his knowing quietness, his humour.

And by his music. She had had no musical education. Her only contact with music had been haphazard, although generous – the parties of the tenements where almost anyone who had ever sang in the shower was a musician, everyone played an instrument, and someone's aunt always hollered to shut up and someone else threatened to call the police if the racket didn't cease. And there had been carnivals, a dizziness of colour and music. She had always waited eagerly for the last conga, which, as advertised, was TODA, COMPLETA Y ENTERAMENTE NEGRA – completely black – so that only the drums gleamed in the soft night.

She was ashamed of knowing so little about music, and nothing about notes and chords and written music. *Soy analfabeta*, she confessed softly. But he smiled and threw the lock of hair off his forehead with a small toss of his head, lit a cigarette and snaked his other arm around her waist. He smiled with his face held at an angle, listening intently to his friends at the Café Paradiso.

220

She had moments of panic – when Daniel insisted she meet his parents, for instance. But their house was less grand, although more stylish, than Miss Douglas's, of whom she had not thought for many years. And Señora Cancio could find little fault with the quiet, demure beauty, other than her pedigree.

Against her lack of good family Daniel placed her knowledge of French and English, her fine manners, and her intelligence, so that his mother grumbled but restrained herself, and his father restrained himself and studied his cigar.

Consuelo's life lifted into a crescendo, into a relentlessly faster beat, until she started to unravel around the edges. She felt light-headed, as if she were sitting on a spinning disc, round and round, the music faster, the music louder, but she was spinning too fast . . .

At other times it seemed to her that her heart was pinned to a kite, where it fluttered violently in the thin blue ether, exhilarated yet terribly afraid, held to earth only by the thinnest of threads.

Young Ladies

The Cancio house in El Vedado was a three-storey terrace with a wrought-iron fence and a stately Cuban royal palm on the front lawn. I had been invited by Daniel's sisters, the plump and sour Lourdes and the small, thin and jolly Margarita, to an afternoon tea.

It was the sort of thing I dreaded. I felt I had been invited to enter the lion's cage without the tamer. I couldn't understand why Daniel wasn't coming with me. I considered refusing but he laughed at me. They're just my sisters, he said. Relax, you'll like them when you get to know them.

I arrived in a sweat, the blouse I had starched and ironed for an hour creased and damp. I was met at the door by a *criada*, and ushered into the formal parlour where the sisters waited.

It was only my second visit to the Cancio residence. This time I was more able to look around. The dimensions of the rooms, the height of the ceilings and the airiness, the tasteful and sparse decorations, all intimidated me. The wooden floors felt slippery and I was melting with insecurity.

Margarita welcomed me with a gracefully extended hand that was heavy with jewels and offered *una tacita de café*. Or perhaps *un cóctel?*

Sitting down, I didn't know where to put my hands. Lourdes asked whose clothes I preferred, LaFayette's or the English tailor's in Fin de Siglo. I was embarrassed but too transparent not to admit I made my own clothes, and then I felt angry. I realised they had been toying with me, *chupándome el pelo*, sucking on my hair, as we Cubans say, because of course they could see my clothes were not sewn by a professional. And then I didn't know what to think when Margarita, all smiles and tinkling laughter, said she had a dress – a LaFayette – which didn't fit properly and perhaps I would like it?

I was confused. I didn't in the least want the dress and wished we could talk about something else – books, perhaps, or the latest Errol Flynn movie – but couldn't think how to lead the talk away. As I hesitated Margarita left the room and returned with a plaid dress, loose at the waist, a style I would not ordinarily choose.

But before I could say, It's very nice, Lourdes was on her feet. You can't give her that dress! I gave that to you! Why are you giving it to her?

Bueno, cariño, it doesn't fit me. I thought perhaps she would like it –

But I gave it to you. *Mira*, give it back. If it doesn't fit you, it will certainly fit me! Let her buy her own dresses! And as I slumped into the sofa in mortification, murmuring that I didn't want the dress, plump little Lourdes swept from the room, the dress waltzing with her.

I wanted to escape, considered rushing to the door, but already Lourdes was back, parading the dress like a squat model on a catwalk. And Margarita was offering me *un dulce*, *un mazapán*, perhaps, or *un merengue?* And smiling so broadly, her vivacious eyes flashing so merrily, that I felt trapped in that house where all appearances were deceiving.

It was downhill from there. I couldn't envision a future in that household, couldn't see how I could ever become the mistress of that inheritance. I began to step back from Daniel, and to brood, and I think that my pessimism plunged him into a cold sea. At times he seemed as passionately in love as before, but other times he stayed away for days, and after the third day of one such absence I told myself that it was all over, it could never be, it was hopeless.

And then Pedro began to *hacerme la corte*, to smile sweetly at me and stare with his dreamy green eyes. And I knew him, had known him all my life, he had always been there, in the same *vecindario*, the same slummy neighbourhood where we had played with the same families, walked to school and back along the same roads. And I could take him to see Dolores without any shame. But even as I considered this, I was mourning a love not yet lost. I was letting go of Daniel, releasing him, telling myself that he wanted this release.

In the end, I was left with Pedro, with his green eyes and loud voice, and it was some years before I discovered the profundity of my mistake. By then, the music had gone, all the music had left with Daniel, and all I could ever hear was the sound of a needle that had slipped across a record, a gravelly sound, a dry monotonous empty nothing sound.

But he loved you, Mami! You could have married him!

The waters of Port Phillip Bay before them are darkening, a cold wind blowing from beyond the curve of sea. Lights blinking on the Westgate Bridge. Ana wants to use her arms to fend off the cold, but needs them to lean on the rickety wooden rails of the pier because the story has been long, has been told over several days. But this final instalment has been longest and hardest, like a reluctant birth – what Ana does not yet know lies ahead of her. Ana balloons more each day the baby is overdue, her shape is grotesque – it does not seem humanly possible, but still the baby waits, listening.

Sí . . . Bueno. But there was no future in it.

Pero, ¿por qué, Mami? He loved you! You would have been good together! Why did you give up so easily?

No, it wasn't like that.

Pero, ¿por qué no? I don't understand.

Bueno, chica, I'll tell you. I don't like to talk about these things, but I'll tell you . . .

¿Sí, Mami?

Well, it couldn't be. Because of Dolores . . . Dolores took a dislike to him. You know how she was . . .

Ana knows how she was, but still she waits. Her scepticsm breathes words into Consuelo.

Bueno, I think it was what he represented . . . wealth,

225

security, social status . . . legitimacy . . . I think she was afraid she would lose me if we married, that I would be ashamed of her, that I would cast her away.

I could see that something was growing inside her. Just the set of her jaw when his name was mentioned. Her looks. I knew them. She was becoming frightened, and angry, and in your grandmother that was poisonous.

One evening we were going to the cinema. I remember he had on a tie; we were celebrating something or other. He said good evening to her. We always tried to get away quickly. But this time she told us to wait, she had news for us.

She sat on her chair, in the corner, her hands on the armrests in that imperious way she had. I noticed that she was worked up, she was furious. Her face was mottled, contorted.

She said, Listen well to what I'm going to say to you. This one is my daughter, whom I bore, and I tell you that you are not to ever come near her again.

It was so unexpected, so unjust, that for a moment there was silence.

Señora, be reasonable, said Daniel, half smiling.

His smile incensed her. Laugh, clown, because tomorrow you'll cry, she hissed.

Señora, I have only the noblest intentions towards your daughter.

But again she answered cryptically – she was always, you know, like an actress in a bad drama. *Chaleco, te conocí sin mangas* – Coat, I knew you when you were just a vest.

I told him to go. But he did not understand Dolores. He

thought she would respect him because he was a fine young man from a good family, in love with her daughter. How could the woman not be pleased? He became impatient with her cryptic insults. He spoke forcefully.

Señora, think about what you are saying. It doesn't make sense. We love each other. If you stand in our way, you run the risk that I'll take your Consuelo away from this hole and you will never see us again.

Consuelo pauses, as if remembering that moment, perhaps seeing a distant self, seeing paths that that self might have taken if life had been different, trying to look down that path she had nosed but never travelled. And then she draws a deep breath, a sigh, and continues.

That was the worst thing he could have said. It was exactly what she feared most. Even as he spoke, Dolores bounded towards him, revealing a knife – a machete, really – in her hand.

Consuelo looks straight at Ana as she says, She stabbed him.

She stabbed him?

Sí. Así mismo. He yelled out when he saw the thing in her hand, What are you doing? Are you crazy? even as the machete came down towards his pleading hands.

If she had meant to kill him, she would have. But she cut through the skin, through the tendon, right down to the bone. And as he stepped backwards, in shock, his hand streaming blood, she reached out again. She took his tie and chopped it in half.

Consuelo looks at Ana, roams her face for a beat, as if gauging her credulity.

It will be your *cojones* if you ever come near my daughter again, Dolores told him.

~~~

Do you remember the heaviness of your children's bodies? Do you remember their breath like freshly baked bread? How happily you sang, walking down a dusty lane, your father's hand in yours? Of course you remember. These things one can't forget. We carry them with us, from one life to the next, and they sustain us in the dry waiting times.

I didn't have children, but I loved Consuelo. When I saw Dolores settle on that knife like a mad hen, when I saw what was under her ass and in her heart, I crept forward. The darkness gathered in the corner of the room, behind the pole where they hung dresses on sunken hangers, and I gathered with it. We retreated when a car full of quiet men with blunt sticks and sharp intentions drove down the sloping road outside, its headlights probing my corner. But when Dolores lunged I was there. It was my arm that held her back, my breath in her ear. Aguanta. Aguantate mujer. And when Dolores did not head or heel, I threw myself on her. Forgetting how insubstantial I was. Still new to it. Shocked that my girth could no longer help Consuelo. But there are greater things than bone and flesh and fat. We're never entirely impotent, alma mía.

~~~

Ana heard Consuelo's voice, which was right and as things should be. She listened carefully, tried to imagine it the way Consuelo told it, aware that she was not likely to talk about this again. But there was a strange seeping throb down below, a widening and a racking, and she was finding it harder to concentrate on an old story.

And you never saw him again?

No.

Ana hesitated, breathed for a second as if thinking, waited for an intermission and then probed delicately, because something didn't sound quite right. Didn't he try to see you again?

¡No, chica! Impatiently, angrily, as if Ana were too dense for her patience.

And after a time, during which both were silent, Ana feeling her labour's first pains and Consuelo more ancient ones: But can't you see that she attacked his hands? Imagine it . . . And she turned away. Ana thought she might cry.

Her mother was sad, she had grown thin since Ana left her side. Ana didn't want to probe too deeply. Already her mother's story was receding in significance: there was a baby finally starting to show signs it was on its way.

But even as she hobbled off the pier, as she thought about suitcases hospitals placentas and all that lay ahead, she considered the story. Maybe it was true that she had never seen him again, that the damage to his musician's hands had been insurmountable, that his love had evaporated that night. Perhaps he had realised she came from the loins of a madwoman and the realisation had doused his passion.

This was what she was saying but Ana didn't believe it. She wasn't even sure that she believed Dolores had ever stabbed her mother's boyfriend with a knife. And it surprised her that she could have a reservation about this, because she had never known Consuelo to invent anything.

But something did not ring true. Even if Dolores did attack him, Daniel did not sound like the type to be put off by a crazed woman. To disappear so completely, to be vanquished, to give Consuelo up at another's command, like a coward . . .

The thought of cowardice reminded Ana of what would soon be happening to her. She wondered how bad the pain would be and how she would bear it. Knowing that she would – women do, what choice is there? – just as Consuelo had. Consuelo, her mother Consuelo, who was now asking her if she felt all right, who was finally wrenching herself from her past and noticing her daughter going into labour at her side. Consuelo, who – thought Ana, even at this moment – would have been such an interesting and delicious woman to love.

Dolores was the only grandmother Ana had known. The only *abuela* she had ever known was Dolores, who had been angry, who, like Pedro, had suffered from chronic fury and displeasure with life. Her anger was even more ancient than Pedro's and just as immutable. But while Pedro's rage was white-hot and clean, Dolores's was an acid, had welled up from a clever woman's heart and eddied inside her through labyrinthian distortions. Sometimes Dolores seemed calm but always her rage lay where it had twisted into her bones and muscles and organs. Eventually, in her late years, with less and less understanding of herself, and with darkness closing in on her but no peace, she narrowed her life even further. In the end she turned off the radio and even turned her back on her magic, honing in solely on torturing her body. Her small, ebony-black eyes, when you stood close to her, never stopped shooting sparks.

Ana woke from the anaesthetic calling for her baby, and when the nurses told her to calm down, that the baby was on another floor being looked after, Ana knew the baby was dead. She remembered Dolores's words, her *promesa:* I will haunt you. I will fuck up your life. And she knew the haunting had started, the baby was dead, she was with Dolores, Abuela had her, Dolores had taken her and Ana's screams were soundless, were held in, could be seen in her eyes but were not yet rending the air because perhaps, just perhaps, the nurses were not lying. Ana lay trapped in her bed; the Caesarian had cut through too many muscles and left her pinned like a butterfly, and when the nurses returned she grabbed one's hand and pleaded, Please, please, bring me my baby. Please let me see her.

They did not bring her. They told Ana to sleep, but Ana could not sleep. If they had brought the baby to her side she would have been able to sleep, but she was trapped in a nightmare, convinced that if she screamed they would pronounce her crazy and keep the baby away on that pretext.

It was still not morning. It was somewhere in the dead of night and Ana was alone with her pain and her fears, without her baby.

With the memory of a thirty-hour labour – her mother hovering nearby, Consuelo saying, I can't believe this is happening to me. Repeating it several times. Ana feeling guilty that she was putting her mother through such an ordeal. The escalating pain, her husband urging her to breathe, reminding her what the book said, Breathe like this, and Ana wild, wild-eyed, wild woman Ana trying to save her strength rasping out, Fuck the book.

The baby in distress. The baby unable to take any more, even if Ana could. The emergency Caesarian. Her last words, as she was being wheeled to the operating theatre, to the welcome ether, We'll be all right, Mother.

Who had been 'we'? You, Mother, me, my unborn baby girl, the whole line of us going backwards and forwards, this unbroken line – please, God, let it be unbroken. Let my baby be all right. Please, Abuela Dolores, watch over her, do not take her, I'll name her María, after your mother, your blessed mother María, *qué en paz descanse*, only don't take her . . .

—•—

As if Dolores would. As if there were not enough dead babies in her arms already, enough to keep her busy. As if Ana hadn't already, in those dark teenage years, half known all that and more.

But when you are a mother with a one-day-old child you have not yet seen, you take nothing for granted.

PART THREE

Adiós, Mi Caballero

A Strong Creature

La Habana in the first months of 1960 was tense and insomnolent. People drank last night's bad news in acrid little coffee cups each morning. The children moaned in the night and woke Consuelo. When she couldn't get back to sleep, she caught the rumours seeping through the city like underground sewage. Now they stopped with her.

They made her so nervous that in the morning she forgot to water the geraniums clasped to the outside walls of the house in small clay pots. They withered and died, remembering her tender tending fingers. She spent her days looking after the children and the women of the house – Dolores and an assortment of aging aunts from Olvidados who had ostensibly come to help with Ana and Carlos, replacing the maids and nannies who were no longer politically justifiable. In reality the old aunts needed constant reassuring, constant thimbles of coffee and back rubs to steady their frayed nerves. Their nervous hands patted *tamales* and *croquetas* that were not there. When they looked at their damp hands and found them empty, they threw them up in fright.

People misplaced packages, forgot appointments, hurried

inanely, and shouted platitudes a foot from their listeners' faces. Everyone was scared, even those on the ascendant were nervous, the situation was volatile. The future was unresolved, and Consuelo was panicked: she had no confidence in Pedro's ability to cope with the new exigencies of their lives.

A year earlier when Ana entered the world, Pedro had been leaning on a bat in the wire-mesh dugout of a baseball diamond near El Parque Forestal. His eyes blazed. El Liceo de Güines was not doing so well. Winning meant a lot – meant everything. It didn't matter to Pedro at that moment that the new year, just last month, brought with it a new government, a new country, an end to everything known – in short, a revolution. What the wind took with it didn't matter right now. What they were left with was momentarily unimportant. The anxiety, the turmoil, the fear and confusion – none of it mattered to Pedro today.

The sky was blue, the clouds were brave, and Pedro Santiago, star of El Liceo de Güines, *campeón*, had the chance, again, to prove that he was a man, that he had *cojones*, in the area of his life in which he was most confident, the thing he most loved to do.

The main thing he was thinking about was the game. Which was not going too well. And then, also, Consuelo hadn't been home this morning when he entered the house to get into his baseball flannels.

The knowledge niggled at him.

The batter ahead of him, Francisco Corva, swung and missed. Pedro sucked hard on his cigarette as Francisco gripped the bat tighter and missed again. Strike two. Pedro threw the cigarette to the ground in disgust, pulverised it with the tip of his cleated shoe, and began to move onto the diamond.

His eye on the stadium to his right, scanning for Consuelo's bloated figure, Pedro made an uncharacteristic mistake. He walked into a pitched ball as it swerved at the end of its trajectory. He turned slightly away just at the last, but it grazed the back of his uniform.

He did not realise at first what everyone was shouting about. Miguelito El Flaco was the only one not doubled over in hysteria or screaming things about Pedro's ass being on fire. Still, when he touched Pedro's arm Pedro flicked him off with a furious shrug. But then the slow combustion in the wool of his pants finally penetrated. He looked down and saw that indeed his *culo estaba encendido*.

He slapped at himself, spanked himself in sudden panic, and it was his flailing hand that first realised what had happened – the ball had met the matches in his back pocket when it thudded into him.

¡Coño, *qué fenómeno más grande!*

He was incensed, beside himself, *fuera de quicio*. He muttered curses, outraged at being the object of laughter. His face dark, his rear smouldering, he strode off the field.

In another part of La Habana Consuelo was lying on a stretcher and telling a nurse through clenched teeth, It's coming, I tell you. Right now, ¡aquí va!

But the woman did not believe her and bent over Consuelo's legs as Consuelo screamed and arched her back. The nurse was rewarded with a great jet that hit her full in the face.

What did I tell you? The child is coming, Consuelo

screamed. And there was no time for the anaesthetist or for anything else – the child came right then and there, in the corridor, in a puddle of water and amid its mother's stools because there was no time for the enema either.

The first words said as the baby emerged into the light were *¡Pero qué criatura más fuerte!* – what a strong creature! This from Doctor McDonald, who appeared at the eleventh minute.

Pero qué es, Doctor? What is it?

Una niña, a beautiful girl. But so strong, Señora! *¡Qué fuerte!*

Now the child was in the stuttering hands of the aunts from Olvidados. Now – the counter-revolution ricocheting throughout the island, dissidents being executed against any wall – it was too late. That was what she told herself. That was what she knew for certain. Pedro could not be trusted to keep his mouth shut, to keep his family safe. Pedro was affronted that the new regime was heading towards Marxism. The pious Catholic in him was outraged. He spoke up at every street corner, every *cantina*, every bar. It terrified Consuelo. There was nothing left for her to do but get out, save her children.

Outside, above her head, floated the skeletons of her dead geraniums, still attached to the greying walls. She did not dare water them in daylight. And at night all she could think about was the cries of *¡Paredón!* and the sirens bisecting the night. In the morning other walls were blood-splattered.

It was a stubborn mosaic. No matter what, she could not hold it in her mind.

The first one had been different.

Fourteen months earlier, before the earth quaked, before the bloodied walls, Pedro swaggered. Pedro looked around with studied nonchalance. Pedro clicked his fingers as he walked.

He had entered into partnership in a sporting goods business, a shop next to El Encanto. He found he had a talent for selling sporting equipment; he could harness his endless enthusiasm for any sport. His good looks helped. Business boomed.

He took Consuelo out at night to cabarets. The crystal arches zooming heavenwards promised a gaudy paradise. She wore black silk and pendulous gold jewellery. She sat heavy. Carlos fidgeted and kicked. She watched her husband dance with her girlfriends. His hips lisped. His lips hissed. *¡Ay! ¡Qué rico!* He sent her long, slow winks.

For eight years they had been honeymooners. He was deliriously proud of her beauty. Almost as much as of his own. When she became pregnant his ardour knew no bounds. The sight of her shapely legs and arms jutting out from her grotesquely extended stomach drove him into the bathroom at night, his handkerchief in his hand, for fear of hurting the child.

He got the message while sitting at a *cantina* at lunchtime, during a quick game of dominoes with a group of his *socios*. He ran out into the street and stopped the first passing taxi by stepping in front of it. By the time the car pulled up in front of El Hospital Calixto Garcia, he had regained his composure, his sense of who he was. He stared hard at the building, as if making sure he had been brought to the right place. Then he drew out a wad of bills from his deep loose pockets and peeled several from the top. He smacked them down on the seat and stepped out, his door slam a detonation.

He did not drive, but then he didn't need to. He enjoyed being chauffeured. He saw a future where he would be even richer, stronger, still more *macho*. He took no notice of the political uncertainty in Cuba in 1958. Even as a baby, when he had soiled himself in his lonely cot and smeared himself as his mother's feet came around the corner, he had had no vision.

He burst through the swinging surgery doors, unmasked, ungowned, unhygienic. He insisted on standing by her side as the doctors prodded and pulled in the blood between her legs. Not able to bear their gaze on her satiny thighs, he repeatedly twitched her furled gown over her straining legs. She pushed and moaned, arched and grunted. The nurses were made frantic by his being there. *¡Qué escándalo!* But he would not budge.

When Carlitos emerged, mossy and reptilian, Pedro had stood still, disarmed, beaming soft green light from genuinely smiling eyes.

The rap on the door was officious. Consuelo answered it, half alarmed, as she was by nearly everything those days.

In the doorway stood a short, plump *miliciana*, a woman Dolores used to call the bulldog because of her sagging jowls. *Saludos, compañera,* she grunted.

Ana María, who had just turned two, came toddling around the corner, round eyes inquiring. Behind her was

Carlos, his forehead creased in his perpetually worried expression. The children crowded the doorway.

The woman's red lacquered forefinger jabbed towards Carlos. *Ese niño* is too old to be at home. Why isn't he at school?

He's only three years old, murmured Consuelo, her breathing shallow. In what way can I serve you?

I am enrolling children for a new school. I want to put your son's name down.

What school is that?

La Habana was boiling with rumours of children being wrenched from their parents, taken far, sometimes even to stand on Red Square. Consuelo gripped the door a little tighter, pushed her children away with her other hand.

It is an honour to be asked, said *la miliciana*. He would be one of the privileged. Think it over carefully. The mandate comes from *El Máximo Líder* himself.

Stained teeth had never encouraged Consuelo. But where is this school? What will it be called? Would it be a boarding school?

Sí, claro. With all the latest facilities. Every advantage! To be asked is like winning the lottery. Where? *En* Santiago, *compañera!*

Consuelo blanched, her heart raced. *Bueno*, this is a big thing, she stammered. So far away . . . I will have to speak with my husband about it. It is not the sort of decision I can take alone . . .

The *miliciana* studied Consuelo suspiciously, disappointed by her response. *Piénsalo bien, mija.* Her words dropped dry like spat olive pips.

Consuelo closed the door quickly. Her mind raced, exploring terrifying possibilities. They will take the children. I will never see them again. They know we are not with *el partido*.

Carlos and Ana were scuffling over something – Consuelo's surge of anxiety had communicated itself to them. Carlos was crying, holding up the shattered wing of his favourite toy, an aeroplane, which Ana had ground with her little black heel. His lips curled in goblin anguish. Consuelo would not look at him. By the afternoon she had lodged a request for an application to leave the country.

El Caballero de París surprised Consuelo.

He handed her a thin envelope without a word. His face showed an ineffable sadness, the tears bubbling out, and from the way he turned away, so morosely, it must be very bad news, she thought.

The telegram was dated the third of October 1961, 'The Year of Education' stamped under the date.

Consuelo read it quickly, and then read it again slowly, and yet again. She looked up from behind the wrought-iron gate at her street, as though trying to see further, trying to see her whole city, trying to see to its very shores. Where cannons had been recently placed. All along the city's wall, grim black cavities pointing north.

She repeated the slogan under the date. It was true. Truly it was the year of her education.

Ay, *Dios*.

She stood frozen as a car sped up her quiet street. It seemed to be coming for her, coming to get her, now! But it raced on, the sound diminishing, on towards the walled shore and through the tunnel that slithered under the bay, not stopping nor slowing down until it was in the ancient angry fortress.

The wind raised great waves that leapt across the city's wall. Consuelo listened to the sound of their rushing assaults, the murmur of their retreats.

She saw a neighbour peering at her from behind venetians. Hastily stuffing the telegram into her dress pocket, she smiled directly at the woman, a tense, tough grimace. Then she walked into her house.

She was alone. Carlitos and Ana María were out strolling with their grandfather, breathing *el aire libre* – still *libre*. She saw their faces before her, small and solemn, staring at her.

She had not known where to turn.

And now, to have to pull the children out by their roots! To take them from their country. *Adiós*, Abuelo. *Adiós*, Abuela. *Adiós*, uncles and aunts and little cousins. *Adiós* forever, Caballero.

The Year of Education. It occurred to her – not for the first time – that she was guilty of having been optimistic, of having misunderstood life, of briefly thinking the world a good place. She felt culpable.

This was not something the revolution had taught her, in this year of her education. This they allowed her to realise for herself. Now she must pay for it.

The children must pay, too.

The decision to leave had been an immense, an almost unbearable, load on her. Pedro, while detesting *el partido*, had been against leaving. Despite her pleas, her hissed threats through clamped teeth late at night, he had continued to let his tongue go, to mouth off to any friend – he insisted all were friends. Whereas she had surrendered the notion of friendship. She was sure he was about to be arrested. He would disappear, like so many thousands of others, executed against a bloody wall for a look, a word, a trifle.

So she had forced the issue. She had applied to leave without consulting him. When the first batch of papers came, she faced him.

I'm going, Pedro. I'm saving the children. You can go with us, or stay, it's up to you. But I'm getting the children out.

And now here it was. A yellow scrap of paper, more precious than gold in La Habana.

Images wheeled. She held her life in her mind, gathered it all carefully for a moment, terrified that it was about to slip through her fingers – the world was tilting and her life could spill out, would lie spilt on the cold white tiles.

There was Carmen. Carmen, in a lacy pink dress, holding a hoop threaded with *claveles* over her head. They were sixteen. They were seventeen, and out strolling along El Malecón, *helados de mamey* in their hands, matching the red of their lips. Carmen, her friend from the time of Daniel. The last time she saw her, Carmen had hurled herself into her arms. They killed my boy, she had whispered in her ear.

Consuelo had drawn back from her, looked in her eyes, sobbed once, and than staggered away. She had not stayed with her, had not tried to comfort her. She had perceived, from the corner of her vision, a *miliciana* watching them. Everyone was watched, always. There was finally full employment in Cuba.

244

She had turned away from her friend, feeling as though she had to walk through a wall of glass, as though the very air in front of her were glass, about to rain around her. She had hoped that the hailing shards would stop her, pierce her, drive her into the cobblestones of La Habana Vieja.

We are going.

They gave Eduardito *paredón*. The boy had only been fourteen. The walls of our city will never be the same. No one will ever be able to wash the blood away. At least not in my lifetime, thought Consuelo.

Carmen will never recover. They played with that boy like cats with a dying bird. He never had a chance.

An image came into Consuelo's mind, unbidden, unfolded a memory as encompassing as wings. She was in Henrietta Douglas's house. She was sixteen, perhaps seventeen. One of the last times she was ever there – just before she met Daniel.

Her mind reeled away from Daniel like from a wound that cannot be touched without risking a haemorrhage.

She is in the house, in Henrietta's house in La Habana Vieja, in the hallway outside the library.

She has never explored a thing in this house, has touched nothing and tasted nothing except Henrietta's books. But this afternoon she finds herself in a tiny panelled room just beyond the library, standing on new roots before a bold red painting that looks as if its maker did nothing more than throw a bucket of blood at the canvas. The splotch it left, wine-red at its centre, fading to a luminescence at the edges, is a chronicle of something else. It tugs with surprising vigour, as if at some unsung memory, something primitive and protective, nourishing, yet also repelling, expulsive . . .

Under the painting is a piece of furniture, a chiffonier of old blond wood with brass handles. Two portraits sit on it, on a roughly woven red cloth – of a young man and a young woman. The woman, she knows, is – was – Miss Douglas, long ago, when she had been a beauty, before she had died and been saved but never completely spared.

The man, a Cuban boy in a loose white *camisa*, has light eyes. At first she thinks it is her Tío Domingo. But then sees that it isn't.

Entranced, her left eye flickering at her daring, she gently pulls open the chest's top drawer and only glimpses a baby's white sateen jacket and, under it, a sheaf of papers, and the thought flies by that they have the crest and insignia of her own school when a hand grips hers and she goes two inches into the air while trying to sink into the floor.

Henrietta's face, the half that Consuelo saw, held nothing but cold contempt. Consuelo thought she would be thrown out of the house. But Henrietta only said, I thought you knew better. And when Consuelo dared to glance at her full face she thought she saw sadness, and remorse, as if the hard *americana* had been holding tears that should have dropped a lifetime ago.

Remembering the scene, wondering why she should be thinking about something so inconsequential and trying to get past it, Consuelo was overtaken by an urgent need to have her children with her, to embrace them, to cling to them, perhaps. They would be with Abuelo Fecundo at El

Parque Florestal. She left the house, bolted from it, stepped into an abyss without a ramp.

Across the road a thin brown man in a white T-shirt leant against a wall, watching Consuelo. Pepe, the head of the block's vigilance committee, was annoyed by the look on her face, the grimness, the panic. But the chest was good. The chest was great. The taut cloth across it – that's good. He settled further into the concavity of his wall, raised a cigarette to his lips.

Consuelo walked with her hand slightly extended. It stroked the grimy sides of the buildings as she passed. She was moving by feel.

Something hard shunted inside her anus. She pressed her buttocks together as she walked. She squeezed hard, pushed it back, held onto it, reabsorbed her hard little pellet as she had learnt to do so long ago, waiting for a turn at the hole in the boarding house that had served as a toilet. As she had had to do in all the moments of crisis – the many! – in her life. She held her hard little stone, stored it, indefinitely.

She was going. She was fleeing. She would leave everything behind, her house that she had worked so hard for, her books, her country, her past. There would be no trace. She knew that. They would wipe her handprints from the rocking chair where she had lulled her babies. She knew that her children would have no memory of an infancy in their homeland. Memories, too, would be lost.

Other things, things she would rather leave behind, would cling to her. She would not be able to forget her Aunt Josefina's aged face after a day's interrogation.

247

She went over in her mind the list of what the family would be allowed to take into exile:

An umbrella or a cane
A coat as long as it is not a fur
A small ladies handbag
A portfolio containing <u>only</u> documents [they had under-
    lined 'only', so that there could be no confusion]
A small bag with infants' needs
THREE long-playing records, recorded in Cuba
A bottle of Cuban spirits, bought at the airport
An engagement or graduation ring
A watch without gold straps

Pepe stood before her. Pepe, the head of the local vigi-lance committee. At every fiesta, every celebration hon-ouring *el Máximo Líder* during the last year, she had danced with him in the street. Her smokescreen. Doubt sown, a weed for him to harvest. To allay the moment when he would begin to suspect that they were not with *el régimen*. That she had applied to leave.

Soon I won't have to dance with you again, she thought.

Already, earlier this morning, he had looked at her strangely. At the market he had glared at her, turned away. Her knees had gone soft, she had thought she would faint. She had rushed home, and minutes later, there was El Caballero, the telegram. Of course, the *comité* had already known. That was Pepe's look. She glanced at him, expect-ing words like blows. His look was acrid. The word *gusana* hung between them, waiting to fall.

248

She would not answer back. She would dance in the street with him again, if she had to.

I will move a world, to get out.

Consuelo walked along the banks of El Río Almendares, glancing at the sky from time to time. Every day she walked through a section of her city, bidding it farewell. She took the children to monuments, parks, theatres. Sometimes she talked quietly to them, but more often the monologue was internal. She was too worried about being overheard. She worried about everything. She used to yank the children under the nearest shelter whenever she heard a plane overhead, but Carlitos began having nightmares, woke up crying and pointing to the ceiling every night. The planes, the planes, he had babbled, making bombing noises and sobbing. So now Consuelo walked boldly under aeroplanes, but still kept an eye towards the sky.

Thus she saw the little white paper butterflies streaming from the small plane's belly, hundreds, thousands, fluttering on delicate white wings. It took ages for them to come down, they floated so slowly, and when they finally approached, Carlos chased them, bolting here and there, arms swinging, tilting, drunk. Ana stared from her stroller, fingers in her mouth in amazement. Carlos caught the leaflets, ran a handful back to Consuelo. She scanned them quickly, then dropped them quickly. They were extremely dangerous. They were seditious.

They had been seeded in the clouds by Cubans who still had some money when they got to Miami, by Batistianos, by former Fidelistas who had believed him when he said he was a nationalist but couldn't believe their fate when he said he was *comunista* after all.

Later that afternoon, pegging diapers onto her clothesline, Consuelo heard dull thuds from the bay. The television news that night mentioned in passing that a ship in the harbour had experienced spontaneous combustion. Another one, thought Consuelo.

The next day the city shook with tremors that originated just beyond the still-manicured lawns of the presidential palace. Then El Encanto, the luxury department store, burned to the ground, a result of phosphorous that got into its air-conditioning system.

Consuelo and Pedro took Ana and Carlos to a political rally. It was important that they be seen, that all go smoothly until their departure date. On the far side of the plaza, barely visible to them, there was a movement of people, a whooshing of air, more than the usual excitement. They were too far away to see what had happened, there were too many bodies, but the news eventually reached them, passed from mouth to mouth. A *guajiro* from Oriente had been killed and two others injured when a giant cardboard cut-out of *el Máximo Líder* collapsed during the rally. The 32-metre portrait fell into the crowd, responding to the vibrations of their stamps and roars of *Paredón* – the call that had sent so many to the city's bloody walls.

Walking along Prado on the way home, they passed El Caballero de París. Consuelo did not approach him, knowing that he knew she was leaving. Knowing that she was a pariah, a *gusana*, trouble on two legs. But he saw her, walked up to her, arms open, kissed her on both cheeks in the French fashion.

Conchita!

Mi Caballero!

He pulled from his jacket pocket a package, somewhat greasy, slightly thicker than an envelope. Consuelo took it up to her nose, smelled it. Smiled at him. *Gracias, mi* Caballero.

For you, my heart, Conchita, he replied, unchanged, as if Pedro were not at her side, scowling to see another man, even one so old and venerable as El Caballero, courting Consuelo. As if they were not in the middle of a great upheaval, and she not a *gusana*. She guessed from the smell that in the envelope there were a few slices of ham. It was no longer eaten in the capital. Lizard steaks and frog legs were replacing chicken and fish in kitchens throughout La Habana. Soon people would learn to remove the vocal cords from pigs so that they could keep them in the bathtubs of their apartments.

As it turned out, it was the last time she saw El Caballero on the streets of their city.

On television, Consuelo watched *el Máximo Líder, El Caballo*, Fidel himself, feet on desk and cigar clamped between beefy lips, address a rural delegation. She turned it off after a few minutes but he went on for eleven hours, hectoring and beseeching in turns. (When the delegates finally filed out, he ordered three gallons of icecream, two of *mamey*, one of mango. He ate daintily, his little finger pointing graciously, until there was only a pink rind left in the bottom corner of the carton of *mamey*.)

¡Cuba sí! ¡Yanqui no!

The standard sentence for listening to the Voice of America was ten years. It was the same for black-marketeering. Both flourished. The G2, the secret police, operated at La Habana airport, about three hundred metres from the airfield. A police photographer stood in the terminal, photographing the crowds behind glass waving goodbye to families and friends boarding Pan Am flights. The photos from what was known as the goldfish bowl were printed immediately in the airport and a G2 officer went over them with a magnifying glass. Every so often he tapped a face in the crowd – we want him – and a couple of militiamen trotted away.

Thousands disappeared.

People fought back by hoarding coins. Fifty-, forty-, twenty- and ten-centavo coins were swallowed. Even Consuelo, who would not do anything to endanger herself or her children, carried bulging envelopes full of one-centavo coins. Anything larger she left at home. *Milicianos* were handed their change in the fat little envelopes. Consuelo stood impassively as they cursed and counted.

Whenever El Caballo was about to speak, Czech trucks raced through the streets, rounding up audiences. From loud hailers the *Internationale* played with a calypso beat.

The centre of the city died slowly, from strangulation. At two in the afternoon it was deserted by everyone except an old man who carried home buckets of water on the shoulder yokes he once used to sell *maníes*. In front of the Ministry of Education, nervous dogs tried to sun themselves, startling at every distant thud.

Machine guns rattled like venetian blinds dropped too quickly.

Tomorrow morning more people would stream into the countryside, pushing carts laden with what they held dearest – babies and grandmothers jolting on the rubbled streets.

Daniel Lay in a Coffin

Daniel rested in a coffin, in a funeral parlour, but he was not dead. He was sick, and was being nursed by the undertaker and his wife. When they managed to bring a doctor to his side, the *médico*, harried by visions of patients missing eyes, feet, fingernails and chunks of skull, or released from the baseball stadium with black testicles, could not concentrate long enough to understand that Daniel had been infected by tropical worms. They were eating him slowly. Before his condition was diagnosed in a Hialeah clinic in thirty years' time, they had eaten a path through his internal organs.

The worms had attached themselves to the souls of his feet as he hid in a swamp that had recently been fertilised for rice planting. In the Sierra he had played his guitar for the revolutionaries. After the heady first weeks of triumph, the bloody walls began to turn his stomach, ultimately affecting his conscience. Now he hid from the men he once serenaded. The worms coursed up and down his legs.

What Ana Remembers

Ana walked into Consuelo's room. The room was a chaos, was in revolutionary ferment. Clothes were strewn everywhere. Shoes and books and toys and hair ribbons and the contents of her mother's jewellery box – the three little turtles with their mock jade backs – lay tossed across the bed. It was startling to see no order and no peace here. As if there had been a hurricane.

The whole house was in turmoil; people rushed about, whispered and made meaningful silences, and then violently broke those silences. Ana felt the tension everywhere, in everyone's words and in her mother's house. But no one would talk to her about what was happening and Ana was anxious. So anxious, that she, who rarely said anything at all, now found it necessary to speak.

What are you doing, Mami?

We are packing to go on a little trip.

Where are we going? Are we going to visit Abuelo?

No. Not to visit Abuelo . . .

Where are we going?

We are just going on a little holiday.

Will we come back soon?

Yes, *sí, claro, mi amor. Pronto.* Very soon.

When you know your mother is lying, there is no comfort.

Ana says that she remembers.

People look at her sceptically. You can't remember, you would have been too young. It all happened before you were three.

It doesn't matter, she says. There are some things I know that I remember.

I remember the rooms in my mother's house, the house she bought in La Habana with the money she had saved from a dozen years of working at the *Havana Post*.

They were white, bright airy rooms, sparsely furnished, a rocking chair here, a soft couch like an elephant squatting over there. There was lots of air in those rooms, and lots of breezy space, as you would want in a house in the tropics.

I remember my mother and father crouching in front of a window, their ears pressed to a radio. I remember that I knew they were doing this because they had to watch who was coming up the path, because they would be in trouble if they were caught listening to this voice on the radio.

I remember anxiety.

I remember the bombing of the Havana tunnel by the counter-revolutionaries.

Well, that's not strictly true. I remember a childhood of being scared that tunnels would crash down on me, would bury me, and always clutching my mother's neck in a stranglehold whenever we drove under the tunnel north of

Miami on the way to Pirate's World in Dania. And I remember the day, very recently, when I discovered in a book that the Havana tunnel, which was near the part of El Vedado where we lived, had been bombed, and how I dialled my mother's number in Miami. Yes, that was the one you remembered, she said.

So you see, we remember, even when we don't realise that we remember.

I remember the goldfish bowl.

I remember my grandmother on the other side of the glass, and my mother and father and me on this side.

I am clutching my mother's hand, and my doll Gavicito is clasped to my chest. Mother is wearing a dark woollen suit, a tailored suit that looks expensive but also looks as though my mother is in mourning.

Which, of course, she is.

We are surrounded by glass.

Mother looks severe and nervous and her face, taut and stretched like that, is not too pretty. My mother is gripping my hand too hard and I am worried, but I do not cry because I never cry.

I watch.

My father is holding a giant clear plastic bag. Inside the bag are all the most beautiful things in my life. These are our toys: the bright tops and wonderful balls and the pretty dolls who are my friends and the train set and my panda bear that I would like to hold very much right now. And Papi is telling the *miliciano* that they are only children's toys and surely it would be all right if we take them with us.

Who is it going to hurt?

La revolución. You are stealing from our revolution.

And now he is handing the *miliciano* the bag of toys, and the *miliciano* is taking it away, through a white door.

Mami is whispering to me to hush, that there will be many toys where we are going, but I am screaming, I am trying to hurl myself on the floor. I am crying. Grief and rage.

My exile has begun.

I remember sitting on the aeroplane, feeling hot and tired and itchy in my hot little woollen suit with the Bambi in felt sewn on the skirt. We have been sitting here forever and there is very little air in an aeroplane and it is unbearable.

The aeroplane doesn't move and Mami and Papi are very nervous, Papi is bent over his knees with his hand over his eyes and he is praying silently so only I know because I crouch down and look up and I can see his lips moving.

What I don't understand – will not know for many years to come – is that there is a problem with my mother's papers and my parents have been told and the plane is being delayed while they check to see if it is all right for Mami to leave after all because there is a problem about her name.

And so of course I don't understand why my *mami* is being led away by several *milicianos*.

And I can't remember whether my mother hugged and kissed me just at that moment, when she didn't know if she would ever see us again, because to remember this part of the story would simply be beyond endurance.

And I know that they must have relented, Mami must have said or done something that she has never spoken about, because they did relent and Mami did come back to us and the plane did fly and I fell asleep and when I woke again we were in the United States of America.

What I can tell you, with considerable authority, is that my mother, even now, is trying to recover from that moment when she was led away.

Now that I come to think about it, so am I.

How the Streets Were Paved, 1962

Consuelo moved fearfully through those first months in Miami, sniffing the wind. Vague anxieties stalked her through the city's incandescent streets, past parks locked in by a steaming fecundity. She could not find shelter.

She seemed to be always listening, yet never absorbing anything. The clamour of the streets was interspersed with English sounds, an English that she did not understand. It was not, somehow – inexplicably – what she had studied at La Habana Business, or learnt so long ago from Henrietta Douglas.

The pervasive and invisible menace she felt was different from the political mayhem she had left behind that winter of 1962. She was frightened, she had been frightened for a long time. There was so much lacking. She wondered if she would ever feel herself again.

She was tired, life was tiresome. Sometimes she had to carry Ana, who could not be bullied into walking further and whose heavy head nodded, nearly asleep, on her shoulder. She had to half drag four-year-old Carlos by the hand, force herself and her burdens through the heat. When she glanced at the boy, she found that his vulnerable frame and pinched face somehow angered her, so that she could barely stand to look at him. *Vamos*, hurry up, she said, yanking his hand. Moments later a wave of pity, tenderness and guilt engulfed her.

The little boy tugged at his shorts, splayed his legs, suppressed a whimper. Underneath his underwear his skin was alive, looked as though it had been flayed. They were returning from the *farmacia* on Calle Ocho, the one called Los Tres Apóstoles, where they had bought a new ointment.

Consuelo thought of the life she had lost. She thought of her stylish dresses and leather pumps and the pearls that had adorned her neck. She thought that she should be strolling along El Malecón at this time of the day, with Ana María in an expensive stroller and Pedro holding Carlos's hand, pausing to greet friends, to buy *un helado de mamey*, to watch the sun set on their city. She should be ignoring the admiring glances of men, safe in her world, the world she had worked so hard to etch out.

Whatever she had believed *los Estados Unidos* would offer had been a bitter trick. Not that she had thought the streets would be paved with gold – she had read too much Steinbeck in Henrietta Douglas's library for that. Still, the wrench had been incredible. It was best to forget there had ever been another life.

The Santiagos had been *reclamados* – reclaimed – by Pedro's cousin. Not a first cousin, a *primo-hermano*, but a cousin nonetheless, the only relative who was qualified, according to US Government criteria, to reach out to them from *el exilio* and pluck them from the chaos that had overtaken *la isla*.

The cousin, Mario, was a small man with a pretentious little moustache and black laughing eyes. His wife Rosafina was much taller, and grim. They had a daughter, Marta, a thin, stressed child just a bit older than Ana María, a bit younger than Carlos.

Mario and Rosafina Santiago had been in Miami a year. Mario, a policeman in La Habana, was working in a lamp factory. Like most Cuban refugees, they had lost everything; they had fled Cuba relinquishing everything. They had signed the forms that had been requested of them reclaiming Pedro and his family but they were not too happy about all that was being asked of them in the name of a thin blood tie.

Mario and Rosafina and sad Marta lived in an apartment building owned by a Mr Peters, on south-west Tenth Street and Second Avenue, just two blocks from the street known as Calle Ocho. The building was a three-storey affair on the corner of the block, built right up against the sidewalk during the housing boom that followed the hurricane of 1926. The walls were of peeling pink stucco, three wings embracing a grassy courtyard at whose centre sat a fountain shaped like a squat mushroom. The courtyard doorways were ornate, with swirling pillars and rococo arches and plaster adornments. But from the street, the opening in the wall for the stairs presented itself as a dark, gaping mouth.

Behind the apartment building, on the other side of the alley, was a one-roomed structure in the same pink stucco, but without adornments. Barely eight feet across by eight feet deep, it had once been a laundry room servicing the apartments, but the washing machines had been carted away to make room for the refugees streaming into the city.

This is where Mario had taken Pedro and Consuelo and the children, after Pedro had been interrogated and processed through the US Government facilities at Opa Locka. (And Pedro, too frightened and worried to be indignant, answered the questions meekly. The outrage would come later, would last a lifetime. *¡Qué coño!* They asked me if I had ever been *un comunista!* Me! *¡Qué coño!* Did I ever know any *comunistas? ¡Imagínate!* I knew them – they strolled around La Habana *al tolete*.)

The door of the laundry room had fallen off its hinges and was being held in place by planks nailed across the jamb.

Mario stood back on the sidewalk as Consuelo and Pedro looked at it. Consuelo felt a surge of panic. Pedro poked and prodded. *Pero* . . . How does one go in? he asked, bewilderment vying with rising anger in his voice.

Mario couldn't wait to get away. *Bueno, compadre,* he said weakly. It was all I could manage. There is not a single apartment in all of south-west Miami for the sort of money you have.

I don't have any money, Pedro said gravely.

Por eso-o-o-o, compadre, said Mario, sweet reasonableness. *Mira, mira,* the window is unlocked. Climb in through the window.

And then, as Consuelo gave him a look of bitter disbelief, he tried to joke. Don't worry, Señora, don't worry. As they say here in Me-a-mi – I'll meet you at the Hilton *mañana*.

Consuelo, who was forever ready to mistrust relatives, had taken her eyes off her husband's cousin slowly, after raking them over his face – making a final judgement about the man and then dismissing him forever. She passed Ana María and Carlos to Pedro through the window. She had to hold on to the ledge to pull herself through, because Pedro did not hear her say, *Por Dios*, Pedro, give me a hand. Or else he ignored his wife's request. The room had a chilling effect on everyone; even the children fell quiet.

It was dark; Mario pointed out a string for the globe which dangled in the middle of the room, and seeing how little else there was to see, took Carlos by the hand. *Vamos, mi socio*. Your *tío* Mario is going to give you your first lesson in America.

Ignoring Ana, he took the boy next door, where a corner store sold the sort of bread that looked, smelled and tasted like thick slices of tissue. He bought Carlos bright pink balls of bubblegum, almost as large as his eyes. As they returned to the laundry room, Carlos stopped singing the *Internationale* for the first time since the plane landed. It was too hard to form the words around the wad of gum.

Inside, no one had moved. The tension, instead of leaving with Mario, had grown and threatened to ignite. Consuelo could not get over it. A double mattress on the floor took up almost all the space in the room. The mattress was bare, and old, and stained, and instantly spun her back to the horrors of her childhood – memories she never examined but which, when touched, shot her through with panic and depression.

There were no sheets anywhere, no blankets, no other

furniture except a rotting wooden table that could only have been pulled from an alley, not large enough for two people to eat from, and a single chair.

In one corner of the room was a toilet, which had never been scrubbed in its lifetime, and next to it a tiny, grimy sink, not big enough to wash a plate. But there are no plates, thought Consuelo in grim despair; but there is no kitchen either, so this is not a problem.

There is also no food, anyway, so things are working out nicely.

And no money to buy any.

In the catalogue of what there wasn't, one must add goodwill. There was precious little goodwill among the panic-stricken adults.

There was tension, in abundance, and grief, and tears. There was heat, and heated words. There were cockroaches, and mice, and even a scorpion in the linoleum near the toilet. There was anger, and rage, and much despair. Life had suddenly become, as they say, *imposible*.

They had to walk long distances to obtain necessities; Miami, unlike La Habana, was not considerate towards pedestrians. Now, returning from one such shopping expedition, Consuelo struggled with the children past an empty lot where a group of boys were throwing a ball amongst themselves. Carlos pulled at his shorts and Consuelo ignored him. She hoped the ointment she had just bought, at great cost, from *la farmacia* Tres Apóstoles would repair the skin on his backside. The boys on the lot were tall and rangy, just entering puberty, with tough faces showing the first shadows of moustaches. Some were dark-skinned with

265

tightly curled hair; they were Cubans but they spoke Miami English. They belong to the first lost generation, thought Consuelo.

She eyed them nervously, glanced at and quickly away from a bare stomach that displayed raised and puckered scars. They frightened her, and they knew it.

¡Oye, qué rica! ¡Qué jeva! they sneered, lewdly imitating a woman's walk. Hey baby, see you tonight, they called, practising what they had only learnt recently and then grabbing each other, falling about with laughter.

Her grip on Carlos's hand tightened. Consuelo dragged him along faster, so that he had to run to keep up. He saw the white on her face and he was frightened, without understanding what had happened, or why. But then, he seldom did.

They reached Mr Peters's property, passed the gloomy doorway. Consuelo rushed to the side of the laundry room. When Anita hesitated at the low open window that they still used as a door Consuelo pushed her forward. *¡Apúrate, muchacha, apúrate!* And when Ana began to cry, Consuelo, feeling life was unendurable, smacked her sharply on the bottom, propelling her inside, and then reached for Carlos, pushed him, too, inside. Without releasing him, she stepped in and began hitting him, her hand fast and hard, again and again on his shoulders, as he stumbled past her.

¡Desgraciado! she screamed. Ana ran to hide, to wedge herself next to the toilet. Carlos stood rooted, staring up at his mother, with no idea what he had done wrong.

Why didn't you stand up for me? Coward! You didn't say a thing to them! *¡Cobarde! ¡Cobarde! ¡Cobarde!*

He put his hand up to shield his face. Her hand fell on his shoulders, his bare neck, thumped hollowly on his back, and even fell on his raging buttocks. He was lost.

I'm just a little boy, he sobbed, cowering in a corner. But by then she had stopped. She did not hear him. She was on the mattress on the floor. Crying.

Another apartment building abutted what became known in the family's lore as the little room – *el cuartico*. The diminutive was not used affectionately.

In *el exilio*, Consuelo questioned herself over and over and over, nearly drove herself crazy with wondering if she had done the right thing in insisting they leave Cuba, as night after night the children nibbled a soda cracker for their supper, and Pedro refused to talk about what doors he had knocked on for work, and to discuss who had given him the five dollars which had bought the soda crackers and a carton of Pall Malls, which he smoked despite the fact that the rent was fourteen dollars a week.

Pedro did not speak English, did not drive a car.

Ana remembers *el cuartico* as hot. Yet paradoxically, it was also damp. She remembers the ledge of a window that faced the wall of the building next door, only a few inches away. The ledge of this blind window was high – as high as her chest. It was her place. Here, she played with shells, tiny off-white shells that appeared, as if by magic, on the sill. They were either perfectly round, flat little buttons, curling towards their centres and smaller than her smallest fingernail, or they were conical. Ana played with them for hours, days weeks and months, a year, her back turned to her mother and brother and whatever was happening in the room, which was usually nothing more than Consuelo crying. Ana faced the window that let in no air and no light, that looked directly onto a dark, mossy wall.

Things became worse. Carlos and I were sick, we had high temperatures and blisters throughout our bodies and Carlos had a skin fungus that ravaged his back and kept him naked on the mattress on the floor. There was very little money for medicines or doctors. Mother became thinner and her face was taut beyond recognition. I do not remember the rubella; Mother has told me about it, and Mother does not say very much at all about this time.

We celebrated my birthday in *el cuartico* with a bottle of Pepsi and a chocolate donut. She had thought these were symbols of an American party, but Carlos and I, if we had ever tasted these things, did not recognise them. We were too new to America – we could not eat the donut, we could not drink the Pepsi. I do not remember whether Mother ate them herself. I do not remember whether she cried on this occasion.

I can't understand how we all slept on the mattress. And even more puzzling, what did we do when Mother's friend from La Habana, Carmen, arrived with her son Joe. Carmen's eyes were puffed like a goldfish from her endless lament about what they had done to her other son, Eduardito. They stayed with us for several months before moving on to New York, never to be heard from again.

So you see, there is very little I actually remember from

this time. Except that sometimes I would go with my mother to the corner store and, when no one was looking, slip a bar of chocolate – *un Peter* – into my hand.

The little grocery store is still there. It strikes me that perhaps I could pay someone for those stolen chocolates. On the other hand, I don't feel I owe anybody anything for those years.

Sometimes I would walk over to Marta's house to play with her. I don't remember what we played. I do recall the day I went to play and followed her screams right into the bathroom, where Rosafina was catching Marta's vomit in a bowl and attempting to force it back past her lips. Marta would scream and push the bowl away, gag and gush more vomit which her mother then tried to catch again.

What do you think? That money grows on trees? Eat it, *condenada!*

Carlos walked everywhere, singing the jingles he had learned the year before, parroting them gracelessly.

Somos comunistas, pa' alante y pa' alante,
Y al que no le guste, que pite y espante!
We are communists, onwards and onwards!
And anyone who doesn't like it can whistle and piss off!

Consuelo shushed him, pinched him, lived in dread that he would break out into a chorus of the *Internationale* in front of a government official, or merely an American, or a

Cuban informer. She worried that he would again, despite her pleas, ask some zealot in his polite reedy voice if she were a communist, or a *gusana*.

Consuelo did not believe in political freedom. She still felt eyes pressing into her back, saw the ears on the other side of stone walls. She knew from memory how trees and shrubs recorded secrets, and betrayed them in rustling murmurs to passers-by. And here she was, holding by the hand a child who could not forget his indoctrination and did not know the difference between Cuba Roja and Little Havana.

And he was addicted to bubblegum. Consuelo suspected that if he could not get someone to buy it for him, he stole it from the shop next door. It was responsible for the clumps in his hair, the way his sleeves wadded up in his armpits, the slowness of his steps. It enfuriated her, and she blamed Mario for this addiction, forseeing others, forseeing how America would corrupt her son.

She would have died had she realised that Carlos was telling the truth when he avowed, just before a beating, that he was not stealing bubblegum. Pedro and Consuelo did not believe him because he would not say where he was getting it from, if not from the corner shop. They did not know that when Carlos darted out the door, he headed down the sidewalk, eyes down, searching for the riches that paved the streets in America. These he scraped off carefully, and popped into his mouth, no matter how grey or black they were, although of course he preferred it when there was still a trace of pink. Then he knew it would still be sweet.

The Rhythm of the Raft

At about this time, Consuelo began to see Daniel in Miami. At first it was always at a distance, in the hot haze of the next block. Her heart would quicken as she recognised – or thought she recognised – the shape of his head, the outline of his figure from the back, his honest stride. She would momentarily surge forward, dragging the children by their hands, but always he would disappear from her sight and she would relinquish him, as she had done before, as she was now bound to do. But for a long time she was deaf to the children, drifted in her mind, was not aware of anything at all until some furious thought finally swam to the surface and anchored itself there. Then she would hiss at Ana for putting her fingers to her nose, or smack Carlos for dragging his hands along the wall, and think grimly that she hated Miami, hated life.

Later she saw him clearly and beyond confusion, and although they did not speak to one another, no one else existed for a moment, not even the children.

It was a December day when the heat of Miami was cut by the vaguest, gentlest breeze, like a promise or a whisper – nothing else. In this freshness, people were invigorated and spilled out of their homes, to the theatre to see movies about the thin ridiculous man, Cantinflas, or to the Miami Dade Auditorium where the first of the annual nostalgic extravaganzas – *Añorada Cuba* – was being staged. That was where she saw him, in the foyer where she nervously waited for Pedro to buy the tickets. She was nervous because they should not have been there. They scarcely had enough money for two meals; they needed clothes and furniture and a million other things and she knew it was simply insane. Yet the program, *Our Beloved and Much Missed Cuba*, seemed to promise some relief from an even deeper hunger. So she waited desperately, hopefully, and the children felt her anxieties, as always, so that Carlos darted about her legs in a little white shirt too small for him, and Ana, in a lacy dress with many flounces that was also too small and which Consuelo had hand sewn in Cuba in another life-time, stood staring about her and biting her nails to the quick. Consuelo wore her one good dress, a green and yellow sheath like the upholstery on a sofa, too warm for a Florida winter. Her gaze was severe and unhappy. She was calling to Carlos to come stand at her side when she raised her eyes and saw him, stared in disbelief, and then faltered, leant against a pillar, lowered her eyes and waited for Pedro.

Añorada Cuba indeed.

That night, when Consuelo lies down on the mattress on the floor, the blood in her veins throbs so that she has the disconcerting sensation of movement; she feels she is being rocked on the surface of a dark, inhospitable sea. She lies still, listening to the rubbery gurgle of air in Pedro's throat, the lap of tides on the raft.

She drops her foot over the edge, searching for firm ground. Even with this anchor, the lurching continues unabated. When she presses her ear into the mattress, the beat she hears is the rhythm of a raft.

She creeps out of bed, motivated by a half-formed desire to sit still somewhere, to still herself, to stop the rocking, to stop herself.

The night is moonless, black. Her foot edges cautiously around the mattress, scouting ahead. She is the furled mast of an unmanned boat. She is navigating by instinct. When she has made three turns, she looks up, expecting to see a window, a square of muted light.

But the square is smaller than it should be, and not where she expected it, and she is lost. She feels insane to have lost her way in the dark in this tiny, hellish cube. Her hand reaches limply, all tentativeness, but she almost falls when there is no wall to her left where she expects it. Her hand arcs across the night, gropes air, and her brain tries to make some sense of it all.

She has stumbled through an unknown door. She is somewhere else, not where she thought she was, but in the past. She is in Cuba, in a marble-tiled house in El Vedado . . . There is the window . . .

She stands like this for many seconds, for minutes, for a very long time, for years that spin backward, for the erasing of years. She does not think about anything at all. She allows herself to rest in the past. The night streams past her, dreamlessly.

In the ensuing weeks and months she saw him often. She found herself dressing with more care, discovered, with helpless shame, that she was dressing for him, knowing their paths would inevitably cross, that inevitably they would find themselves in the same room, at the *bodega* where she went for saltine biscuits and milk, at the *farmacia*. (*Enviamos medicinas a Cuba* – but she could not afford the medicines her children needed here in Miami; how could she think about sending any to Cuba, from where Dolores was clamouring for various pills already?) She saw him at the *lavandería* or at the street corner where steel tubes held a television aloft and people gathered at sunset to watch the American news for information about Cuba. Anywhere Cubans congregated, their paths were likely to cross.

They would not look at one another, would not speak, would not acknowledge the other by the tiniest glance or gesture – only by the deep inward and unseen palpitations of their hearts.

This was the dance of proud passings Consuelo and her former lover performed the year she was thirty-five, both of them looking into a future where the other would not be.

Pedro knew nothing of it. Consuelo never confided anything at all to him, never spoke of her past, and the few things she ever mentioned he did not hear, such was his egotism (which at times provided welcome cover for what she did not want him to know). Of course, the children also knew nothing, and in fact, there was nothing to be known, except that two souls suffered in each other's presence, that this was the bleakest time of Consuelo's life.

While he shadowed her by day, he wove in and out of her dreams at night. Even in her dreams she did not allow herself to recognise him, to speak to him, to lift her gaze towards him, so desperately seriously did she cling to honour. Nearly every morning when she awoke, stiff from the mattress on the floor, cramped from her children's bodies pressed against her, her first thought was that once again he had accompanied her all night – accompanied but eluded her.

They could neither touch nor let go.

Still, she felt he was a given in her life, dependable as the moon.

After each dream of Daniel, it took her days to return to her family, to her life, to stop living in the more vivid reality of the memory of her dream, in that faraway place located on the fringes of her past.

After seeing him, she thought she would go mad.

Then, for weeks, she could not stand the sight of Pedro, his tobacco breath, his booming voice – his toenails! – his maulings.

The strain of hiding so much feeling, the realisation that Daniel had loved her, that his love had ultimately proved stronger and truer than her own – all this and all that had been denied to her as a child, and all that had been within her grasp had she but had the strength to seize it, all this and the hardship of exile – further and deeply embittered

Consuelo. She became ever more serious and solemn and stiff and stern. Something wavered and died in her – the last remnants of conviction that life could be good – and she began a long and bitter slog to live for her children, to never cry and never reveal herself, to soldier on for their sakes alone.

Daniel, for his part, began to find himself once again in the company of the plotters and schemers and the *desesperados* – the hot-heads who longed to splatter their blood in the dirt of *La Patria*. In his mind, in his torment, Daniel's desire to regain his past with Consuelo merged with a passion to regain Cuba.

In this he was not alone. The Cuban refugees found life in Miami a caricature of what they felt life should be. Their pining for home was so intense, so purely an expression of life lost, that it infected everything they did. When Consuelo and Pedro took the children to Miami Beach for the first time, all they could talk about was the beaches of Varadero. Their superlatives were so exaggerated, their nostalgia so acute, that always afterwards Ana María would imagine a place where castor sugar ran to greet the sea.

As Daniel began to disappear on secret missions for long periods, for months at a time, an old acquaintance re-entered Consuelo's life. At this time, El Caballero de París also fled Cuba, found his way to Miami like so many thousands of others, and, as so often before, sought her out without even seeming to remember her name.

He appeared before her again and again, in the laundry room doorway as the sun set behind him, or in the soft glow of dawn, any time Consuelo felt herself sinking into the abyss, losing all hope, ready to give up. At such moments she would close her eyes and picture herself in the grip of some giant unknown hand which held her by the ankles and swung her in a smooth arc that ended against a wall, dashing her cranium in a vision of relief.

And always, within seconds, as if responding to some vibration from her soul, would come a rap on the window, and the sad, aging visage of El Caballero de París would be standing before her, holding out a carnation, and then, bowing with a flourish that made one imagine he still wore a cape, he would present his flower.

She stood before him, thinner than in the old days, yet somehow heavier, dragged down by apprehension. Time had thickened her waist, set into the line of her jaw, whittled her cheeks, retarded her dreamy step. Yet from another perspective – from that of El Caballero de París – time had not touched her.

Señora, *con su permiso*, he would say, handing her the flower, and as she hurried to get her purse to pay him something, he would put his hand up in respectful protest. *De 'so nada, Señora. Para usted – mi corazón*. She smiled grimly at the absurd courtly language, looking around at the poverty of her home, but accepting the flower that somehow always rescued her from total despair.

She had thought it was out of her hands – the next decision, the next place to place her right foot, to put her left. She told herself that the road had taken an unexpected turn that had knocked her feet out from under her and left pieces of her scattered everywhere, and Daniel was out of her hands.

She thought that when the needle slid across and the droning nothing sound began it had all been taken out of her hands – if it had ever been in her hands and not in the arm that held the needle or the arm that held the knife. But really, you and I know it was always in her power, and in her powerlessness – the arm, the needle, the scratched record, the gravelly noise, and even the music behind the gravel and even . . . even Daniel. Even happiness.

Consuelo had always had options; what she did not have was the strength to take what was available. Her fingers had curled around happiness, had held it in their grasp. But it had proven an infinitely soft grasp, a grasp like a baby's, like a baby that had been abandoned by its mother on a rubbish heap and had never once been acknowledged and had been raised by a woman who understood more about mourning ghost babies than raising real ones.

Consuelo dreams.

One night she dreams she has run into a friend, a woman named Alicia, a phantom from her past. Alicia is at a laundromat, perhaps the one that used to be here before, perhaps the windswept, fluorescent-lit place on Calle Ocho with the Coppertone sign where a little black dog pulls on the panties of a blond, curly-haired child, to the delight of the onlookers at the beach but surely not of the child's mother, thinks Consuelo grimly.

Alicia is beside her, shovelling clothes into a washing

machine. Alicia mentions his name. Conchita, *figúrate tú*, I spoke with him just yesterday!

¡Sí, muchacha! ¡Ese mismo! He is living in Georgia! My man had to call him. *No seas boba* – don't be silly! Everyone remembers the two of you together – in that other life!

And somehow, recklessly, appalled at herself, Consuelo finds herself confessing to Alicia. *Sí*, I loved him. *Sí*, I never stopped. *Sí*, I can't seem to stop, even in this arid exile, and *sí*, I would give up everything, I would leave – and here she amazes herself, she can scarcely believe her own words, how could she say such a thing? – I would leave *mi marido* and *mi hija* even now, for him, for a word, a sign from him.

And she dares not look up, because Alicia's eyes are boring through her. And she hears her friend's wordless thought: You would only stay for the son? You would leave your husband and your daughter, but never the son?

And now Consuelo is trying to hurry her dream, is trying to skip over this embarrassing admission. But it hangs onto her heels, it pursues her as she races off – how could you leave Ana María? When would you see her? What does this mean, Señora?

But her dream manages to carry her off, to carry the moment, and she sleeps on, and she dreams, and in her dream she is remembering El Vedado, the corridors and yellow stone walls of his university, and the way he had once clasped both her hands in his, there, in front of the statue of the *Alma Mater*, and held her hands, like a captured butterfly, up to his heart, held them there while she spoke earnest nonsense, while her heart fluttered, stuttered, stalled, fell a few precipitous flights, while her mind recorded the look in his eyes for eternity.

And her mind whirls in its sleep, and she dreams, she remembers the day at a party, *una fiesta*, at someone's house, a fine house, and he asked that mouse-girl, Maida, to dance, perhaps because no one else had, no one ever did, the girl had atrocious acne, but Consuelo felt the acid of jealousy seep through her. And how she hated herself for her jealousy, and how her jealousy possessed her, so she couldn't stop herself from sulking afterwards, from reproaching him, and the disappointment in his face still shames her, so many years later, in a dream.

Beside her Pedro's snores catch on the jagged edge of some invisible object, and the snores unravel, become a low whistle before stalling completely, and this rouses Consuelo.

She wakes with the feeling that she has been in his presence, that she has seen him again in a dream, that heart-racing feeling, that plunging feeling – yet she cannot conjure up the meeting, only the feeling.

She clings to that, releases it reluctantly, refuses to open her eyes long after she is awake, as the morning sun illuminates the wretched room, and the cold of the concrete floor seeps into her, and the smell of Ana María's wet diaper and Carlos twitching in his sleep like a spastic child, and they all huddle on the mattress that is a pitiful raft plying the waters between the life that was and the new land where hope will be quenched.

She knows without looking that Pedro is sleeping with his mouth agape, his nicotine-tarred teeth more yellow than ever in the morning sun, one hand lightly on his chest that beats like a slow drum, like a death march.

His yellow teeth are ragged cliffs beyond which – she swears! – she never will pass.

And she wonders, as she wrenches back into her life, rolls onto the floor on all fours so as to not wake her family before pulling herself upright, gingerly, because her back is stiff, when he will leave her, finally release her, stop haunting her. Her bones creak, the cold of *los Estados Unidos* is seeping into them, decalcifying them.

But still, she thinks – she indulges herself in the thought – it is temporary, all this is temporary, and perhaps she will leave it all behind for a word or a sign.

María Rides the Night

Consuelo knew she was afraid of heights, and knew she had been contaminated by Dolores's fear. She had less understanding of her fear of darkness.

She thought it had to do with María's death. María died running away from Lisandro. In his dotage, he had become convinced that she was trying to murder him. He accused her of poisoning his beer, of hiding a nail spiked with tetanus from horse dung in his *huaraches*, of attempting to smother him with her bosoms at night while he slept – the most laughable accusation, her little *masitas* hanging so pitifully after nourishing so many. His conviction and rancour grew so large that María was forced to flee the man she had slaved over for fifty-seven years. Her daughters hid her in their homes, passing her from hand to hand when the old *gallego*, now shaggy and mangy but still powerful, came roaring for her. *¡Cabrona!* he would bellow about a woman everyone else considered a saint. *Te voy a descuartizar.*

His threat to slaughter and quarter her proved unnecessary. She died of a stroke while hiding on the floor of a closet in her daughter Esperanza's house in Olvidados.

Consuelo dated her fear of the night to María's death, but she was kidding herself. It was older. It had been planted by Dolores and nourished by her own fears, had grown subterranean roots, and if it flowered at the time of María's death, that was not where it had begun.

But it was María, at the time of Consuelo's greatest need, who came to end it.

In the laundry room, in the depths of her despair, a memory came to Consuelo – dredged up by her, or perhaps sent by María. What was the difference? From the long ago she remembered sleeping under an open window in a *bohío* in María's embrace, María's hands holding hers, her smell like a perfume in her nose, her hair in her mouth.

The memory massaged her, soothed her, but did not settle her spirit as you might have expected. That evening, when Pedro stalked in reeking of rum and with *El Diario de las Américas* tucked under his arm, both exorbitant luxuries considering the cost of the ointment needed for Carlos's bottom, Consuelo spat so many insults at him in the course of a minute – about his mother and the circumstances of his birth, his lack of *cojones* and brains and his all-round smallness – that he left, spluttering as helplessly as a doused kitten. And later, alone in the tiny room with only Carlos and Ana, who had heard everything, as usual, she threw open the windows at night for the first time in many years and let in the cool breeze.

And realised, despite her agitation, that the night was friendly.

Sleeping a little less crowded on the mattress than usually, Consuelo was disturbed by strange creakings and shiftings in that place that had never known anything except the ghosts of washing machines. Flopping on the ticking, she dreamt of other nights, nights spent on a pine-needle mattress, and saw a flash of light in her sleep like lightning and dreamt of things she thought she had forgotten.

That is how María returned – riding the night air in a torrent of soothing memories. María, who had loved her. María, who had let her go but had now come back.

And she dreamt of El Caballero de París, who gave her bushels of flowers in her sleep, and of Pura la Puta, who had a *pirulí* in her still-smiling mouth and seemed to be wanting to embrace Consuelo, and even of the peanut vendor on the corner of the old tilting house, whom she had once thought was her father. And María was also there, always there, in the room, which at times seemed to be other rooms in other houses, but then again seemed to be this very room of her exile. And somewhere, on the outskirts of her dream, like a vague awareness, she dreamt of Daniel. Of course.

She woke at dawn, on a mattress dry for once, and she thought Ana and Carlos must have also slept sweetly. She noticed that the golden light streaming in was tinted with the perfume of gardenias and jasmine, although there were none nearby.

She woke thinking of Dolores, of how she had always controlled everyone's life, and narrowed it, and she realised that in this tiny room, in the wretchedness of exile, and even though she had Pedro to deal with, still, she was free of Dolores. For the first time in her life, Dolores was far away, she was free of her, and she was free to love.

And then she realised that she did love, that she had never loved so much. She loved her children. And she would always love Daniel, even when he was far away, as he was now.

It was as if a door had been temporarily opened, there, in that tiniest of houses. There was a doorway, and it led to other things.

No one ever saw her draw a curtain against the night again.

After almost a year, Pedro found work in a plaster factory. Consuelo went house-hunting. She settled on the biggest place they could afford, an old dairy in north-west Miami. She thought she had taken it because of the extra space the children would have, because of the overabundance of rooms they would enjoy after having been squeezed so hard in the laundry room. She chose to ignore her misgivings – that most of the rooms were senseless, that the house groaned and shook and babbled too much to be normal.

Actually, Consuelo did not so much choose the house as the house chose her. The house on 25th Street spoke to Consuelo, saw something of itself in Consuelo and invited her inside.

Shortly after the family moved to 25th Street, Dolores and Montero arrived in Miami.

Consuelo Stared South

This is when the photographs start.

I have seen fuzzy black and white photographs of Carlos and Ana visiting sad Marta, sitting in front of the fountain in the courtyard. Ana's fringe is brutally short, half an inch from her scalp. Her hair is pulled into many tight plaits and caught up in ribbons. The girls' dresses balloon around their knees. They all look well-cared for, and on the verge of crying.

Consuelo's face is cold, and hard, a rocky windswept place. The door had closed. Dolores was nearby. She had Consuelo in her grip once more. It was as if Consuelo knew, knew rightly, that Dolores would never relax it again.

There are small colour snapshots of Christmas 1963, that year Ana was four. Consuelo shopped at a Winn Dixie that gave out stamps, which she pasted into little books with a collector's lust. She redeemed the bulging books for toys.

Of course, the children knew nothing about the bulging books. In Cuba, the three wise kings – *los Reyes Magos* – had come on January 6; now Santa Claus came on December 25. Among all of the changes in their lives, this one did not perturb them.

The photos show the inside of the house on 25th Street, a red armchair stacked with dolls and a doll's house next to it and a teaset, and a little stove with miniature pots and pans – things Consuelo perhaps needed more than Ana. There is the blue plastic control panel of an aeroplane with buttons and dials for Carlos to twirl (but which can not fly them back to Cuba) and a red fire truck and a walking robot and a red fireman's hat on Carlos's nearly shaved head.

In this photograph, their smiles are less strained.

In the mornings, Consuelo combed Ana's hair and picked it up off her nape with rubber bands. She pulled the hair back grimly, gave the bands one too many twists. Ana was made miserable by the fire in her scalp. One day when Consuelo was talking to one of their new neighbours on 25th Street Ana ran up to her mother to complain.

Leave me alone, *hija*. I'm talking.

But Mami, Mami, it hurts, it hurts.

Leave me alone, *muchacha!*

Ana retreated in tears into the house. She looked in the mirror above her mother's dresser, tugging at the tourni-quets, until her eyes fell on a pair of scissors. They were long and silver and clever. Suddenly she realised she could solve her problem without bothering her mother. She cut at the tension, snipped it until it was gone, and then went outside, cheerfully, to play the long day.

What she had done was not discovered until that night, when Consuelo was undoing her plaits before bedtime. Ana sat on a stool in the kitchen. At first the curls wafting down like feathers amazed everybody. Then, as the locks of hair fell more rapidly and a bare patch near Ana's scalp emerged, Consuelo understood.

Her first blows knocked Ana off the stool. Then she hung on to her arm, hitting her on the face, the head, the back – an unleashing of fury.

When Consuelo later spoke about those years, it was usually in passing, about something trivial. For example, she often remarked that one must have extraordinary patience with young children. People used to say how incredibly patient I was, she would say. They would watch me with Carlitos, who could not be still for a single moment. He was so nervous, and he jumped constantly, was never quiet, ran into everything, broke everything. People would say, Señora, you have extraordinary patience.

It seems a great injustice that Carlos and Ana do not remember the many long hours and days and years of her patience. As Cubans say, *Hay que verlo para creerlo*. You have to be there, see it, to believe it. And even so, you have to be old enough to remember right. Because it was the other moments that seeded in their memories.

Sad Marta's mother Rosafina had trained as a nurse in Cuba. She worked at Jackson Memorial Hospital in Miami. The Santiagos said she was a nurse, but in fact she cleaned floors and toilets. She was the one who helped Consuelo get a night job at the hospital.

The work was simple, if arduous – it involved bedpans and changing soiled sheets and stepping in and out of Lysol. Consuelo did it because she had no other choice. Until the night a black woman – a very large lady – said to her, over and over, I wanna mo' mai bowels.

It was not a phrase Consuelo recognised. It was not in the books that Miss Douglas had used to teach her English – Dickens and the Brontës and even Lawrence. She looked at the woman in confusion.

There was urgency in the woman's voice. Mai bowels! I need to moo mai bowels!

Consuelo moved all sorts of things around the room, smiling and saying, Yes, this? And even straightened the woman's clothes, pulled and heaved at her to prop her up more. The poor woman never stopped complaining about her bowels, and Consuelo lost the job.

A week later she was working at the plaster factory and learning more about reptiles than she had ever wanted to know.

Sums scrawled on butcher's paper on a three-legged table have no way of giving optimistic news. Consuelo toted them up again and again, always getting the wrong answer, the one she didn't want.

Pedro was sitting in bed, fiercely flicking through *El Diario de las Américas*, grunting and flicking paper. He let it fall. Closed his eyes. Put his hand to his forehead. Sighed.

Something stirred in him. He knew he needed comfort. With nothing in his pants but the edge of his singlet and an empty wallet, something else stirred, auguring a moment's respite. He watched her adding figures irritably, yanking her hair behind her ears, and all he wanted was to put his head in her lap and feel her hand on his forehead.

No man whose mother died before he was ever held enough and called darling enough is likely to take such a risk. So he squatted on his haunches like a catcher and extended a hand to her shoulder.

Consuelo?

She glanced at him and went dark. Don't even think of it, she said. Don't even think of it.

It wasn't just that *he* was out there. She knew he was out there. The *invasión* had failed, was already known as the Bay of Pigs fiasco, and many had died and many more had been taken prisoner. The Cubans had been betrayed, Kennedy had lacked *cojones,* at the very least, and the planes that had been promised to the invaders had never materialised. The Cubans in Miami were spitting chips. But Consuelo felt Daniel was not dead, knew it in her bones. Beyond that, she had no idea where he was.

In fact, he was in a cage already, loving a lizard, engaged with it, holding on to it with the softest of touches. Because a lizard's tail will slip off as easily as a man can lose his sanity sitting in a dark stone cage six by two.

A lizard's tail slips off and even though it's still wiggling in your hand you know you've lost it and this is no lizard, only a dead tail.

He was there, but she didn't know it, and that wasn't why she told Pedro to think about something else. There are more ways than rocks and bars to make a prison, and Consuelo was in one of her own making.

She was trapped, and pacing, blinking in confusion and

sliding back her ears. Growling if Pedro came near.

Nothing in a cage will mate. It takes freedom to reproduce. Captivity is no aphrodisiac. Consuelo paced, and stared into the darkness, towards the sea. On dark nights she sometimes took a wrong turn trying to find the window, and got lost. She paced and snarled and bit at herself. And stared south, at her life, which was receding.

Daniel stared north.

PART FOUR

Remembering Paradise

That Giant Drum, Her Childhood Home

Ana has spent the cold nights this winter hanging on to the phone, her umbilicus to her mother. She rings doctors, wastes money listening to their secretaries' voices on answering machines. It's no use leaving a message; no one will ring the other side of the world.

Once in a while she gets through, and gets a small kick from telling the Cuban ladies on the other end that she is calling from Australia. Eh? What dit you say? they tell her, their voices rising in angry suspicion, and so she says it all to them again, this time in Spanish, in Cuban Spanish, like their own. And then they say, Okey. Jew wait, and then they call the doctor, and Ana hears when they say, I think iz a practical joke.

Ana hangs up the phone. She hears her own voice reverberating in her cold and cleanswept kitchen.

When Consuelo and Pedro arrived in Miami, they considered the streets deserted; they were tortured by their nostalgic longings for Cuban men loitering on corners, playing dominoes, *haciendo guardia* with their *socios* – marching up and down the street in front of their homes.

They missed women's voices calling out from balconies,

from behind half-dozing shutters, the strident, chummy, *confianzudo* clamour that was the sound of the living. That they were cut off from.

In this ambulatory death-dream, they drifted towards their compatriots, the other *exilados*, to huddle together around Calle Ocho, throwing scornful glances at the cold, mean and loveless American Life.

When we left home, Ana has heard Consuelo say, I found the heat unbearable. The sun baked us as we dragged you – poor creatures – up and down Miami looking for work, for food, for medicines, for a life.

But wasn't it just as hot in Cuba, Mami? It's even closer to the equator.

No. No, no. There, there was always a sea breeze. The sea breeze lured *los enamorados* – the lovers – along El Malecón.

Remember it is an island. It was a paradise.

Ana has moved further and further from paradise. Where she lives now, the air is thinner; the people are even more conspicuously absent from the streets.

So what does she do with her thin air, her depopulated life? She calls Miami during the night, and sleeps during the days. She wakes to find herself entwined in her dreams. She dreams of Miami, and of Cubans.

She dreams of the heavy, redolent air of the tropics. She dreams of white-hot streets with music in a *sssss*, *chi-chi-chi* rhythm crooning from loudspeakers over café stalls. She recalls the swooning smell of jasmine, and frangipani, and the aroma of *café cubano* percolating and stale *pastelitos de guayaba* and *lechón* roasting in a pit in a neighbour's back yard, and *arroz con pollo* cooked on the verandah of her childhood with beer – *una taza de Materva*, and half a cup of Budweiser as well.

She thinks of the heavy stillness of a Miami evening, the air on her bare shoulders a soft shawl.

Ana feels she is being kept from it. She is on the edge of a disappearing circle of water. It began when a stone was thrown into a relatively calm pond. The ripples from that revolution (whose ideals were soon murdered against stone walls) have left her washed up here, unable to rejoin her current.

But maybe it never had anything to do with the great gestures of our times, she thinks. Maybe it all started with a much smaller thing, something as small as an unwanted baby, something whose power lay in a bottomless rage, in an unfathomable quest, in the inscrutability of the past. Love withheld, affecting generations, scattering them to the corners of the earth, like so much dust. Sometimes Ana cries. And sometimes she is furious. And sometimes she is just confused, and, still, can't understand why.

In the place of Ana's exile, the winter rains are cold. The air is thin. The people are inside. And the rain doesn't stop.

Ana hears echoes. After twenty-five years, that giant drum, her childhood home, is sending out a message, speaking in the pounding rhythms of heartblood.

She hears it when she least expects it, in the shower, standing by the sink grating a carrot; she hears a call, the way her family called her when she was a child.

297

Ana María! Ana María!

At night, the calling continues. But along with the urgency, there is something else. There are oblique reminders of the things that chased her away. Half-forgotten voices crowd her dreams. Nostalgia and her love of Consuelo vie with the gloom of her childhood. Her sleep becomes congested, erratic, unrestful.

Last night she dreamt she was a girl, lying on her mother's bed in the house on 25th Street.

Ana's legs were open on the bed and she pulled something out from between them.

It was a child's small white toothbrush. It looked like her daughter's toothbrush, the daughter she had not yet had, except that time collapses in dreams. She wondered how the toothbrush had come to be inside of her. She must have forgot she put it there, she thought guiltily.

Then she pulled out broken pieces of popsicle sticks, with jagged wooden ends. Then globs of matted hair, the kind that need to be removed from around the shower drain. She scooped out handfuls from her vagina, amazed by it all, when suddenly she looked up, realising Abuela Dolores was watching her.

She slunk away to the bathroom to wash her hands.

Ana has kept the world of her childhood and her adulthood separate. Now the two are about to touch. How can she leave this world? Re-enter that one?

But over and above anything else, she hears her name being called.

Ana María! Ana María!

Her mother is sick, and she will go to her.

She pictures the house in March, in September, in December – it's all the same. She sees a suburban street with too few trees, too much asphalt, two lines of houses whose paint has been dulled by relentless, seasonless years. Always summer. Always humid. Always hot.

Ana María! *¿Donde estas?*

Consuelo Determined to Move, 1970

Consuelo reached over and snapped off the singer's love plaint. For a few seconds they sat in silence, staring at the house's low green fibreglass awnings, further darkened by mould. It was hot, they were tired, but they sat and looked. It wasn't just that two of the old Chevy's doors didn't open – they had always been able to stumble over window ledges into a house, to slide over hot seats to the car door that worked. They all lingered, as if arrested by something new in the house on 25th Street.

The house was surrounded by bushes; the hedge had grown taller than the front porch railing, and the ornamentals in front of the picture window reached the awning. The garden was taking over: it was neglected and too, too green but this wasn't what discomfited the family.

There was a dull brassy din of traffic at the other end of the street and the rare tit-switch of a neighbour's sprinkler. A group of black boys at the intersection three doors down were tossing a football and yelling things that might have had to do with their game or perhaps were disparaging comments about the Santiagos. Carlos never looked directly at them but Pedro gave them a stern glare. The boys kept laughing and rollicking and tossing the ball and stopping to stare with slack, unfriendly faces. They were not in the least intimidated by Pedro's glares.

Almost all the front yards were overgrown on 25th Street and the red trims had fallen off front porches. Where curlicued numerals wrought in iron once bragged the number of a house there was now only a shadow on a wall. It all looked very tired and although they did not notice, it made them tired. The radios now played soul and jazz, nothing that the Santiagos could dance to, let alone understand. Certainly not WQBA *La Cubanísima*. Elderly Cuban men no longer patrolled the street as if atoning for some military duty they had failed to perform in another life. The new neighbours bent their venetians slightly and dark faces peered but did not approach. *El comité de persianas* – the venetian blinds committee, muttered Dolores.

As the others unloaded groceries, Carlos wandered over to the side of the porch where there was a switch and several taps and a machine that he knew was a small motor. He could never resist tinkering with mechanical things and now he twirled a tap. It was something he had done regularly for years and nothing ever happened except in his imagination, where he was steering a shuttlecraft past Klingon destroyers. He was about to make the *putt-putt-putt* noise when he was surprised by the ground beneath him trembling slightly. The motor shook and spluttered but he was too interested to turn it off – he needed to know what would happen next, that was the sort of kid he was.

The front yard sprinkler squirted a stream of yellow water into Pedro's crotch, all over his well-pleated slacks, just as he stepped off the porch step for another armload of groceries.

He bellowed. He pulled Carlos up with one hand and smacked him with the other. The boys playing football stopped to gaze, cynical smirks all around.

Pedro beat his son in the front yard not just because he was incensed that Carlos hadn't been carrying things in, and not just because he was overstrained by the tensions of his life and not just because he was terrified of all mechanical things and couldn't remember what the landlord had said about the sprinklers all those years ago. He was also beating Carlos because their neighbourhood was changing, was becoming impossibly foreign and unfamiliar.

The house on 25th Street was tired. It wished it could twitch its mossy shoulders and shrug them off. Then they would go, like so many other Cubans, off to Hialeah, to Miami Lakes, to Kendall and North Shore, anywhere the ground was still raw because only lately sawgrass grew there. Raw ground offered a pretence of affluence. Sprinklers not only worked but were never turned off.

It had been seven years since they had walked into a staid house and made it lively. It had moved. Pounded with Pedro's cha-cha-cha music, gloomed over with Dolores's radio *novelas*. Heaved and bubbled with their rage, shuddered and shook, quaked at Pedro's step, rose with the sun and Ana's early morning hummings only to find itself hunkering down by mid-morning and flapping in the wind by evening. Too much living, too many lives lived all at the same time, too much of the past and too many memories in the attic. It had left the house old. Stiff. Crippled with arthritis.

By now nothing worked and nothing met and nothing fit. It came from all that heaving and living. No door met its jamb, no window could be shifted. Not a bolt could slide home.

The house wanted to see them go. It was weary, and wanted the memory of their backs to be the lasting one. Despite her years, all the rain on her roof, the cavernous attic and basement, she lacked wisdom. How could it be otherwise, when there were so many corridors that led nowhere, so much dead space, so many hollow walls? She did not realise how empty they would have left her. And – worse – she had no way of knowing that Ana would haunt her.

Consuelo decided to move. She complained that the land-lord never fixed anything. She cited the hopeless distribu-tion of rooms in the house, the wilfully wasteful spaces. They had to go.

While these complaints were reasonable, they were not her true motivation. Her real reasons she wanted to keep hidden from herself.

Consuelo's dreams had lately settled in the attic. She, too, had begun to roam the extra rooms upstairs. In her waking hours, on those rare occasions when she was alone in the house, voices whispered to her. They urged wild and wanton actions on her – that she leave Pedro, that she quit the reptile-infested office, that she run. They encouraged her to find the strength to be happy. Perhaps that strength could be had on an island in the Bahamas, or in Costa Rica, where politicians were benevolent, or even in the snows of New England? She was still good-looking, spoke two languages, had a fine mind. Perhaps there was a rich *americano* who could give her the things Pedro would never offer?

Perhaps, the voices hinted, Daniel was out there, waiting for her?

Despite the amiability of their advice, the voices scared her. It wasn't just the things they were saying: they were ideas she had always toyed with herself. They were the escape routes she never used, that heightened the poignancy, the exquisite sadness, of her life. It was the very fact that there was something up *there* that worried her so much. Consuelo did not want to learn more about life than she already knew.

She thought moving from 25th Street would silence the voices. In this she prefigured the mistake Ana would make ten years later. Ana and Consuelo did not realise that no amount of space, not city blocks nor even enduring mountains nor deep seas, can be sufficient barrier when it is the past that is pursuing you.

The sun streamed into the little bedroom at the back of the Hialeah house. It was to be Ana María's room. It had a bathroom; an ensuite was attached, not to the main bedroom at the front of the house which would be her parents' room, but here, tucked into her room, even though there was another bathroom just next door. And somehow Ana had been promised this room because the second bedroom was slightly bigger – just big enough to wedge in a bed for Dolores and a nightstand for her collection of medicines and a bed for Carlos, who had agreed to share with Abuela Dolores for the rest of his life. No one seemed to notice that his adolescence was around the corner.

The room belonged to a little girl and it had light pink walls and the ensuite bathroom was also tiled pink. There was a bed with a pink and white coverlet that looked like something from the Cuban bakery. On the bed sat a floppy clown and there was a goldfish bowl on the white dresser. It all looked fine. Ana stayed after everyone went on to inspect the rest of the house. She would also have a bed with a flounce around it and she would put her panda bear right there, on the pillow, like the little American girl had put her clown.

She looked out the large window behind the bed, and seeing the realtor outside with her family she moved quickly to the toy chest at the end of the bed.

It was empty.

She opened the closet but it only had a jacket on a hanger and a red velvet dress – very pretty, but not what she had expected. The shelves held no games and no toys. Ana managed to sneak a glance under the bed but that too was swept clean and now the family was moving back into the house, they were in the kitchen. Dolores called. She went.

Passing through the lounge room she saw a photograph on a table of a little blonde girl with a cheeky smile in pyjamas in front of a Christmas tree. A man behind her had his arms around her and his face turned away. Ana memorised the picture before moving on.

Everyone threw themselves into the task of saving for the move to Hialeah. Dolores pocketed small change and scattered it around for good luck and wealth. She wanted to leave the house and its attic and its disturbing presence which had long fought her for ascendancy and had proven a worthy foe. She tossed coins like corn to chickens. Copper and silver rolled behind sofas, chairs and dressers. Carlos and Ana wanted to leave just as desperately but they no longer put much faith in Dolores's powers. They tried to remember where the coins stopped so they could retrieve them later.

Dolores's friend Aída was staying with them. She had been pitched out of the house she had thought was home when Señora Ramírez became menopausal. Her hormones had compelled her to rid herself of her husband's mistress so she could re-establish relations with him. Aída was crying herself to sleep on the verandah of the house on 25th Street and trying to be useful during the day. She swept the floors and washed the children's clothes. Sensitive since her recent tango with Señora Ramírez, she neither brewed coffee for Pedro nor cleaned the matrimonial chamber. She compensated by zealously cleaning the bedroom Dolores still shared with Ana and Carlos.

Aída showed Ana how to sweep. She pointed the sharp end of the straw broom towards the door and swept in small tight motions. When she gave Ana the broom Ana swung it in joyous curves that rarely made contact with the floor. The red and black carpet on the floor was worn and the smells of too many people in one small room rose up in a cloud.

You'll have to clean your house for your husband one day, said Aída. She wore a tight skirt and a sleeveless knit blouse that showed the damp crinkled edge of her bra. Relative to the stout *cubanas* Ana knew, Aída was tall and slim and refined. But her hands were clammy and her nose almost always red. Her eyes shone like a seagull's.

Así que you will be a *señorita* soon. You have to be clean, very very clean.

She fixed Ana with a false smile. Ana did not smile. She was not a child to invite confidences from too many people other than Consuelo. That was enough.

Así que you will soon have your *quinces*. The boys will crowd around.

The mournful look that accompanied this remark seemed to say that to be at the centre of a huddle of boys was an unenviable situation.

Aída glanced nervously behind her, as if checking to make sure no one was listening.

A woman has to learn strength. You must pray a lot. Here, why don't you make a little place where you can pray, here in this corner? I'll show you.

Aída went to the coffee table in the living room. She plucked up a plaster figurine of *el Niño Jesús* with a crown of gold metal spiked into his painted curls and his legs kicking in the air. She carried him reverently. She knelt with a flourish in the corner and placed the plaster infant there.

307

She stood back, a finger on her lips, inspecting her work. Then she left again and came back with a crucifix, with Jesus now grown, suffering on the cross, and leant him against the wall behind the Baby Jesus.

You can kneel here every night – and in the day too, if you want. You can beg *la Virgen María* to make you pure and to forgive your sins.

Ana stared, her face smooth and expressionless. Aída faltered, smiled, then decided to continue.

Perhaps you will grow up to be a nun! Wouldn't that be wonderful?

Ana didn't answer. She was thinking of all the things she had overheard about Aída and the family she used to live with. She was thinking that Aída used to kiss a man who was someone else's husband, who was her friend Armandito's *papi*. She wanted Aída to take her perfumed scent away and leave her alone.

Aída finally got up from her knees and smoothed her skirt with her jewelled hands and said, I'll leave you alone now in case you want to pray. She smiled once more in that slightly uncertain and false way of hers. Ana waited only a second before gathering up the plaster Jesuses and carrying them back to the living room. She dumped them on the coffee table without trying to hide them from Aída.

Aída was not the only one aware that Ana was approaching womanhood. Dolores never seemed to forget it. She had always imagined she could see into the future – as if, never being able to recall the past with any clarity or judgement, she had somehow been compensated.

As often as not, these visions of the future came to her as she helped her afternoons slip past by taking a siesta. Sometimes Ana and Carlos toyed with her during these naps. They hid her dentures. There was often a strand of thread dangling from the corner of her mouth where she had bitten off her sewing thread before nodding off. Carlos would carefully pick it up and replace it with another thread he had tied to a lamp or to the dresser's leg. These games delighted Carlos. It was his way of tolerating and even enjoying Dolores, of making distance between himself and her. He would stand, looking at what he had done, bent over in helpless laughter.

Ana had more trouble manufacturing any distance between people. As soon as Aída found somewhere else to stay, Ana began to beg for a bed on the back verandah. And this despite the fact that both children had been infected by Dolores's fears. But Ana was reaching the stage where she disliked Dolores more than the night, or the spirits, or the presence in the attic. She had been doing battle with Dolores for six years, and felt ready to take on other things. Unlike Carlos, she felt little affection for Dolores. True, Dolores had always preferred the boy, but that wasn't the only reason why Carlos tolerated Dolores. He was tenderhearted and, like the other Santiagos, prone to inertia. It was not in Ana's nature to take things easy.

This Wednesday afternoon Dolores woke from her nap, sat up in bed, and called Ana. Her voice was alarmed, but it was an alarm which Ana knew and distrusted.

Ana María, come here, quickly! Quickly, daughter, you'll never believe what I have just witnessed!

Ana came reluctantly and slouched in the doorway.

I just had a vision, Dolores declared, crossing herself several times, clasping her hands to her chest and lifting her small brown eyes towards the ceiling.

I saw you, not this you, but the future you, *una mujer, Dios Santo!* I saw you matured, I didn't think I would live to see it, but I have, *gracias a Dios!* There you stood, as real as you are now! Did you see her, my son? She stood right there, at the foot of my bed.

I didn't see anything, Abuela, said Carlos.

How could you not see her? She was there, I tell you, solid as a miracle!

So I stood there. *¿Y qué?* said Ana.

¿Y qué? Daughter, don't be prosaic! I tell you it was a vision! A sacred thing! I saw the future, with these eyes! Your hair was piled on top of your head. You were a bride.

Dolores focussed beyond Ana, penetrating time instead of space.

You had on a beautiful gown. Lacy, soft, satiny . . .

Suddenly Dolores hardened. She remembered something: a bad smell.

But dirty. You never learned to keep your clothes clean. Your dress was filthy.

Beside you was your groom . . .

Her dark face, which she attributed to the equatorial sun – but it was almost certainly a genetic legacy, since she took such pains to deny this – had an intensely sour expression.

He was black, she spat out. No white man would have you.

Consuelo felt able to save for a deposit on the house in Hialeah because Pedro had got a promotion at the plaster factory. For the first time since their early years in Havana, she felt capable of optimism. First he had been the star pitcher of the baseball team sponsored by the factory. He had led the team to the top of *la liga cubana*. This victory had made him a hero at work, had lengthened his stride and deepened his voice, so that Maceo Pérez had noticed Pedro and promoted him to factory foreman. Maceo still kept snakes at the office, but his plaster business had prospered and he increased Pedro's wages. For a while life had looked good to Consuelo, despite the reptiles at work.

But she couldn't live too long like that. Consuelo had long ago acclimatised herself to despondency. If there was too much cheer in the house, if good luck seemed too sustained, she became jittery, uneasy, a caffeine addict without a *cortadito* at ten in the morning. She needed that bitter aftertaste.

And it was never long in coming. It began with Carlos. He had always been different – he had refused all sports, playing strange games instead, his butt between his haunches as he stirred an ant's nest or took apart a gadget. But as the neighbourhood changed, Carlos stood apart even more. The other boys on the street began to hound him, waited for him after school to beat him up. Carlos ran like a rabbit through the streets. When Pedro got home he accosted him. *Mariquita*, he bellowed. He demanded that Carlos stand up and fight the boys. Told him he was a boy who would grow up to be a girl.

But Carlos knew there were too few other Cubans left on 25th Street. His only chance lay in his speed. Pedro's frequent beatings did nothing to harden him and his taunts did not rankle as they were meant to.

Carlos fought Ana instead. They were the same size, of a similar strength, and could vent their frustrations on each other. They grappled in the barn like wrestlers. They pulled out tufts of hair, gave each other hot beaded bracelets, their arms in each other's mouths.

The Caldwells who lived at the corner and who all had round sheared heads and were slow at school called out Cuban spics! whenever any of the Santiagos passed by. Pedro would have liked to get out of his car and slap their faces for them and kick them in their *culos* until they rolled on the ground but he didn't dare and he couldn't speak to their parents either because he was ashamed of his English.

At school the teachers were middle-aged and matronly and worried about what the Cubans and the blacks were doing to their town. They were scared of the blacks and couldn't believe their impudence but the Cubans were sometimes worse, with their rude chatter that you couldn't understand in your own country and their loud clothes and louder radios. They were not pleased to see Carlos and Ana in their classrooms, even such well-behaved and bright children as Carlos and Ana did nothing to please them. If anything, the fact that the two did not conform to their prejudices was

312

even harder to handle, was quite disconcerting. When the boys scuffled in line and reached over to torment Carlos it was Carlos who was sent outside to run laps. Carlos ran in the unbearable heat of the middle of the day until the blood pounding in his temples was way too thin and tears mingled with the sweat in his eyes. The teacher forgot to end the punishment, and Carlos's migraine lasted for days.

Ana decided to show her teacher how bright she was, to dazzle her as she had once dazzled Miss Fuchs that first year at Fairweather. Her Sixth Grade teacher had her in the group with the slow readers and Ana knew this was wrong and waited for the teacher to realise it. When she didn't, after several weeks, Ana shyly took a book from home up to Mrs Stuart's desk. It may have been Dickens or perhaps Victor Hugo – it was certainly something Consuelo had enthused about at the Kennedy Library. Ana tried to explain that she was reading well and Mrs Stuart looked impatient and this discouraged Ana, and then Mrs Stuart pursed her lips and Ana faltered. And Mrs Stuart said sternly, I'm not interested in what you read at home. Just try to do a better job with your reading at school and see if you can learn to enunciate more clearly.

Ana knew what she meant. Whenever Ana's turn came to read aloud to the class, there was always some word like yellow which Ana would mispronounce as jello. It never failed to send the class into fits.

Mrs Stuart sent Ana back to her seat with the terrible sinking feeling that she had been trying to show off and she had got what she deserved. It was not until much later that she understood neither she, nor any of her family, were any longer welcome at the school or in the neighbourhood or even in the old house on 25th Street.

Pedro hammered on a baking Saturday afternoon. The hibiscus drooped and the ornamental bushes threw shiny splinters of light from too-glossy leaves. Everyone else was inside. Fans and the odd air-conditioner buzzed dozily but not Pedro. Pedro was hammering crates in anticipation of the move to Hialeah, sweating hatless as he nailed palings a friend had given him from an old fence. He was mocking the sun.

Consuelo was in her room with the venetians down and the curtains drawn. It infuriated her and ultimately exhausted her to think he was out there working on a day like this. He was trying to prove that they would still move to Hialeah, trying to negate the evidence she had just thrust under his nose.

Idiot, she had yelled at him, when once again the monthly figures didn't tally in her cheque book. You pathetic idiot, she had snarled. Look, she said, waving a handful of green dollars at him. There was 372 here two months ago, 372 *cocos*! But you knew what to do. You couldn't just wait and save like anyone with half a brain. Oh no. ¡*Los numeritos*! You can't keep your hands off *los numeritos*! *Dios mío*, you're an idiot.

No, no, he had said, wagging his finger. Ten dollars. Ten dollars is all I ever took. Anyone can lose ten dollars.

So where's the rest?

What do I know? You spent it. You spent it on your

314

books, you lunatic woman. You fill your head with shit and then come attack me.

They had squared off, staring at each other, until she spluttered in disbelief and frustration and threw the cheque book into the garbage can and went to her room to lie down. And now there he was, slaving under the sun, building crates that they did not need because she knew there would never be a new house. How could there be? She was tethered to an idiot. She was an idiot herself for having married him. She closed her eyes and tears slithered out the corners. She turned on her stomach and beat the pillow with a fist and wished herself dead.

Pedro nailed planks into sheets. He would show her. His luck would turn any day now and she would regret her words. And why shouldn't a man spend a bit of money now and then? Someone with his kind of luck, his kind of knowledge of numbers? Who was she to snarl at him, to insult him, to begrudge his spending the money he earnt, slaving all week like a *burro*, choking on plaster. Right now he could be lying inside, the fan directed at his bare chest and a Budweiser sweating on the floor by his hand. Dozing through a baseball game. A man's prerogative.

But it was Consuelo who slept. Each thud pierced her dream but didn't rouse her. Her dreams swirled, confused, bordering on wakefulness. Ebbing, plotless. They took in the children outside, the first skeins of a tangling. An argument. Voices rising, petulant as the day. Their shoves and thumps and shrieks of outrage a tiny moving holocaust that passed from the front to the back of the house. Past the papaya trees. Past the banana grove. Innocently heading for danger.

315

Mierda. Puñetera mierda.

She was awake then.

Stop it. Be still. *¡Coño!* You'll knock over my nails. Don't make me tell you again!

And then glass breaking. Pedro bellowing.

Damn kids! Now you'll see what are *cajitas de dulce de guayaba!*

And then new shrieks. A higher pitch. More forceful thumpings. Different thuds. Not a hammer on wood.

So. He needed a reason to come inside, thought Consuelo. *Qué cabrón.*

And that was my nap. My treat for the week.

Two hours later Pedro called for Carlos. He had gone back outside to admire his work. He had stood with a Budweiser in his hand in front of a litter of palings, surveying the half-finished crates, when a sudden realisation spread over him, singularly welcome news from on high.

Carlos's face was still streaked and the red handprints had not yet faded from his legs. He kept his distance. He was afraid he might start crying again. Pedro did not notice.

Carlos, come here, *mi socio.* I want you to do me a favour. It's something important. Just between us. *Hombre a hombre.* Can I trust you?

Carlos didn't dare look at him, trying, as always, to gauge the moment. He had already forgotten. Carlos also tried to forget, made a huge effort because Pedro was offering redemption. Perhaps if I do this thing for him well . . .

Can I trust you?

The boy squinted into the sun sinking behind Pedro's head, wiped his face with his sleeve and nodded. *Sí*, Papi.

Pedro looked towards the staring windows of the house. He drew the boy closer. He took his wallet from the seat of his pants, fished out some bills.

He spoke quietly. Do you know what this is? Twenty big ones. Twenty *cocos*. *Bueno*. This is what I want you to do. Ride your bicycle to Pipo's house. Give it to him. Tell him fifty-nine and forty-three. Can you remember that? Say it. Fifty-nine. Forty-three.

Let's see, where are you going to put it? No, not there! Don't be an imbecile. The minute you bend forward it will fall out.

Give it to Pipo. Go around to the back. Don't forget! Don't let me down!

No, Papi.

Bueno. Vete. Go.

The twenty *cocos* were, strictly speaking, Consuelo's money. Not even the money for the deposit, which he had already plowed through, but other money, a special cache that she had thought he didn't know about. It came out of her pay cheque, parings that she had been putting aside for Christmas. Three months of denying herself such things as whole underpants and *cafecitos* at work. It was only September, but Consuelo was looking ahead.

Pedro however was looking back. Remembering the time he had had the big win. Thinking of what he owed Pipo, and Cheo, and his other *socios*. Feeling lucky today. Or desperate enough.

Perhaps it had been the unusual Saturday exertion that

317

had purified him. Perhaps it was the children, who so often forced him to lose his patience. Perhaps her words still rang in his ears. Assaulting his manhood. Perhaps this was as close as he got to analysing the whys and wherefores of his actions. He was betting on forty-three, a box, and fifty-nine, a move. It seemed a sure thing. Of course. He was sending Carlos because *un fulano de tal*, some poor unfortunate, was arrested the other day at the house of another *banquero*. Pedro was keeping away, even though on any other day, for any other business, he would not have hesitated to visit his friend. But the numbers were *candela*. Pedro respected fire.

He watched Carlos drag his bicycle out of the barn and ride away. He scratched his crotch. With a little luck. It was a sure thing.

But the twenty *cocos* didn't grow. They evaporated into the hands of those who ran the lotteries, those who peddled that and other drugs, they fell like uncountable grains of sand into so many pockets through so many holes, and piff! – they were gone.

¡Qué fenómeno más grande! Pedro stared at his hands, and they seemed to him so *manzas y fuertes*, so strong and tame yet empty, and he shook his mane and wondered how he would tell Consuelo. Because now it came to him – as if he had not known before – that the money had been for the children's Christmas presents. It seemed incredible. Of course, he told himself, he hadn't known. Already he was furious, imagining her accusing. *¡Que mierda! ¡No comas mierda!* Of course I didn't know it was for them. Do you think I would have taken it if I knew it was their money? *¡No me jodas!*

And indeed she persisted in her accusations. You liar. You liar. Of course you knew. You weak imbecile. It's not you who does without *café* thrice daily. It's not you wearing rotten rags for underwear! It's me! she cried, pounding her chest with her palm. She thought about the worn diapers she still used monthly to save on sanitary pads, but hesitated to hurl them at him. Still they enraged her.

We've lost all hope of the house. You ruined it for us! But still you're pissing it into the wind. While I, I have to work *como una loca. Mira. Mira*, go away. Go away, *por Dios*, before I do or say something I regret.

And he went, he always did. He stormed out of the house, eyes blazing but head down. And she lay in bed and allowed herself to remember that most of the presents had already been bought. Well, how could she not? How could she leave it to the last minute, knowing how he squandered money on luck, on such a shiftless thing as chance, on *los numeritos*. And she heard her voice in her head, repeated to herself the things she had said to him, he said to her. None of it made her sorry. She would not apologise for a single word. What an infant he was! How tired she was! How had it all come to this?

She wondered if she would dream of Daniel tonight. She felt a pang at the thought. Perhaps we're both children, in different ways. Perhaps I'm destructive too. And then she let that go. And fell asleep. Eventually she dreamt of him. Daniel was eating a custard apple and teasingly spitting the pips at her.

She would not be getting the desk for her birthday in February after all, said Consuelo. It had been promised to Ana for years, for all her good report cards, and year after year it did not come. Ana did her homework on the floor in front of the fish tanks. Gravel dropped from fish mouths disturbed her concentration.

Ana made herself miserable thinking about the desk they had picked out, a French-style thing with curving legs and gold edges. Pedro, ashamed, borrowed five dollars from Cheo and bought Ana a handbag, blue vinyl, large and rectangular. It was an old lady's accessory and Ana could barely bring herself to kiss his cheek when he gave it to her, patting her head hopefully, asking forgiveness.

The bills knocked one against the other, faster than they could bring money home. Consuelo fought with Pedro over every cent. Dolores would saunter up when she heard their querulous tones, waiting grimly for their attention.

What do you want, *por Dios?* demanded Consuelo.

You know you can count on my money.

Pedro snorted, but Consuelo, never able to distance herself from Dolores, took the bait.

Por favor, Mami. Leave us alone. Don't come with your *mierda* right now.

She waved a packet of bills in the air. This is serious. She flicked them onto the bed. I need real money for this. Not your mendacious promises!

Dolores shrugged. As you like, she said, infuriatingly.

The bills spawned. Pedro drove the blue Chevy away and

came home with an even more beat-up station wagon and fifty dollars. He gave thirty to Consuelo and put the rest on hope, on eight and twelve, a sure thing, always, of that you can be sure, *sí señor*, some things you feel, here (a light hand on his heart). In March he drove away the station wagon with its stalled windows and itchy plastic seats. He came back with a different car and sixty dollars which Consuelo took, meeting him on the nature strip before he could pocket any of it for luck.

The new car was like nothing Ana had ever seen. It was black, a lustreless rusting black, and tiny, not large enough for four, let alone the required five. Now only one door opened and *all* the windows were paralysed, some half open so that rain poured in along with wind and sun. The seats were thin and the black upholstery marbled with mould where it was not split. It was twenty, thirty, maybe older. On rainy afternoons, when Pedro left the factory early to wait at the front of her school to save her getting wet, Ana wanted to bolt for a back door and run across the playing fields, dodging into alleyways and down the banks of canals, like in a nightmare. But she could not do it, and she got into the car next to him, water pouring in through the window, wishing she could ask him not to bother.

Pedro took the 'A. María' bracelet to a Coconut Grove pawnshop, along with Carlos's ring. He got a hundred and fifty dollars and bet on eight, the number for gold, and sixteen, twice the gold. He lost ten, lost twenty, lost every week until the jewellery was discovered missing, by which time there was not enough money in the house to recover it.

Pedro docile, Pedro ashamed, was given no quarter, not by Consuelo and not by Dolores and not much by Ana. Only Carlos. Carlos felt sorry for him, brought him a glass of water when he sat on the front porch, his hands between his knees. Here, Papi. Pedro grunted and took it, and then called him back and patted Carlos, clumsily, because the little boy was almost a man.

Carlos, you know I love you, don't you?

Sí, Papi.

Pedro's eyes filled. Carlos, I've done my best. And then the tears were spilling, his hand was covering his eyes, his shoulders shaking.

Sí, Papi. It's okay.

Carlos loved his father like never before. His was the only hand on Pedro's shoulder not shoving.

Pedro woke up in the middle of the night and shook his head in amazement. He put a hand to his cheek and discovered it wet.

He lay down again gingerly, hanging on to his dream. It was so rare to dream of his mother. She had appeared before him, walking across the sea, along a highway of sand and blue water. She was moving towards Miami from Key West. She was dressed as La Caridad del Cobre, the patron saint of Cuba, the guardian of fishermen, and that made sense because wasn't he drowning, wasn't he as low and despondent as you could get? Consuelo would not speak to him about the jewellery fiasco, but Dolores never missed an opportunity to hurl it at him, to taunt him with accusations

322

that he was stealing from his children what she had given them, their fortune, their only wealth. *Qué ladrón* – what a thief – what kept him from soiling himself in shame?

And he *was* ashamed, and desperate. He saw it as his duty to provide for his family and he saw himself as an honourable man, not a basher of women, not a drunk, not a womaniser; a good Catholic, and life was turning to diarrhoea all around him.

But she had seen his suffering, and had returned to him, appeared before him. Why are you worried, my son? she asked, and he said that his hands were empty and he feared he would have nothing to give his children.

Don't worry, my son. I will look after everything.

And he woke up knowing what he had to do. Tomorrow morning, the first thing, straight after his *café con leche* and his *pan con mantequilla*, he would go out and find Pipo. He knew what numbers he should play, he had never been surer. He would put thirty – no, sixty. No, if ever there was a time to go for it! He would put a hundred *cocos* on numbers that matched the day, month and year of her birth: sixteen, five and six. It was a sure thing. *Sí señor. Gracias, Señor. Gracias, madre.*

But still he had to wait a week before his money came in, before his numbers came up, and in the meantime Ana needed glasses.

When Ana closed one eye and looked up with the other, the bridge of her nose made a perfect egg-sized oval with her forehead. Close that eye and it didn't work – all she saw was a fuzziness of space, and a tiny triangle of nose in the lower corner.

Pedro took her to the optometrist in his clanking black beetle with its riven doors and glassless windows. There was a smell of petrol fumes in the car and of baking plastic and of rot, and also of fear. He had put everything – *todo, todo, todísimo* – on his faith, his knowledge, a vision of his mother as La Caridad del Cobre. How could he go wrong? That had been his feeling this morning but now it had evaporated like the dew and he was no longer so sure. No, no, of course I'm sure, but it's a lot of money, that's all. Of course I have faith, *madre mía*, don't punish me for lack of faith, no, banish the thought! *Sí, claro*, I have faith, how could anything be surer?

Ana sat beside him and knew he was worried. She knew he was defeated, he was sinking, but he was still there – terrified but hanging on. He was small in the corner of her field of vision. She did not speak to him.

He was holding her hand and she was four and he was going to buy her a chocolate bar. She was three and riding *caballito* on his knee. In her memory he patted her head as if she were the cat.

But she would not look at him. Pity could not erase the rest. And anyway it didn't matter that much. Not now. Not any more.

It was her. Him in her. In her chin. She saw his jowls in the curve of her cheek. She imagined she'd be a female version of him one day.

Once she wanted to take an axe to him. Now it was herself that she wanted to crack open, and let drop the viscous part, see the stale yolk splattering on the ground. Then pick up the shards – whatever's left, even if it's just a handful of crunched shell – and take them somewhere clean to try to make someone else.

But she can't. It can't be done.

That night, Pedro again dreamt of his mother. This time Doña Rosario was dressed as a Cuban dancer, she was doing a samba, frilly open sleeves ballooning around her.

But the samba costume was black, and although at first it seemed she was shaking her rear in a carefree dance he suddenly saw that she was actually wagging her finger at him. He awoke, sweating profusely in the cool milky dawn. The nightmare was too terrible to sustain. His pious mother, who never, ever, sambaed. Never, never, never. Her sacred memory. How could he dream such a thing?

And then, a worse knowledge. A darker nightmare. Suddenly he knew that he had screwed up, that he hadn't bet on the right numbers after all, that he had put his hundred dollars on sixteen, five and six, the anniversary of her death. *¡Qué fenómeno! ¡Dios mío, qué fenómeno!* How could he have done such a thing, forget her birthday, remember only her death day, confuse the two, *¡Qué fenómeno!* Everything his sacred mother ever said about him, everything Consuelo said, they were right, he was an idiot, a fool, unworthy of saving, and he sat up in bed, hitting his forehead with the palm of his hand, over and over, so that Consuelo woke up and laughed. When he would not stop, when she realised he was hurting himself, her laughter died. Feeling guilty, she tried to put her arms around him. But it was too late, it had been too long since the last time they had touched, too many years. He could not be comforted.

Ana was growing up in a concrete landscape, squares of grass dictated by asphalt, a flat congruity of square houses on square blocks.

She had never seen a stream. A meadow. A mountain. Woods.

Her images of these came from her earliest readers, when Jane went to the farm to see the lambs and to run. See Jane. See Jane run. Ana kept these naïve images. One day she would know a place like that – a real farmhouse set in green pastures. She would walk towards it and never turn back. See Ana run.

But right now she was in a darkened house searching for the light switch, for the windows, for the open door. To get out you had to go through a room where light had never penetrated. She edged along the threshold. A lip. A precipice. Before her was her life. She would leave the place of square houses. She waited to leap.

The house held her. It imprisoned her while it sheltered her. At night she dreamt about it.

Already she haunted it, in the way that all houses of unhappy childhoods are haunted. We return to them nightly. They have changed – now they are a luminous white, now they have two storeys, now there is a presence in the attic. Like real ruined houses, they have evolved, transformed themselves. We walk through vaguely familiar rooms. Voices echo in chambers. It is only when we wake that we recognise it. Our childhood home.

Daniel

It was a spring day or a fall day, or even winter because it was the tropics, after all. A cool, breezy, *wistful* day. The sort of day that called for clam chowder and spinach salad and beer bread, or, if you were from a different culture, *camarones enchilados* and a *guanabana* icecream. By the evening, walking along Miami Beach Pier with the water sloshing and creaming in the darkness underneath and a velvet sky falling above, Consuelo felt a full moon rising in her throat and moonshine swamping her chest.

Carlos at the legs of the pier, almost in the water, catching tiny crabs, scuttling on his own haunches in tight determination, head down.

A dozen different calypso beats combining to echo a heartbeat before drifting across the water.

Ana dreaming from pillar to post, singing tunelessly, happy as a drunken sailor in a white seaman's hat.

The fishermen settling in for the evening, and Pedro striding around, stopping abruptly to inspect buckets, a half-grunt, half-sneer as he dropped a lid.

Consuelo swinging her arms at her sides, thinking of a dress pattern for Ana who liked dressing up so much but hated to stand still for fittings, fought the pins, you would think they were torturing her. Thinking of that and trying to stop herself from thinking about the plaster factory tomorrow and her bastard boss's accounting methods and his perfidious promises and roaming hands, not to mention the roaming reptiles. Hard to know which were worse. No, drop that line and think about the sky.

Drawing up to the end of the pier where there was an office that issued fishing permits, or something of the sort. An employee sitting in front of a flickering black and white set with his feet on a desk that had seen too many fish on its laminex top. The news on. Consuelo stopping, first drawn by a voice, and then by something more abiding.

What I did was not so unusual. Hundreds of our people have gotten on rust buckets and tried to drift to the United States.

Even in English, in strongly accented English, even after the years, she knew the voice. Daniel, back. Daniel, there. She stood, her heart racing, everything else deferred. Incredulous.

Well, I felt I had to go back. If we want our land, we have to fight for it.

The camera moving closer, focussing. Daniel's eyes. Daniel beyond any doubt, and her hand goes out to the window, hangs on to sheer glass lest she swoon.

They suspended me from the ceiling. Like a lightbulb. When they beat you, your nerves receive such a shock you can't control yourself. The worst thing is to be denied the freedom to die. That's how they tortured me.

When she was sure the commentator's voice had moved on to something else, to a rampaging elephant fleeing its

328

keeper, Consuelo dropped to the floor, let her feet slide forward and her legs fold and dropped quietly. And stayed there for an hour, ignoring Ana's plea of *Vamos* Mami, Come on, get up, and Carlos's quiet, worried study of her, until Pedro strode up. *¿Qué te pasó*, Consuelo? Get up, *mujer, por Dios*.

I hadn't known, she thought. She had heard rumours but she had not known. Her life had gone on, that dreary treadmill she lumbered through each day, while he, he was being tortured. And she had not known, had not dreamt it, and if she had, had not remembered the nightmares in the morning. Had not heard his screams, or his moans, or his prayers – only the conflicting hearsay at street corners, names passed like illegal lottery tickets, whispered through calloused fingers. They have Daniel.

And so they had. And now here he is. Back. My God my God my God. He's here.

Driving home. For once not seeing the lights of the bay, the glittering necklaces tracing the causeways. She didn't hear Pedro declaiming. Didn't see Dolores's face turning bright red and didn't help her find her vaporiser. Chewing her nails, removing them methodically, each one left bloody whenever she managed to get a purchase on a bit of claw or skin. Devouring herself.

Pedro shook his head, muttered, She's losing it again. Pedro felt like shitting himself. He hated it when she went into one of her trances, when she ate herself *como una loca*. It prodded memories of his mother in her final days, when her mind slipped its moorings and went wandering, never to recognise him again. And he only ten.

By the time they were in bed that night, Consuelo had given herself enough Valium to sleep through a quick war. So she scarcely turned her head when Pedro, lying next to her, feet crossed at the ankles and his cigarette balanced on his protruding ribs, riffled *El Diario Las Américas* significantly, cleared his throat.

Oye, here's something on *un tal* Daniel Cancio. Remember him?

A low whistle that barely pierced her consciousness.

¡Coño! They had given him twenty-five years. *En cadenas*. And he escaped. *¡Coño!* No one escapes! *¡Qué fenómeno!*

And indeed, Daniel, having his third go at prison life, had known it was escape or die. Who knows why he chose the harder course. The one that had him baking on a disintegrating raft, dehydrating daily, watching his mate die inch by inch and himself losing so much lucidity that eventually he talked to the rotting corpse in front of him, talked to it for days, knowing how stubborn Manolo could be and believing that he was perversely ignoring him.

The raft rose and fell so many times that in the end there had been nothing left of it but two crossed planks. Daniel hung on to this as the sea devoured him slowly, playfully. Manolo resumed talking to him. It was Manolo who paddled at his side, who told him when to rest and when to move to keep himself warm; Manolo who kept telling him that he was, after all, drifting in the right direction. Manolo who, like a friendly dolphin, nudged him toward land and into the arms of the US Coast Guard. Who searched for his friend for two days, at

Daniel's insistence, until he recovered sufficiently to remember the rotting corpse.

He was the first man, outside my family, that I can remember thinking was handsome, so attractive that I was totally aware of him, drawn to stand close to him, to clamber onto his lap when Papi talked to him, and there to sit quietly, *contenta*.

He was a short man, barely my mother's height. He had straight hair that fell across his round forehead, rich, black hair – one of my mother's expressions comes to mind, 'as black as a poet's night'. I am not saying she referred to him in this way. I cannot recall her ever speaking of him at all.

I remember his voice as soft and melodious. I used to love to sit on this man's knee, although I was dimly aware that my mother did not want me to.

I wish I could remember more about him. I wish I could remember his name, although the name Daniel Cancio does not sound implausible.

I know he talked with Pedro about politics. I cannot remember Consuelo speaking to him, only her hand extending a *tacita de café* to him in someone's house – offered in a tiny, thin and exquisitely fragile cup. Her extended hand seems to quiver, in my memory.

I remember knowing that he was one of those Cuban men fighting to regain the island. I knew that Pedro was in awe of him, looked for him at Cheo's house, or Pipo's, at *la farmacia* Tres Apóstoles and at *la bodega*. Papi leaned towards him, put his arm around his shoulders, smacked him on the

331

back. Papi asked him to talk, pumped his handle. Pedro wanted to hear of his covert adventures combating Fidel, to gather, as every Cuban did, stories of young Cubans being trained in the jungles of Guatemala, of Panama, or south of here, in *los* Everglades, and of *invasiones* and *contra-revolución* and small acts of desperate heroism. To gather hope.

He never visited our house, although Pedro asked him often.

Now, with an adult's cynicism, I see Pedro also trying to gain something of the man's esteem among other Cubans through association.

But I am very uncharitable. I have to remind myself that Pedro was also suffering, that he was also thoroughly frightened and dispossessed and homesick, and yearning for his past.

I am six. I am eight. I am four, and the dress I am wearing is too short; my bloomers, plumped by rows of lace at the rear, show. We are at *la bodega*, I am tired. I want a *pastelito de guayaba* from the cafeteria. The man is there.

As I try to remember – and remembering seems very important now, now that I am casting back – it does seem to me that his name was Cancio. And if his name is slippery, at least his image is fixed and saturated with colour; I particularly recall the smooth blackness of his hair.

But is that what I really remember? Now it is hard to distinguish what I remember from what I have since imagined: the image conjured up by my mother's voice, an image of a man which materialised and took its place in my mind amongst my own lived history.

So now I believe it was Daniel.

Only the men speak. I do not recall the women even being present, except for myself, of course. But doubtlessly they were. How is it I could have been so unaware of my mother, of her feelings? How could I not see my florid and irrepressible grandmother? Where are the women? I cannot find them in this memory.

He hints, quietly, that he will be going back soon. There will be more missions. He will not rest until he regains the past.

(Here, does he glance, for the briefest second, at Consuelo? Or is the look conspicuous by its absence?)

In prison, says the man, I wrote in the dirt.

(Here he does not look up at my mother, in this scenario I am reconstructing).

In prison, I kept sane by taming a lizard, he says to my brother. The lizard became so trusting it would walk into my hand and rest quietly there.

I imagine a prison, a man in chains on a dirt floor, his body racked, his hand extended towards a small grey wrinkled lizard. I imagine him hiding the small stick he uses to write on the ground.

(Now I wonder: was he obsessed with a woman named Consuelo? And how many other prisoners would have scratched the sweet syllables of my mother's name into the stone of Cuba's prisons?

Consuelo: solace, comfort. Hope.)

Ana Imagined a Kind Stepfather

Dolores's stories dwindled. The children never asked for them. They stayed away. More and more Dolores's mind wandered, strayed into foreign gardens. Her edges were thickening. She dropped broad hints about inheritances, money that was somewhere, that only she knew about, that would make them rich when she died. The stories she told, when she rounded them up and compelled them to listen, had lofty purposes.

Respect your elders, she intoned, holding up a forefinger. God's commandment. Disobey and sell your soul to *Satanás*.

Ana was eating bright pink guava cups which Dolores had cooked in sugar until they were tissue-soft and served with warm cream cheese for the children's after-school tea, the years of the swirling black *potaje* finally over. Ana tried to think of something sufficiently disrespectful to say.

Carlos was more straightforward. I'm an atheist, Abuela. He savoured the vowels in the word *ateo*.

So what? God expects you to obey him anyway. Don't you breathe his air, metabolise his food? *Mira, hijo*, I'm not long for this world. Let me instruct you. I have lived long. Known many things.

Carlos listened in mock respect, enjoying the old charade. Ana sighed and pretended to read the book at her elbow.

I knew a woman once whose father almost killed her for disrespect. He held her over a bridge by her ankles and threatened to drop her into the water below. She was only eight. By the ankles, here, like this. Twelve metres, nothing less. People heard her shrieks. They came running. They called the man a savage. Took the girl away.

Was she adopted?

Someone took care of her. But that's neither here nor there. *Oyeme bien*, pay heed, my point is this: she never stopped loving her father. Never. Never.

Ana looked at Dolores. A thought came to her, a revelation, and she was quick with it.

That happened to you! she exclaimed.

Dolores was stunned for a second. She had so many stories, it was hard to know which had happened to her and which were merely stories which belonged to her. She had always been a victim, things had conspired against her, life had it in for her, of this she was convinced, and the stories of her victimhood which she told herself were different from the ones she told other people. Perhaps the child was right. Perhaps that had been Lisandro, her ankles. A fast-moving river, another life.

But there was a danger there. No, no, it wasn't me, she said, a door banging shut. She never trusted the girl. Not Ana. Loved her, but never trusted her.

335

It was another – a girl I knew. Not me!

Carlos plied her with questions. Who took her home? Did the police arrest the father? Did he go to prison? Why not? And what sort of house did she go to live at? Was it better than her old house? Did they give her toys?

Dolores tired of the questions, gave short answers and then dried up altogether. They were on the wrong track.

If you grow up with a feeling, you get to know it, can recognise it even by its smell, and can anticipate it many years before you ever have a name for it. Ana imagined a kind stepfather. A nervous man, who chewed his nails to the quick, whose eyes could get no purchase on your face when he spoke to you and always slid down. His skin was pitted by the ravages of a too-sensitive adolescence and his seat pants sagged. And the rescued girl rarely touched him – he was too skittish for that – but she basked in his sweetness.

And she would have grown up – this saved person – not bitter over the loss of her real parents but with a wordless, a boundless, an almost quivering, sensitivity, because of her stepfather. At an early age she would have understood, thought Ana, certain complexities, and she would not have been glib, or resentful, or awkward.

She would have been steeped in gentleness, having seen its other side. She would have clothed herself in it. She would have been permanently transformed.

As Ana felt herself to be – by her father's rage.

Sometimes Ana's dreams changed, like a record turned to the other side. Sometimes she didn't dream about their old farmhouse and the evil in the attic, or of the child buried in the back yard, or even of falling from bridges. Then she dreamt of the little blonde American girl who used to live in the bedroom of the house in Hialeah which they almost bought. The girl lives with a woman who is not her mother. The woman does not love her.

The girl has no toys and the clown and the bedspread and the goldfish are her stepmother's tricks to fool visitors into believing the child is happy. The child lies in her pyjamas all day long in her bed and is sick and unhappy.

Ana awakes from her dreams drunk with sorrow, a sadness like a heavy weight oppressing her and the dreams cobwebbing her days.

The Santiagos tried to leave their old house for a house that was young and small and clean. But it had not been young enough; it too had had ghosts, which hitched a ride with Ana.

Now they lean over Ana's fold-up bed and whisper their stories to her.

An Incredible Phenomenon

My father began dropping plaster effigies during my fifteenth year. They slipped through his hands as if greased. After all his years of service, he was fired.

It was a terrible blow to his self-esteem – a real *golpe de estado*. *¡Qué fenómeno más grande!* And it was absolutely unbearable that Maceo Pérez – *ese Ache-Pe*, that SOB – had retained Consuelo in the factory office while firing Pedro. Pedro and Consuelo would have very much liked to be able to afford for Consuelo to quit. Pedro was desperate to tell Maceo to stuff the job along with his pet snakes up his *culo*. But there was the rent to pay and too many bills and they had known dire poverty in their childhoods and far from strengthening them, it had left them scared.

It is an evil myth that the bad things that happen in your childhood strengthen you. They never do.

A Baby Has Plans

Consuelo had hoped for something better, and being who she was she had identified that something better as a life among Anglos in the slightly more affluent suburb of Hialeah. It did not enter her mind to want to move to south-west Miami where Cubans had established a strong-hold and were leeching towards Coral Gables. She was such an unlikely Cuban – she had been an outsider for so long – that she was free to come and go. But she had wanted to run, from people who spoke her language and knew her history and perhaps knew more about it than she did. But when Pedro lost his job after all the other losses on *los numeritos* she finally understood that there would be no escape from the house on 25th Street. That no matter what, Pedro would keep them there – Buried up to our necks in your shit, she told him.

She relinquished her dream. There was a certain perverse joy in it. There was no use saving anything. This realisation freed her. She need no longer bank on hope, a thing alien to her nature. It was as if something had been held taut in her for months – optimism – and now she released it, and it snapped around her ankles and she sighed. She relaxed,

339

and then went one further. She searched out despondency. She courted disaster.

She found her wallet and took their meagre expendable wealth and, against all logic, went shopping at the new mall that had just opened at the end of Forty-ninth Street.

At Northland she bought things for the house. She bought cheap things – plastic tables and rugs that went bald within weeks and ugly lamps with rococo curls at their waists. When she took these things back to the house on 25th Street they all looked good for a few days and then they stopped looking good and looked cheap and ugly. And then their bad moods returned – Pedro was knocking on doors that would not open enough for him to even put his hand over the threshold and too many of his former *socios* were demonstrating a lack of respect. As he watched his luck dribble through his fingers Pedro tried to snatch it back by betting on the meaning of numbers again. He played thirty-seven, a star, because for a while he had been *campeón* of the league, and he played twenty-five for a storm passing overhead, but the numbers didn't come up. The money they kept in the cigar tin under the bed dwindled dangerously and Consuelo had more trouble balancing the cheque book. Now it was *arroz con maíz* three times a week.

Ana, sleeping alone finally in the curtained-off part of the back verandah, started to wet herself again even though she really was almost *una señorita*. Carlos began rising from his bed in the quietest part of the night and bumping into furniture while trying to evade boys. The cheap objects in the house mocked them and caused

Pedro and Consuelo to seize them suddenly and hurl them at each other. What they did not dash against the walls they set out on the nature strip on Monday morning to be collected.

The next weekend they went shopping for a new set of props. They changed the props regularly. When prints of Yosemite waterfalls with sappy bits of Desiderata failed to bring wisdom to the house, they tried a rustic cowboy look. Consuelo threw out the chenille bedspread where Ana had harvested so much fluff while pining for her mother. She returned from Jackson Byrons with a quilt and matching sheets in mustard yellow and hot orange, a repeating pattern of thrusting cacti in an arid desert. Finally they reverted to a Spanish look. The plaster Jesus that had never before been ousted from the coffee table lost his place to a pair of Spanish *bailarinas* stamping a *flamenco*, their hands thrown back proudly, their backs arched so that Ana wanted to strip the male dancer of his glued pants to see what was causing the bulge below his waist. Angels succumbed to bullfighters over the stereo cabinet. When all the money they had saved for the deposit was gone they were left with the Spanish decor. It was as if, after much jostling, they had managed to find something meaningful. The mustard desert and the thrusting cacti stayed on Consuelo's bed. This she never thew out, for the rest of her life.

Outside, the scenery changed and changed again, new families came and left, each wave progressively darker, and Ana began to play with Paula, a Jamaican child from a poor and troubled family, feeling both their houses were uncomfortable in similar ways. Because despite the changing props, the lines spoken in the house on 25th Street always stayed the same.

Consuelo stewed in a bathtub rimmed with mould. Green-grey slime flourished in the twin rails of the sliding door. It overflowed. It contaminated the slits above the taps. It spread up the tiles, crawling on soft plaster, inching forward, cancerous. She never noticed.

The purple-tiled walls were also hairy. Pedro was shedding. Consuelo too. Their short dark hairs curled on the tiles. No one wiped them.

Consuelo hummed bits of songs. She couldn't remember the words. She couldn't finish anything, couldn't connect. Words images songs memories and things she would have to do tomorrow passed through her mind like meteorites. She forgot to use the soap. She pulled herself out of the bath by hanging onto the spigot. Water sluiced off and swamped the floor. She threw on a greying housedress. She lay down, looked at the ceiling. Somewhere the television evening news was on. Happy was howling outside. Dolores was thumping in the kitchen. Someone was crying. Ana. Consuelo was asleep.

In the dawn, as the first birds called each other across the tufted lawns, Consuelo washed dew off the ancient black beetle because the windscreen wipers didn't work. She held the hose limply in her hand. She drove off. Ana heard the engine, whirring, clanking, catching. Building up, receding, then purring hard again as if suddenly closer, before disappearing into a distant quietness.

Ana felt a pang of envy. Perhaps Consuelo was making

good her escape. The world out there was new this morning, the horizons farther than ever. There was also the melancholy of being left. It always tightened her up into herself, any car speeding away, no matter how irrelevant. But above all there was the moment's reprieve. She herself didn't have to face the day yet. She curled under the thin blanket. There was a refuge. She held the minutes. Sixty. A hundred if she stretched it. She stretched it. She poured them out slowly, one at a time.

The marine life was disappearing from the salt-water aquariums. Carlos still went down to Mr Christie's and bought seahorses but they were only around for a couple of days before they disappeared. Carlos scoured the floor under the tanks and lifted up the curtains and tried to work out how the seahorses could jump out despite the hood that covered the tanks for lighting and to prevent evaporation. And then the little red-eared turtles that Ana María had always kept in a bowl also went and so did the clownfish and the angelfish and even the shells of the hermit crabs were found empty. No one could understand it and it seemed as if it should be a bad sign, as though the animals sensed impending disaster, but Dolores did not read it like that. Dolores said the cat was to blame and took it all with an equanimity that should have made everyone suspicious.

Consuelo drove home white-knuckled through the late afternoon heat, part of the sullen hungry snake of cars on

South Dixie Highway. After a glum meal and the dishes and the next day's lunches and Ana's spelling list she wandered through the house, searching for peace.

In this quest she gulped two Librium and lay down, and looked at her nails.

Having chewed her fingers in the early years with Dolores she would never be one of those people who unwind by meticulous attention to their hands. She had given up devouring them but still clipped them fiercely at times, and gnawed them when driven by anxiety. Something had been cut back in her – she had been raised by María and then handled by Dolores – and she could not totally relinquish the habit of pruning hard.

So she relaxed by removing things – clipping cuticles and snipping at her corners, tweezing hairs and forcing them out. In this mood she also went to the toilet and sat for several minutes. Nothing helped.

She glided through the house, muttering as she stepped over Ana's strewn books, looking darkly at Pedro's shoes left to air near the front door. There was something she craved at the end of a day – some recompense for her daily unselfishness, the lack in her grinding days. She wanted a spark – more than a *dulce de leche* from the Cuban bakery, more even than a good movement on the toilet. Some couples make love at night, but that was not what she wanted. No, not that! Not when she looked at his shoes. Not when she saw the petulant look on his face as he stared at the television, one hand in his lap ready to scratch. No, not even the drums and the unrelenting rhythm of the music her neighbours played – loud – could make it *that*. That was not the thing that would release her.

But every night she made the rounds of the house, prowling like one of the cats, and never did she find the moment's pleasure that justified the day, that filled her or touched her at all. Not once.

Her desires were as old as her habits, and had everything to do with running to the corner through ringing afternoons to look at him and see if today he would give her more than a *pirulí* – if today he would give her a father, and with it, a name, acceptance and the filling of that tugging void. But what had always gripped her behind the hibiscus and held her there was another girl, a child not much older or younger than herself. It was his daughter, who had every right to sit on his knee, and if her nose was hooked and her face unwashed, still she was lovable and beloved on his knee, and that was the hand that came from the wall next to the hibiscus and stayed her, scooped her empty and left her like that.

When she opened the door and found a suited man in a humble smile and two older women in recent perms collecting for charity, Consuelo said, No thank you, the words falling like brown pebbles into a bowl of water. She did not give to anyone. Not to the women at the office at Christmas, not to charities, not to Pedro. Her void was too deep, her memories too blighted. She never doubted that she had nothing to give.

The neighbourhood became poorer. The bulldog woman next door sold her house and the new owner rented it to several families, all living in the space that one fat white

American had previously occupied. The schools couldn't handle the influx. Ana's junior high became the second most overcrowded school in the nation. Consuelo dropped her off at seven in total darkness before driving on to the plaster factory. Ana stayed at school until noon and then walked home, passing the Seventh-graders who were just beginning their day.

When she got home she opened the refrigerator and began to eat. She ate anything that was readily available – cakes disappeared under her flying hands and so did last night's leftover *picadillo*, and if any icecream was in the freezer it was demolished spoonful by spoonful.

Then Ana took out the loaf of *pan americano* and broke several slices into a deep bowl and took out the carton of eggs and broke half a dozen and threw away the whites. The yolks she stirred with sugar into the bread. It reminded her of the marzipan fruit Pedro used to buy her from the Cuban *dulcerías* when she was a child and of the *pudines de pan* she used to help her mother make. And then, reeling with food, her stomach distended so that she looked six months pregnant, she lay down to sleep away the afternoon. Food was a sedative.

She was roused in the late afternoon by the sound of Dolores's ravings. Dolores sat in the red plush armchair. She screeched at Pedro. She still looked imperious but she was beset by her past, she was being driven crazy by the voices in her head, and day and night she demanded operations. She declared that she needed surgery, right now, this minute. She demanded to be taken to hospital, screamed that if he wouldn't take her she would call an ambulance herself, Here I go!

Screw the cost, she hissed to her son-in-law. And screw you too! Here I am, *una viejita*, dying, and you, *hijo de puta*, are counting pennies. *Me cago en ti* – I shit on you.

That's it, she cried, pounding the armrest. I'm writing you out of Consuelo's inheritance!

Don't eat shit, muttered Pedro, half intrigued by her persistent talk of Consuelo's elusive wealth.

It's you that will be eating shit! You thought when you came sniffing around Consuelo that she was common, like you. Well, she's not, I tell you. She has an inheritance! A fine inheritance. Millions, squillions, *cabrón*! You have no idea, *bruto*! No idea, no idea, no idea!

When Pedro stormed out of the house, frenzied by her untenable promises and her unveiled threats, Dolores put her face out the back door and called to the family across the alley, the only other Cubans now. The Santiagos hated them because they caught the ducks that wandered off the canals and fattened them in cages in their back yard and then feasted on them.

Ondina! Ondina, hurry, I am dying, *socorro*! Call an ambulance! *Este hijo de puta* that is my son-in-law is killing me!

Ondina never responded, if she ever heard. They were no more friendly with their only remaining Cuban neighbours than with the Anglos. Pedro raced out of the house to escape the *loca* that squatted inside, but Ana stayed trapped, trying to do her homework in front of the fish tanks and picking at her pimples and watching her waist thicken as Dolores bellowed and screamed.

Carlos was also trapped. He was sixteen years old and

still sleeping in the same room as Dolores. He and Dolores protected each other from their mutual fears of the dark.

He was still being bullied by Pedro. Carlos was loyal, and unwilling to attack Pedro, but it did him no good. Pedro spent most of the month languid, despairing and hopeless and meek, but as Consuelo's payday drew near he became irascible, struggling with himself to give up the numbers, yet arguing that one good win was all they needed, would be their salvation; that bad luck could only walk with you so far. To take Consuelo's money, to play with it and risk losing it, he needed to work himself into a fever-pitch of fury, into a righteous indignation like a reawakened volcano.

Ana had learned to goad Pedro, to challenge him when he was in one of his rages. When he lifted his hand to hit her she said, Yes, that's right, hit a woman! You're having a bad day, a bad year, a bad life – go ahead, take it out on me. She did not flinch, did not cry, did not take her eyes off his face. The look in them astonished Pedro and he could not believe her words. His hand wilted like a man's passion and he stopped hitting her so that he would not have to hear her challenges. He roared that she was twisted and told her that she was as ugly and insane as her Abuela Dolores, that they both had the same horse-face and were both impossible. Then he walked away.

But Carlos still flinched when he roared, still made to run when his hand snaked out. Carlos was thin and not quite as tall as Pedro and he was gentle, gentle and noble, and he infuriated Pedro beyond endurance – drove him *fuera de quicio* – each time he flinched. Pedro could not allow anything in his son that had been denied him, because that would have touched his deepest pain. To keep it buried he had to repeat what had been done to him. Any weakness, any misdemeanour, any infraction had to be punished severely, any gentleness squashed. He had to make him a man. He had to beat Carlos, for the sake of young Pedro who had once been beaten by his parents.

Carlos was trapped in that tiny bedroom with his grandmother. At night they shared the same stale air and she was there a foot and a half from him when he woke in the mornings with wet sheets and an erection, because despite what Pedro said – or perhaps in spite of Pedro – there was absolutely nothing unusual about Carlos.

But when Dolores spread her bloomers over his school books or shoved his model of the starship USS *Enterprise* onto the floor to make room for a new haul of medicines from the pharmacist, it was all Carlos could do to keep from screaming at her. But he would not scream, he did not believe in violence, he longed for self-control despite all provocation, so instead he clamped down on his exasperation. He took his hand to his mouth and bit down on himself and in time a callus appeared on his hand. He was very ashamed of the callus and always tried to hide it. It was the nature of the family and the bad time they were living through that he was ridiculed for this as well.

Dolores tried a new tactic to get herself hospitalised. She declared that she had lost control of her bowels and looked for the best times for this loss to manifest itself. It happened as often as not in the kitchen, when she would grab whatever cooking utensil was handy. And then she left a turd in the hallway when one of Pedro's *socios* was visiting, but she knew she was playing with fire. She stayed in her room and complained feebly that she could not clean up after herself because she was too weak and was in dire need of hospital care.

It was too much – too much madness, too revolting, too ludicrous and embarrassing – and the family rounded on her, the whole team clotted around her and screamed that she *would* clean it up and she could make the three steps to the toilet and this simply was not on, Señora!

But she had broken the family's will; the family was reeling and staggering and soon after that Dolores was admitted to the Mercy. There, in the course of some exploratory surgery, her heart stopped beating, and by the time she was revived her mind was changed.

After a week in intensive care the hospital staff could not stand her curses, and they sent her home attached to a cylinder of oxygen and with the chaos in her mind set loose. She insisted that she was being watched through the television screen, that the air-conditioner spewed poison fumes and that Ana María was sneaking drugs into her food. She talked of the inheritance non-stop, her eyes blazing, forefinger wagging. But where is this money? demanded Consuelo. Tell me, where is it? I need it to pay your hospital bills. We can't wait for your death! I need it now!

It was the only thing that could make Dolores shut up.

Now she really could not make it to the toilet, and Ana María and Carlos when they came home, and even Pedro – because Consuelo was at work all day – carried bedpans for her and changed her bed. The family fed her mush and had the pleasure of having it spat back in their faces when she declared it was poisoned. Life in the house on 25th Street had again become impossible.

Ana stood in front of the refrigerator, her hands moving like a harvester's. Consuelo came home raw-nerved to find the eggs that were to have made a *tortilla* for the family's dinner had disappeared, along with the leftover *dulces* and the half-gallon of milk, the two mangos and the slightly stale bread. *¡Puerca!* she screamed. Pig, cow! she screamed. *Estás obesa*, she yelled – you are becoming obese.

Ana believed it. Believed it all.

Ana did not see that, in her penchant for self-punishment, she was like Consuelo and Dolores. She did not see anything at all.

Ana was changing Dolores's sheets, trying to get at the corners in the narrow confines of the bedroom and thinking that Abuela looked more than ever like the witches in her stories. She had gone into hospital a stout woman, agile and strong, and had come out a wizened crone.

Dolores had hurled her dentures in rage at the family so many times lately that the teeth were cracked and useless. They now sat quietly next to her while she raved gummily from the other bed. She had just finished talking to her friend Aída on the telephone. Aída had discovered the Jehovah's Witnesses and found solace in their midst, as well as a tiny apartment in a converted garage that she rented for next to nothing from a Jehovah's Witness family. Aída felt better now that she was in a place where *el* Señor Ramírez, were he so inclined, could visit her. She wanted to convert Dolores to her new-found faith. Her influence was already evident in Dolores's ravings.

Hija, I'm dying. Soon I will be in Heaven with the angels of Jehovah. But you look more like a *puta* everyday!

Dolores examined Ana María's waistline with a beady eye and asked directly, Have you gotten yourself pregnant?

Ana would have seethed at the irony of the question were it not for what her fingers had discovered in the pillow in her hands. She believed she was so ugly that no boy could stand the sight of her. Sometimes she harvested the fridge but more often she starved herself. She was starting to waste away, just like Dolores, but when Ana looked in the mirror she saw fat. Dolores saw the curves of a pregnancy and Ana saw fat and neither realised how similarly skewed their vision was. Ana didn't have a boyfriend and she didn't think she ever would, but her fingers had found a hard lumpy ridge running all along the hem of Dolores's pillowcase.

She walked away with the pillow, ignoring Abuela's screeches to come back here with that, *demonia.* Ondina, *esta desgraciada chiquilla* is robbing me, she yelled towards the window, but Ana took a pair of scissors from the kitchen, picked at the crude sewing along the hem until the pillowcase opened to reveal the desiccated corpses of the marine animals that had gone missing last summer. There, along the edge of the pillow, Dolores had sewn the seahorses, tail to snout, and the empty little shells of the red-eared turtles and the remains of the clownfish. Ana

352

threw it all down in disgust and ran out of the madhouse to the refuge of the John F. Kennedy library.

Cheo's daughter Rosa was celebrating her fifteenth birthday – her *quinces*. It was a low-key affair in the back yard of their house in East Hialeah, with no more than a hundred guests and dozens of little white-clothed tables scattered under the mango trees. Carlos was bored and would not dance. Pedro was holding forth on the political situation in Cuba with a group of old men. Ana wandered on the outskirts of the party, in places where the spotlights did not reach. She was sure her white polyester party dress, sewn by Consuelo before Ana had stopped eating, made her look fat. A pimple on her forehead throbbed like a beacon.

She was friendly with Rosa. They were the only two Cuban girls in the Dade County Gifted Students program and they had been able to overcome the hurdle of knowing each other since childhood and had become friends. Ana watched Rosa dance with Cheo on a platform lit by spotlights and moonglow.

Rosa was having a Napoleon Bonaparte craze. While Ana read Steinbeck and the poems of Rainer Maria Rilke, Rosa carried a thick, cheap novel about Napoleon everywhere she went. Ana once asked Rosa what she saw in it and Rosa answered simply that Napoleon reminded her of her father.

Ana could not understand her friend's naïvité. How could she compare her grocer father to Napoleon, for God's sake? It bothered Ana a lot. How could Rosa say such a thing without embarrassment? It was even somewhat sickening.

Ana felt superior. She watched Rosa dance turn after turn with her little Napoleon. Both Rosa and Cheo were round and squat and swarthy and danced with abandon. They stamped and twirled and shook their hips like lovers. Ana couldn't do any of that. She wouldn't have minded dancing with her father if he were interested but he was over there *descargando* – flushing the toilet, as Consuelo called his diatribes – and Ana wondered if he even knew he had a daughter. She herself had not had a *quinces* party. Music was not played in the house on 25th Street any more and no one in the Santiago family danced.

Ana was curled up, naked, on the floor of the purple-tiled bathroom. There was vomit spattered on the floor and vomit on her cheek drying like a chunky glaze. She had cried for so long that she had fallen asleep on the moist cool tiles. She had not eaten for three days – she had been so good – but she could not resist a spoonful of the pecan ice-cream Pedro had bought at La Vaquita and then she had felt so bad that she needed to punish herself. So she ate the whole carton and left it in the freezer with only a crust of icecream in one corner. And then she ate almost everything else in the refrigerator.

Consuelo studied the pattern of swirling cement on the bedroom ceiling. She had given up sleeping. She left for work before it was light and returned at dusk to cook the family meal and look after Dolores and listen to her raving because she wanted to be hospitalised again. There was something wrong with Ana, but then adolescence was always difficult and Ana was a strong girl. Consuelo felt herself to be nearing the end of her tether with the strain of keeping the whole madhouse afloat. Perhaps if she could save some money they could convert the garage into a unit for Dolores and then perhaps there would be some peace. Her fights with Pedro were becoming more rancorous and they had not spoken to one another for three weeks. Consuelo's face had a perpetually hard, strained look, as if she badly needed to cry. But Consuelo did not cry. She worked, and at the end of the day she lay on her half of the bed with the lights off and stared at the ceiling.

Things broke down in the house and were never fixed. The house absorbed their angers, and had learned to loathe itself. Nothing looked right, no piece of furniture was comfortable, and even though Consuelo cleaned, and Ana when she was not too desperate, and even Dolores sometimes tottered around with a rag, it never really smelled good. It smelled of stagnant rainwater, of which there was a lot, and of old smoke from damp smouldering fires and of unwashed bodies, for which there was no accounting.

Ana's bedroom behind the drawn curtain was the worst. It still had the old sewing machine. Bolts of cloth lay around, and half-cut patterns and dresses begun for Ana but left unfinished because she lost so much weight every day that it was no use making her anything.

Ana sat on her unmade bed. She ignored the clothes leaping out of drawers and the books splattered on the floor, the shoes tangled with bedclothes and the bits of food dehydrating on plates. It was chaotic; it was the house in Havana the night before the trip.

· Tonight was junior prom night. The kids in her class would all be dancing. Ana sank down under her pillow and cried until the pillow was sodden with tears and snot and sweat. And then sat up and banged her head against the wall. Banged and banged. The windows above her made an icy rattle. Plaster fell like wet snow. Blood matted her hair. Still she couldn't stop the pain inside her head and she couldn't understand her life and she didn't know how to live. She wished she could dash her head against the wall and stop the world.

The others were watching television and no one went to investigate the banging.

Around midnight Ana, dry-eyed, slunk to the kitchen for a glass of water. She found Carlos and Dolores sharing a midnight snack, a heaped *medianoche* sandwich. Dolores was telling Carlos about his mother's secret wealth.

You will be rich.

Consuelo had an inheritance.

For her. It is all for her.

It is your mother's inheritance.

On my death, all will be revealed.

You will be maharajahs.

I have my secrets. Those I will take with me to my tomb.

Rub my bottom for good luck.

Dolores spun in the kitchen like a dervish. Carlos smiled to see her. Her eyes crossed, her face advanced through the shades on the warm end of the spectrum. She wheezed. She turned on Ana.

Nothing for you, Ana! You, I will see in Hell! *Satanás* will arrange our reunion!

Long after her parents slept, Ana went to her mother's bedside table and gently pulled open the drawer. Her hand slipped over the pile of childhood drawings Consuelo kept there and over the rolls of Pedro's discarded socks which Consuelo had handy because she suffered from cold feet. Ana's hand found the old cigar box with the little capped bottles. They were her mother's tranquillisers and sleeping pills and blood-pressure medications. Ana took the box out of the room lest she rouse her sleeping parents. She took ten tablets from each bottle and then a handful from the aspirin bottle. She put the cigar box back in the drawer. She carried the pills in the palm of her hand. She went to the kitchen and opened the high cupboard where Pedro kept the whiskey bottles he had collected at Christmastime in the days when he was still working at *la factoría* and which no one in the house – except Ana, surreptiously – ever drank.

She filled a glass with the pale gold liquid and swallowed the pills like so many M&Ms. Then she went to her bed to wait.

Ana slept for three days. They left her alone. She had been so odd for so long now, nothing much seemed amiss.

Once or twice Consuelo shook her shoulder and ordered her to dress for school. When Ana groaned Consuelo shrugged and let her sleep. She thought she was lucky to be young and carefree. She wished she could sleep endlessly herself. She went off to the factory and thought about more pressing things than Ana's marathon sleep.

On the fourth day Ana awoke mid-afternoon to find herself still alive and the following day she dressed in the morning and took herself to school where she continued to make good grades and that was all.

The Kennedy Library was icy-cold and smelt of the printing chemicals in new books and the stale mouldy odour of old volumes. Ana dragged herself in. She was becoming weak but still she felt fat. Her bones rubbed together and her pants were empty in the seat and held up by a belt that flapped halfway around her waist again. Still she knew she was fat and she also knew she was sick because she was not fat and over and above it all she remembered what it used to be like when she was younger. She grieved for that loss and she didn't realise how young she was, but thought she knew it wouldn't get any better. She checked out ten thick volumes on psychology. Six by Freud or on Freud. And Erik Erikson's *Childhood and Society*.

Funnily enough, at first she read more about Dolores than about herself in the books. There were chapters on the compulsion to punish the body, on the many ways one could crave the knife. The books claimed that the source of this compulsion was often guilt. This was a revelation. Dolores, like Pedro, never confessed to anything, never admitted anything, never apologised. But Ana thought Dolores might feel guilty about something. She found that idea interesting enough to stop her thinking about herself for an afternoon and half an evening.

In the next days and weeks Ana read and tried to puzzle it all out – her mother, her father, Abuela Dolores, herself. She thought Dolores might be the riddle, its answer, the problem and its solution. She thought her grandmother was haunted, was haunting all of them and wrecking their lives and fucking everything up because she was driven by a madness, a rage, that was beyond her control. Ana tried to work out what its source was, what was in her history that forced her to punish herself and everyone else, that made her crave the knife, that led her by the hand into doctors' rooms and clinics and – if she got her way – into hospitals where, to her joy, she was operated on yet again. But always, thought Ana, her grandmother's joy was short-lived. Whenever she awoke she found that whatever organ had been extracted was not the right one, the one responsible for the pain. Dolores never realised that the pain came from elsewhere, was in her history, was not flesh and blood but lay curled there and could never be removed by any surgeon, no matter how skilful.

Ana tried to fathom what had happened to her grandmother. She knew she had left her parents' *bohío* against her father's wishes, chasing after a man she could not marry because they were too closely related. She had worked in the city, done whatever she could. There had been several abortions – more than several. *No sé, hija*, Consuelo said. *No sé por qué* she had to have so many abortions. *Sabe Dios*. Well, perhaps she worked as a prostitute. Why else would someone need to have so many abortions? I don't know. She never told me. Let's talk about something else. *Tu abuela me enferma*.

Ana could get nothing else out of Consuelo except these half guilty half-confidences.

But Ana was smart, having lived other lives, more than

the one, her mother's life as well as her own, simultaneously. She began to imagine, and her imaginings were close to the mark.

A baby about to be born has plans. It lies squeezed up in a dark, bubbling, murmuring little swamp and it sucks in with its thumb plans to see more than blackness – to see sunrise purples and glowing pinks and even eye-squinting whites and to feel that white burn its throat; to feel lost and tortured and expelled and then know the sweet consolation of a blue-veined mound of flesh in its vacuum hold.

A baby on the verge of life has giant plans and dreams and aspirations for a world about to open and reveal itself, and when all that comes its way is the sharp point of a metal clothes-hanger that pierces the brain arms legs and heart the scream that cannot be heard continues in its mother's ear – continued in Dolores's ear – the rest of what should have been the baby's life. And even when her dead baby tucked Dolores in at night the plans never born became dead whispers in her ear.

Other babies went different ways. Because Dolores could never face up to anything, because she had to curl the truth so many times that it was disguised even from herself, she never aborted her babies early. By the time her stomach burgeoned before her like a hoary truth, it was too late for any but the most brutish means.

The clothes-hanger led to septicaemia so bad she landed in a clinic with a 104° temperature and a clamp dangling from her uterus like a tail for two weeks.

A girlbaby came after she swabbed her ravaged cervix with pimientos ground with kerosene (and then had to sit in a tub of water and milk and think of *granizado* for three days to try to cool the fires on the lips, the entrance and even the surrounding mound).

Another was disturbed in its sleep by a slow steady rhythmic massage that left it wishing it had left earlier, but then the stroking pressure grew until it became a pounding so insistent its soft jelly brain was crushed and its soft tissue heart dissolved into dust.

The fourth decided to leave of his own volition as soon as he knew for certain that the poisons she took that racked her lungs and had her heaving over a bucket were meant for him.

The fifth knew nothing because she had fallen asleep in an alcoholic stupor and by the time Dolores passed out – she had been told to drink herself into unconsciousness – the girlbaby had also passed out and lay on the floor next to her in a sea of blood clotting with flies and only because Josefina found them did one of them live.

Dolores did not mind working the cool nights and sleeping in the glare of day. She did not mind the looks the smells the rancid breaths the mauling hands the grazings and the rhythmic poundings because she had learnt with her father how to look men in the eye to stay their hands and she was rarely beaten.

She did not mind the work. It was what millions of country girls had done for as long as the sun's only purpose was to light their way into the city until they found their dreams had been too big for the space between their legs.

She didn't mind that part of it. But in the end it was the babies that drove her to shut her legs and get down on her knees amid swirling lye and scrub until the tiles reflected her fading looks and her fingers peeled and peeled again. Yet no matter how much she put them in buckets of hot soap the blood never seemed to wash off her bleeding stumps.

The blood drove her mad. Her madness took the form of a surge of desire for a child, for a real baby to give life to all the dead babies who were haunting her.

She stole a doll from the room of a little girl whose house she cleaned in Miramar. She took to sleeping with it at night and clasping it to her bare breasts and just when it seemed she would die of grief and longing she found that life was once again shifting inside of her.

But time and again the swelling turned out to be caused by phantom babies and the doctor that her brothers and sister took her to prescribed pills to calm her and a rest in the country but said with finality that he could do nothing to return her mutilated organs to their original purpose.

So they sent her back to Olvidados where her brothers and sisters that had stayed there got her work with a rich American family that owed them because it had stolen something from them and squandered it.

Dolores cleaned and carried and watched and served so well that she became *criada* to the grief-stricken *señorita*. And Dolores watched as her dreams grew inside another.

Dolores cared for the grieving *señorita* with an assiduousness that slid towards obsession. She safeguarded her, to protect her baby.

It would be a mistake to think she did it because she knew too well the darkness a dead baby lays across your house. It wasn't that. It wasn't that she was saving Henrietta Douglas from anything at all. Dolores was simply helping herself. Taking. Grasping with both hands. Grabbing what life would deny her. She had that much will. She believed in herself that much. She believed – she always said it – in no one and nothing.

She hugged her doll at night and listened to the murmured reproaches from the pines of her home town and she patted her stomach and inched her finger in gingerly just to see but there was nothing but the stale black blood. She fell asleep listening to the resentful pines and praying to La Caridad del Cobre to safeguard the child that was growing inside *la americana* and which only she – Dolores – knew was there and knew was to be hers.

Ana Soars

Ana arrived home from school and found Dolores in the kitchen, peeling potatoes. Dolores had recovered much of her strength in the year since her last tango with the knife but the FBI still had her under surveillance and there was always the danger that *los comunistas* would try to poison her food again. She had written a letter to Richard Milhaus Nixon protesting her treatment at the hands of medical bureaucrats and letting him know that she had been the victim of human rights abuses to rival those of the USSR's, but she had not yet received a reply.

Ana threw her school books down on the table and sat down next to Dolores. She did not ask about her health because that would be the wrong tack. She looked her in the eye and said, Abuela, I am worried about Mami.

¿Y por qué?

Well, she looks very thin lately. Haven't you noticed the dark circles under her eyes? I think she cries at night. I think Mami is very unhappy, Abuela.

Bueno, perhaps if you did more to help her, *desgraciada*, your *mami* would be better.

But Ana knew she had hit her mark, and left it at that.

Ana and Pedro wandered in the K-Mart on 49th Street. It was the Saturday afternoon before Mother's Day and Pedro wanted his daughter's advice on what to buy for Consuelo with the forty-seven dollars he had won last week on sixty-three – a light – and forty-four. In her bedside table, squashed amongst the faded red construction paper hearts with their curling edges that the children had made for her at school, Consuelo kept cards that Pedro had given her on other Mother's Days. His heavy cursive hand, grinding with all the pressure the Jesuits put on him as a youngster at La Salle, always surprised Ana with its noble messages: *A mi queridísima esposa,* from the man who adores you. It always seemed at odds with their daily, monthly, yearly rancour, their unending disparagement of each other.

Pedro and Ana chose a pale blue cardigan for Consuelo, after looking at many and Pedro each time grunting, *No, eso no,* rubbing the fabric between the ball of his thumb and his middle finger and dropping the garment as though it stank warmly. *Eso es basura,* he had grunted, wanting something better for his beloved, something nicer, the very best that he could afford.

While Pedro chose some new socks and underpants for himself, Ana drifted across the aisle to the book section. Her eye fell on an orange paperback – *My Secret Garden: Women's Sexual Fantasies.*

Ana picked up the book, read two pages. Found it

immeasurably interesting. Knew that she wanted it. She carried it nonchalantly as she followed Pedro around the store. When they got to the cash register, Pedro dumped his purchases on the counter. Ana placed her book on top of her mother's cardigan, next to Pedro's socks and underpants.

She was betting that he would not read the title. She was taking a punt that, as always, his mind would not bother taking in the words in English that lay there in stark black capitals, that even he must surely understand, after almost fifteen years in *el exilio*. If he were to read them, to pick up the book, she would not know what to do. How to face him? How to ever face him again? But he would not. She had never in all her life seen him with a book in his hands.

Pedro watched the cashier punch in the amounts with the vigilance of a starved cat. He was ready to pounce and savage the young woman for the smallest mistake. He grunted when she arrived at the correct answer, threw bills and coins from his wallet down after counting them twice, picked up the bags and headed for the doors with Ana trailing. He strode past the invisible beggars and the Salvation Army lady with her bell and her cup.

He looked at his daughter, smiled at her. He was happy to have bought a present for Consuelo, pleased with himself. And then he looked at Ana again. As if seeing her for the first time in years, he took in her clothes, the flared gabardine polyester pants with the wide belt that all the Cuban women, old and young, were wearing that year and the clinging shirt with the scalloped neckline. She was radiant. She had been gaining weight, she had found a measure of peace in the last few weeks and it showed in the soft slim rounded edges everywhere. And he patted the back of her head as if she were the cat, and told her, *¡Qué linda!*

The moment froze in her memory, became one of those mundane moments, going through the K-Mart doors on a sunny noisy Saturday afternoon, that her mind, when it was blank, would wander back to time and time again.

The book, which she pulled out of the bag when they were in the car and carried to the loft of the old barn, was an open door into rooms her parents would not ever have knowingly let her go. She lay amidst old books and discarded clothes and masturbated so vigorously that after a week she was no longer a virgin. She wondered how anyone could remain a virgin when this silent flight was possible. She flew frequently.

As Ana soared in the barn, Consuelo was earthbound on her cactus garden and trying to get aloft.

A grizzled face grazes her cheek, a sunburnt arm gently parts her thighs. Would he remove his cape to make love to her?

Only afterwards did it occur to her to feel ashamed, and if not ashamed, at least ridiculous. El Caballero de París was toothless by then, scarcely had eyes. She had seen him examining a garbage can on Flagler not long ago. He would not look her in the face. Pretended not to recognise her.

Look at you, she had fussed, patting his clothes. No cape these days. Let me buy you *un café* and a midnight sandwich.

But he shrank from her touch, shook his head, pawed the ground. And she had let him go. Out of pride. His.

It was only when there was sufficient space between them that she could no longer smell him, and he knew it, that he stopped, and turned towards her. We lost it all, didn't we Conchita?

Sí, mi caballero. They took it all away.

Except the fantasies, and the dreams, and the memories. Now he is young, and virile, and although the face is out of focus, she knows, somehow, that it is handsome. Now he strokes her bare breast. Bends over. Takes it tenderly. Sucks gently.

Now he does things to her that Pedro never did, for lack of imagination. Nor did Daniel, for lack of time.

Now he lifts her high atop the cacti.

Sí, mi caballero. Some things they couldn't touch. A few. A very few.

Ana walked home from school through snow. It was the only time it had snowed in Miami in recorded history and she had a short-sleeved blouse on. When she came out of class and realised it was snowing, she stood at a phone booth for fifteen minutes trying to call Carlos to ask him to come and pick her up. Carlos had graduated from high school and was spending a year trying to decide whether to go to college or look for work. Consuelo had given him the car in case he needed to go to a job interview. When he didn't answer the phone, Ana knew he was watching *Star Trek* and wouldn't let himself be interrupted. She walked the mile and a half home with snowflakes spinning around her, her notebooks clasped to her chest.

When she arrived at 25th Street her brother was indeed in front of the television. The bits of furniture not sold or pawned had been turned upside down. Armchairs waved their legs uselessly in the air. Dolores said she did it because she had bought the furniture with her own money and she had a right to keep everyone off it so it would not wear out. The sight of the house like that infuriated Ana.

Her grandmother's madness remained firmly coiled around money. She still talked endlessly about her inheritance, a secret source of wealth that she could not divulge but which would be known upon her death. All will be revealed, she promised. Rub my bottom for good luck! I will leave you a glorious inheritance!

When they pressed her for details – who, why, where, what – she clammed up. That I will take with me to my tomb!

They no longer pressed for details. It was just Dolores. They scarcely heard her at all. Yet they never seriously considered her madness. No one except Ana. To admit that she was mad, disordered, unhinged, would entail a level of awareness, of sanity and control and maturity, that they could not sustain. So they fought her as an equal, sank to her level.

It was true that she had paid for much of the furniture. Consuelo complained bitterly that Dolores never contributed her government money to paying for utilities. That was money that evaporated. Piff, it's gone, Consuelo said. But when you buy armchairs you can always pull them out from under someone's ass just as they are about to sit down.

Ana walked into the house and immediately began righting furniture. Dolores came running and grabbed her arm. Ana flicked her off with a shake.

With amazing dexterity for a person of her years Dolores leapt into the air and landed on her rear. *¡Bicho!* she screamed. You've killed me, *maldita*. *Auxilio*, Carlitos, *por Dios*, call the police. Your sister is trying to finish me off!

Carlos wrenched his eyes away from the television long enough to take in what was happening and laugh at the new turn in the household drama, and then resumed watching *Star Trek*. Dolores dragged herself along the floor like an injured soldier under enemy fire, making for the phone in the kitchen. When she reached it and began to dial the police, Ana pulled the cord out of the socket.

Abuela, listen to me, she hissed. You are driving all of us mad. I know you don't care about me but Mami is your only daughter – the only thing you have in this world – and if you don't stop she will go crazy and have to go into an asylum.

Abuela, you know what I'm saying is true. You have to move out. If you don't find somewhere else to live Mami will go insane, and it will be your fault.

Is that what you want? Do you want that on your conscience? Haven't you got enough there already?

Dolores did not cave in all at once. At first she fought back. *Maldito* the day you were born, she cursed. And she cursed the rest of Ana's life.

I am dying, she declared. I hope I die soon, the sooner to start haunting you.

She clasped her hands together, intertwining her fingers, kissed each finger, one at a time, announced, By all these crosses – and here she shook her laced hands up and down – I'm going to ruin you. I am going to fuck up your life.

A promise.

You've done that already, Ana said, feeling honest. You might as well go.

Ana kept working on her. It was part of a general effort to get better. At times she thought she was making progress. At times she binged again, or fasted, tore at her hair, peeled skin off in lumps.

No one in the family acknowledged she had a problem. No one took her to a therapist, or to a priest, or even to the school counsellor. It was in the nature of the family to accept her as they accepted Dolores, and to deny that there was anything wrong. That's just what Dolores is like, they said to Ana when Ana said she had read in a book that Dolores was suffering from paranoic delusions. There's nothing wrong with her mind, said Pedro and Consuelo. *Bueno, sí*, she has always been difficult – *pero* she is not *loca! Sí, sí, sí*, she is difficult, for as long as we've known her. *Nada es nuevo*.

Every afternoon when Ana arrived home from school, she sought Dolores out and worked on her. Abuela, have you looked at the ads for apartments today? Did you call Aída and ask if you could live with her? Time is slipping by, Abuela. You must give your daughter a life. She needs to rebuild her relationship with her husband. She needs you to get off her back. Can't you see that now, Abuela?

I am at death's door. That is when I will leave this house. They will carry me out in a six-sided box, you demon! And it will be your doing. You are killing me, heart-of-concrete. I will haunt you all your life for what you have done to me!

Leave now, Abuela. If you wait for your death, it will be too late for Mami. Save Mami.

Ana thought she was doing it for her mother's sake. She believed she was saving her mother's sanity.

Driving Jehovah to Murder

The day came when Ana María arrived home from school and Dolores was not there.

Dolores's old friend Aída was involved in a new religion. A splinter of the Jehovah's Witnesses, it also wove together aspects of Cuban Catholicism and Cuban/African *santería*. What attracted Aída so strongly, and would suck Dolores in as well, was that the group's guru, an ancient, ailing *santero* from Güines called Nene Rey, promised his followers he would reveal to them the secret of eternal life in the here-and-now.

Although Aída knew Dolores too well to take her into her own home, she had found a place for her with three old Cuban ladies, *tres viejitas* who were members of this sect. They rented a house on Palm Avenue.

Dolores was to have the back room, the enclosed verandah.

She left one Monday morning when no one else was home. She left behind her furniture, much of her clothes, even her bed. As soon as Consuelo came home and discovered Dolores was gone, she and Ana packed the rest of her clothes, dismantled her bed, and arranged to have it all driven to her new home.

Consuelo and Ana and Carlos went to see her on Saturday and took her cooked meals for the week. With Dolores's leaving it was as if a fresh breeze had swept through the house. A weight lifted from their souls, and although not exactly happy, they all nosed the path to salvation.

But Dolores immediately regretted her decision. She begged the family to let her return. She did not like the three *viejitas*, and the nights on the verandah left her apoplectic with asthma by morning. She shoved chests of drawers against the windows. There was an amazing amount of furniture and boxes in the room. Ana wondered whether Dolores was again placing pleas for donations in newspapers and on the radio. She did not ask – it didn't matter.

When they finished their visit and were preparing to kiss her goodbye, Dolores knelt in front of Consuelo, blocking her path in the crowded room. Throwing her arms out in supplication, like the saints on religious cards, Dolores begged to be taken back.

Por Dios, *hija*. In the name of everything holy. Find it in your heart to have some compassion for me. Do not leave me in this rat's nest. And then, glancing fearfully towards the main part of the house, she whispered loudly, You have no idea the sorts of things that go on here. Those three are possessed by the devil. They are Satan's handmaidens. I beg of you, take pity on me. Don't leave me in their clutches.

Ana and Carlos and Consuelo craned around the doorway to look at the three little old ladies who sat in the dining room watching television. On one's lap a baby's jacket was materialising between clicking needles. The three looked plump and sweet. One of them noticed the

Santiagos and called out an offer for a *tacita de café*. She heaved herself up and moved towards the stove, but Consuelo graciously declined. *No*, Señora. *Gracias*.

Consuelo thought of her teenage son, who finally had a room to himself. She thought of Ana, who seemed to be blooming in her niche on the back verandah. For once she stood firm. *No Mami, tú estás de lo más bien aquí.* This place is fine for you.

Carlos attempted to shift Dolores with a joke, as he always had. Lightly, politely, good-naturedly he asked her, Abuela, tell me, how are Jehovah's testicles lately?

The Spanish word for testicles, *testículos*, is very close to the word for witnesses, *testigos*. Dolores's eyebrows shot up and she turned her thin beak towards the young man. *Chico*. Don't be prosaic. It's Jehovah's witnesses, not Jehovah's testicles, we talk about here.

But she could not be sidetracked. Still kneeling, Dolores looked at Ana. She shook a witch's finger in her direction and hissed, This is all your doing, *desgraciada*. It is you who are keeping me from my daughter's house. But I'll get even with you. I am at death's door, I tell you. And I will haunt you all your days. *¡Oyeme bien, maldita!* I will fuck up your life!

Ana was reading on her half of the back verandah, the curtain pulled across for privacy. It was February, the best month. Her space was tidy today and the windows open. The radio on the floor played a song she liked. Under her bed was a suitcase that had been packed for two years,

375

waiting for the day when she would finally leave her mother's house.

The day would soon be at hand. Yesterday she had received a letter offering her a university scholarship in the fall, and suddenly the sky had no horizons and the world was fresh and full of promise. She thought that life could perhaps be good after all.

Ana was lying on a pillow that her Abuela Dolores had sent her. Dolores had sent many presents from her exile and all of them Ana took straight to the garbage can – except for this one. It was a pink and white pillow edged with lace that Dolores in a sweet mood said she had sewn especially for her, Anita María. Ana had left it lying on the floor in a corner of her curtained room for several months, but today she placed it on her bed and she was resting her elbow on it as she turned the pages of her book when suddenly she felt something large and stiff inside the pillow.

Ana's heart lurched and she ran to the kitchen but the scissors weren't in the little drawer where they usually were. So Ana grabbed the sharp kitchen knife and plunged it into the pillow and ripped it open. There among the soft white cotton stuffing was the dried corpse of a rat.

Ana's screams brought her mother to the kitchen. Consuelo picked up the pillow with the rat and carried it to the garbage can at the end of the back yard. And when Ana calmed down, Consuelo said, I don't think she did it on purpose. Mami would not do such a thing. Perhaps the rat fell in while she was sewing.

The phone rang at midnight. Ana was the only one awake, reading. She ran to answer it before the peals could rouse the rest of the family.

¿Quién es?

Tu abuelita, hija. Dolores's voice was drippingly sweet. The sound in the background was street music; she was calling from a phone booth.

Hija. Tell your mother she must come and get me right now. *Estoy desamparada.*

What do you want, Abuela?

Put your mother on the phone, you daughter of Satan.

Where are you, Abuela?

Pues I am at the temple. We are awaiting the awakening of El Rey. Tell your mother to come get me.

Consuelo managed to placate her without leaving the house, but Dolores called again at three in the morning. Consuelo had been dreaming of a garden in her grandmother's pueblo. She had been digging in this garden; now she remembered the dead child's curving cheekbones, its staring doll's eyes. She had found it as she was planting *yuca*.

Dolores was weeping. It worried Consuelo. She drove to the temple, a turquoise building, formerly a house, on the corner of 49th and Le Jeune.

Inside, the smell of decomposing flesh rammed into her, pushed her back. She saw Dolores at the fringe of a group of people sitting on folding aluminium chairs. In the centre of the room, amid a profusion of flowers, lay Nene Rey.

The features on his thirteen-day-old corpse were no longer recognisable. They had melted.

His followers awaited his awakening. They were buoyed

up in their faith by miracles he had once performed, which were well established as fact. Twenty years ago he awoke from a deathlike trance that had lasted seven years. The old ladies around him prayed, and waited.

Consuelo rang the police, and then the Department of Health.

It was full summer and the household slept, exhausted by the relentless heat and humidity of the day, when a midnight phone call again stalled their dreams. A man's voice yelled at Consuelo and it took her a while to wake up enough to understand him.

Consuelo and Carlos and Ana dressed and drove to the man's house. It was the sixth or seventh Jehovah's Witnesses family Dolores had lived with since Nene Rey's death. This time she was in a unit they had made from their garage, with her own kitchenette and bathroom.

The man took Consuelo by the arm. You have no idea how difficult your mother is, he told her. We are Jehovah's Witnesses but there are limits to what is tolerable, he insisted. He showed her his telephone bill, where the numbers 1-999-9998, 1-999-9999, 1-666-6666 and 1-900-0000 were listed repeatedly.

Look! She keeps ringing Nene Rey! She thinks she can get through to his spirit! It is costing me a fortune!

He showed her the bathroom, pointed to the bathtub, which was filled with a creamy, murky liquid. Look! She pees in the bathwater. Now tell me, why does she do that, when here, right here, is the toilet?

She's old, murmured Consuelo, but there was a doubtful look on her face. As if she were straining to remember the tin bath at the boarding house which had to be filled by hand. Dolores had peed in that as well. She had always let the warmth relax her. Her age, now, was only causing her to forget to pull the plug.

¡Y mira! Mira, mira mira mira mira. He took Consuelo's arm again, steered her into the living room and pointed.

They stared at a hole in the wall large enough for a person to crawl through. Something had busted through the plaster, the plywood underneath, and the plaster board on the other side. It was as if a small bomb had exploded there. The man shook his head, still incredulous.

Look what she has done, he said. It is unbelievable! Just look at it! Her room is on the other side of that wall. She uses her cane to summons us! Like a queen! She bangs the wall there, with her cane, until one of us goes to her. She calls my wife like that three dozen times a day! For petty things! And to scold *mi señora!*

I have to tell you something. Your mother is an incredibly strong woman. She will live to be a hundred. But she is difficult. She would drive Jehovah to murder.

Consuelo listened. Then she took out her chequebook and wrote a cheque. She apologised for not being able to offer more. She told him that Dolores had been on waiting lists for two years for a government nursing home.

Gracias, muchas gracias. But let me tell you something, your mother is impossible. *¡Imposible!*

And then, leaning closer to Consuelo, he asked quietly, Is she really a doctor? Can she really prescribe medicines?

She sounds so learned when she talks. And she makes up such amazing poems. Is she a poet? What is she?

She is not a doctor, said Consuelo dryly. She is only a poor *guajira* from a town called Olvidados. Who never spent more than a year at school. But she is brilliant.

In the last months of the summer of 1977 the sunsets over Miami were more beautiful than ever; the sky was more bruised than before and more tuggingly sweet. The smells as Ana bicycled into south-west Miami in the late afternoons were sharper, more *criollo* . . .

The city seemed to be waking; the whole low sandy soggy place with its cement cube houses was changing before her eyes. The quiet, sombre, mysterious shadows that had lived there for a generation or two were slinking north again. They were being replaced with live people, lively brown and coloured people with loud voices – singing voices, fighting, yelling, lovemaking voices. Expansive people who were used to inhabiting their allotted space in life and then claiming more.

The whole city breathed, stretched, expanded and began, also, to fray around the edges, to gather garbage in the chain-linked fences of its frontiers, because the puritan, civic-minded ghosts were going and there was a new *gente* in Miami . . .

The ducks were lured away from the canals and into the newly paved back yards, penned in amongst the savage dogs, a distraction for the beasts. The ducks were fed, fed often, *se hartan* with *pan* and *arroz criollo* and the *picadillo* with its raisins and olives. They were fed until they were fat, until they were ready to burst, and then they disappeared . . .

As Ana bicycled what she smelled was *arroz con pato*.

And Ana, that girl who hated herself, who picked at herself, a bit of flesh here, a lump of scalp there, that adolescent obsessed with putting things in and taking things out, began to understand a little about the things that gripped her mind. Ana María, coming and going, moving between the rooms in her mother's house like an indifferent shadow, found a bit of space for herself and took it . . .

Carlos did not go to university, but got a part-time job in an occult bookshop, part *botánica*. The *botánica* specialised in *santería*, that shady mix of African vodoo and Catholicism. Carlos advised a customer not to put mercury into her straying husband's food. (*Bueno, sí*, Señora, if you give him mercury he'll stay faithful to you, but he'll be dead. Here, try this – a more benevolent solution, Señora.)

In that time, black men began to be beaten up by white policemen with greater and greater frequency, and the black Americans, marginalised by the whites and the Cubans until they could scarcely breathe, began expressing their rage on the smouldering streets . . .

Pedro's moods were meaner than ever, and he and Consuelo fought about everything. They fought about the amount of coffee Pedro demanded be brought to him in thimble-sized cups. Consuelo seethed and seethed, and then exclaimed that he needed a hose from the *cafetera* to his snout, to save him the trouble of lifting up the cups that streamed to his lips all day . . .

Bars started going up on windows. People began to disappear from the expressway while in transit from their office to their home. New marks appeared on the walls of the Santiago house. Mundane objects were compelled to fly . . .

And in Cuba, the grip on the lives of the people was, if anything, tighter than ever . . .

Consuelo waited. She lay in her bed and wished that everyone would stop, that time would stop and everyone would freeze, like the family of dolls in Ana's old doll's house.

But the house was against her. It was impatient. Clocks ticked the passing minutes too quickly. Screens flapped even when there was no breeze. Flour bought just last week came out of the cupboard with weevils and the peanut butter turned rancid. Even the summer, the tropics, didn't account for it. Foliage threw itself into the task of surrounding the house, penetrating it, despoiling it. The roots of the mango and the avocado and the ficus and its hairy tangles moved towards the house, bent on rocking its foundations.

Dolores went into a government nursing home. The last time Ana saw her, her radio was chained to her bedside to keep it from being stolen by staff. Every week Consuelo took her a new nightgown and underpants to replace what had disappeared in the laundry.

Dolores had stopped eating. She was sure her food was being poisoned. It was not such a ludicrous idea any more.

The medication she was given to sedate her she stuffed

into her anus when the staff weren't looking. Then she went to the toilet.

When Ana visited, she took a tape recorder and asked Dolores to recite some of her poems. Dolores had by then forgotten many of them and no longer had the ability to create new ones on the spot. But she still remembered snatches from old favourites, such as an ode in honour of her mother María. It reminded Ana of Rilke's poetry.

It was the only tangible thing Dolores left behind when she died.

She had begged to be allowed home. Do something for me, Ana María, she said. Don't let me die here. I need to be with Consuelo.

She was crying, and Ana felt sorry for her. She knew that what she asked was impossible, and tried to think of something to say.

Abuela, they take care of you here. It's like a hospital, what you always wanted.

There is nothing wrong with me, Dolores declared.

Abuela, there have always been a hundred things wrong. You always wanted to go to hospital. What about the asthma? The emphysema?

That's cured. I haven't had asthma in months.

So they're looking after your health.

No. I cured myself.

How did you do that, Abuela?

I decided I wouldn't have asthma any more.

That I can believe, Ana thought. She remembered all the attacks at propitious moments, all the attention-seeking. Pity gave way to ancient angers. It hardened Ana.

No, Abuela. This is the right place for you.

The last time Ana saw her, Dolores was kneeling in the middle of the main corridor of the nursing home. On her knees, arms outstretched, Dolores was asking to be taken back to her daughter's house.

No one realised it would have been kind this time to listen to her. Ana hurried away, embarrassed as families visiting other patients stared and the staff made jokes.

In the end, her heart failed. She was skeletally thin.

It was impossible to say exactly how old she was. That, along with her many other secrets, she took with her to her tomb.

———

So what? I also died alone. And don't say that ultimately we all die alone, that's rubbish. Some of us live well, and some die well, and others live miserably and die miserably and never get over it. I was one of those.

It shouldn't have been like that, of course. Of course I should have called her to my side, told her I was hers, told her she was mine. Flesh of my flesh, bone of my bone. I reclaim you, I could have said. Claim me. Make a claim. Know that I am yours. These things are yours. This porcelain cup, this vase. This land. My eyes are yours. See?

I had the time. Cancer of the womb, when I finally managed it, was slow and gave no quarter.

My father did it better, and with less time. That was a mercy. Herman died quickly, struck down while still a fine figure astride a horse. Yet still he had time to have them bring me, and I went, even knowing why.

I wanted to give him my pain but only if it would add to his own. To say, You killed my beloved and robbed me of my life and there is no forgiveness on earth.

But he didn't give me the chance. He read all there was to hear on my face the moment I stepped into that darkened room. Because he said, Henrietta I love you, and closed his eyes and died, and he made it look easy although it couldn't have been. Leaving me more angry. More bitter. More alone and more lost, leaving me leaving me leaving me.

Still he had reclaimed me. And all that he was I am, except the parts he took, which he could not give back even on his deathbed. So that despite the money, the jewels and the rugs and the chandeliers, the acres of cane and the acres of swamp mud, I was poor at his death. Too poor to call her to me when my turn came.

Too poor to hand anything on.

Too poor to help her, leaving her in the hands of that madwoman, that Dolores. And of course I knew. I knew who she was, and what she was. We know. For God's sake. We know. Did you think we didn't?

One knows.

What Consuelo Remembered, 1995

Images appeared unbidden in her mind. Niggardly, baffling things. The face of a youth shot on a white-hot Havana street. The way the flies had congregated around his nostrils, fossicked in his mouth. It had perplexed her all those years ago. It still did.

She remembered the sweet weight of her children newly born. The condensed weight of them, how they were denser than one expected at their core, lighter towards their skin. This had made their sleep, in her arms, extraordinary, enabled that heavy soft melting, that moulding, that weightless sinking, flesh returning to flesh.

Their smells. The different feelings each had evoked. The sweetness of Ana. The protectiveness of a lioness that she had felt towards Carlos when gazing at his round head on its stalk-neck.

Ay, Dios.

The light of the setting sun shone brilliantly for a few minutes, illuminating the tiny room, twinkling it, before receding, a slow let-down. In its wake soft shadows emerged. They waited patiently, now that there was so little time to wait. Consuelo closed her eyes. Sighed again.

Dios mío.

A bright blue day . . . bluer than the eye of a cat . . . Seagulls stalling mid-air above a sugar-white beach. Herself in bathers, in two bits of a handkerchief. Slim-thighed and honey-armed. El Caballero de Paris in the distance. Coming closer. *¡Granizado! ¡Maní!*

¡Corazón!

Ay Dios mío.

El Caballero hands her a Coca-Cola with one hand, a white carnation with the other. Won't accept her coins. Never did.

How much did her debt grow, over the years? How will she ever pay him back?

They said he went crazy in his last years. Don't we all. The mind prepares for the night, closing windows one at a time.

She never shrank from him. If anything, she loved him more than ever. It was not just that he alone, of all the men in her life, never disappointed her. It was also that he became more than the father she never had, the brother, the husband, the lover.

He became her lunatic.

The one with the cape, even when the others couldn't see it. The flower, even after all the flowers had wilted. The gesture. The touch.

My lunatic. My lunatic. Mine.

She had always thought her last thoughts would be of Daniel. She had rehearsed this moment so many times, lying beneath the cacti covers of her bed with Pedro. Now she wondered that she was not thinking of him. She did not realise that even this was another way to think of him, and a more fitting way. Daniel, after all, for the most part, had always been conspicuous by his absence.

She never saw Paris. Would the late-afternoon sunlight in Paris be like this? No, it wouldn't be. I doubt it.

Dios mío.

I've had two falls, *Dios mío,* and now I'm heading for my third. The one from the lamp post where I clung that hot hazy day, Batista at the head of ranting crowds. The typhoid pulled me down, and I fell five feet . . .

And the earlier, more devastating, fall. When she had fallen from innocence. Discovered María was not her mother, and Dolores never could be. She had tumbled into this knowledge with a great, dauntless, conviction. Still, it took her breath away, and knocked her off her feet. She is not my mother. Neither is María. The person who was my mother never claimed me. I am no one.

Consuelo, in these last days, recalled the smell of soaked earth, her earliest impression. An image played on the edges of her memories: the donkey-drawn cart of the trashman.

She remembered Olvidados, walked again and again over its two dusty, chicken-pecked avenues: the Street of Forgetting, and the Street of Miracles.

She saw herself, a young child, kneeling in the mud of María's *bohío*, patting mud *torticas* while chanting in tongues the stories of her former lives.

She remembered leaving the countryside, passing from a world of crude hoes and sunken chests, young men who

388

shuffled like old unless beating their families, gap-toothed smiles and bare feet, where everyone knew which was the road that led to their pueblo.

She backed out along that road at a tender age, facing her pueblo, clutching her grandmother's hair.

She remembered swimming pools in paved back yards flashing by, the greenest of eyes.

Stately fountains, bougainvillea-choked mansions, hibiscus-covered courtyards, private aviaries.

And then, closer to her destination, the *solares* with their noisy *cantinas*, the life in the streets, the boarding house.

Voices echo down the years. What would you do without Dolores?

Thank God.

She once ran everywhere she went. She clipped on skates and flew. When Dolores took the skates, she constructed kites, took them to El Parque Central. Flying at the end of a thin, humming string.

That time her aunts from Olvidados visited the house in Havana. Tía Ofelia, Tía Esperanza. Visiting Josefina, not Dolores. No bond of sister-love was strong enough to withstand Dolores's personality. They talked as if Consuelo wasn't there. Perhaps she wasn't.

What a woman!

What a woman, *Dios Santo*!

What a headache.

It hurts my head to think of her.

Así mismo.

She doesn't believe in anyone.

In no one.

Ramón . . .

May he rest in peace . . .

She says she did it for him.

For him! Heh!

She says lots of *mierda*.

She was always *egoísta*.

She doesn't believe in anyone.

She was obsessed with the child.

Bueno, es tía.

We're all aunts.

And *la americana*? What can you tell me about *la americana*?

They don't know how to be mothers.

They're cold. A cold race.

They don't get milk in their chests.

What they don't have is a heart.

Bueno, they say she went crazy when they killed Ramón.

I almost went crazy myself.

¡Qué miseria!

¡Qué vida puta!

Her father arranged it.

He did it.

May God punish him.

He finished us.

Poor creature. Without mother, without father.

In God's hands.

In God's hands.

May God help her.

La pobre.

Pobrecita.

And when Consuelo had stepped up to them, questions bouncing from her eyes, accosting them, their faces had shut like slammed doors.

Who are you talking about, Tía? Choosing the softer one, Ofelia, the more beaten one.

De nada, mi amor.

We're talking about how frogs grow in little girls' panties if they don't wash.

Run and play.

Take this *galleta.*

Anda, muchacha.

There had been a tangle there. They had meant Dolores wasn't her mother. But who was? Who was, *Dios mío?* She would die not knowing.

And with this thought her mind slipped a few rungs, twisted along well-trodden paths, from the mother she had lost to the lover she then had to lose. And she thought of Daniel.

She had lived her entire adult life always in his arms, every night. She had met him in a place by a river, more often than not the same place, and she had only ever left it as dawn approached.

Even dreaming, she had known she was living two lives, another one at the same time, that one more filled with strife and anger, where there was no river and no Daniel. She had lived these two lives simultaneously.

The river . . . She remembered the river. It was of unspeakable beauty, the land on the other side at once far away and yet distinctly beautiful, the sunshine causing high contrasts between very bright but never glaring light, and deep dark comforting shadows.

The gardens along the river where they strolled and loved had been marshy and seaweedy, as if at the edge of a sea. As if decaying. He would touch certain places, and children with flower wreathes on their heads would step out from the vegetation wastes. Children and flowers had been everywhere, if only one knew how to touch, where to seek, how to open the earth and release them.

¡Pero qué tontería! What nonsense! All her life she had been a hopeless romantic. She had indulged in melancholy, preferring dreams and shadowy remembrances of things past to vibrant life. But she had been a good woman. Well, she had tried. God be merciful. She would have to confess it, now, soon, very soon. She would have to tell the priest. Her most painful secret. The third fall, the one she could not bare to even think about . . .

Daniel had not always danced just in her dreams. And the flower children that the dream-Daniel could bring forth from the ground the real Daniel, Daniel Cancio, had put between her legs.

Ay Dios. Forgive me.

How many years can two people spend dreaming the one same thing while living something else entirely before worlds collide? If there is power, unseen but pure and direct, in prayer, if the human mind is a universe and our knowledge of it only skims its edges, then surely it was their love and their dreams, and not coincidence, that reunited them.

It was Havana, 1958. Khaki-clad figures slunk in the foliage of the Sierras, and an American journalist, flush with the naïve idealism of youth despite not being young, scurried after them. The echoes of the reverberations of their detonations, by the time they reached the city, were mild, familiar and comforting in their dissonance. The maracas or the castanets or the cymbals in the Cuban beat. The drum beat, in the late tropical spring of 1958, still came from the Presidential Palace, and did not give any warning of its own demise.

So how could Consuelo have known? And had she known, how could it have changed anything? When so little, after all, was in her hands?

Consuelo, following Pedro into the main hall of El Centro Gallego, had no prescience of the future, not of her own nor of her country's. Her solemn face sought out a familiar one so that it could break into a radiance no less dazzling for being feigned. Nor did Pedro have a care or a worry that moment, snapping the fingers of one hand, hips already swaying, his other hand pushing the small of Consuelo's back, claiming rather than guiding.

Nor did Daniel, sitting on a makeshift stage, playing a guitar. At least not until the moment when he saw Consuelo, and lost the beat.

At the time, Daniel had not played for many months. For nine months this particular song he was now playing had grown inside him, gestating an inconsolable lament, a song of love lost and life denied, the only music Daniel was capable of composing. He did not usually play in public.

But what is a musician without an audience? Daniel was asked to play and he accepted. Daniel played. Daniel strummed his guitar and Consuelo sat, the music the only thing between them.

It caressed. It stroked. It washed over her gently and then it pummelled its reproach. It fingered her and it entered her and it was the music, too, that shuddered in a joy like agony and then the music receded and it was the music, that night, which conceived Ana.

When he stopped and placed his instrument down and bowed slightly and moved off the stage, Consuelo waited. Then she stood. Patted Pedro's shoulder in a treacherous reassurance. Moved through the room in zigzags, greeting friends, nodding as if she heard the chatter, accepting a drink from a lacy waiter and all the while heading for a door, then a corridor, then, unthinkingly, refusing to think, opening another door beyond which Daniel waited.

After that, even guardian angels and guilt-ridden spirits can't say what happened. Such a room is too full with two people, with all the longing of lifetimes searching and missing each other, with all the energy of a universe of love, and there is no room for anything else. But this is what he might have said:

He might have said, Consuelo. I love you. You love me. How could you have married him?

Or. He could have looked up when she entered the room. Stared long into her eyes. And then looked down again. Fumbled with his guitar as he put it into its black-as-night case, stroked a wrinkle in the velvet lining, flicked away a thread. Asked, So? How have you been?

These, and a handful of other things would have been possible had not the music come first. But the music had said all there was to say, had been embarrassed enough, tentative enough, reproachful to sufficiency. Had been coy, had overcome these hurdles, had found its stride. Had strode. Had surged, had exclaimed love and disclaimed time and the laws of men and, having discussed everything, had left them to simply rush into each other's arms.

For this moment we are born. For this moment we would die. Without such a moment our lives have little meaning. Only at such a place do we feel a respite from our loneliness.

Suddenly there is nothing we cannot touch.

Consuelo emerged from her skin and entered his. He enveloped himself in her. Knotted fingers, pounding hearts, thigh to thigh and chest to breast. No one else in the world, nothing else but one's love. Daniel. Consuelo.

Her every muscle trembled. In fear at her daring, at her sin. In joy. In ecstasy. She came the second his hand touched her breast, came again when he touched her vulva. Many times more as he entered her.

He loved her tenderly, every brother, every father, every beloved. And then savagely, unforgivingly, from behind. For having left him. For being weak.

The masochist in her was understood. No other lover, she knew then, would or could touch her the same way again. Because only Daniel had known her, had understood her from the first minute their eyes had met across a shrieking street. And because of everything else they did to each other after that first moment, and everything they didn't do.

She had not even gone to a priest. She could not have confessed anything, even to herself. She did not flesh it with words even as her body had fleshed the fruit of what she had done. She never stopped to consider that the wheel had come full circle. She had not put a name to her feeling because she had obliterated his name from her mind.

Another woman might have left. Perhaps. Perhaps if things had been different, if she had been different, she could have gathered the strength into herself, the energy generated by an evening when the moon failed and the wind lost itself in the palms, the hands of clocks froze at awkward angles and cars dozed on inland roads. Nothing moved, nothing breathed, nothing but two people finishing something that had waited fifteen long years. Consuelo had known then that nothing else existed – not religion, not family, not the heavens above nor the ground below. Just his hands his back his waist his neck, his hair the dear dear face and this sweet melting frenzy.

But afterwards, how could she have left Pedro, Carlos's father? Her husband, after all. And for what, *Dios mío?* During that tense and insomniac period when strange forces had been gathering strength. The rebels in the mountains had been gaining assurance every day; the wind moaned through the capital, frightened by the rumours being bandied at street corners. There were assassinations, power shortages, buildings experiencing spontaneous combustion.

There was madness afoot, and Daniel was part of it. Daniel was in the Sierra Maestra he was in Miami he was in Santiago he was certainly not at her side. Pedro had been by her side, strutting like an Arab stud, buying ridiculous presents, overjoyed at the prospect of another child, perhaps a daughter. Pedro had bought presents in anticipation of this daughter – absurd things, dolls that cost a week's wages and were twice the height the child was when she came.

She had blotted everything else out. She had carried her child in fear, and lived a lie.

She could never hold on to anything. Not her birthmother's house, not her grandmother's hair, not Pura's laughter. Even Ana left her to split the oceans and live on the far and under side of the world.

Yes, yes, but those are the women. What of the men? Could she not have held on to the man who truly loved her, and whom she loved? But what of the other men? Her son Carlos? His father, to whom she made vows in a cathedral, with a veil whose train covered the aisle from altar to door, and trailed outside?

And what of a bastard child who doesn't know her own parents, whose birth is illegitimate? That is who she felt herself to be, forever a baby lost in a confusing miasma of names and aliases, half-truths and rumours and whispers overheard, all of which added up to less than an identity. Could she do that to her own child?

The fact that by turning her back on Daniel and raising a second child as Pedro's was doing precisely this, living a lie, was lost on her. Her need was great enough to fool her into believing that the smallest, narrowest, dimmest and saddest path would be the best. It was the only path she had ever walked. It seemed familiar. She could do nothing else. It was never in her hands.

My Mother's Face

My mother's face traces her passage through time.

The curve from cheek to chin is still, even now, harsh and abrupt. Her mother, who left her, let her go. Whose love she never had.

These lines around her eyes follow the traintracks that led away from her grandmother María, to the boarding house where nothing good was ever sustained. And then her mouth is sunken, and dark, and the grim lines can never be lifted. Dolores.

Now the road takes her away from the island to a single room, the narrowest, most hopeless time in her life, when she also loved the fiercest.

Now her roads branch out, to all the corners of her face, rivulets that go nowhere, that dissipate into the fine tissue of her still-glowing eyes.

I hold her hand, keeping it the same temperature as my own because it is so thin and fragile that the light seems to pass through the webbing between her fingers. But still it looks much like my hand, I can see the same shapes, the same veined boniness in these large hands of ours.

There are clouds on her fingernails, little smoky smudges

that float up from the cuticles, self-assured only in their centres and lazily drifting. In no hurry, as if they knew they would never arrive at her moon-shaped fingertips.

My mother is dead.

I have sat next to her for hours, for days, for days that turned into seasons and swirled around me into years, for an impossibly curved passing of time.

My old bedroom, begrudgingly shared for so many years with Dolores and Carlos, because it is closest to the bathroom has become my mother's last room. From the window I see the pawpaw trees she planted outside, ripening fruit hanging onto their slim trunks like hungry puppies.

Beyond the pawpaws stands the old ficus. The swishing of its leaves comes and goes in waves. A rustling sea.

I am on my way home. It is night. There are very few passengers and everyone has several seats to stretch across, if they want to, and I am lying across three seats with two pillows and a blanket. I feel as though I am in a spaceship, as if I could lift up the plastic covering on the windows and see galaxies swirling past. The hum of the plane's engines is strangely comforting.

I expected to feel sick with loss. But somehow I feel all right. Perhaps it is shock. I am taking a spaceship back through space and time and oceans and cities and aeons and instead of overwhelming grief all I feel is a mellow sadness and anticipation at the thought of being with my children again, home again.

Only last month, while driving past Albert Park, I

showed María the house on Beaconsfield Parade where we had lived when she was born.

I walked all along here with Grandma Consuelo, I told her, pointing to the beach. When you were overdue and we were trying to shake you out.

But no matter what, you wouldn't come.

I know, my daughter said. I was hanging on to your heart.

I think about María and Elena María, who are so much like their grandmother.

And I feel sleepy.

Ana is sitting on the red plush chair in her mother's house, much as Dolores used to sit when she was demanding to go to the hospital or simply ruling the house from her throne. Pedro walks in, and the look of him is a surprise. He is looking surprisingly young, dark-haired and unbent. He is carrying in his hand a bouquet of flowers. He drops the flowers with a disdainful gesture, quite what she would expect from Pedro but Ana also knows the gesture is meaningless, no more than a habit.

She bends to pick up the flowers but realises she was mistaken. They are not flowers; they are actually a sheaf of papers. They spread on the floor like an open fan and it occurs to her that they are letters, some very old and yellowed and written on thick paper like parchment and some perfectly contemporary.

Pedro takes out a cigar from the pocket of his shirt and unwraps the plastic from it and even this surprises Ana because he gave up smoking years ago. Pedro lights up and inhales.

Whose are these? Ana asks.

Pedro is smoking and staring out the window as he answers, Yours, Consuelo, *claro*.

Ana inclines further to look more carefully and sees, from the repetition of certain words, that they are love letters. The dates span eras, span a lifetime, but all are written in the same strong sloping hand. It is not Pedro's writing.

Papi, who wrote these letters? Ana demands. But Pedro merely nudges the papers with the tip of a brown polished shoe so that the fan opens further. Ana looks down again, looks for a name, but her eyes are blurry and she can't seem to focus.

He turns from the window and Ana looks at him. She meets his eyes. She notices how deep green her father's eyes are and wonders why he called her Consuelo just now. She feels panicked for a second and looks down again and there are the words, beautifully drawn in the script of an earlier era: From he who can never forget you, Daniel.

So you knew?

Of course, *¿qué tú crees?* Do you think I didn't love you?

And then Ana sees the tears in his eyes, notices how his clear green eyes swim in tears, how they seem to hold all the water in the world and are spilling over and it seems unlikely they will ever stop. And Ana feels a great wrenching tenderness for him, feels as proud and loving of him as she did when she was three, is suffused with that love that she had so long ago vanquished.

Later Ana dreams of other things. She dreams of sky-blue houses in neighbourhoods where decaying cement vies with flamboyant clothes and happy music. She sees Consuelo and María sharing a cigar in that sky-blue house now topped by a thatched palm roof. She sees Dolores's babies lapping up against María's knees, chubby gurgling messy lively babies with not a scar on them anywhere. She sees Dolores, her forearms like *jamones* and her thin stick legs flying about as she dances with her grandfather, the one with the hair on his face not his head, the one who turned his old-world granary into a tax collector's tomb. And around them all she sees vague apprehensive faces, half-shadows missing arms legs ears and mouths, and she realises these are the Caribs, the real people of Cuba, the ones robbed by her people. They are present, too, even if unreconciled. The rising and falling of their talk is the roar of the sea. Ana strains to hear what they are saying. They have a message for her, a message about homelands lost and families divided and love lost and the residue – what remains, what prevails – but in the end she wakes without understanding.

She wakes heavy with this dream but the many images fade immediately.

What she remembers instead is a detail from the previous dream – her father's cigar.

But now he is standing at the counter of the *dulcería* with his *socios*. Ana María, what is that thing they make you say at school?

Pero, hombre, she said it yesterday! protests Pepe. What do you think this is? A government office?

He smiles good-naturedly, undissuaded. No, no, no. You have to listen to this, Pepe, the girl is a *fenómeno. Anda,* Anita.

403

I pledge allegiance, to the flag . . .

And she says it all, in one careful conscious stream for him and his friends, yet again, although she said it yesterday, and last Monday, she says it almost nightly, and he is bending over with mirth, proud laughter is erupting from him, he is smacking his knee and patting her head and handing her five cents.

Now I remember. I remember him taking me trick-or-treating, carrying my plastic jack-o'-lantern brimful with candies, patiently following, arguing that it is ten-thirty, my greed is boundless, no one is left in the streets. But still he follows.

Una más, Papi. Please Papi, just one more.

———

Some people are born into their lives completely, with no memories protruding like unfleshed femurs and no traumas trailing them, pulling them back.

They sleep deep and almost dreamlessly, with light airy visions passing for dreams. They move mountains, these people, and they will talk to you about engines and transmissions, the theatre and geology and astronomy and the stock market and the secret life of the pygmy possum and God knows what else. They have interests and they enjoy company.

They don't obsess about leaving their children in someone else's care because they don't half remember how the baby drowned in a bucket of milk when they left her with the half-witted maid. They don't remember hanging themselves in the pantry a few months later.

They don't see the hands in the blue sea waiting to pull down

404

the children now hurling themselves at the waves. Or else they think it's only a bit of floating debris.

They don't remember how easy it is to die because they have erased the time the quilt smothered a first child and they don't remember all the empty rotten years after that and how long a life can be and how hard to die.

But others remember. Others are only half-born. They are heavy, weighed down by their pasts. They know plagues come. And droughts. And despots. They remember slavery. They are tired, and their sleep does not rest them. They awake slowly, the way they were born, and incompletely. Dreams trail them, yapping at their heels. You seldom hear them laugh, but they sigh a lot. They sigh all the time, and the wind wafts through the soughing pines to mock them.

The Multiple Effects of Rainshadow   Thea Astley

In the little hours of a January morning in 1930, on an island off the Queensland coast, a man goes berserk with a rifle and a box of gelignite. Is he evil? Or crazy? His violence is in fact a mirror for the brutality of Australian life – and is a dim reflection at that, in a country where atrocities by whites against blacks are so ingrained few question them.

The effects of the rampage ripple out to link the lives of those who witnessed it, across the north and down through the decades. It is a time when silence in the face of tyranny is at its loudest. When allegiance to English niceties is confounded by the landscape and by the weather. And change is a slow wind that brings little real difference.

The Multiple Effects of Rainshadow finds Thea Astley back in the territory she is a master of, writing with the iconoclastic wit and insight that are her trademark, in a voice that marks her as a diva among contemporary novelists.

Before I Wake   John Scott

With evening, cloud begins to close across the sky. Blanket upon blanket. As if it wished to hatch some unnatural thing from this town.

I will tell you what these clouds, what this incessant humidity, have hatched. In me. They have hatched the past.

Jonathan Ford, childless at 43, moves restlessly through other people's lives. From Australia to Europe he pursues a series of ill-fated relationships with the vulnerable and the insecure. In turn he is pursued by his past, whose echoes he finds all around him: in Danielle, a young French poet condemned to perpetual childhood. In his mother Violet, wickedly irreverent even as she struggles through her days alone in a council flat. In the flawed genius of the painter Malcolm Richardson. In many lives, ordinary and extraordinary, that he changes in the profoundest ways. It is through two sisters, themselves once hostage to the past, that Ford finally awakens to the present.

This is a story to treasure, a journey through what it means to be human, told with exquisite feeling by the award-winning author of *What I Have Written.*

'The most appealing and engrossing novel I have read in a very long time. John Scott is, quite simply, one of the best writers of fiction at work anywhere in the world today.'

Deirdre Bair